Books by B. V. Larson:

STAR FORCE SERIES
Swarm
Extinction
Rebellion
Conquest
Battle Station
Empire
Annihilation
Storm Assault
The Dead Sun
Outcast
Exile
Gauntlet
Demon Star

REBEL FLEET SERIES
Rebel Fleet
Orion Fleet
Alpha Fleet
Earth Fleet

Visit BVLarson.com for more information.

Armor World

(Undying Mercenaries Series #11)
by
B. V. Larson

Undying Mercenaries Series:

ISBN-13: 978-1093774672
BISAC: Fiction / Science Fiction / Military

Report: The Dangers of Economic Expansion
Authored by the Hegemony Economic Directorate

Possibly the greatest genius of the Empire is its economic design. The system is simple and therefore easily understood by even barbaric races. It is also crushingly effective.

Every world must produce a single product to sell in the Imperial marketplace. There is *one* and only *one* allowed product per planet—that's the genius of it. Once each monopoly is established, it is locked into place for all time. Unless another world proves they can produce a better version of the same product, they are not allowed to do so. In practice, this rarely happens. There is therefore no competition, no advancement, and no strife. The result is a dramatic slowing of technological progress among all the non-core worlds. This dampening effect has kept the peace along the frontier provinces for generations.

Recently, Earth scholars have begun to comprehend the very different set of rules under which the Galactics operate at the center of our galaxy. Unlike the quiet frontier provinces, they have free and open economic interchange. Any of the twenty-odd elder species are free to buy and sell, to arrange treaties, place embargos or make any other arrangements they wish with one another. Essentially, they have the sort of relationships humans once endured in Old Earth's past.

A century ago, nation-states ruled our planet, and humans struggled chaotically just as the Galactics do now. This author shudders to contemplate those bygone days. There were countless ad-hoc trade agreements which inevitably resulted in countless wars. The same state of confusion now exists among the Galactics.

Out here on the frontier, for all the complaining one might hear about stifled development, unemployment and poverty, at least we have peace. There is almost never a war between two member civilizations in the non-core worlds.

Why not? For one thing there is very little to fight about—but even if we did dare launch fleets at one another, we would be rightfully subject to extermination by our wise benefactors from the Core.

What could be more pleasant than our sedate pace of life? Those who wish for the old days are thinking only of the benefits, not of the horrors.

In recent times, however, the Hegemony government of Earth has seen fit to move past the old model. They're actively expanding Earth's borders and influence. The Empire looks the other way because they are weak and need local military support. It is this author's opinion that we are on a dangerous pathway. We are breaking the rules, and others are sure to follow our shameful example of wide-open capitalism and expansion.

Do we dream the saurians of Cancri-9 will be content to mine and sell metals forever? What about the ingenious engineers of 51 Pegasi who produce all our AI goods? Already, the Skrull have been slighted. We build starships with abandon, destroying their economy without a care. Will they remain placid forever, or will they build warships for other planets that fear our growing strength?

Our future is dark and unknowable. Already we face barbaric aliens at our gates—Rigel, the Wur, and all the others still lurking. Infinitely worse, we will soon have to look to our flanks, where former friends have been turned into enemies by our greed and neglect.

"I will kill thee a hundred and fifty ways!"
—Touchstone, of Lord Frederick's Court.

-1-

The sky was a golden hue. The sun was going down over the land out to the west, and a warm night was setting in.

Down in Georgia, when the sun sets in late spring, people like me go outside to sit on porches and enjoy a beer. That's what I was doing now.

Etta met me on my porch. That wasn't unusual. We'd finished dinner, and we'd helped my parents clean up. There were always a lot of chores to do around the old place, and Etta was really pulling her weight these days.

To tell the honest truth, there was a slightly haunted look in her eyes ever since she'd returned from Dust World. I could see it, and my mom could too—but nobody had dared say anything. Etta had come back to the nest, but since she was old enough to make more huge mistakes, I figured that just having her home again was good enough for now.

But... that light in her eyes.

I'd seen it before. It was the light of the stars. An odd, glazed-over expression people get after they've traveled to other worlds and had their minds blasted open.

Normally, when I saw that expression it was on the sad-sack faces of legion recruits. In some cases, new people never did adjust to the grand dance of life and death, both of which

3

were cheap when you traveled off-world. Soldiers that couldn't get used to dying had to be kicked out of the service entirely, returning to Earth bewildered and ashamed.

Fortunately, nothing *that* dramatic seemed to be happening inside Etta's head. She wasn't broken or abused. But she clearly had *seen* things… things she'd never forget in this life or the next.

As a father, I naturally wanted to pry. She was our family's only child and only grandchild. She was all the family's eggs in one basket, and we naturally felt protective.

But despite all this, I'd contained my curiosity for weeks. I kept telling myself that Etta was a grown woman now. If she wanted to talk about things, she'd do so.

On that hot Georgia night, she climbed up my creaky old steps. I kind of expected her to set up her autoscope on the porch to look at the stars—but she didn't. I guess she'd seen enough of those cold, glittering points of light.

Etta didn't say anything. She just handed me a beer and opened up one for herself.

I frowned at that, as she was technically underage, but I let her drink it anyway.

"What are you thinking about on this fine evening, girl?" I asked in a cheery tone.

She still didn't look at me. "I'm fine," she said.

A new frown grew on my face. She wasn't even hearing me.

It had been months since she'd come back from her adventures abroad, and she hadn't told me squat.

All at once, I lost patience and decided to push, just a little.

"I see the light of the stars in your eyes, Etta," I told her. "That's not a good thing—not to a starman like me. What ghosts are haunting you tonight?"

Slowly, she turned to look at me. She tilted her face, opened her mouth—but then stopped and shook her head. "Nothing. Nothing's bothering me, Daddy."

I laughed at her. "You big fat liar!"

A smile flickered on her lips, but it went out.

I waited patiently, and we both sipped our beers.

4

"I..." she said at last. "I don't want to join the legions. Not anymore."

"Oh?" I said, trying to keep the pure joy out of my voice. "And why's that?"

"I saw you," she said, staring at the weathered floorboards of my porch. "I saw you dead. I saw you as a blob in a tank. I saw you growing back... That tank... the stink of it..."

"Ah..." I said, feeling relieved.

Back on Dust World, I'd died shortly after arriving. Then Etta's grandfather had regrown my body in a home-brew tank—a Galactic crime if I'd ever seen one.

Etta had witnessed all this firsthand. She'd seen her own father, crushed and dead, being slowly reborn out of a vat of slime.

I guess that could feel creepy to a young girl.

"Yep, I get it," I said. "Life and death—then more life, then another helping of death. It's a cycle that takes some getting used to for any of Earth's real soldiers."

Her eyes met mine fully. "Are you really my father? Or are you some freakish mutation? Some construct of flesh that Grandpa shocked into life? A biochemical robot that—?"

"Hey, hey, hey," I complained. "You can't go and talk to a legionnaire like that! That's plain rude."

"How do you handle big questions like that, then?" she asked me.

I squirmed a bit in my seat and downed my beer in a guzzling motion to buy myself a little time. After a belch and a long sigh, I started again.

"Listen, I'm an old-fashioned legionnaire, and I play by the rules of such men—the rules we've lived by for about a century now."

"Meaning?" she asked.

"Meaning we don't talk about crap like that."

She studied me intently. "You don't think about it, or dream, or—"

"No," I said flatly. "Not anymore. Early on, say before you were even born, I fussed a bit. But I got it out of my system."

"I'm almost the same age you are now, Dad," she said quietly. "That's another thing that's bothering me."

5

"Nah," I laughed. "I might look young, but I'm as old as dirt. I don't mean that I'm physically weak, but my mind is older than it would appear. That's a blessing, a curse, and a twist of fate all wrapped into one."

I was telling her the truth now. My mind had moved along in years somewhat—but not my person. My skin was still smooth as glass. My eyes could see everything, and my muscles could twitch like a jackrabbit's if I was in a fighting mood. That's what dying and being reborn over and over did for the body.

But my mind was older, wiser. My brain could remember witnessing thousands of deaths, for example—millions, if you count aliens.

"So dying doesn't bother you at all?" she asked.

"I wouldn't say that. It's just that legionnaires don't dwell on death. If we did... why... I suspect we'd all go crazy."

Etta shrugged and turned to look out over my overgrown yard and upward, above the shaggy trees. The sky was darkening, and the stars were just beginning to pop.

"That's odd," she said, pointing to the brightest pinpoint of light in the sky.

"That must be Jupiter," I said. "The king of the Roman gods."

"I guess... but it seems almost too bright."

"What else would it be? You want another beer?"

Etta didn't answer right away, so I waited. Finally, she sighed. "You were right, Dad. About the legions, I mean. You tried to protect me. You tried to tell me the service wasn't right for me, but I didn't believe you. I thought you were trying to smother me."

"Yeah... well."

"I just had to go out there and watch you die twice, didn't I?" she continued. "My grandfather wanted to resurrect you a second time, you know. He said he would control the experiment better on the second try, that he'd done it improperly the first time around."

"Hmm..." I said thoughtfully. "Control it better? I don't like the sound of that. I did break the needle he was trying to

6

stick me with when I woke up…. Do you think that upset him enough to make him want to keep me sedated or something?"

"Probably. Grandpa doesn't like chaos. He likes order, and he likes to do things right."

"And by 'right' you mean things need to be done *exactly* like he wants them to be done?"

Etta shrugged.

Instead of railing on her grandfather, who was a strange man by any accounting, I decided to pat her and fake another smile. Her mouth flickered in response.

"So that's it then," I said. "You saw what death really looks like—and you didn't like it."

"No, I didn't. Not when it's someone close to me. I can't imagine making friends and watching them die… Even worse, dying myself. Finding my own corpse later…" She gave a little shudder. "Did that ever happen to you, Daddy?"

"Uh…" I said, envisioning a half-dozen horrific scenes. I decided to lie and kept on smiling. "Nope—but it could have. Anyway, what do you want to do now that you're out of high school?"

"I think I'll try to go to the university."

I brightened for real then. She'd always been a clever student, when she cared to apply herself.

"That sounds great, honey. What would you major in?"

She looked evasive again. I braced myself—but when the answer came, it didn't sound bad.

"Medical stuff, I guess. Biology. Something experimental…"

"That sounds perfect! But Sector U isn't cheap. Real university tuition… that can cost upwards of a million credits a year, you know. I've got enough cash in my accounts to get you started, I guess."

She shook her head. "Don't worry, Dad, I can pay for it myself."

"What…? How?"

"I, well… I'm not talking about the Sector University in Athens. I'm talking about going to the biggest school. Up in Central."

I blinked a few times, baffled. "Central City?"

"Yes... I signed up for a research center internship. I'll play lab-rat and do whatever needs doing. They'll cover my college as long as I can get good grades."

My frown returned. "You've already... wait a minute, what do you mean you signed up? With who?"

"Hegemony. They liked my test scores... If everything works out, I'm going to be working at Central in the defense labs."

My mouth hung open for several stunned seconds.

I thought of Floramel right off, one of my ex-girlfriends who worked down there in the secret labs under Central. She hadn't had such an easy life.

With an effort of will, I stopped gaping and forced that smile to come back. Because even this new life Etta had signed up for, locked-up in a secret vault where the sun never shined and never would, that was better than seeing my little girl die over and over again as a grunt in the legions.

"You're not upset?" she asked.

"No," I said honestly. "I'm happy for you."

She hugged me then, and I could tell I'd made her evening.

As for my own thoughts... I wasn't delighted. Certainly, disaster had been averted, but I hoped against hope she wouldn't come to regret her choices someday.

2

Bright and early the next morning, my summer vacation came to a sudden end with a call on my tapper.

"James?" Galina Turov asked. "We need you up at Central."

"Uh… What's up, Tribune?"

"Just get on a sky-train and be here by morning—faster, if you can."

She dropped the channel before I could ask for more information. The official activation notice came through a few minutes later. I was furloughed no longer.

That was the legion life in a nutshell, I guess. You never knew when you might be called upon to solve a crisis or just to shine someone's shoes. At least they were paying me double now.

Shrugging on a jacket and pulling out the duffle I kept under my couch, I didn't make it across the yard before my family spotted me. They knew the truth right off.

They were upset, of course. My family always was when I was called back to duty. But, they didn't fuss about it overly much. We'd lived this way for decades.

Eyeing my parents, I had to marvel… they were doing pretty well. A few years back, I'd freshened them both up with a good killing and an illegal revive. That had erased lots of long term wear-and-tear—scars, organ damage, stuff like that.

But their aging had been checked more recently by a different technology. There were over-the-counter longevity drugs in every market now. Cell-stim, Nu-cream and the various injectables. Altogether, if a person was careful not to get too banged up, a decade could go by and you looked like it had only been a year when you examined yourself in the mirror each morning.

We all hugged, and I headed to the family tram. To my surprise, Etta was sitting in the driver's seat when I got to the garage.

"Uh…" I said. "I don't really need anyone to drop me off, honey. We've got the autopilot. She'll drive herself home."

"I'm not going home—I'm going with you."

"Uh… what?"

She looked at me seriously. "I'm checking into Central U in a few weeks, Dad. I might as well have a look around."

Naturally, I was worried that having my daughter along might cramp my style when it came to evening activities… but I couldn't think of a good reason to leave her behind.

"Hmm…" I said. "Okay."

We drove off and left my folks behind. Etta seemed happier the further she got from home. It wasn't that she didn't like living with my folks, but a young person had ideas of their own by her age.

We took the sky-train to Central, flying all day and into the night. When we landed, I thoroughly expected Etta to stay with me—but she didn't.

Instead, her mother met us at the station. Della had lost none of her looks or her odd charm. She gave us each a hug and led us out of the station.

"Daddy," Etta said, "I'm going to spend some time with Mom. I want you to come look at my dorm room tomorrow though—you promise?"

"I promise and hope to die!"

A shadow flickered over her face, and I instantly regretted my choice of words. As I couldn't take them back without making a bigger mess of things, I stood there and grinned like an idiot.

The women both seemed to buy this. I got another round of hugs, and they were gone.

Heaving a sigh, I looked around for a bar. Before I'd sipped my second beer, I was rudely interrupted.

"McGill!" shouted a small man with an impatient, bird-like step. It was none other than Primus Winslade. He marched toward me as if his feet were on fire. "There you are! Damn you man, can't you keep your location settings on?"

"Oh, right..." I said, working my tapper. While I was off-duty, I didn't like how much the computer embedded in my forearm spied on me, so I turned off every tracking option I could.

Winslade glared up at me. "So," he said, "what do you know about all this?"

"About what, sir?"

He sighed. "I never know if you're playing dumb or if you really are functionally retarded."

"I suppose it's a little of both, sir. But I honestly don't know why I was ordered to come up here. What's happened? A surprise assignment on some dumpster of a planet?"

"Nothing so mundane, I'm afraid. Come with me."

I did so, and we soon reached the street. A hog specialist driver was waiting, and he was playing jockey on one of those government fliers with ass-injuring metal seats. We climbed in, and the specialist zoomed us straight toward the obsidian-black fortress known as Central.

We were breaking lots of laws along the way, I could tell that right off. Other air-traffic darted and dashed to the side, letting us pass. It was either that, or slam into us. A few drivers cursed and waved their middle fingers against their canopies as we soared by.

A frown was growing on my face as I thought all this over. Something serious seemed to be happening. Winslade had been Turov's sidekick in the past, but these days he was a Primus and a hog. It seemed odd for him to be fetching me from the airport at all—but I decided against asking him about it. I'd find out what was going on eventually.

We landed on the roof. That was unusual, too. I hadn't been up here for years. One time, I'd shot a Galactic on this roof...

11

On another occasion, I'd participated in a rebellion of sorts, starting right here.

I shook my head and smiled at the memories.

"Are you drunk?" Winslade demanded.

"No sir—but I'd like to be."

He made a snorting sound, and we got out of the car. The specialist zoomed off without a word, throwing grit in our faces.

"Damned hogs," I complained.

"Careful. Have you forgotten where you are?"

"Not at all, sir. This is hog-Central. Now that we're alone, can you tell me what the hell is happening?"

"You haven't heard about the... artifact?"

"Nope."

"Nothing at all? Even the local news is talking about it."

"Uh..."

Suddenly, I thought about the bright object Etta and I had spotted earlier the night before. Craning my neck, I looked up into the darkening sky and peered to the south.

There it was. A bright, bright light. It was even bigger and brighter than it had been the night before. I was sure of that much.

It had to be a planet—didn't it?

3

After staring for a time, I wasn't so sure. I knew the planets in the Solar System pretty well by now. I could tell something wasn't quite right with the heavens above us, the same way a sailor might learn to recognize a coastline or a brewing storm. Being an interstellar traveler built a natural interest in a man concerning astronomy.

"That's no planet, is it?" I asked.

Winslade was standing at my side, staring up with me.

"No, it isn't..." he said without his usual sarcastic tone. "It's something... unknown."

I didn't look at him, and he didn't look at me. We were both staring up at that single point of white light which grew ever brighter in the darkening sky.

"How can it be unknown? We've got lidar and a network of optical—"

"I've heard a few details," he said. "It's metallic and assumed to be of artificial construction, as it's unnaturally smooth and round. Most importantly, it's hurtling toward Earth at about a million kilometers an hour."

Still craning my neck back, I took a step forward. The gritty puff-crete roof of Central crunched under my boots.

"This is why I've been recalled to Central? What the hell does Turov think I can do about it?"

Winslade released a dismissive snort. "On that score I'm as baffled as you are. Do you recognize it?"

"At this range? It's only a speck."

"It will grow bigger soon as it draws near."

I frowned and looked at him at last. "What do you mean? How far out is that thing?"

He sniffed and shrugged. "Twenty million klicks, I believe."

"Twenty million..." I said, doing what limited math my mind was capable of. The object was already larger than Mars or Jupiter. Granted, they were both farther away, but...

"It must be the size of a planet," I surmised.

"Yes. Something like that. We must go downstairs now. I'm being summoned."

I saw his tapper glowing redly. That was why I kept mine as difficult as possible to locate. If people could find you easily, they tended to give you more things to do.

Mine began to glow red too, however, filling with urgent messages from my superiors. I didn't bother to check. Instead, I headed to the roof access doors, passed security, and we walked into the elevators.

"Yes," Winslade told his tapper. "Yes, yes—I've got him here right now. No, he seems as baffled as everyone else. Of course he might be lying, I'm not an idiot—sir."

I ignored Winslade. I was thinking hard.

Going back over his statements in my mind, I could assume the object hadn't answered any radio challenges from Earth. So, the spooks here at Central didn't even know where it was from. It could be a ship, in which case it was the largest vessel I'd ever heard of, or just a chunk of flying metal.

The details of its origins and identity didn't really matter if that thing struck Earth. An object like that, drilling its way through space without a care, would smash into my home planet like a bullet hitting a balloon.

It would destroy the world.

Who could have sent it? My mind conjured up a dozen suspects. The Rigellians, the Wur... Maybe even a pocket of rebel squids. Lots of local aliens hated Earth.

The elevator stopped and Winslade got off. I followed him. I didn't bother to figure out what floor we were on. It was somewhere up in the five hundreds—brass territory.

14

He stopped in front of an ornate set of office doors. I saw the insignia of a praetor on the wall outside, and I knew it had to be Drusus' office.

Drusus had once been the tribune of Legion Varus. But that had been a long time ago. These days Turov ran the outfit, and Drusus ran Central.

Winslade hesitated at the door, reaching up a hand to knock. He wasn't moving fast enough for my taste, so I reached out and opened the door. I strode past Winslade into the vast chamber beyond.

The office was very large and mostly empty. A dozen steps away, Drusus and Turov faced one another over the praetor's massive desk. Drusus was behind that desk, while Turov was in front of it, sitting in a steel chair.

Now, none of this was too surprising. In fact, the scene looked quite innocent at first—until I noticed that Turov's right wrist was handcuffed to the chair, and the chair was gravity-bolted to the floor.

Hmm...

So, she was a prisoner, and she'd summoned me to Central...

Making the best of an unknown situation, my face lit up with a broad Georgia grin. I threw them both a salute, then stepped up to the praetor's desk and offered him a hand to shake.

"Good to see you, sirs!" I boomed out.

"You too, McGill, I'm sure," Drusus said, ignoring my hand. "Take a seat."

There was a second steel chair, and the gravity bolt was clamped on that one, too. But I sat down on it anyway like it was a velvet recliner.

"Got here as fast as I could, sirs," I said. "People are all snarled-up about this new light in the sky. You don't happen to know anything about that, do you?"

They both looked at me carefully. Turov seemed sullen, irritated, and worried. Drusus seemed deadly serious.

"We think it might be a Mogwa ship, McGill," Drusus told me.

"You don't say…"

"Who else would have the technology to build something like that?" Turov snapped suddenly. "An artificial sphere roughly the size of our own Moon?"

"Uh... could be any number of alien types. Take the Wur, for example."

Drusus shook his head. "Not likely. The Wur aren't good with metal. It's their primary weakness, remember?"

"That's true..." I said, detecting the first trickle of sweat under my arms since leaving Georgia.

"What would you suggest next?" Drusus asked.

"Uh... the saurians? They've got plenty of metal to throw around."

"True, but to my knowledge they've never built a ship. They rent them from the Galactics, like they're supposed to. And before you mention our local ship-builders the Skrull, I'd ask you to get serious."

"Yeah... They're sneaky, but not really this kind of aggressive. You're right. It's obvious who's behind this: Rigel."

Drusus frowned while Turov rolled her eyes. Drusus rubbed at his chin. "That's not absurd on the face of it. Rigel hates us, they have excellent ship-building capacities, and they might have the balls to pull a stunt like this."

"Drusus," Turov said. "The odds on that scenario are very long. Don't let McGill distract you."

Drusus flicked his eyes to her, then back to me. "Ever since we first detected this object, we've been tracking it and trying to communicate with it. The object has ignored us. It has no obvious means of propulsion, no weaponry in evidence—but it does move. It has been accelerating and changing course, in fact, as it approaches Earth."

"Well, *that's* good news!"

"How do you figure, McGill?"

"Maybe they're just a new species coming to pay us a visit. They still might slow down and slide into orbit quietly. You should never pre-judge a houseguest, my mama always says."

A smile tugged at Drusus' face. "That's a very optimistic attitude you have, McGill. Unfortunately, I can't take chances like that. I have to know if this vessel is a threat to Earth or not."

"Uh… it *might* be, of course. Have you gathered the fleet? Are you going to blast that thing before it gets any closer?"

"Yes," he said firmly. "We're going to make an attempt to stop it. But I thought that in the interest of gathering all the facts I can before taking drastic action, I should talk to people who tend to be involved in unusual events around here."

I glanced at Turov and her chained wrist. "I see… you figured the tribune here might know where this UFO came from?"

"That's right. She's actually been quite helpful. She suggested that you might have the answer we seek."

Looking over at Galina in surprise, I saw her study the floor.

Right then, I knew the truth: She'd sold me out. She'd blamed me for this sudden threat out of the blue. Apparently, judging by her manacles, her gambit hadn't been entirely successful.

Galina and I had what could only be described as a twisted relationship. In our personal lives, we'd become quite friendly. We frequently had sex when we were off-duty and sometimes even when we were on.

But that didn't mean we were some kind of pair-bonded soul-mates. It was treacherous moments like this that proved the point with regularity.

Galina liked me. She might even love me a little bit—but she loved her career and her ambitions even more.

"I see…" I repeated, deciding two could play at the blame-game. "So, she mentioned that I'd recently been on an unsanctioned trip to some distant planets—is that it?"

The incident I was referring to had happened right before I'd shipped out to Storm World. On that occasion, I'd been killed then revived on Mogwa Prime. As an unfortunate by-product of that particular adventure, I'd ended up killing Xlur, our local provincial governor.

"Yes," Drusus said. "If that ship up there is of Galactic origin, I can't imagine a better reason for their visit than to follow up on whatever crimes you might have committed while visiting the Core Worlds."

Nodding my head in Galina's direction, I decided to spill the beans a little further.

"Did she happen to mention that she killed me and then had me revived on Mogwa Prime? That the whole trip was her idea?"

Galina's head snapped up. First shock, then rage flashed over her face.

"Shut up, McGill," she hissed. "No one wants to hear your lies!"

I lifted my tapper, which now displayed no less than thirty-one urgent messages from Galina herself. I hadn't bothered to read any of them, but it demonstrated clearly that she was quite interested in what I had to say today.

"Seems like you were interested an hour ago," I said calmly.

"Look," Drusus said. "I don't want to hear about any personal problems you two might have. But what's this about Mogwa Prime? What did you do out there, McGill?"

My jaw worked for a second with my mouth hanging open. I hated when it did that.

"Uh…" I said. "Look, sir, let's just say that me and Galactics don't always see eye-to-eye. However—and this is the big thing—there's no way this ship is coming out from Mogwa Prime for vengeance."

"And why's that?" Drusus asked.

"Because Sateekas is on my side, that's why. He likes what I did. We discussed it at Storm World, and he considered my actions to be proof of loyalty on my part."

Drusus blinked. That was a big tell. As much as he knew about this situation, or thought he did—he was out of his depth. We all knew it right then.

"Sateekas? The ex-admiral of the Battle Fleet? The Mogwa who rules this province today?"

"The very same, sir."

"He knows about your unsanctioned journey? How?"

I told him briefly, in a highly edited form, how I'd been forced to interact with the Mogwa who was now our local governor while serving out at Storm World.

"So, you see sirs, we've got nothing to worry about. That ship isn't a Mogwa vessel. It's somebody else."

"You can't know that," Galina said. She looked at Drusus. "You can't risk Earth on the basis of one rogue centurion's hunch."

Drusus looked at each of us intently. He was thinking hard, I could tell. After all, life hadn't dealt him the easiest hand of cards.

"What's the big deal?" I asked. "I mean, I'm just giving you information. I can't see how it would impact our current situation, other than to clarify—"

"That's because you don't *think*, James," Galina said. "If I thought you'd come here and bring up that trip, I wouldn't have called for you."

"The big deal is this, McGill," Drusus interrupted. "I'm trying to decide right now if Earth is going to deliver a first-strike against this approaching ship—if it indeed is a ship. Galina has been urging me toward caution. To support her case, she confessed to having interacted with the Galactics recently."

"You mean interaction… like airmailing me naked out into the cosmos?"

"Now that those details have been unearthed, yes."

"I see…"

And I did see. Drusus had to deal with this threat. But if he played it wrong, and it turned out this vessel was coming to arrest me, or Galina, or thousands of other humans, then attacking them first would widen our crimes and make us into rebels.

On the other hand, if he waited too long to take action, Earth might not survive at all.

Drusus paced for a few minutes while staring at his desk. There on his desktop the image of the alien sphere grew larger ever so slowly, like the movement of the minute-hand on an ancient clock.

"I recall, McGill, that you once told me your loyalties resided with Earth, your family and Legion Varus in that order. Do you still feel that way?"

"Sure do, sir."

He nodded and paced some more.

I noted that Galina was looking less carefully made-up than usual. A drop of sweat fell from her hair.

"We have to do it," Drusus announced at last. "We have to strike first, and strike hard."

He released Galina and threw us both out of his office. When we were alone, she turned on me.

"James! This isn't a game. You have no idea who is coming at us, and whether or not attacking that ship will trigger our doom. What if you've just killed us all?"

I shrugged. "Sometimes you can't know the truth, Galina. You just have to take your best shot."

Looking sick, she accompanied me to the elevators.

I wasn't all that good at reading women, but she didn't look like she was in any kind of a romantic mood to me. All hopes of a warm and fuzzy rekindling with her tonight were fading fast.

-4-

Galina wouldn't look me in the eye when we rode down in the elevator. That was kind of a big deal, as elevator rides in Central took a long-ass time. The silence grew uncomfortable as hundreds of floors flashed by.

"Uh..." I said. "Where are we going now?"

"You can go anywhere you like. I'm going to the command center to watch this disaster unfold."

"You mean the fleet action? That would be cool to see. I bet our boys will blow that steel beach ball right out of the sky."

"It's not made of steel," she said, "not according to our spectro-analysis."

"Well... titanium, whatever."

"It's not titanium, either. It's something odd. Something with a reflective coating, but underneath that, we're sensing a very dark surface. Like charcoal."

She glanced at me about then. Her eyes were intent, and worried.

"Why exactly were you handcuffed to that chair?" I asked. "If you don't mind my asking?"

"Because Drusus is an unreasonable oaf. He assumed that this visitation might have something to do with me—just because of past events. So, he had me arrested."

"You're talking about when the squids invaded Earth, and you wanted to help them?"

21

She shrugged and checked on the floor numbers. We were down in the one-hundreds now and still going strong.

"You got away with selling out Earth back then," I said. "Why would that come back to bite you in the ass now, after all these years?"

"Because I don't have the level of support I once had on the Ruling Council. They've become like you, arrogant and prideful. They believe Earth can beat anybody."

"Uh-huh, I get that feeling too. You still think we should take a knee whenever a scary alien shows up? What about Rigel? Do you want to sign up for enslavement by those mean-ass little bears?"

Galina glanced at me again, troubled. "No... I don't think so. You proved to me on Storm World that they can be beaten. It's such a risk, though. You should understand me of all people, McGill. I'm thought of as a wild card—but really, I'm not."

Galina was right about that. She was one of those people who looked for dangers ahead of time and took decisive action to avoid them. She was pathologically cautious, in a way.

"You're right," I said. "I know how you think. What do you say we should do about these aliens? Just let them come close and hope they're in a good mood?"

She sighed. "I don't know this time. Their approach is very threatening, I admit that. It just seems so final for us to attack them. At that point, war will be unstoppable."

I nodded, and I reached out a clumsy hand to her shoulder. She flinched a little, but she didn't snarl and pull away.

"Listen," I said, "high level command is about making hard choices. Drusus is doing that now. He doesn't know the perfect answer, but he knows he can't let some trillion-ton alien ship roll right up to us and kill the planet without a fight. Sometimes, even a lowly skunk can fight off a wildcat by being ornery enough."

She looked up at me wonderingly. "For a moment there, you were making good sense. But then, you lost me."

I smiled, and she smiled back.

Taking a big chance, I gave her a light hug. I don't mind telling you that my balls were crawling in fear as I did it.

Galina could change her attitude and react violently when you touched her the wrong way.

But sometimes, a man has to take a chance, or nothing ever happens.

She went with it, and she even hugged me back. She rubbed her wrist and leaned against me. The handcuffs had left a red loop on her skin.

"I don't like being arrested," she said. "The moment they came to my house yesterday—I sent for you."

Suddenly, things made a little more sense.

"That's why you called me yesterday, huh? Because they were arresting you?"

"Yes. After that, all I could do was send you a few texts—you took forever to get here, by the way."

Just texts… that figured. Galina was a master at working her tapper. She could fire off a text-wall with her hands tied behind her back if need be—I'd seen her do it.

"That's when you messaged me and sent Winslade to pick me up. Why me?"

She shrugged. "I don't know. Maybe I needed some protection."

Looking into her eyes which were locked with mine now, I knew she was partly telling the truth and partly lying. She'd probably needed me nearby to throw to the wolves in her place if things went badly enough.

But at the same time, I could see that she *had* needed help. She had plenty of very serious enemies up here at Central. A big scary Moon-sized spaceship on a collision course with Earth might be just the thing an opponent would use to bring her down.

I gave her a light squeeze and let go of her. I naturally wanted to pick her up and kiss her—but it wasn't quite time yet. I've grown an instinct for these things as I've gotten older.

By the time the elevator stopped and dinged, letting us out into the lobby, the energy between us had changed completely.

Galina and I had become more than casual lovers lately, but our relationship was still an on-again, off-again thing. For instance, when in public we tended to play it cool by reflex.

We stepped off the elevator, and I turned toward the big front exit. I was ready to go out on the town and get her some dinner—if she could be persuaded.

But she was already striding purposefully to the east, toward the darker, quieter quadrant of this giant building.

Sighing, I followed her. She glanced back and stopped, putting her hands on her hips.

"Where are you going?"

"To see this fleet action firsthand."

"I didn't mean—"

"Look, Galina. Do you want some help or not?"

She frowned. "What can you do for me in the strategic ops room?"

I snorted. "Ask yourself this: how many of those officers down there really like you? How many would have your back in a crisis? Or, a better question might be, which one of those hogs ratted you out in the first place?"

That last question made her blink. Her fists came off her hips.

"All right. Follow me—but try not to do anything embarrassing."

"Don't worry," I said, "this will be like Sunday school all over again."

"That's what I'm afraid of."

From the ground floor, you could take the elevators going up, or you could take the ones going down. We took the ones that sunk rapidly into the earth.

After about a hundred floors, and a few ear-cracking moments as the air pressure grew slightly, we got out. Next, we went through some very persnickety security people, losing all our weapons and electronic gear—then found a third set of elevators.

These went all the way down to the bottom—at least, I think they did. I've only been down about five hundred floors. Some people say there's more below that, but I couldn't swear to it.

At somewhere in the minus three hundreds, we came to a dead zone. It was a region under Central so deep the floor numbers stopped flashing—but we kept going deeper. For several seconds, I had the eerie sensation the elevator had jumped the tracks and fallen away into an abyss... but then right before I said something, the elevator slowed and stopped.

We'd come to our destination at last, but nothing happened. We weren't moving, but the doors didn't open.

"This is the War Room," Galina announced, turning toward me.

"Uh... I don't remember it being like this."

"It's been newly expanded. About thirty floors have been torn out and collected together into a large underground cavern."

"Okay, but why aren't the doors opening?"

"Because they're watching us," she said. "Checking us out. If we fail some test, we'll be sent back up to the lobby—or worse."

"Hmm… what would be the worst case?" I asked.

"If we're determined to be a threat, this steel box will be our tomb."

"That's encouraging…"

So saying, I walked up to the video pickup and squinted at it. The camera was a tiny thing, but I knew it was very high res and contained countless other sensors as well. It was even reading the nature and quality of my breath right now.

"Hey! Hey you hogs out there! Can you smell my breath? There's no booze in it, none at all."

I blew a puff of steamy air on the pickup, and Galina kicked me lightly in the back of the knee. I ignored her.

"Get away from there," she hissed at me. "I told you not to antagonize these people."

To my mind, the hogs were antagonizing me. But I straightened up and waited impatiently. Getting bored, I considered resting a hand on Galina's shoulder but dropped the idea as unworkable. There was no way she was going to warm up when she knew we were under scrutiny by a pack of hogs.

At long last the door opened. On the other side stood a team of guards in a chamber of rough-hewn rock and puffcrete. It looked like someone had dug a cavern in the midst of Central's countless basement levels—because that's exactly what had happened.

"About damned time," I complained. "Were you boys eating donuts or something?"

I strode out into the midst of a six man squad of armed veterans. They weren't smiling. No smiles at all.

A familiar voice spoke up from behind them. "McGill? What are you doing down here?"

"Primus Graves! Good to see you, sir."

26

He frowned back at me. "You haven't answered my question."

"I'm here as Tribune Turov's attaché," I said.

Graves slid his eyes to Galina, then back to me. Shaking his head, he turned and walked away. "Follow me."

We did so, and he led the way toward a roundish opening that gave us a view of an even larger chamber. As we passed through the opening, I realized we'd been in an elevator lobby, but now we were in the main hall.

It was *huge*. Easily as big and tall as the Mustering Hall in Newark itself. That was a stunner, considering the fact we were a kilometer or so underground.

The ceiling and walls were lit with LED panels, but the size of the place was so great it felt shadowy all the same. It was kind of like being in a football stadium at night.

On the main floor a thousand people and robots were moving around. They were operating workstations, updating screens—there were countless huge holographic screens all over the place.

"This is a restricted area," Graves told us as we walked down some uneven puff-crete steps. We were several floors above the main hall.

There wasn't a rail or even a handhold next to the stairs, and it was a long way to the bottom if you slipped. The modern military wasn't big on safety. If you screwed up and died, well, they'd just print a new soldier and give him an earful for being dumb.

"I know the security rules, *Primus* Graves," Turov said.

She outranked him, and we were all in the same legion. I could understand why she was getting irritated. By all rights, she was Graves' direct superior in the chain of command.

"They made me leave my meeting and come up here to the elevator lobby to approve McGill's admission," Graves continued. "That's not helpful at this critical time."

Graves was slapping at Galina for bringing me—and she knew it, too.

"Since when did you become a hog, Primus Graves, sir?" I asked.

27

He stopped marching down the steps and turned to face me. "I'm not a hog, McGill. God willing, I never will be. But today Earth is in crisis, and I'm doing my part at the request of Praetor Drusus. Please try to be part of the solution rather than the problem, all right?"

"Uh…" I said, feeling somewhat chastened. "All right sir. Sorry sir. You're no hog, I know that."

We followed him in silence after that. He showed us to a station that had only one seat and one touch screen. I tried to sit down, but Galina slapped me out of the way and slid her small butt onto the chair instead.

Graves left, and I peered over Galina's shoulder at the ops screen.

"All right everyone," a voice announced over the PA system. "We're about ten minutes from go-time. Our first beams should be landing sooner, but we won't get measurable results until the T-bombs hit. We're going get all our data at once. Be alert, and man your stations."

My mouth sagged open a little. "The fleet is hitting that big steel marble out there? Right now?"

"Ten minutes…" Galina said, "it isn't much time, is it?"

"It's going to feel like forever."

And it did. We watched the countdown, examining the placement of our ships and other assets.

Earth's space forces had come a long way over the last decade or so. After Earth had been invaded by the Cephalopods, we'd launched our first destroyer-sized puff-crete abominations. Those early ships were like molded bathtubs, flipped over and filled with oxygen and weapons. They'd been slow, ugly and easy to take out with one missile or long-burn beam.

But we'd advanced a lot since those days. We'd been given license to do the job of the Skrull—our local ship-building species—as long as it was in the name of Empire defense. As a consequence, our vessels weren't allowed to carry trade goods or play passenger ship—but they could be warships.

Our fleet designs had gotten much more sophisticated. I suspected this was due largely to the influence of the near-human scientists we'd captured from Rogue World. They'd built a ship on their own that had held off the Empire's entire provincial battle fleet for quite a while—destroying perhaps twenty percent of the Imperial vessels.

That violation had nearly gotten humanity as a whole permed, but we'd survived it. Today, I got the feeling I was going to witness all the advances we'd made since then with the help of Floramel and other rogue researchers.

The invader was only about eight times as far away as our own Moon now. That was as close as anyone down here on Earth was willing to let them come before taking a shot at destroying the vessel.

Hundreds of our ships stood between Earth and the approaching super-ship. In addition to that, we had orbital platforms, bases on the moon, lots of mines and other things hidden out there in the infinite dark of space.

The fireworks started at promptly T-minus eight minutes.

All of a sudden, every screen in the place lit up.

"What the hell is that?" I asked.

"Enemy defensive fire," Galina answered. "It has to be. She's responding at last..."

We watched tensely, and the crowd quieted. Battles in space are pretty much silent, as there's no air to carry a vibration from one spot to another. There was, however, plenty of energy and mass being thrown around out there.

Hundreds of missiles popped. Some discharged their warheads in glorious spheres of destruction, but many were disintegrated by defensive fire. They never blossomed into massive explosions, but instead became tiny pinpoints of light on the screens.

The crowd around us murmured, and there were some gasps.

"What?" I asked, leaning over to Galina's chair. "What's going on?"

"We're not sure..." she said tensely. "Maybe it's a force-field, or an aerogel—the missiles are running into something. They aren't reaching the target's hull."

I straightened up and searched the crowd for a familiar face. At last, I spotted one—Floramel.

A lot of the spooks down here who worked in the darkest bowels of Central were near-humans. Sometimes, I wondered if it was such a good idea to rely on outside help here in our holiest of holy command-centers—but nobody gave an icy damn what I thought about it.

Striding away from Galina, I crossed the distance quickly. None of the hog guards tried to stop me, which was just as well for them. They were all gaping up at the big screens like everyone else.

"Floramel?" I asked.

She craned her long lovely neck around to gaze at me in surprise. "James? What are you—? Please, don't disrupt my thoughts now."

"Sorry," I said. "I'm here strictly as an observer and advisor."

Her head had turned back to a screen full of numbers, but she frowned and glanced back again. "An advisor? An advisor to whom?"

"Praetor Drusus of course. Not an hour ago, I was briefing him on this threat up in his offices."

"James," she said tiredly. "I don't know how you got down here, but impressing me by name-dropping will not grant you sexual access. I've told you before—"

"Look," I said, putting a hand on her chair. "Just tell me what's destroying our missiles? Are they hitting force fields?"

"No... There's been very little defensive fire, and we would have detected a repelling energy field of some kind. I'm suspecting it's a smart-gel."

"A what?"

"A cloud of nanites, microscopic in size, but programmed to mass up when a missile approaches to destroy the swarm."

I nodded slowly. "That could be it... How are we going to get past that?"

"We're launching T-bombs next—they're already counting down."

My face brightened. "What kind of warheads do we have?"

She nodded. "We've developed a new delivery system to use with our standard fusion bombs."

I touched her shoulder, giving it a slight squeeze. "That's good work, girl. I know it was you who helped with a lot of these breakthroughs. You're saving Earth's ass right now."

She smiled, a flickering thing, but then she eyed my hand on her shoulder critically.

"James…"

"Sorry!" I said, pulling my hand off again like she'd burned it. Her kind considered any kind of touching as a prelude to sex.

Now, we were longtime friends and we'd been lovers once in the past, but a lot of time and lightyears had gone by since then.

"It's all right, but *please* stop distracting me."

I did my damnedest. I shut the hell up and stood there—hovering over her while she watched her screens.

A few minutes later, a series of flashes began to shower the hull of the great ship.

"Is that those T-bombs?"

"No… they haven't launched yet. They're having trouble getting a fix on the enemy."

"How the hell…?" I asked. "That ship is as big as the Moon. How can they fail to lock-on?"

"I don't know. The enemy have several advance defenses. We're working on the problem now."

"Where are the T-bombs?"

Floramel lifted a single, long finger. "On the floor above this one—are you sure you're cleared to know these things?"

"They let me in the place, didn't they?"

She didn't argue the point, so I stared up into the darkness overhead. It was alarming to think that a warehouse full of fusion bombs was sitting directly overhead.

My mind and my eyes fell back to her screens. "But… something made it through and hit the invader. I saw it."

She shook her head. "That was our particle beams. They actually hit a few seconds ago. We're far enough away for a delay in what we're seeing."

"Yeah, yeah, I know about that—but did our beams do any damage?"

31

She shook her head again. "We're not measuring any significant hull damage, just a little discoloration—the ship has shrugged off our guns."

That was a shocker. This hurtling beach ball wasn't just a dumb rock, that was for sure. Somehow, it was evading and deflecting everything we had to throw at it.

"Is it dodging around in space somehow the way your ship did, back at Rogue World?"

"No, I don't think so. I'm still suspecting a field of particulate matter—tiny motes of dust or metal that interfere with our sensors and our strikes."

"Well, just launch the damned T-bombs blind then," I said. "Lay down a pattern right in front of this big prick—something they can't help but run into."

Floramel gave me one more glance. "Are you listening in on command chat?"

"I don't have the authorization."

"Well, you should feel vindicated. The brass has decided to do exactly that."

A moment later the T-bombs flew, and everything changed.

-6-

At first, there was a wild series of ripping flashes. I saw a dozen strikes, then a hundred—a thousand? I couldn't tell, but it looked like we'd lit up a sun out there. Automatically, I threw my hands up to cover my eyes. The screens were so good and so accurate, they blasted a pulsing blue-white light that dazzled us all. Stark shadows grew behind us, drawing silhouettes of the milling, wincing crowd of operators and officers.

"Gee-zus!" I shouted. "What in hell's name was that? Did it blow up?"

"They got through!" I heard someone shout.

My shock faded. Grinning, I whooped, and all the nerds around me gave me an odd glance—but I didn't care.

"Hot damn!" I said. "Did we tear up that wrecking ball or what, Floramel? I can't even see the thing anymore."

Patiently, she regarded her screens and instruments. Numbers played there rather than pretty pictures and interpretive graphics.

"We definitely hit it. They must not have been expecting a shower of T-bombs. We gave no hint up until this moment that we have that kind of technology."

"That's great, girl. But is it destroyed?"

"No... There's a field of vapor around the object, but our magnetometers, our gravimetric sensors... the object must be relatively intact. No significant reduction of mass. No signs of a catastrophic break up, either."

"Are you sure? What kind of a rock takes dozens of point-blank fusion bomb hits in stride?"

She turned slowly in her chair toward me, but she didn't look at me. She was staring at the deck, frowning hard.

"You've got a point," she said. "Normal matter would have been vaporized or at least seriously ruptured. It's clear this invasive object is not only massive but unnaturally rugged as well."

"Like what? What could take that kind of a whuppin'?"

Floramel shrugged. Over her shoulder, I saw the big screens clearing. The flashes, the clouds of displaced radioactive gasses, had subsided.

And I'll be damned if that big-ass cue ball wasn't still there, and still barreling down on us.

"Shit…" I said. "At least it's all black and scarred up now. Hey. Maybe the ship is intact, but the people inside are dead from shock. What do you think about that?"

Floramel turned back to her console slowly, thoughtfully. I could tell she was surprised and unhappy. She'd thought the T-bombs would do the trick. We all had.

"The object is slowing," she said. "It's reducing speed dramatically."

"Well, that's good. At least they don't intend to smash into us, cracking our planet apart like an egg."

"No… That doesn't appear to be their plan. Unfortunately, the fact they're still able to maneuver means we haven't killed the crew with the shock of our attack, or the radiation. In fact, we haven't disabled it at all. They seem to be gliding in with a controlled, smooth deceleration."

Graves showed up then.

"Your T-bombs didn't work," he said.

"Evidently not, Primus," Floramel said.

"What other kind of fancy stuff have your nerds got in store for this kind of emergency?" he asked.

Floramel licked her lips. She didn't meet his eyes, or mine.

"The fleet failed. Special weapons failed. I'm not sure that even our monitor ship, the one that held off Battle Fleet 921 single-handedly for over an hour, could stop this enemy, Primus."

He nodded. "That's great. All right, we're stepping things up a notch, then. McGill, come with me. Maybe you'll be useful today after all."

While Graves and Floramel talked, I'd been examining the data on other people's screens. News vids were pouring in from the city outside.

Down here, we were locked inside a fortress. There was no place safer on Earth, unless you counted a few mile-deep mining holes that no one knew about.

People had been permanently blinded by the flashes. Others had been sunburned—right through the clouded sky.

Sirens rolled out over the streets, and armored troops jogged to defensive positions. I hadn't seen this kind of alert at Central since the Squids had hit us—maybe not even then.

"Uh…" I said, "can you give me two minutes, Primus Graves, sir?"

He slid his eyes to Floramel, then back to me. He sighed. "All right. Come to the upper deck conference room in five minutes, or I'll send a squad to arrest you."

"Thank you, sir."

My hand reached out, and I touched Floramel's shoulder again. She stiffened slightly.

"James, this isn't—"

"I'm worried, Floramel. I need your help."

She frowned at me, and I was sad to see a hint of suspicion in her eyes.

"Della and Etta, my little girl, they're out there in those streets."

Her expression changed, and she swept a glance over the continuously playing news vids on screens all around us. There were scenes of panic, traffic snarls, even fires in the old wooden buildings on the east side of town.

"Oh… your daughter is out there?"

"Yeah. She wants to be a lab-monkey, like you. She's already been accepted by Central U."

"Really? She's not neuro-typical then?"

"No, not at all. She's half Dust-Worlder, remember? The granddaughter of the Investigator."

"Yes, yes, of course," she said, as if a great mystery had been solved.

I didn't take any offense at this. I'd never been much good at school, and I didn't care who knew about it.

"My mama always said I was one-part genius and three-parts retard," I said. "Maybe Etta inherited the right part."

"I understand your concern, James," Floramel said, "but I don't know what I can do for them. If Della insists she has important legion business at Varus headquarters, she might be able to get inside the upper floors here at Central, but your daughter... she's not even an intern yet."

"Can't you just print her out a pass, or something?"

"I don't have that authority... and security is going to be unusually tight."

Thinking about the hogs that examined Turov and I in the elevator, I had to admit she was right. My heart sank. My little girl had come to Central just in time to fall into a magnitude 9 shit-storm.

"All right," I said. "I'll try something else."

"But Graves said five minutes..." Floramel said, but she was talking to my back.

"He'll get over it," I said over my shoulder. "He always does."

Striding with ground-eating steps, I moved at a pace that only a man of my height can do without jogging. Turov came into view a few moments later, and I caught her frown of disapproval.

"Where the hell have you been? Flirting again?"

"We're in trouble, Galina."

"No shit, McGill. That ship is not only slowing down, she's coming here. Right *here*."

"What?" I asked, catching her arm and turning her around to face me.

Startled, she looked up into my intense face. Something there told her I wasn't fooling around, so she didn't get angry. Maybe she was too surprised for that.

36

"They think the ship detected the source of our T-bombs," she said. "They traced our attack to this building. They didn't *like* that attack. Right after the bombs detonated, that big ship changed course. Instead of aiming at the Indian Ocean, it's now targeting Central."

I loosened my iron fingers from around her elbow and studied the screens.

"Della and Etta... they're out there in those streets."

"Ah..." Galina said, rubbing at her arm slightly. Her anger and confusion drained away. "Your daughter came back to you from Dust World?"

"She sure did... but right now I kind of wished she'd stayed out there."

-7-

"James?" Galina said to me. "James!"

"Huh?"

I'd been staring at the screens. Panic was spreading across the city, and the displays were full of chaos. The big ship was decelerating, and it would make planetfall in about ten hours. The word was spreading and people were freaking out.

"I can try to help," Galina said.

That got my attention. I looked up and spoke to her at last. "I can't even get through to them on my tapper. I'm blocked."

"I know, it's a security thing, but I can get past the firewall with a text. I'll see what I can do for them."

My eyes searched hers, and I smiled in relief.

"Thanks, Galina, I owe you one."

She waved for me to leave. "Go to your meeting with Graves now. He's got something, um, *special* for you to do."

I felt an urge to kiss her, but I knew that wasn't going to fly in public. I could see in her eyes that she felt the urge too. That had to be enough. Turning away, I hurried toward the upper galleries.

They were really apartments, or offices, or something like that—parts of the basement floors that hadn't been demolished completely to make the big chamber in the middle that was serving as Earth's War Room today.

There were ramps made of slabs of puff-crete. It was the only path upward from the main floor. In the hall, it was half-dark—lit up like a movie theater by random flashes of light from one screen or another. The strobing effect made it hard to see where I was going. I almost fell off one of the ramps when I reached the third floor and took one step too far. They hadn't even bothered to make any handrails or patch all the cracks in the walkways.

The final ramp just ended, some ten meters above the main floor.

"Shit," I muttered, looking down. That would have been a nasty fall—maybe ending in a revival.

Reaching out a boot, I managed to feel my way onto the broken slabs of puff-crete that connected the ramps to the corridors. Once inside the corridors, it was relatively safe and easy going. After another fifty steps I found a door my tapper was indicating to me with a big green arrow.

Pushing my way inside, I discovered the room was full of people I recognized.

"Sargon? Harris?" I said, putting on a grin.

They nodded back to me coldly. They didn't look happy.

At the front of the place was Graves. He was inspecting equipment of some kind.

"So good of you to join us, Centurion McGill," he said. "You're only seven minutes late."

"That hamster's maze out there almost killed me, Primus!"

Grave's made a disgusted face. "Maybe you'll wish it did before this briefing is over."

Sliding into a seat in the back, I listened in. Normally, I was bored and mentally drifting during any briefing—but somehow, this time things felt different. The stakes were higher today. This wasn't going to end up with Legion Varus going out for a cruise on some inhospitable rock. This was Mother Earth we were preparing to defend.

Harris raised his hand, and Graves nodded.

"With all due respect, Primus," Harris said, "this sounds like a job for hogs. We're on Earth, after all. It's not even legal for us to—"

"Hegemony has suspended their normal rules for the duration of this crisis," Graves told him. "Specifically, they've dropped the prohibition concerning independent legions performing military operations on Earth."

"That was quick," Harris muttered. "I didn't think the Ruling Council could do anything in less than six months."

A few people whistled and shuffled their feet. Legion Varus hadn't fought on Earth since we'd last been invaded, but it was hard to be surprised. If you scared anybody enough, even a hog, he tended to wake up and take action.

"If you don't have any more comments, I'll get back to the briefing," Graves said. "We're in the planning stages, naturally, and we don't know if our services will even be needed. Maybe these aliens are friendly, and they only want to ask to borrow a cup of sugar."

No one laughed, but at least *I* knew that Graves had made a joke. His jokes were always grim and delivered with a stony expression—people rarely laughed.

"What's the plan, Primus?" I asked him.

My tone was serious. Normally, I would have been calm and collected, if not bored. But today… today I had a kid out there in the city, and it sure as hell looked like someone was coming to kill her.

Graves looked at me for a moment, and he nodded. "The ship is headed directly for Earth. It's slowing down, and we don't know where it's going to land yet."

I raised my hand. Graves sighed and waved for me to speak. In the old days, he would have told me to shut the hell up—but now that I was a centurion, technically only one rank below him, he allowed me to talk a little more.

"Sir," I said, "that's old news. The ship's course has been plotted. She's coming right here, to Central."

The crowd of Varus officers mumbled again. Harris growled at me. "How the *fuck* do you know that? You just got here."

"That big bastard cue ball of a ship sensed the origins of the T-bombs—at least, that's what the nerds running the ops stations down there think."

Harris frowned at me fiercely. When he got bad news, he tended to get angry—at the messenger. Turning back around,

40

he crossed his arms over his wide chest and glared at Graves sourly.

In the meantime, Graves had checked his tapper. "I can see here from the live updates you're right. The ship is homing in on Central. We'll have to speed this up…"

Moving to a control screen, he began making gestures and touching big colored blocks of text. The wall behind him transformed into a map of local space. The Earth was down low, in the bottom left corner. In the center of the screen was the Moon, and far, far up in the upper left corner was another object. It was something metallic that followed a trajectory line all the way to our planet.

"It will pass Luna in about three hours. As it's reducing speed, it will hit us tomorrow morning just before dawn."

"That's great. That's just frigging great," Harris complained.

"Legion Varus will play the part of first-responders in this crisis."

We looked at each other and grinned at that, but our grins faded as Graves continued. He displayed a layout of the city.

"It's possible they will lay waste to this city for daring to effectively attack them. The xeno-people say their behavior patterns indicate arrogance and decisiveness. No matter what their intentions are, there can be no doubt they didn't like our surprise attack—ineffective as it was."

The grins were gone by now, but Graves wasn't done.

"If, on the other hand, they don't dust us off into our component molecules, it's predicted they will land here and at the very least inspect the origins of our attacks—meaning the vaults below Central."

Total silence met his statement. It hadn't escaped any of us that we were standing directly in the path of this hurricane of shit.

"Accordingly, Central will prepare to defend itself as best it can. To that end, we'll not just lock the doors and set up auto-cannons on the roof. We'll counterattack the moment they arrive."

"How the hell are we going to do that?" Harris demanded. "We teleported bombs into that ship, and they didn't do crap."

41

"No," Graves said, "we didn't teleport bombs *into* the ship. We tried, but failed to penetrate their hull. The bombs therefore came out of... wherever the hell a teleporting object goes through when it's in transit and struck the hull. That's partly why they were so ineffective. Most of them struck with kinetic force only and didn't go off properly."

"Still, I don't see how—"

Graves lifted his gauntlet. "We're going to get another chance when they arrive. If they want to land troops here, they'll have to open some kind of door, something like that. Then we'll be able to breach that hull and enter the ship."

"You mean," I began thoughtfully, "we're going to teleport *troops* into the ship the second they open up?"

"When commanded to do so, yes. We'll send commandos aboard to deal with the crew directly."

"I volunteer for that duty, Primus," I said loudly.

"Well, you can count me out," Harris said. "I've committed suicide lots of ways, but they clearly have a force field or something protecting that monster ship, and I'm not going to smash into those walls like our bombs did."

"Wrong," Graves told him. "You're in this, Harris. We all are—my entire cohort."

"Why us?" Harris demanded.

"Because this outfit has the most experienced teleport operatives in Earth's armed forces. We've been called upon by Earth to serve, and by God we'll do it with distinction today. No choices, no options."

"Shit..." Harris breathed.

That was pretty much everyone's opinion. This was a bad situation, and it wasn't getting any better.

The briefing broke up, and we were told to go upstairs We were to gear up and catch a few hours' sleep if possible. The third cohort of Legion Varus was playing commando at dawn.

-8-

Instead of searching for a bunk or teleport gear, I headed right out to the main floor. In a stroke of luck, I located Galina and Floramel together. My mind immediately leapt to the possibility they were working on a way to get my daughter to safety—but that wasn't what they were doing at all.

"This isn't possible..." Turov said, frowning at the data. "This kind of chemical signature—it's not *possible* in a manufactured object."

"We don't know how this ship was built—or if it's even a ship, really," Floramel told her. "We have to examine more remote possibilities. They might have found this shell of super-dense material and turned it into a vessel."

"Like turning a hollowed log into a boat? Preposterous."

Now, I knew you couldn't just go at Floramel that way. She always had her ducks in a firm line before she spoke, especially about something technical.

"And yet the ship exists," Floramel responded. "It's approaching rapidly, and it's clearly under powered flight. How would you explain its apparent composition? Even the gravimetrics support my theory. That object is a powered ship, and it is also made of compressed stellar dust."

Turov pursed her lips like she smelled a skunk and stared at the data.

"I still say it's impossible. Could this thing be an illusion of some kind? A phantom made to distract us?"

43

"That phantom is pretty damned solid," I interjected. "We just smashed a volley of T-bombs into it."

Turov glanced at me. "Ah, there you are McGill. About your daughter—something has been arranged."

"How's that?"

"She's been... advanced to candidacy. This means she is eligible for an immediate internship here at Central. Floramel has been gracious enough to become her mentor. We've relayed this to her tapper, and she's been ordered to report to this office immediately."

I frowned. "But did you talk to her? Did you tell her what's happening?"

Galina frowned. "That's your response? No thanks or anything? I'm busy defending the planet here—none of us really have time to do more."

"Okay, sorry. Thank you ladies—both of you."

Turning to go, I left them to their argument. Before I could take ten steps, however, I heard small, slapping boots behind me.

"Tribune?" I asked Galina when she came to walk next to me. "What's up?"

"I... I'm sorry James. I shouldn't have been rude just now—I'm stressed."

"Yeah, I bet. That's okay. We're all on edge, seeing as some kind of alien moon is falling on our heads. What were you guys talking about? This ship is made of stardust?"

"Yes, apparently so. It's very odd... how would you build such a thing?"

"Right now, what matters to me is how we go about unbuilding it."

She shook her head. "I don't think we can. Compressed matter is incredibly tough. Even if that ship's hull is only a hundred meters thick and the region inside is hollow, it still will have as much mass and gravity as our own Moon."

"And all the gravity readings support Floramel's theory, don't they?"

"Yes... it's very strange. If they have the technology to hollow out a neutron star, or something... I don't see how we can beat them."

"Don't worry. I'm involved in a plan to do just that."

As she was my tribune, I gave her the details of Graves' plan. She listened in concern.

"Graves has not yet approved this with me. He's working directly with Drusus, bypassing me again. But in any case... it sounds to me like you'll be splattered into a million pieces— just like our bombs."

"May be."

We'd reached the elevator, and we began the long ride up. She put her hand on my arm and squeezed.

"What are you going to do before your scheduled suicide in the morning?"

"Uh..." I said, looking her over. It seemed like she was making an offer. One which I found very appealing.

But I sighed resignedly. "I have to find Etta. I have to get her to safety first—I don't have very long before this mess begins striking the fan."

"I understand... What if I help? My air car is parked in a nearby garage. I'll take you to her, and we'll fly her to safety."

"That would be great, Galina."

Without thinking about it, I swept her up and kissed her. I'd wanted to do that for the last hour or two.

She went with it for a few moments, but then she gently pulled away. "We're on camera, you know."

"Yeah, but our affair isn't a secret anymore."

She pulled away farther, and I let her go. We rode up to the surface then walked the streets to the parking garage.

People were out there protesting. A swarming crowd was held back by police barricades. They waved angry fists at us and threw stuff—but neither of us was fazed. After you've fought and died on a dozen planets, a riot at the capitol seems like a high school dance.

Climbing into Galina's air car, we soon launched above the throngs. Now that we were outside Central, I began getting all the texts that had been censored while I was in the War Room.

For once, I paged through them eagerly. Etta had written me and so had Della.

"They're in the harbor district," I told Galina, flicking the address from my tapper to her onboard autopilot.

After she tapped an approval, the car slewed around and lost altitude, heading for the new destination.

Not ten minutes later we'd located Della and Etta at an outdoor mall. There wasn't much shopping going on—but there was looting.

They climbed into the backseat, laughing and showing us the stuff they'd picked up. It was clothing, mostly. The expensive smart-kind that the younger ladies liked to wear.

"Did you two just steal that?" Turov demanded sourly.

"Not at all," Della said. "We chased off looters, in fact. Unfortunately, when people drop their goods in the middle of the pathway there's no easy way to return it to the rightful owner."

Etta fell quiet. What had no doubt been a fun time had turned into something serious. She wanted to join Central, not be labeled a criminal.

"There's a way," she said suddenly. "We can scan for nano-markings. They'll be registered to a corporation somewhere."

Galina laughed. "You *are* the smart one," she said. "Are you sure you aren't Natasha's daughter?"

"Natasha Elkin? Well… she did raise me for several years. Maybe some of her—"

"I'm her mother," Della said firmly.

She was getting steamed, and I couldn't blame her. Galina was a great lover, but she tended to change people's moods for the worse when she got to talking to them.

This was all about petty jealousy, of course. Della was my ex, and Galina never played nice when there was a potential rival around.

Deciding to intervene, I laughed loudly. "It's great how that green dress keeps crawling around on your leg, Della! It's trying to figure out what you want it to do."

"Yes…" she said. "It is amusing. I'll try it on later if you're still with us."

"Uh…" I said, taking a quick glance at Galina. She shook her head ever so slightly, and I forced a smile.

46

"I think it would be best if you ladies were transported out of town and dropped off in a safe place. We could go to Bridgeport, if you like. I—"

"No," Galina said. "We're going to Central. Floramel did an excellent job with the internship invitation, I'm afraid. Maybe too good."

"What do you mean?" I asked her.

"Remember when you wanted Etta to come to Central? Well, her application was already on file, and she has been accepted. She's government property now, just like you and I are. And you, Della—you've been added to the roster for Graves' project in any case."

I groaned aloud.

"What project?" Della asked.

A slightly evil smile played on Galina's lips. "You haven't heard—? Oh, of course you haven't. You've been out... *shopping* while Earth is being invaded. The situation is classified, but you're all cleared now to hear about it. James? Please brief them."

Sadly, I gave them the bad news. Della was part of the same cohort I was in, under Graves' command, but she'd become a ghost specialist recently, and I hadn't thought they'd want her for this mission.

Apparently, I was wrong. We were all going into that ship together—or getting permed in the attempt.

The worst part was informing Etta. We were her only parents, after all, and she already knew what dead legionnaires looked like.

Etta didn't cry, but she was in mild shock. Her face was pale as she gazed out the window at the city sliding by underneath us. Now and then, she craned her neck upwards.

"I can see it," she said quietly. "It's always there now, even in daylight."

None of us asked her what she was talking about. We knew Earth's new moon was coming. It grew larger and more threatening every hour.

-9-

That night, we all went back to Central. There were plenty of quarters for troops in emergencies. The building had been built with a century's worth of expansion in mind.

After checking in with my unit and arranging a short-range teleport harness for each soldier, I managed to slip away with some excuse about a briefing.

Galina met me at her office, shooed away everyone else, and made sweet love to me on her couch.

"I'd like to spend the night with you," she said, "but I know you have to get back to your troops."

After a final hug, we parted ways. I found a bunk about seventy floors below her office and slept a few hard hours until Veteran Moller began hammering on the walls to wake everyone up.

Pulling myself together, I inspected my yawning troops. It was briefing-time.

"3rd Unit," I said, "we've been called upon this fine morning to defend Earth directly. It hasn't been since the Cephalopod invasion that we've been able to make that claim."

"You're scaring me, boss," Carlos said.

"You should be scared," Harris muttered.

Everyone else stayed quiet, staring at me.

"That's right. We're first-responders today. When that big ship arrives, we're going to board her. This is the kind of opportunity we've all dreamt of."

They looked stunned. Not even Carlos had a snappy remark for this occasion.

"Legion Varus has more experience, more battle creds and more support from the brass than any outfit in history."

At this point I was lying my ass off, but some of them were buying it. Not Carlos of course, or Harris, or Cooper—but people like Moller and Sargon. They liked and needed a good pep-speech before they got their asses handed to them by some heartless alien menace.

"Accordingly," I continued, "I've been authorized to hand out combat bonuses today to everyone under my command. That's right, double-pay for a month!"

There were a few cheers. Not many, but a few.

Carlos was making that twisted-lip look of disgust, but it was Cooper who raised a hand to speak. Reluctantly, I called on him.

"Sir, that's great news and all, but it's got me wondering— is Central offering this to us because they expect a mass-perming?"

Right then, I wanted to kick his ass out the window and into the streets a thousand meters below us. That was the urge Graves had undoubtedly felt toward me on occasions like this when I opened my mouth at briefings.

"Absolutely not," I boomed loudly. When I lie in pubic, I like to go big. "That's damn-near impossible. Hell, we'll probably be in wifi range of the routers right here in old Central herself. How could we get permed under such circumstances?"

"Well," Natasha spoke up, "from what I understand, the hull composition is collapsed matter. That's going to stop all kinds of electromagnetic radiation more efficiently than a wall of lead."

My mouth twitched, but I managed to hold my smile and shake my head. "Such paranoid delusions! Should I call up Graves right now and tell him we can't go? That we all wet our collective beds last night?"

"No, sir!" a half-dozen of the more gung-ho types replied. Among my officers, only Adjunct Barton was among this

49

select group. I was beginning to like her personal style. Legion Varus could use more people who were as eager to serve.

The briefing broke up, as I didn't have many operational details to provide. The truth was we weren't sure if we were going to be deployed at all. We'd suit up, stand on the launch pad and be ready to pop into the enemy ship at a moment's notice. It was the sort of thing we'd drilled for and had lots of practice doing.

We were given light rations to eat, and after that, we made our way to the teleport rooms. I organized my first squad in harnesses without a lot of heavy gear. They were to jump first, clear any immediate resistance, and cover the rest as they came in hot right behind them.

Leeson sought me out as I fitted people with harnesses.

"McGill," he said, "can I ask you a private question?"

"Shoot, Adjunct."

"How did we draw the short straw on this one? Did you shit on Graves' lawn again?"

"Uh… how do you mean? The whole cohort—"

Leeson began to laugh, shaking his head. "Oh right, sure, we're going to get a thousand men popped aboard this enemy ship, all wearing their skivvies and ready to fight. Did you notice that we're pretty far up on the roster? As in: first?"

My eyes crept over to the scheduling boards. Leeson was right, 3rd Unit topped the list.

"Hmm…" I said. "Well, that just means he trusts us. We're some of the most experienced teleport troops Earth has."

"Yeah, right. That's because you keep getting us assigned to crazy-ass stunts like this. And while I'm in a complaining mood, what's the deal with these harnesses? Aren't these kind of flimsy? What if the internals on that ship are burning hot or icy cold—or not pressurized with oxygen at all?"

"Each soldier will be equipped with an emergency oxygen tank, a full-pressure suit, and enough juice in their harnesses for one more port back home."

"That's beautiful," he said, shaking his head. "They'll open some kind of bay door into their cargo hold, we'll pop into a vacuum-filled ice-hole, and get five minutes to shoot our way out."

"More like fifteen," I said, but that didn't sound good to me either.

Giving Leeson a hearty slap on the shoulder, I told him I'd toast him in Hell and moved on.

"We'll go in by platoons," I said. "Barton, your lights go first. Next up will be Harris with the heavies, last is Leeson. I'll be joining Harris."

They grumbled, a few prayed, one of the new recruits even puked—but they were all game. I could tell. You didn't get far in Legion Varus without accepting what you were: fodder for the nearest cannon.

While we were moving Barton's nervous team onto the launch pad the ceiling lit up. It transformed into a giant screen.

Staring upward, it was as if we could look out through hundreds of floors of puff-crete, and through another thousand kilometers of sky and clouds. Space was revealed, with a soft, blue-white glow at every edge of the huge chamber. That was the limits of Earth's atmosphere.

The big sphere had finally arrived. We could see it clearly, without telescopes or interpretive graphics.

It was a moon—but a scarred moon. Smooth white metal in most areas, there were dozens of blast marks. Splotches as big as cities dotted the surface. These revealed the real hull of the monster underneath. It was a black, crusty surface of compressed matter.

"She's in orbit, right on top of us," Natasha said, gaping up at the ceiling in wonderment.

"It's Hell's own angel, come to collect," Leeson said.

"It's way too big," Harris complained. "It's just not right."

We all stared and gaped at the ceiling. Somehow, until that moment, the enormity of this thing had escaped me.

A surge of acid burned my guts. A tickle of dread fluttered down there, inside me. I couldn't help it. Our task seemed beyond suicidal—it was hopeless.

Recovering, I looked around at my silent troops. Even Moller was staring upward as if the Almighty himself had come to dinner.

Clapping my hands together with painful force, I made a series of loud booming sounds. They blinked and looked at me.

51

"That's our cue, boys and girls! Time for the fun to begin! First squad, on the launch pad!"

They wavered for a few seconds, but Barton and Moller recovered fast. They were slapping helmets and kicking asses until the first group was assembled on the raised section of floor.

Instead of activating each harness one at a time, Central had made advances. They were able to launch a whole group at once if they stood on that pad a few meters apart.

"James," Natasha said in my ear. "I'm getting all kinds of reports from other techs—the ship is so big it's disrupting our local tides. The harbor area is being flooded. There are waves in the streets, James!"

She sounded a little panicked. I thought of the shops where Della and Etta had been enjoying themselves just yesterday— but then I moved my brain to here and now.

"Not our problem, Natasha. Get your head in the game, girl. I need you."

"On it, Centurion. I just thought you might want to know."

Natasha was well known as the best tech in the cohort. Graves, in his infinite wisdom, had decided to put my unit on point, and he'd embedded Natasha with me for support. It was a nice gesture at least.

All we had to do now was wait for the go-signal, and we didn't have long to wait. The big ship, looming not so far over our heads, soon opened up a section of its massive hull.

A door bigger than a supertanker slid away, revealing a dark maw within. In very short order, sleek-looking objects began to drop out of it.

"Are those fighters?" Carlos asked.

"They look more like landing craft," Sargon said. "They're the size of our lifters."

"Are you crazy? They're tiny."

Sargon laughed at him. "Those tiny little bat-winged craft are big enough to carry a thousand troops. You've got to wrap your head around the size of this thing."

"Oh yeah..." Carlos said. "It is the size of the Moon..."

The signal came in about then, as I'd been expecting. I lifted my hand and chopped it down, waving to Barton. A countdown started, overlaid on the ceiling above us.

"Ten... nine..."

"Button-up!" Barton shouted. "Check your gear. Safeties off, O-2 on!"

"She's a pro," Sargon said at my side.

"She's hot," Carlos said from the other side.

We watched as Barton marshaled thirty-five terrified light troopers. Some of them were confident veterans, such as Cooper and Della, but most were the greenest people in the unit.

When the countdown hit about four, the teleport effect began. Their outlines began to waver, and soon they transformed into standing regions of blue-white light.

This effect grew rapidly, and they all winked out together.

"That's it!" Harris roared. "Heavy platoon, we're up! Come on, come on, come on! You didn't join Varus to live forever!"

Hustling forward with something that bordered on eagerness, the heavy troopers massed up onto the launch pad. I stepped up with them, and we quickly spaced ourselves out by sidestepping.

Each heavy trooper wore powered suits. We looked like hockey goalies in armor. Every man was encased in whirring metal that weighed more than he did, but we moved easily enough with exoskeletal suits underneath that were trained to respond and amplify our every motion.

Soon, the countdown began again. Ten short seconds after that we left the surface of Earth—possibly for the last time.

-10-

Blinking out of existence and appearing again in a different place is always upsetting, but this time it was worse than usual.

We didn't land on a solid surface. Apparently, there hadn't been time to aim that precisely. Instead, they'd just thrown us into the open door of the alien ship during the short period it was open.

We were floating, weightless, unanchored—at least, that's what I thought at first. Then I realized we *were* falling. Our acceleration curve was kind of slow, but we were moving toward a distant dim-lit wall.

That wall—it was gently curved. It had to be the outer hull of the great ship.

"Oh shit..." I whispered aloud. "Unit leaders, come in! This is McGill—give me a sit-rep!"

"Harris here—and our situation is that we're completely fucked, Centurion."

"Barton here—I have to agree with Harris."

We'd all realized the problem. Central had been so anxious to get us inside this ship, they hadn't thought things through.

We were inside the vessel, but this hangar area the smaller ships had come from was *huge*. It was so big that we were probably going to be smashed to a pulp once we fell all the way to the hull.

"Natasha? Talk to me!"

She didn't answer, and I realized she wasn't with the rest. Not yet. She was coming in with the third platoon led by Leeson.

I tried to raise Central, but coms were out. Maybe the ship put out too much RF, or maybe the crew was blocking us. I didn't know which, and I didn't much care. We were cut off from Earth.

Earth.

I caught sight of my home world then, as seen through the yawning doorway that provided most of the light inside this massive vessel.

Clouds like streamers ran across a hazy surface of brown, green and blue. Those clouds looked like cresting waves from orbit.

"I need a plan," I said. "What have we got?"

"Let's bug out," Harris said immediately. "We can't do anything in here, it's ridiculous. We're like a swarm of gnats inside a football stadium plotting how we're going to take it all down."

"I'll tell you what. If you're about to go splat, and can't escape that fate, you can port home. The harnesses are more valuable than we are, and we can always try again."

"I'm not so sure about that, Centurion," Barton said.

Looking around, I saw what she meant. A final trio of invasion shuttles left the mothership, gliding out of that gaping door. Their engines flared white with radiation as they nosed downward toward Earth.

How many troops were on those shuttles? Surely it had to be more than we'd sent back at them.

The bad part wasn't the escaping shuttles, or a radioactive backwash of their engines. It was the massive door that had let them out. It was rolling slowly closed, moving back into place.

"We're gonna get shut in!" Harris shouted. "We'll be trapped!"

"Where are you bastards?" Leeson spoke up, having just arrived.

I craned my neck upward, to where I'd first appeared. I could see Leeson and his men, distant metallic dolls. We'd already fallen a kilometer or more, if I had to guess.

55

The trouble was that on Earth, there would be a terminal velocity due to atmospheric friction. Here, the air seemed to be pretty thin. That meant that even though the gravitational pull of the hull was lower than it was back home, making our acceleration lower, we didn't have anything holding us back .We were falling toward the outer hull, faster and faster as we went.

"Natasha!" I roared, ignoring Leeson, "I need you, girl. Can we survive a landing on the inner hull of this ship?"

"I… I'm not sure, sir. I'll do some measurements and calculations."

"Hurry it up, we're running out of time."

"Once that door rolls shut, McGill, I don't know if we can get out of here. Can these teleport suits take us through solid star-stuff?"

"It sure can," I said with utter confidence, despite the fact that I didn't think it was possible.

Straining to spin around again, I looked toward the door. It was half-way shut already.

"Natasha, give me something to go on!"

"Uh… according to my calculations, we'll hit at about forty meters per second."

"Great. What's that mean? Splat or walk it off?"

"If you're in a light suit, you're dead. If you're in full body armor—you might break a bone, but you'll probably survive the impact."

That was good enough for me. "Barton! First platoon, withdraw! I repeat, bug out back to Earth!"

They didn't hesitate. First platoon was full of nervous nellies to begin with. They initiated the sequence. I watched them, far, far below my heavies, as they began to flutter blue-white.

Splat!

Splat-Splat-Splat!

A shower of bodies hit. Some of them had been too close to the point of no return, apparently. They'd crashed into the inner hull of the great ship before the teleportation sequence could finish.

As they smashed down with killing force, every terminal fall made me wince. There were gasping breaths from a few, but most had died instantly. It all depended on whether they'd come down on their heads or their feet.

Maybe half of Barton's platoon escaped. It couldn't have been more.

"If you've got no armor, you have permission to bug out back to Earth right now,'" I broadcast to the entire unit. "Otherwise, aim your air tanks at the approaching surface. Release up to half your air to slow yourself down."

"You crazy mother..." I heard someone say. It was probably Harris, but I couldn't be sure.

Dutifully, some of the troops winked out. The bio people like Carlos, the techs like Kivi and Natasha—they all took off.

The rest of us, falling in our metal suits, braced for impact. We turned on repellers and fired vital O-2 downward, trying to slow our fall. It had some effect—but that floor was still coming at me way too fast.

"Bend your knees!" I heard Moller and Sargon shouting. "Bend your damned knees, you pathetic splats!"

We did as the veterans said. We'd all been in combat jumps before. No one gets heavy armor without earning it.

So I bent my knees, bled out my oxygen, gritted my teeth and prayed.

Then the inner hull of the great ship came up at me like a giant's hand and smashed into the soles of my boots.

-11-

Most of us survived without broken bones or compromised suits. A notable exception was Leeson—and he wasn't happy about it.

Somehow, he'd gotten into a tumble during those final moments before impact. He'd probably fired too much gas out of his tanks without aiming at the precisely correct angle.

He'd come down cracking one knee, then his faceplate, then he'd gone into a violent rolling spin. As the gravity was Moon-level, his body bounced up a dozen meters before smashing down again.

I staggered from my landing spot toward him. He was on his back. His faceplate was cracked like a mirror smashed by a hammer. He managed to groan and wheeze at me.

"I'm dead," he said, coughing weakly. "Back's broken, I'm pretty sure."

I thumbed his suit's diagnostics. His prognosis was correct. After you'd spent a few decades in Legion Varus, you got know how injuries worked and what they felt like.

"Laser or faceplate?" I asked him, looming into his field of vision.

"What? Can't you just let a man die in peace?"

"Nope. I need your air, your power, your harness and your weapon. You're carrion now."

"Fucker..." he said, and he flipped up his faceplate.

58

I shot him in the right eye socket. That was a lot better than freezing solid, as I could attest.

When everyone was down, we counted bodies. I had thirty-nine effectives left. About a third of the troops I'd jumped with.

"What about the other units?" I asked. He was my only surviving officer. "Any sign?"

"No," Harris said. "There wasn't time, I guess. The big door is closed."

"Maybe they saw how badly our jump went, and they scrubbed the rest."

"I suppose they might be here somewhere inside this giant ship. Long-range coms is out."

We both spun slowly around, panning and examining our new world. We were inside a chamber that was bigger than a city. Above us were hundreds of claw-like docking systems.

"The assault ships must have been hanging on those things," Harris speculated. "They probably dock there, then fall out of the ship when the door opens, and they're released."

"Yeah..." I agreed. "Come on. Let's get all able-bodied asses up and moving again. Have everyone pick up an extra O-2 pack and ammo if they find it."

We stripped the dead like pros and moved on. It only made sense to me that we'd been detected by now. There had to be someone on guard duty, and I wanted to get off the LZ before they arrived.

It had only been ten minutes since the first platoon had blinked out from Central and appeared here. My survivors were jogging smartly toward the nearest interesting thing we could see—a big segmented tower of dark metal.

It took some time to get there. When we were halfway to the goal, some of the troops in the rear sounded the alarm. Breathing hard, we stopped running and looked back.

A swarm of alien flying-machines had found our dead lying sprawled on the deck. They seemed baffled. Floating and swaying, even doing little loops, they circled around the bodies and poked at them.

"I rigged them up a little surprise," Sargon said, walking up to me and grinning.

He thumbed a detonator. A gush of plasma swallowed the fluttering objects, and when it cleared, they'd vanished along with the dead they'd been poking at.

Harris slammed the back of Sargon's helmet with his gauntlet.

Sargon whirled around, raging, but he lost his urge to kill when he realized who was standing behind him.

"You damned fool!" Harris said. "They'll know for sure they've got commandos aboard now!"

"Easy Harris," I said. "That had to be pretty obvious to them once they found that graveyard full of splats."

"How would these aliens know we weren't all dead? Now, they *know* we're here."

I shrugged. "Don't worry so much. We're here to break things, not make friends."

"What are we going to break next, Centurion?" Sargon asked. He, for one, was ready to kill something.

I pointed into the distance. "The only thing we can reach without running out of air is that segmented tower over there. Come on, it looks important."

"I'll beat you to it," Sargon said, and he began clanking away by using his exoskeletal suit to move his armor faster than a mortal man could run.

For a moment, I wanted to call for him to slow down. He was using up valuable power and oxygen recklessly—but then it hit me. Harris was right, and Sargon knew it.

The enemy had pinpointed us. No matter what we did now, it was only a matter of time before we were hunted down and destroyed—if we didn't suffocate first.

"Sir!" called out a voice behind me. I turned to see it was Moller. "Permission to port out, sir!"

"What's the problem?" I asked, but I saw what the problem was almost before I finished the thought. Her faceplate was cracked. "You low on O-2?"

"Yes, I'm down to my last minute. I've sealed the crack, but I'm still leaking."

"I can give you another bottle."

"No sir," she said firmly. "I'll just waste it. The air will all leak out."

"Moller, I don't think we can port out of this ship. Our T-bombs couldn't penetrate the hull, and the door is closed now."

"I know all that sir, but I'd rather try than die gasping."

After thinking it over for a few seconds, I nodded to her. "Give it a shot."

She began to grow a blue nimbus. A moment later she vanished.

A smile appeared on my face. It looked like she'd done it. But then Harris trotted by looking disgusted.

"She bugged out?" he asked. "Serves her right then."

He pointed, and I saw something at my feet. It was Moller's gauntlet, fingers outstretched, sprouting out of the hull of the ship like a flower.

She'd tried to teleport through the dense matter, but she'd ended up getting stuck about meter or so down. She was beyond dead. She was encased in star dust forever.

Grimly, I turned back toward the tower Sargon was running toward and picked up my pace. There was no escaping this place. Our best option was to do some fast dirty damage right now while we could.

Kicking on my own exo-suit, I began charging in Sargon's wake. "Come on! Everyone, top speed!"

Like a herd of kangaroos we set off, bounding in huge ground-eating leaps. The low gravity, combined with our power armor, sent us flying with each stride. Our steps were ten meters high and thirty long.

We ate up ground very quickly. Overhead, I saw something—but I ignored it. A swarm of flying objects was coming after us—but it didn't matter. We were running out of air.

Before we could make it to the big tower, which now looked to me kind of like a giant coiled tube or cable, the enemy bird-like things caught up.

I don't think I'd ever been attacked by stranger creatures. With the body of a metallic manta ray, they had flapping wings that shouldn't have worked in the nearly airless environment—but they seemed to operate to anyway. How could something so ungainly fly? I didn't know. But they were doing it.

The first time we slashed one down with force-blades, we learned more about them. They weren't robots—not exactly. They were part metal, part meat. They flapped, and they clicked. We cut them out of the air, and they sprayed dark blood all over. They seemed to be full of blood that had the consistency and color of reddish motor oil.

Oddly, they didn't try to kill us. They tried to capture us instead. They gripped our armor with metallic claws and lifted us into the air. Usually, this was a bad idea for the flapping manta-ray things. We slashed them apart, and they fell back to the deck—and we kept on running.

After a hundred of them were down, the rest flapped away into a darkening cloud.

Glancing up, I realized the cloud they'd formed consisted of thousands more of the same kind of nightmares.

"Centurion!" shouted Harris. "We've got more trouble! There are bigger things charging up on us!"

I looked this way and that, then my HUD went red with contacts, and I turned around.

Harris was right. Running across the giant hangar on foot was a herd of strange-looking things. I couldn't be sure if they were robots, or walking vehicles or maybe just armored giant beasts. Whatever they were, they walked on four legs in a predatory run. It was hard to get the scale right due to their distance, but I would have to estimate they were each two or three times the height of a man.

"Some kind of walking machine?" I asked aloud.

"I don't know. They're shaped with curves and move like they have muscles. Metal and meat mixed together just like those flapping things."

For a moment, I couldn't tear my eyes away. They kept coming at a methodical run. Each one moved like the others, coming our way with deadly intent. It was like watching a vast pack of predators coming to feast. Some instinct of mind sent fear through my nervous system. Part of me knew I was being attacked by an army of monsters, even if my brain was too stupid to admit it.

"All right!" I shouted. "Listen up! We're not going to make it to the target before we're overwhelmed. Sargon, take your package and sprint toward the coiled thing. The rest of us will head in the opposite direction."

Sargon was far ahead, but he heard me. "Got it, Centurion. My football will reach the target, or I'll die trying."

"Come on everybody, get moving!" As I said this, I reversed course and raced off in the opposite direction.

Sargon was carrying one of our few bombs. We didn't have many A-bombs left, mostly because antimatter was very difficult to make. Using supercolliders to knock the unstable stuff apart from standard matter, antimatter had one useful property: total conversion from mass to energy when it contacted normal matter.

Just keeping it from exploding was the most difficult thing about making an antimatter bomb. You didn't need to have a detonator or some kind of compression system. All you had to do was let it touch any normal mass and *boom*! Everything went up. Even our best fusion warheads using plutonium only converted mass to energy about a tenth as efficiently.

Unfortunately, we'd blown up most of our strategic arsenal with the T-bomb attack, and Graves had entrusted my unit with one of the precious few A-bombs we had left.

All of us were running now. Instead of following him, we were moving as fast as we could away from Sargon.

Above us, the metallic flock grew, and those bastards finally began to plunge downward. This time, there were thousands.

We slashed them down and shot them, but they kept coming down and trying to capture us. Some troops, swarmed and screeching, were carried off. Wriggling and wrestling with their captors, they couldn't break away.

Most of us fought and died more naturally. We killed hundreds, but hundreds more took their place. They seemed absolutely heedless of their losses. They didn't seem to feel pain, either, when you cut them down. The broken halves crawled around until their bodies no longer functioned. It was like fighting giant insects.

We'd been inside the enemy ship for around fifteen minutes now, and we were running out of oxygen and men—but I knew it didn't matter.

This attack had been insanity from the start. How could a hundred men hope to best a ship the size of the Moon? If we'd sent in a thousand, it wouldn't have mattered.

Then, a brilliant explosion flared behind me. My right eye glazed over, going white, and it never saw anything again.

The other eye—my left, still could make out my surroundings. Perhaps it had been more protected by the back of my helmet than the right.

A moment later I was struck by a wave of superheated gas and hurled like a leaf into spinning flight. I was sure I'd been captured by those manta rays—but there were none in evidence.

Flying ass-over-teakettle straight up, I saw the sky again.

Such a beautiful sight. The door—the massive, roll-away door—it was sliding open again. Outside was space, and Mother Earth, shining with a blue radiance.

My mind wasn't working too well. I was shot-through with gamma rays and ionizing radiation. I was as good as dead. But it still occurred to me what that massive coiled up tower had to have been: a big spring. Or maybe a cable. Something that had kept the outer door shut.

Sargon must have reached it and lit off his bomb. In doing so, he'd broken the mechanism that shut the outer door. It was now falling open like the yawning mouth of a sleepy giant.

Earth had been revealed again because we'd broken the monster's jaws. One of the massive springs had been cut, and now the whole system had malfunctioned.

What's more, I suspected there was some amount of atmosphere in the great ship. Maybe only the region around the door was depressurized when it opened. Or maybe it was just the vaporized gasses released by the bomb.

In any case, gas puffed out into space. The surge of air pressure drove me up into the sky and now sent me hurtling out into open space.

Once I passed through the mouth and out into the blazing light of our own home star, I began trying to transmit.

No one answered me. Not my own troops, not Central, not even space traffic control.

But I kept trying. My armor was leaking air, my body and mind were barely obeying my brain's commands, and I was spinning in an uncontrolled tumble.

But I still kept trying to transmit everything I'd recorded on my tapper. It was the least I could do.

Eventually, I knew I'd fall down in a decayed orbit, burning up in the upper atmosphere like a meteor.

Long before that, I choked up, stopped breathing, and died.

-12-

Groaning, I awoke and almost fell off the gurney. I couldn't talk yet, but I could sit up—kind of.

"That was outstanding!" A gravelly voice said. After a second, I realized it was Graves. "Here's a man who's eager for the fight!" he continued with unusual enthusiasm. "How's it feel to be Earth's hero, McGill?"

"Mmph?" I asked. For some reason, my mouth wasn't able to form words yet. With a fantastic effort of will, I forced my eyes to flutter open and squint.

"What's his score?" a woman asked. She pawed at my face, and I let her.

"He's an eight," an orderly said. "But his nervous system isn't hooked up to his face quite right yet."

"You're telling me he's a bad grow?" Graves complained. "What shitty luck."

"His scans were hard to get," the bio specialist explained. "His engrams… they were sketchy. Where did you get this file, Primus?"

"From orbit," Graves said.

"That explains it," she said. "I'll get the grinder going."

I heard the whine and whir of the blades spinning. My eyes flew wide, and I blinked. I might have tried to grab a weapon, but I was weak still—and a little dizzy.

"Shut that damned thing off," Graves said. "Let's give him a chance. I don't want to recycle my best soldier without being sure."

The bio nodded to her sidekick. Reluctantly, the orderly shut down the whirling blades.

"I've seen a lot of this emotionalism, Centurion," the bio said. "Sometimes the hardest choice is the right one."

"You don't have to tell me about that," Graves said.

I couldn't believe he was actually sticking up for me. Frankly, I was amazed that I'd been revived at all. Anyone who died floating in space near a giant alien ship should expect a solid perming, and I'd done so—but praise and protection from Primus Graves? Now, *that* was a first.

"Sirrr…?" I managed to slur out.

"There you go!" Graves responded. "Did you hear that? He's talking."

"We have to keep him here for observation, Primus. If you'll just come back in about an hour—"

"No, no, no," Graves said. "You ghouls want to reroll. I'll tell you what, I'm taking him out of here. If he still sounds like a stroke-victim in half an hour I'll shoot him myself and shove him into the recycler."

"Suit yourself," the bio said resignedly. "Place your thumb here, sir."

"What's this?"

"A standard release form."

Graves glared at the tablet and at the bored-looking bio. She had the look of an over-worked Blue-Decker who just wanted her troubles to go away.

"Something that releases you from responsibility for him, right?"

"That's about it, sir."

Graves touched his thumb to the plate and lifted me off the gurney. He helped press me into a smart-cloth uniform, and we exited the place, which stank of new life and old death.

"Thhhff…" I said.

"Thanks? Don't thank me yet. If you can't talk right in the next twenty minutes, hero or not, I'll have to put you down, McGill."

67

"Whaa—?" I asked.

"Why do I have to put you down? Because I can't have a clearly bad grow talking to the troops—or the brass."

"No... Why hero?" I was forming each word with great effort. It shouldn't be this hard, but sometimes part of a man's new body didn't operate at one hundred percent capacity right off.

"Why are you a hero? Because you chased off that ship, man! Don't you know?"

"...been dead..."

"Of course, of course. Here's the short version: by some miracle, we got a transmission from your suit after the big ship's door reopened. The alien crew didn't like you blowing their jaw off, apparently, and they couldn't close the hatch again. The ship spun around so the opening couldn't be seen from Earth, then it withdrew several million kilometers. We think they were worried we'd fire a load of T-bombs into the guts of their vessel and take them out."

"...good idea..."

"Yeah, it would have been, but we're pretty much out of T-bombs. We fired them all in that first attack hoping to penetrate the hull—fortunately, the enemy doesn't know that. With their armor breached, they couldn't take the chance."

I nodded and began to walk without aid. I wasn't feeling a hundred percent, not yet, but at least I wasn't feeling sick anymore. My mind was working better every second, but I never seemed to get out of a revival chamber without some kind of lingering malady.

"That's right," Graves said. "Walk it off. You're coming to dinner with me tonight—before deployment. Praetor Drusus demands to sit at your side. You'll be his guest of honor."

"...deployment...?"

"Of course. You didn't think this war was over, did you? The enemy invaded with ninety-one assault shuttles before their mothership retreated. Each shuttle carried down something like a thousand troops."

That was a stunner. While I turned his words this way and that in my mind, we made our way through Central. Graves talked to me all the way up to the Varus offices. By the time we got there, I'd learned that New Jersey was full of alien troops. It wasn't the homecoming I'd dreamt about, but I did my best to take it in stride.

When I could talk properly they debriefed me for a few hours. I described the strange cyborg creatures we'd fought and been overwhelmed by. They were particularly interested in the way the giant coil worked to open the ship's outer door.

"Are you seriously expecting us to believe you broke the hinge or something?" Winslade asked in a distrustful tone.

"Primus Winslade," I began, "you and I go way back. *Way* back. You might have felt that some of my after-action reports were inaccurate or… let us say exaggerated somehow. But all that's in the past. Today, the fate of Earth is involved. I stand by my statements, one hundred percent."

"I wonder…"

"That's enough," Turov said. "Winslade, you're dismissed."

"Technically," Winslade said, "I work for Hegemony under Drusus now, remember? I represent his interests in this debriefing."

"Fine. I'll just tell him you're not being cooperative."

Winslade's hand came up off the table he'd been leaning on as if a bee had stung him. I got the immediate feeling that he wasn't on Drusus' hot list anymore, and he didn't need complaints going back to the big boss.

"I'll go check in with the dinner crew," he said. "I don't want to eat cold food again."

"You do that," Galina told him.

Miffed, Winslade sauntered out. I was left with Graves and the tribune.

With Winslade out of the room, I found things to be much more pleasant. Both Graves and Turov were pretty happy with me. Graves was prideful that Varus troops had helped drive away the enemy ship—even if the aliens had managed to deposit invaders on Earth before leaving.

Turov, on the other hand, was trying to figure out how to best exploit my unit's success and take credit for it. In any case, neither one of them wanted to hear jealous nitpicking from the likes of Winslade.

"We don't have any of your video recordings, unfortunately," Graves said. "We got something from the platoon that withdrew—but nothing of the enemy you saw. The last pulse of data from your tapper carried the essentials of your mental engrams, proof you were dying—and that's about it."

"It's a pity," Galina mused. "It would be a powerful move to play video of your commando raid at tonight's banquet."

For my own part, I wasn't so sure about that. After all, the operation had resembled a first-class Charley-Foxtrot. We'd popped up there and splatted one platoon right off the bat. Then, another platoon had been forced to bug out without seeing much. Lastly, my dented-up heavies had run around like cockroaches until we blew ourselves up in desperation.

Of course, I didn't describe it that way. It was the charge of the light brigade in my version. We were damned near perfect in our execution and made critical choices under fire.

Now, a person might get the wrong idea while listening to me that I was hamming it up for a promotion or something. That's not really the case. I was pretty happy as a centurion, and most of my superiors would have been very hesitant to advance me any further.

No, my call for glowing descriptions and outright bragging just came naturally to me. When events needed a little dolling-up for public consumption, James McGill could always do the job.

By dinner time, true to Graves' word, I found myself seated next to Drusus. Not only that, but what amazed me even more was the list of big-wigs in attendance. Another praetor was there, Wurtenburger was his name. He was a fat-boy from the Euro-branch that I hadn't laid eyes on for years.

Graves wasn't even invited and neither was Winslade. In fact, I was the only person in attendance under the rank of tribune. Many lower ranked officers would have been spooked by this fact, but not me. I wasn't fazed in the least. I was eyeing the doors to the kitchen, mostly.

"When do we get to eat?" I asked again.

Drusus smiled good-naturedly. "I see you haven't put on any years or any pounds, McGill."

"No sir. My body just got freshened up this afternoon."

"Freshening up" was what legion veterans called dying for Mother Earth. Doing so, then getting pumped out of a revival machine, allowed a man to live again in a copy of his body that was often years younger than the one that had been mangled. Copies of our neural networks—our memories and thought-connections, were updated much more frequently so we could remember our past.

"Of course... that was a spectacular operation. The enemy were clearly surprised and unprepared for a boarding attempt by infantry."

"That's right, sir," I said. "We took the fight to them."

"It is remarkable," Praetor Wurtenberger said, speaking up for the first time. He had one of those Germanic accents and voices that were a little irritating. "Our fleet fired everything we had at the intruder. Not even T-bombs penetrated the enemy hull. How do you think you managed it, Centurion McGill?"

Something in his voice made me look up from my menu. I'd been drooling over it since I sat down. The special today was lamb. I love lamb, when it's done right.

"Uh..." I said. "Well sir, as far as I could tell, they opened a door in the hull. That's how we got inside."

"Oh yes, of course. I've heard that theory, that the stardust is too dense to allow teleportation through its mass—but I don't buy it."

"Huh. You don't?"

"No. There must be something else at work, rather than the density of a relatively thin wall of matter."

"How's that, sir?"

"Think of a journey between star systems. Often, the teleporting individual passes through the entirety of Earth's mass in order to reach another planet far away. How can it be believed that a mere hundred meters of—"

At this point, Galina leaned forward and smiled sweetly at Wurtenberger, touching his upraised hand.

"Excuse me, Praetor," she said in what seemed to me to be an unnaturally nice voice. I knew she was pissed, but she'd always been good at hiding that when she really had to. "Not

71

everything is known or understood about this enemy. I believe we'll have the good fortune to find out more about them soon, however."

Wurtenberger blinked at her and the hand touching his own for a moment. She let that hand linger there, and I knew she was purposefully fogging his mind with it. Galina was a lovely woman who had absolutely no qualms about using every gift God gave her in pursuit of her interests.

"You are speaking of the enemy ground force, correct?" Wurtenberger said.

"Naturally," Galina said, keeping that steady voice going. She was only rude to people she outranked. "The invaders have already been surrounded by six near-human legions. They're trapped in the New Jersey—"

"They have been contained? Is that what you're telling me?"

"Yes, sir. We don't anticipate—"

"No, you do not anticipate. I, however, must do so. We must assume their ground forces are superior in performance, as was their ship."

Galina blinked and frowned. "Do you know something I don't about this situation, sir?"

Wurtenberger gave Drusus a glance, and he cleared his throat. Before he spoke, a waiter showed up. We all ordered food. I requested an extra plate, and no one argued.

When the waiter had left, Drusus leaned toward Galina.

"Tribune," he said. "As you are about to deploy Legion Varus to face this invasion, I feel we have the responsibility to keep you informed."

That didn't sound good. I almost stopped chewing on the breadsticks.

"Please enlighten me, Drusus," Turov told him.

"The enemy landed in a circular pattern. Their ships are arranged to form a perimeter. Inside that zone, approximately two thousand hectares, nothing has come out. The landing ships formed some kind of collective shield. They are essentially hiding under a dome of force."

72

"A dome of force generated by their invasion ships?" she said thoughtfully. "A shield powered by ninety pillars? Is that it?"

"Yes."

"What are they doing under there?"

"We don't know. But nothing has come out, or gone in. There was a small town in the region called Hammonton— we're assuming the worst."

"Hammonton? I've never heard of it... Still, this is alarming. I'd assumed they'd landed in a field somewhere. I don't like to complicate the situation with civilians."

I snorted. "I bet they're not too happy about it down there in Hammonton, either."

Galina's eyes slid to regard me for a moment, then slid back to Drusus. "Nothing has come out of there? None of McGill's flapping bird-robots?"

"Nothing. We've surrounded it, and we're moving in more troops all the time. But we don't really know what we'll be facing when they do decide to come out."

"We should go in," I said firmly. "March right in there and clean them out. Whatever they're doing in there, I'm certain we won't be happy about it when we learn the truth."

Drusus looked a little troubled.

I knew he was thinking about the people. Checking my tapper, I looked up Hammonton. The local population was around thirty thousand. That was a lot of hostages to be responsible for.

"I think your hero is right, Drusus," Wurtenberger said. "You should do it now—before they make their next move."

Drusus was in command of local Earth Defenses. One time, years ago, he'd been responsible for the entirety of the planet's defensive armies. I don't think he'd enjoyed the death toll back then, and I don't think he liked contemplating it now.

At last, he nodded. "Galina, you're going to deploy Varus tomorrow morning. Solstice is already out there, setting up shop."

"What about the Iron Eagles? Or Germanica?"

"They're both on other planets, doing guard duty."

73

Galina knew this of course. I figured she was bringing up these other legions with valorous histories to point out the fact Earth was overextended.

It was a serious problem. We'd gained planets, but that meant we had to guard them all to keep them. We only had so many seasoned legions—and we were spread pretty thin these days.

I'd finished my first plate by this time. The rest dug in, and I felt happy to have another plate waiting. To a casual observer, it looked like I'd waited for them.

The truth was, of course, that I had stacked the first plate under the second. It was a little wobbly that way, but it worked well enough.

-13-

That night I slept with Galina. There was an urgency to the sex I knew all too well. When people think they're about to die, or when they just had a near-death experience, they go at it with intensity.

In the early predawn hours, we were a little fuzzy but relatively happy. We'd worked out our differences and become determined to see our mission through to the end.

Outwardly, we were all business by the time we hit the lifters and were transported to the battle zone. Landing on a green sward of pasture just south of the Wharton Forest, we joined a mass deployment.

From the air, we could see the enemy dome directly. They'd built up something that projected a wall of force. All around the outer perimeter were those strange, bat-winged landing craft. Each one was a source point for the force field.

"Doesn't look like it'd be too hard to pop that bubble," I commented to Harris, who was sitting on my right.

"You're right," he replied. "A few tactical shells would take out the ships and boom! No more dome. I don't know why Drusus even needs us out here."

"You're fooling yourselves," Leeson said from my left. "They don't want to light up a nuke out here in the middle of Jersey. They'd rather see us all die twenty times than lose a tall stack of voters."

Leeson was probably right. The brass didn't think the invasion was all that serious, and it was in the middle of a heavily populated area. No one wanted to see a radioactive dust cloud floating over New York City. Troop losses were far more acceptable to any politician—especially when they could print out new copies of us when it was over.

"They'll mass us up and have us charge under there…" I said, thinking about it. "This will be bloody. They've got hostages in Hammonton."

"Hostages? Ha!" Leeson snorted. "They probably ate them or something by now."

Frowning, I began thinking of tactical dispersal of troops, and how I should march 3rd Unit under that dome when the order came to advance.

When the lifter landed, the big door cracked open, and we rushed out. Graves was in the lead, at least you had to say that for him. The man was no coward.

The first thing I discovered when I got out into the open was a massive stink. All around me, my troops were recoiling, squinting, and shaking their heads like dogs with dust up their noses.

Thousands of Blood Worlders had already deployed here. They marched in ranks that went all the way up the highway, then off the road into Wharton forest. I'd forgotten they had a training facility in there.

The Blood Worlders were mostly heavy infantry—hunched-over men who were about three meters in height. They weighed as much as grizzly bears and were about as physically powerful.

"Hate the way these apes smell," Harris complained.

"You should learn to love that stench," Leeson said. "These boys are easy on the eyes to me. Just think: who do you figure the brass will send under that dome first? A horde of big, ugly near-humans—or us?"

Harris considered. The longer he thought about it, the more distrustful he looked. "I don't know… Look who they sent out here: Varus and Solstice—both of us are shit-outfits. We're only one notch better than a zoo legion to the brass. I doubt they even have a favorite in the field today."

76

I didn't say anything. First, I had no idea who they were going to order to march under there first. Secondly, I was bored with the topic.

"There's nothing we can do about it either way, so shut up," I told them both as their argument began to get heated.

"That doesn't sound like the McGill I know," Harris complained.

After I glared at him a bit, he finally shut up.

Soon we reached our checkpoint. We ate some rations, checked our gear and did a headcount. As was oftentimes the case in the military, we had to wait around after that. Not every unit was in place yet.

The morning wore on, and it soon turned into afternoon, then evening. It wasn't until around 1800 hours that Graves finally contacted me for a readiness report.

"All present and accounted for, sir," I told him. "We're ready to eat steel and shit nails out here."

"Outstanding. You'll be leading this charge, and it will be recorded by drones all around the world. Don't piss on your boots today, McGill."

"Uh…" I said, blinking in confusion. "Leading the charge? Really?"

"No, not really. You'll go in with the first wave, which will come from every direction at once. The point is: the cameras will be on you."

"Really…? Exactly why is that, Primus?"

He frowned at me. "You're the hero, remember? Earth's just had a bad scare. They needed to feel like they're protected. Accordingly, your story has been relayed to every news-vid online."

"I… I see, sir."

Graves closed the channel, and I turned to Harris and Leeson with a wide grin.

"It's our lucky day, gentlemen! We're going to play hero together. Trust me, there's no better way to get lucky later on with the ladies back home."

Throwing out a gauntleted hand at waist level, I urged them to slap their hands on top of mine. After a few glum looks, they finally did it.

"All right, let's move out!"

Trotting away toward the enemy lines with manufactured enthusiasm, I got them to follow me. Sometimes, that was the key to leadership: to lead by example.

Less than an hour later it was dark out, and we were creeping up on enemy positions. Those bat-winged invasion ships were dark metal, and they looked sleek up against the night sky. They were as wicked-looking as our lifters were ungainly.

"Leeson?" I hissed.

"Huh?"

"You think those landers have anti-personnel weaponry?" I asked. "Like ours do?"

He looked at me in alarm. "Hells bells... I didn't even think of that. Of *course* they do. This can't be the first time these pirates invaded a planet. They have to have it all planned out. They'll mow us down on this open ground!"

It was all open fields around Hammonton. There wouldn't be anywhere to hide if we just charged in.

"Maybe you should go talk to Turov," Harris suggested. "Maybe she could be... *convinced* to cut us a break."

I shook my head, knowing that wasn't going to happen. Galina enjoyed my company, and she might even love me a little—but telling her I was going to die wouldn't impress her one bit. She knew I'd come back out of the revival machines as good as new.

"I've got a better angle," I said, using my tapper.

I contacted Turov, and she frowned out of my tapper.

"Can't you see those drones swarming overhead, McGill?" she demanded. "They don't have endless battery power, you know. Get a move on!"

"Well sir, I've just gotten to thinking—"

"Don't do that. Try following orders instead."

"I'm thinking about those drones, sir. Of what they're showing, and who they're broadcasting to."

"They're broadcasting to the entire planet."

"Exactly right, sir. What if, let's just say, these landing craft are equipped with heavy weapons like our lifters? We'll be mowed down before we can reach the barrier—and it will happen on live camera."

"Hmm..." she said, thinking that over.

Galina had a heart of ice when it came to the pain and suffering of her troops—but she understood PR quite well.

"That could spell disaster... All right, hold your position."

My men were flat on their faces in the dirt.

"That was well-played, Centurion," Leeson said.

"It sure was," Harris agreed.

A tall woman walked up to us. It was Barton.

"Get down here, and hug the ground," I ordered her.

She threw herself down beside us and scrutinized the field. We were about a kilometer out from the ring of enemy ships and the force field that shimmered above them.

A voice spoke up nearby a moment later.

"No orders to charge in yet, huh?" Specialist Cooper asked in disgust. He was wearing his stealth suit and invisible.

I looked around, but my favorite chunk of cannon fodder evaded my eyes.

"We're sending in scouts," I told him. "Get up there, Ghost. Do your job."

"Who's idea was it to send in the scouts first?"

"Mine."

I heard him cursing quietly as he crawled forward. "Do you really think an alien task force that has traveled across hundreds of light years is going to be fooled by my Vulbite stealth suit?" he asked.

"You'd better hope so. Now, get out there and start hopping, bunny-rabbit."

Cooper trotted off, muttering unpleasant things.

Checking my HUD and altering the settings, I could see the ghosts. They were blue dots superimposed on my vision. Every ghost specialist in the cohort was advancing toward the enemy position.

Then I got a kick in the ribs. Startled, I rolled over to yell at whoever was thumping on me. There was no one there.

"Who's that?" I demanded. "Another ghost?"

"Yes, of course. We're all going."

I knew that voice, and my heart sank. It was Della.

-14-

Della had finally moved up into the specialist ranks. She'd never been big enough to be a weaponeer, stable enough to be a bio, or bookish enough to be a tech. Instead, she'd had to wait until they'd finally created a specialty rank that fit her perfectly.

That rank was known as a *ghost*—a noncom that operated as a scout.

The ghosts employed a personal stealth-generating system. Invisible to the naked eye, they activated light-bending garments and were able to evade the enemy with ease. In fact, the running joke was that you never saw your unit's ghost until chow-time—and maybe not even then.

Della had been a scout of sorts in Dust World's military back when I'd first met her. She had skills in stealth and tracking that were legendary in my unit. Coupled with new tech that literally made her invisible, she was among the best ghosts in the legion. I'd kind of forgotten about all that until now.

After kicking me, Della walked off, and I lost track of her.

The rest of us hugged the dirt, watching our HUDs and the circle of invasion ships. Nothing happened for what seemed like a long time—then the sparks began to fly.

"That's snap-rifle fire, or I'm a midget," Harris said. "Looks like the ghosts are engaging with… something."

"Which means they've been spotted," I added.

Zooming in, I could make out very little of the scene on the ground near the base of those enemy ships. The shielding was brightest there in color and intensity. It was like looking into a floodlight that shifted constantly. The enemy force field reminded me of the northern lights—aurora borealis.

"Adjunct Barton," I said on command chat, "advance your light troopers into range. Provide covering fire if the ghosts fall back toward our lines."

Butts humped up all over the field as Barton moved her lights forward in the grassy fields.

"Could be a trap, sir," Leeson called out to me. "Those ships… they're like gun towers. They'll blow everyone to Hell and back if we make a target of ourselves."

He could have been right, but I didn't see how that mattered. The brass wanted us to take out the enemy on the ground to reduce local civvie deaths and destruction. Implicit in that goal was the fact they didn't give much of a shit about me and my troops.

The local voters were much more important than we were. They knew they could just print out fresh copies of my men, which was infinitely preferable to everyone on the grid posting pictures of their permed grandma if they struck too hard.

I could appreciate their position, but I still wanted to do this as cleanly as possible. Accordingly, I contacted Graves.

"What is it, McGill?"

"The ghosts have made contact, sir. No news yet on what the fighting is about. There's some kind of interference keeping us from getting voice responses from the ghosts."

"I know about that," he said. "No one has been able to get a radio signal to penetrate the edge of that force field. If that's all you—"

"I'm calling to request star-fall artillery, sir," I said quickly before he could cut the channel.

Graves hesitated. "I can't do that, McGill," he said after a pause. "We have our rules of engagement, and they're pretty tight when we're this close to urban areas."

"I appreciate that, sir," I said. "But as any battle with an unknown opponent tends to go in unexpected ways, I'd suggest we prepare for the worst."

"Meaning?"

"Roll up the star-falls and the 88s. Set them up behind our lines as a back-up measure."

"That's specifically against—"

"Drusus will only know if you use them," I told him. "At that point, he'll call you hero."

Graves shut up for a moment. I figured he was checking on the displacement of our heavier weapons.

"I'll take your comments under consideration," he said at last. "Graves out."

Harris wormed his way over to my position on the ground and looked at me expectantly.

"Yes, Adjunct?" I asked.

"Well?" he demanded. "Did it work? Are we getting some support or not?"

I flashed him a grin. "Legion Varus isn't going into this fight with one hand tied behind our back."

He grinned in return, buying my half-truth immediately. "That's great to hear, McGill! You're shady as fuck, but it all works out for the best sometimes."

Deciding to take his words as a compliment, I went back to studying the tactical situation with my HUD. Officers had abilities and equipment the regular troops lacked, mostly involving our helmets and onboard computers. They gave me a layout of our forces. It was the best view anyone could get short of working one of the battle-tables in an HQ tent at the rear of our formation.

Legion troops were closing in from all sides, and there was a definite firefight going on along the front lines—mostly involving our ghosts.

The strange thing was that I didn't see any counter-fire coming back at us from the invaders. Repeatedly, I tried to get a report back from Cooper or Della—but failed.

"Do you see anything yet, Barton?"

There was some static on the line as she replied. "...not sure... something coming. Troops marching toward us..."

"Dammit," I said, feeling a rare moment of indecision.

Each moment I delayed, I saw more figures come out of that blazing field of colorful plasma. It did look like an

82

advancing army—but then again, when I'd been aboard their ship the enemy hadn't looked like humans at all.

"Shit…"

I could just order Barton to shoot into the advancing ranks—but what if they were civvies? What if some of our local populace had escaped and were approaching our lines?

With a growl, I got to my feet and rushed forward a hundred meters. I threw myself down again next to Barton.

"What the hell is going on out there?" I asked her. "Are those things people or aliens? And what about my ghosts? Are they shooting at that advancing line?"

"Take a look at the base of the landing ship on the left," Barton said.

I zoomed in where she indicated, and I saw one of our ghosts. It had to be ours, as the soldier was crouching and firing for all he was worth. Panning right, I saw the target: A human-looking figure that advanced with methodical, unhurried steps.

The snap-rifle fire wasn't knocking it down. The target jerked and twitched, but it kept approaching.

That was good enough for me. "Barton! Have your men switch their weapons to sniper-mode and knock out those slow-moving humanoids."

"Roger that, sir."

I contacted Leeson and Harris next, ordering them to advance to my position. They grumbled, but they did as they were told.

Then I reported the situation to Graves and moved closer with my troops. Our lights were in the front line, kneeling now and then to take careful shots at the odd enemy. Every so often, a target fell back, knocked off its feet.

But then, a few moments later, they usually got back up again.

-15-

Cooper made it back to our lines first. He was out of breath and out of bullets.

"It's Hell back there, sir!" he puffed at me.

He joined our advancing lines. We were spread out and moving at a steady jog toward the colorful force field and the assault ships, which seemed to grow larger as we got closer.

"Report, scout," I told him. "Make it good."

Cooper resupplied from a pig drone that marched behind my team. He slammed a fresh magazine and battery into his snap-rifle before talking.

"I was out," he explained.

That was alarming all by itself. Snap-rifles fired pellets roughly the size of a BB. The rounds were of very small caliber, but when accelerated they packed a lot of kinetic energy despite their size—equivalent to a traditional nine millimeter bullet.

The best feature of those bullets by far was that they didn't need a casing or any kind of explosive to fire. Since the magazine held only pellets, not cartridges, ammo was plentiful. The assault rifles essentially worked like traditional weapons, but they could spray on full-auto for a long time without reloading.

The alarming part was that Cooper had run out of ammo at all. A ghost specialist typically carried one reserve battery and magazine, meaning Cooper had managed to fire two thousand rounds in the span of a ten minutes.

"At first," he said, "we thought the townspeople were trying to escape. We didn't fire on them, even when they didn't respond to our calls and challenges. But when they got closer... we realized something was wrong."

"What was wrong? Are they people or not?"

"No—not exactly. I mean, I think they were once human, or that parts of them were—but not anymore."

I looked at him, checking to see if he was joking. I could tell by his expression that he wasn't.

"They're not men," Cooper explained. "They have flesh parts—the muscles that move their limbs, mostly. Sometimes you can see a neck or a ribcage, but there's a lot of metal too. They're cyborgs, I think."

Frowning in confusion, I tried to contact Natasha. She was my number one tech. All our radio signals were out now, however. She couldn't hear me.

Using my feet instead of my tapper, I took Cooper by the arm and led him back a rank to where the support people were marching behind us.

Natasha was among them. I had him repeat his story.

She looked upset. "A grim thing—there were thirty thousand people in that town. Thousands more were out in the surrounding countryside."

"What are you saying?" I demanded. "That they aren't human?"

She was flipping through a few shots Cooper's body cam had taken. She showed me a few choice examples.

The creatures—I say that because they certainly weren't men anymore—walked on two legs. They had two arms and a bulbous head. But that was where the similarities to humanity ended.

Each of these things was armored in metal plates and plastic. Here and there, you could see exposed muscle working under there, bulging and relaxing, propelling these nightmarish hybrids of meat and electronics.

"You can tell they aren't human anymore," Cooper said, looking over my elbow. "Just by the way they walk if nothing else. They're not in a hurry. They're kind of out of it. They just keep coming at you, and if they catch hold of you, you're done."

"How do you know that?"

Cooper shrugged and bared his teeth for a moment. He didn't meet my eye. "I saw them catch a few of us. Our ghost suits—they didn't do shit. I'm not sure what kind of sensory systems these guys have, but they homed in on us like we were standing there naked."

"They may not see in the same visible spectrum that we do," Natasha said.

"Anyway," Cooper continued, "when they got close I panicked and unloaded on them. I'd been crouching and hoping they would wander by, but they kept turning to follow me as I sidestepped. That's when I realized they could see through my stealth, and I started blasting them."

"Good move," I said. "How hard are they to kill?"

He shook his head. "They're incredibly tough. A hundred rounds at point-blank range—that might put one down. But he'll probably get back up again. They don't talk. They don't shoot at you—they just come at you and reach for you."

"Did they catch anyone out there?" I asked.

"Yeah... Della got it. There were three on her. I knocked one down over and over, she did the same to a different one. But they kept getting back up, see... Anyway, the third one just walked up behind her and tore her up."

My face was like stone. "You sure she's dead?"

He nodded. "Sorry Centurion. I've seen dead before—there's no way."

I pointed back behind us, toward the rear lines. "You go that way until you've got a signal. Report Della's death, with photos if you have them, along with any other confirmed KIAs you've witnessed. Then you come back here. Soon, we might have more casualties to report."

He ran off, and I went back to marching with grim determination. Della and I weren't together anymore, but anyone who killed her pissed me off.

"James," Natasha said. "Maybe we should retreat. We don't know what we're facing."

"Sure we do. We saw similar things back on their ship. The town is gone—or most of it is. The sooner we get into Hammonton the sooner we might rescue survivors."

"But we don't have good comms down here. We might get killed and permed."

I shrugged. "I didn't sign up to last forever—that's just a side-benefit. These aliens—whatever the hell they are—they like to build armies out of machine parts and biological flesh. That's sick, and I've decided to kill them all."

"Single-handedly?"

"If necessary."

Natasha shook her head and took off, moving back to the rear ranks again. She knew me well enough not to bother arguing.

"Sargon!" I shouted.

He came over to me a few minutes later. "Sir?"

"You got any of those shotguns left—the ones the Rigel boys use?"

"I've got one, so does Moller."

"Good. We might need them."

I described the creatures Cooper had met up with, and he whistled. He scanned the grass and the shimmering force-fields ahead of us.

"I don't see them. They might be farther back in that mess of plasma—or maybe they retreated."

"It could be," I said. "Maybe they sensed our ghosts and came out to stand off their advance, and then fell back within their perimeter again—but that's not going to save them."

Sargon laughed.

"Spread the word on how these things look and fight. I can't broadcast to the unit. Move around and do it the old-fashioned way."

He trotted off, and I got out a new weapon.

It was one of the super-shotguns. Nasty weapons that fired heavy accelerated slugs at short range. They could punch through the hull of a shuttle or the armor of one of our walking dragons.

I only had five slugs left, but they should make a good start.

-16-

We nearly made it into the shadowy region between the big landing ships before we encountered the enemy.

In retrospect, I should have figured out what was going to happen—but I was too pissed off about Della and too amazed by the weird environment to think clearly.

We advanced right into the middle of them when the enemy soldiers stood up, right in our midst. We'd almost walked on top of them.

They were humanoid *things*, part human and part machine. They began getting to their feet right in front of us. They'd simply lain down in the grass and waited there, motionless, until we got close.

When they suddenly rose up, wild cursing and full-auto fire broke out all around me. Snap-rifles from the lights, force-blades, morph-rifles and a few shotguns from the heavies—everyone sent a lot of mass and energy flying at our ambushers.

A few of my troops were cut down by friendly fire.

"Mark your targets!" Moller roared. "If I see blue-on-blue I'm going to return the favor, soldiers!"

The truth was, as seasoned as we were on average, these creatures kind of spooked us. We shook that off quickly, as we were tougher than the usual lot. I could imagine a bunch of hogs breaking and running from this attack—but not Varus legionnaires.

After about two minutes, we had them all down. They didn't like to stay down, mind you. It took several killings each before a given cyborg lay still.

"You have to frigging hack them apart!" Harris said, coming up to me and panting.

I nodded and hefted my shotgun. "One good blast from this does the trick, but I'm conserving my last two shots. I'm using force-blades."

The shotguns were alien-made, captured from Rigel troops back on Storm World. We didn't have ammo to match on Earth, and although I knew the nerds huddling under Central had been working to copy these weapons, they hadn't managed it yet. They were effectively hand-operated railguns that shot a cloud of depleted uranium pellets rather than normal bullets. However they worked, they were damned effective.

Harris watched me sling the shotgun in favor of my morph-rifle.

"You're saving your rounds. That means you know something—that something worse is up ahead."

"Never hurts to be prepared," I told him and left to go find my favorite ghost.

Cooper had returned from the rear lines, and he wasn't much use without the ability to stealth. I decided to keep using him as my communications runner, sending him back to report our status to Graves.

Since we'd lost another six men in the ambush, I sent Cooper humping back to the rear lines to report to Graves again.

Carlos watched him go with wistful eyes. "Maybe it will turn out the guys who cashed-in early on this little monster-hunt were the lucky ones. At least those guys won't be permed."

"Nope. They'll be waiting for us in camp when we get back. Let's go!"

Up until that moment, my entire unit had been standing around, patching up the wounded and marking the dead. So far, no one had taken a single step farther into the force-field. I could tell they were a little freaked out.

Without giving more instructions to my troops, I marched ahead. The flashing plasma loops soon whirled around my armored body as I moved into the depths of the strange barrier these invaders had built.

I was kind of worried my electronics would short out—but I didn't let on.

Seeing me march into that neon display, my troops took heart. I made a point of kicking dead cyborgs this way and that as I passed, which made my men laugh. Soon, they were following me.

I could hear them bitching and cursing quietly in my wake. I knew they would follow me, the braver ones shaming the rest. I didn't look back to see who had moved first. That didn't matter, as long as they all did in the end.

We advanced a hundred meters, then another hundred. At that point, the light-show faded away, and we were in an open field again. It was an odd-looking scene to be sure, but it was just a farmer's field.

Overhead, there were no stars. Instead, a haze of yellowy-white formed a curved sky. It lit up the grasses with an unnatural glow. Ahead in the distance, I saw rows of dark houses and a few taller buildings. That was the direction I took. If I stopped now, it would be harder for my men to keep marching ahead.

We found a road choked with abandoned trams and trucks. The vehicle doors all hung open, but there was no one inside any of them. I had the feeling the townsfolk had tried to form a caravan and escape—but they hadn't made it out.

There was something about this place that filled a man with dread. The vacant cars, the silent enemy, even the very fact we were on Earth, not out in space somewhere—all that worked together on the mind.

I told myself that it was nothing. Even a Varus man could get jumpy now and then.

"This light," Harris said, catching up with me. "It's like moonlight, but golden instead of silvery."

He had a weird tone in his voice, so I laughed at him. "You've got quite the poetic tongue on you, Adjunct."

Harris glowered, suspecting I was making fun of him. He was right.

"You scared?" I asked him, slamming a gauntlet on his armored shoulder.

He brushed my hand away.

"Hell no! These things die—even if they seem to be dead already... Anything that dies I'm not afraid of!"

"That's good. Make sure the troops see that look in your eyes—not the other one."

Harris met my gaze, and he nodded. Walking away, he made a show of talking about how easy these aliens were to kill. How stupid and slow and downright harmless they were. The troops didn't say much, but they seemed to listen.

We made it almost to the outskirts of town before we met up with trouble again.

It was the trams in the town—they looked different. Instead of abandoned wrecks left in random positions, they were in a line. A tight line that stretched on for fifty cars or more each direction.

"Um... boss?" Carlos said. "I don't like the look of those—"

That's about when the nearest one fired up its engine. Human-looking arms extended then from the windows, which were all broken out and dark inside.

Arms. That's what they had to be. Each arm ended with a hand, as they should, and in each hand was a weapon. Some of the trams had six, eight—I even saw one with nine arms hanging out of the various broken windows. And in every hand was a weapon of some kind. I saw guns, hatchets, all manner of deadly instrument. A few had strange-looking tubes of sleek metal that I suspected were alien-made weaponry.

I don't mind telling you I halted, stood and gaped for a second. I didn't know what to make of it all. It was freaky and then some.

The engines roared, revving, and the enemy line advanced. The trams shook and their treads clacked as they beat the road. They rolled over grass, fences and other things I suspected were lying in the fields. They humped over everything that might lay between us and them, uncaring.

91

"Spread out, front ranks kneel and fire at will!" I roared when I'd recovered from my initial surprise. "Weaponeers, stand and take them out!"

The lights in front threw themselves onto their bellies, and the heavies in the middle knelt. Together they opened fire at the haunted row of vehicles that approached us, but our guns seemed to have little effect.

Had these aliens really managed to armor-up the front grilles of these vehicles so fast? Is that what they'd been doing down here, under this protective dome of theirs?

Over our heads, Sargon and his weaponeers unleashed heavy beams. Some of the weaponeers carried guided missiles too, and flocks of drones swarmed from Kivi and the techs.

Any unit in the legion can release a lot of firepower at short range. My group was no exception. The makeshift armored cars were blown up, two or three at a time. Only half of them made it to Barton's lights, who danced aside and threw grav-plasma grenades into the broken windows or rolled them under the treads.

Several more of the trams went up, hopping into the air and thumping back down again on their backs. But some of Barton's people weren't fast enough on their feet. A few were run down, others were hacked by the bleeding limbs that hung from those windows.

Those arms… they were beyond freaky. They didn't have eyes that I could see. No heads were in sight—just arms hanging from windows that had the safety glass broken out.

They worked in a frenzy to kill us for all that. The arms didn't have anything like a sense of self-preservation. They cut themselves on glass, metal shards—anything for the opportunity to slash and shoot at my troops.

Some of the trams made it past the platoon of lights out front. My heavies were up next. We were spread out and ready. Armored up, we were too slow to run out of the way. Some were run over, others bounced off the fenders.

One of the trams came right at me, and I vaulted onto the hood. The machine stopped revving. It seemed insane with a terrible urge to kill me.

Hands clutched my boots. They sawed on my metal armor pointlessly with knives. I slashed their hands off at the wrist, but they still thumped and flailed, splattering dark blood all over my kit.

"Nasty-ass bastards!" I said, shoving my shotgun into the guts of the passenger section.

Boom! Boom!

I released two blasts, and the monstrosity stopped making a coordinated effort to kill me. Some of the limbs still felt the air with trembling fingers, but they appeared to be mindless and blind.

Hopping off the hood, I walked away and checked on the rest of my unit.

After a few minutes of mopping up, the battle was over. But my men—they weren't the same. They'd been shaken up, and I could hardly blame them.

We'd never fought an enemy like this one. Whatever these things were, they seemed to come in countless evil forms like demons spawned in Hell.

-17-

Harris was the first to confront me. The others were looking on, too.

"Centurion…" he said. "That was just plain *wrong*."

"I know," I laughed. "What *losers*! Whoever these aliens are, someone should tell them they don't fight worth a shit. What kind of a half-assed invasion force tries to run trained troops over with trams?"

Harris blinked at me twice. I knew that hadn't been the response he'd been expecting—but it was all he was going to get from me.

"But sir, as the senior adjunct here—"

"You're not senior," Leeson shouted. He was listening from a safe distance.

Harris tossed him a scowl before turning back to me. "Centurion, we're of a mind to march back out of here. We've done our piece. There's no one here that we can rescue."

In the distance, I heard a rippling gush of rifle fire. Somewhere across the battlefield there was another unit encountering God-knows-what.

"Our mission is to eradicate these pests," I told Harris. "I'd say that hasn't happened yet."

"But sir—"

Turning away from him, I pointed a long arm into the town. We were standing at the outskirts, and the roads were choked with vehicles.

"It's less than three klicks from here to the center of Hammonton. Are you telling me I'm going to have to walk it alone? That my whole unit has gone chicken-shit?"

"No sir, it's not like that at all—"

I stepped up to him. "I think it is. I smell the stink of fear on all of you. Shameful. I bet you all wet your pants as kids when you walked up to the big haunted house on Halloween, didn't you?"

There were a few weak snickers. People shuffled from foot to foot.

"Now, let me hear from Barton. If she wants to leave—"

"She got run over and hacked apart by some sixteen-armed tram, McGill," Leeson called out.

"Oh, that's right… We should circle-up and do a roll call. Count off!"

We gathered among the smoking, bleeding trams. Without being told, my men formed a perimeter with their weapons pointed outward in every direction. Walking the middle of the circle, I counted heads.

Normally, I'd have checked the data with my tapper in private—but inside this dome it wasn't working right. We were cut off from any kind of grid service. There was still too much radio interference.

The numbers I tallied up were grim. Barton was indeed dead. Natasha had been killed as well.

"That's a real shame," I told Carlos as he gave me the grim news. "We could really use our techs and weaponeers on a mission like this."

"No shit, sir?" he asked, and I cuffed him.

This knocked him flat, as I was wearing powered metal armor—and he wasn't.

He got back up, spat some blood and went on with his report.

"We're down to about fifty percent effectives, Centurion."

"I'm ready to carry that report back to Graves, sir," said a voice out of nowhere.

"Cooper?" I demanded, whirling around.

He wasn't in sight of course. He was a ghost.

Now, under normal circumstances that would be acceptable. But not today. Not here. Because I knew that the enemy could see through his stealth suit—and he knew it too. That meant he wasn't wearing it to hide from these creatures.

He was wearing it to hide from *me*.

I took a swipe with my boot where I thought he was. He skipped back, but I'm quick and unreasonably long of limb. My metal-encased boot swept his legs out from under him, and he went down on his can.

Leaning over the depression his invisible ass left in the grass. I gave him a stern warning.

"Don't hide from me, Specialist. That's the kind of move that gets a man the most dangerous of assignments."

He appeared immediately, dragging the cloaking suit off. He hopped to his feet and saluted.

"Sorry about that, sir. It was force of habit plus my extensive training that made me suit-up."

That was a good lie, so I accepted it with a nod.

"All right. We've lost a lot of people—you can run back to Graves and make one last report."

"Thank you, sir! Thank you!"

Cooper ran off like a bunny in heat.

Harris snorted. "What a piece of work that kid is. I didn't know chickens could go invisible."

"He's made three solo runs so far to our rear lines, and he's still alive. Even better, he keeps coming back for more. You want his job?"

Harris looked startled. "No."

"Okay then, we're moving forward. We'll check out the town center—then we can call Hammonton scouted."

Normally, I'd have been in contact with the other units or Graves at least. But this was no normal operation. We were still cut off from the outside world and the rest of our units that were presumably under the shield with us.

We didn't make it far into the town's streets before we ran into trouble. Hammonton looked like a pretty normal place to live if you ignored the abandoned look of the place. The lighting was probably the oddest thing, but if you told yourself they had a new kind of yellowy streetlight here, well, you could almost buy it.

But about six blocks in, things went wrong.

It was a feeling at first. A quiet fell over the streets. Now and then, we heard rippling gunfire. There were flashes in the sky, off to the eastern side of Hammonton. They rose in frequency until there was a veritable storm, then they died down again to random popping.

"That's snap-rifles and morph-rifles both," Leeson said. "I bet someone is taking it in the shorts out there."

"At least it's not us—not yet," Harris noted.

Frowning thoughtfully, I stopped marching at a stop sign. It was one of the old fashioned ones made of painted steel.

"Let's head that way," I said.

"Toward the action?" Harris asked incredulously.

"Maybe we can lend assistance. With luck, we'll come up on the flank of some of these freaks."

They grumbled and shook their heads, but they led the men that way. I stepped up to the front lines, where our lights had fanned out. Since Barton was dead, I'd taken over as their platoon leader.

The night was darker on the tree-lined streets than it had been in out in the country. Mostly, that was because the strangely bright sky was obscured. After a ten minute walk, we ran into something.

"Contact!" came a cry from up ahead.

Another firefight lit up the night, but this time it was much closer at hand. Streaks of accelerated snap-rifle rounds formed pulsing lines as Barton's nervous platoon focused their attack on the end of the street.

Peering into the dark, I looked at the concentration-point of those converging lines. At first, I thought their target was a tractor. But then I realized, as we advanced in a rush from tree-to-tree and house-to-house, that it was more like a walking ogre on two legs. Dull metal covered most of the body, and I couldn't see any eyes or other soft parts to target.

The thing had no arms. It had no face—but it did have a bulbous body coated in metal that sat atop two stork-like legs. Protruding from the turret on top was a tube of some kind. It was about the size and length of a belcher, and it reminded me of the long beak of a stork or heron.

The tube swiveled here and there, releasing a wavering gush of energy each time it paused. It was a broad beam, but no less deadly for all that. Everything it touched—troops, broken cars, trees—everything exploded into flame.

"Go for those skinny legs!" I roared. "Cut it down to size!"

My heavies were getting close enough to target the thing, and we lashed its legs. A sizzling sound began, and the thick odor of roasting meat filled the air. Clearly, there was flesh inside that strange, bird-shaped metal body.

Barton's light troopers were helpless. It was immediately obvious their snap-rifles couldn't hurt this monstrosity, and the troops had used most of their grav-grenades during the last battle at the outskirts of town.

Serving only as a distraction, the light troops scattered like rats under the ogre's tramping feet. The walking machine moved eagerly after them. It's single snout-like gun swiveled rapidly, almost greedy to kill. Radiation gushed out from that tube and men died in smoking, thrashing heaps.

From over my shoulder someone fired a belcher then, and they nailed the walker in the left kneecap. It stumbled and went down on one knee.

The turret quickly swiveled in our direction. The beak-like tube lifted, the aperture narrowed, and it returned fire. A precise beam flashed down the street, and I could tell from the angle that it was aiming at the weaponeer in our rear ranks who dared to injure it.

After that, we got in close and tore it apart. It couldn't move on one leg, so we circled and dashed in like pygmies hunting a crippled ostrich. Force-blades stabbed, belchers gushed at point-blank range—we cooked the meat that was hidden inside that armored body.

At last it sagged down, thrashing. When it had stopped moving, I walked up and toed the massive... *thing* we'd just killed.

Was it a machine or a living beast? It was hard to sort out, but best as I could tell, it was a little of both.

"Centurion, look!"

It was Harris. He was standing beside me. Looking up, I saw a group of figures running toward us. We lifted our rifles—but then lowered them again.

They were human troops. It was 6th unit, and they were coming our way at a dead run. They ran up and stopped, sides heaving.

"6th?" I called out. "Where's the rest?"

"This is it, Centurion," a veteran ranked man said.

'No officers?"

He shook his head, wiping sweat from his brow. "Just me, sir. We've got… nineteen left. Mostly heavies. The lights and the auxiliaries, well, those snake-things killed everyone without body armor."

"Snake-things, huh?" I asked, not encouraged by the description of what was undoubtedly another form of alien menace.

Hearing our talk, those of Barton's light squad that had survived looked more nervous than before. That's when I noticed they were mostly standing around in the street.

"Spread out!" I ordered. "Take up firing positions and keep your eyes open. This isn't a frigging block party!"

Turning back to the veteran, I nodded to him. "Good to meet you. I'm commandeering your squad. Fold into Harris' platoon, you'll lead your squad."

"That's excellent, sir," the veteran said in relief. "How are we getting out of here?"

I looked at him in surprise. "We're not. We're pressing ahead to the center of town."

All of the relief drained out of his face as he absorbed these words. I couldn't blame him, but I didn't let on that I sympathized. It would have been bad for morale.

With around seventy troops at my back, I marched toward the city center. It wasn't such-a-much, as they said back home. My grandma might have called it a one-horse town, but that would have been a little harsh.

There were no high-rises or anything like that on Main Street. Instead, there were some brick buildings, a few of them topping out at three stories high. The oldest trees were a good deal taller.

The place was eerily quiet. The sounds of battle in the distance impinged occasionally, but not that often. I suspected one side or the other had won for the most part—could have been either them or us.

We passed a couple of schools and a park. When we came up to the town center, where a puff-crete City Hall building showed on the maps we had on our tappers, we got a surprise.

"Dear Lord..." Leeson said. "What the fuck is that?"

"That's *wrong*," Harris said. "That's just plain *wrong*!"

"Can that be... human?" Sargon asked me. "Can that whole mound of quivering stuff be some kind of meat?"

"I think so..." I said, squinting at it.

The town plaza had a hospital of sorts, really more of a medical center. Next to that was an outdoor row of shops and the government buildings. At least that's what our tappers showed us was supposed to be down here.

But that wasn't what we were seeing. Instead of the medical center, our eyes were offended by a nightmare of overgrown flesh. A tumor-like monster squatted on the building. It had to be ten meters high and maybe a hundred in diameter. Here and there, at what should have been the bottom floor of the building, there appeared to be entrances and exits. Smaller creatures, humanoid in form, were carrying things in and out of there like ants feeding their queen.

"That's an abomination against nature," Leeson said with feeling. "We've got to blow that up, McGill."

"You willing to die to do it?" Harris asked him.

Leeson thought about that for a second, then he nodded his head. "Yup. I'm willing."

"Hopefully, you won't have to," I said. "Let's burn it."

There was a fueling station nearby. We got out buckets and trashcans, filling them with gas. It took a while, but oddly, the worker-aliens ignored us. They didn't seem to see us as a threat. Either that, or it wasn't their job to kill us.

Forming something like an old fashioned bucket-brigade, we began to splash the quivering mass with gasoline.

"It doesn't like that!" Leeson laughed. "Pour more on those knobby sucker-cup things up high!"

We kept working, but all the while, we were looking over our shoulders. Sure enough, a response came before we were through.

I wasn't sure how the weird, nest-thing we'd found had called for help, but the reaction was undeniable. Dozens of those walking things with beam-tubes like beaks appeared on the street and stalked forward.

"Huddle up!" I shouted. "Get close to this hamburger pile! Stand close so if they miss, they hit their nest!"

Racing up with our last buckets of fuel, we threw them on the fleshy mass and stood with our backs to it.

The alien walkers seemed to be aware of our implicit threat. They didn't fire their beams at us. That was a good thing, as they could have wiped us out if they did.

Standing about a hundred meters off, they halted, and their deadly snouts swiveled this way and that seeking an advantage. They tried to encircle, walking around, but we always made sure they couldn't get a clean shot without hitting the flesh-factory, or whatever that nasty thing was behind us.

"McGill?" Harris called out. "What now? If we torch this thing, they'll kill us all for sure."

"Wouldn't that be worth it?"

"Say what? Fuck no! There's gotta be a better way!"

"He's wrong!" Leeson shouted. "Just do it, McGill!"

My rank-and-file troops looked freaked out, especially the guys from the 6th. They didn't know me well, and were therefore new to my surprising brand of solutions to tactical problems.

I'd just about decided to go for it when another army showed up. They were walking on two legs as well, but they looked fairly normal. They were definitely humanoid.

A few of my troops even cheered, thinking they were seeing reinforcements—but the cheering died pretty fast. It was the odd, tottering gait these newcomers used that gave them away.

They'd once been people, I was sure of that. What's more, they wore Varus uniforms in many cases. Some of them even carried snap-rifles.

We called out to them, just in case, but they weren't talking. Not a peep. We shouted and we challenged, but they just marched closer. The only sound we heard from them were whining motors every time they took a step.

"Take them down!" I shouted, and a one-sided firefight began.

By one-sided, I mean the other side wasn't shooting at all. They were just coming at us, getting in close.

We blasted and sprayed them as they came. Often, they spun around and fell, but they usually got right back up again and kept coming. It was kind of spooky to watch. The first row fell, then the second, then the third—but most of them climbed back on their feet and shuffled closer.

The first of them to make it to our thin line grabbed hold of a surprised light trooper. He plucked her rifle from her hands. He raised the rifle, lifting it up like a club. But before he could smash her down, she'd gutted him and cut his head clean off his neck with a combat knife.

All along our line, the things that made it to us did similar things. They grappled us, they punched us with their fists, and they strangled us with long metal fingers.

Behind each wave was another rank. Another hundred—another thousand.

That's when I knew it was time to make my play.

"Burn this bitch down!" I shouted.

A moment later, while I was doing a slow-dance with an armored-up bag of meat, Sargon used his belcher. A wide beam lit up the building-sized nest-thing. With all the gas we'd poured on it, the flames surged greedily. I could feel the heat on my back and my hair began to curl and singe.

The creature that wrestled with me seemed to react, becoming stronger, more desperate. Muscles bucked under its tunic, and it ignored the broken ankle it was grinding on, striving to throw me down.

Instead, I managed to use its motion against it and toss it to one side. It fell into the burning pyre behind me, and the flames surged higher still.

It seemed like we were winning. The enemy was only using their claw-like hands, and although they were numerous and strong, we had better weapons and much better reflexes. I dared to hope we'd kill them all.

But then, the bird-things showed up again. Now that their nest was on fire, dying, there was no reason to hold back. They began to use those beak-like tubes, blasting us with beams of hot radiation. They burned humans and former humans alike indiscriminately.

"Retreat!" I shouted, seeing the bird-things no longer cared if they hurt their nest, or killed their mindless brothers who wrestled with us. As long as they could slay a human, that was good enough for them. Instead of holding our own, we were now losing troops at a rate of about one every second.

"Retreat where?" Harris called out from somewhere to my left.

"Into the building!"

"Shit… I knew you were going to say that."

Those of us who could get away did so. We slammed our armored shoulders into the enemy, bowling them over and racing past. The bird-creatures sang with those slashing rays, cutting down a dozen of their own troops to get just one of us.

Sargon went down. Carlos was gone—I couldn't remember the last time I'd seen him.

Harris and I made it into the entrance—one of the mushy openings in the burning, dying mass of flesh. Behind us were a dozen or so others. Among them was the veteran from the 6th. I thought he was pretty lucky to still be alive, but the expression on his face suggested he might not agree.

Inside, it wasn't lit, and it wasn't pretty. We used our suit lights and stumbled deeper into what looked like a digestive tract. The walls were covered in growths. It was beyond disgusting, and the worst part was the unmistakable impression that the thing was still alive, shivering in pain.

The walls ran with secretions. Choking smoke filled the passages, and we flipped down our visors so we could keep walking and breathing.

In the core of thing, we found the main waiting room—or maybe it was a medical ward. It had once been filled with beds for the sick, but we found a different kind of technology there.

This wasn't meat. It was metal and crystal, and it was hooked up to the rest of the odd equipment in the room by thick humming cables. I recognized it because I'd seen something like it before, years ago.

In the center the machine was a bright spinning light inside a metal cage. It was just like the one I'd seen on Dark World, powering the orbital factory we'd tried to capture in a failed campaign.

-19-

We gathered around the flashing light, and we shot the workers that wandered the place. For a few seconds, we contemplated the strange machine in our midst.

"That's got to be a power-source," Harris said. "It's a fusion reactor maybe—it must run something *big*."

I nodded. "It's a reactor all right. What's more, I've seen this kind of power generator before. I found one back on Dark World, on that space station we tried to take over."

"You mean when we met up with the Vulbites?"

"Yeah. But I don't think this was built by Vulbites. I think this is Rigellian tech. They owned that space factory, and I'm thinking they sent these freaks here to pay us a visit, too."

"Huh... what are we going to do with it, Centurion? Those giant storks can't get in here, but I'm sure something else will soon. Either that or the building will burn down and kill us all that way."

He was right of course. If we were going to do anything effective, we'd have to do it now.

"We're going to turn it off," I said. "These aliens aren't just growing troops like radishes, they're putting metal parts on them and powering a force-field as well. That means they have to have a serious source of power. I think we just found it."

"That's got to be right..." Harris said, circling the abomination. "You found the heart of this alien base, McGill.

You really did. How did you destroy the one back at Dark World?"

"Uh…" I said, remembering.

I'd actually used my helmet. After spreading the bars of the cage, I'd stuck my head into the reactor core. That had shorted it out and destroyed the entire orbital—but I figured that was information that wasn't going to be helpful to my men just now.

"Well… take a look around, everyone. There has to be a switch or something around here."

They all tore their eyes from the spinning light and began searching. While they did so, I steeled myself. If another wave of the enemy caught up with us in here, I was going to have to try once more to short it out personally. I doubted anyone in the Hammonton would survive.

"Hey, I've got it!"

Turning, I saw the veteran from 6th unit bending over a cable on the floor.

"Hold on—!" I began to shout, but it was too late.

These cables weren't like our human equivalents. They weren't shielded for safety.

A massive spark leapt out, uniting the veteran, the cable, and the cage that surrounded the spinning singularity.

"Damn, boy! He lit himself on fire!" Harris said, kicking at the veteran to knock him loose.

The dead man fell away, leaving smoking parts behind. He'd been flash-fried.

"Nobody else touch the cables," I suggested. I needn't have bothered. They'd all scattered like kicked dogs.

"At least it was quick," Harris said, grimacing at the smoldering mess on the floor.

"Hmm," I said, eyeing the cage and the spinning light.

It had died down some when the veteran had made his fatal error. That gave me an idea.

"Cooper!" I shouted. "Come out, now!"

For a few seconds, it was crickets. Everyone looked around in confusion. We hadn't seen Cooper since I'd sent him back to report to Graves. That was hours ago.

Any reasonable officer would figure that he'd lost his way or maybe been killed at some point. After all, these aliens could detect him, stealth suit or no.

But I wasn't a reasonable man. What's more, I knew Cooper very well. He reminded me of a sneakier version of myself as a younger man.

"Get over here, on the double!" I boomed.

Three splashing steps, and Cooper materialized with a smile. "Yes sir! What can I do for you, Centurion? I'll scout the perimeter if you—"

My big index finger hooked him by the collar and dragged him back before he could dance away and vanish again.

"I don't need a scout right now. I need a volunteer."

Harris hooted. "You just volunteered, boy!"

Cooper shot him a pissed look. Then he turned his eyes toward me. He looked resigned. "Is this because I've been invisible since—?"

"It's best you don't remind me about that right now," I told him. "But no, it's because you're the only lightly armed, lightly armored man I have left. Normally, you'd be useless at this point. But I've got a special mission."

"What kind of special…?"

He followed my pointing finger toward the generator, then the live high-voltage cable. The blackened corpse of the first man who'd touched it was a contorted heap nearby.

"Seriously?" Cooper asked in dismay.

"Yep. Get a belcher—or some other long solid metal object. Jam it into the cage and touch it to that cable. Mission accomplished."

He looked pretty unhappy. I couldn't say that I blamed him.

He opened his mouth, and I expected a litany of excuses and dodges. He had the sore-back, stiff-necked shits, I was pretty sure.

But before he could speak, a lot of sounds began in the passageway. Squelching feet advanced.

"Something has found us," Harris said.

"A whole lot of somethings by the sound of it," I said.

"What do I get out of this?" Cooper asked.

107

The rest of the squad and a half I had left alive took up defensive positions at every entrance and exit. Harris took a moment to throw an answer over his shoulder.

"You get the pleasure of knowing you've served the legion, boy. You're about to give your all, Cooper, and I salute you!"

Harris was a bastard. His eyes were lit up, and I halfway considered making him do it, but I passed on the idea. Cooper hadn't done much of anything useful on this mission so far, and I'd much rather have Harris at my side in any final confrontation—even if he was a dick.

"Hey, I found a metal strut!" Harris trotted up to us, his boots splashing. "Damn, this whole nest-thing is dead now, I think. It's getting all goopy."

He was right. The life had gone from the flesh that had overgrown the medical center. The veins no longer pulsed, and the walls had become still and dry.

But there was still the generator. It was spinning, full of malice and powering something.

"Here," I said, taking the strut from Harris and handing it to Cooper. "If you figure out a way to live through it, that's cool. I don't care, as long as you short out that generator. Besides that, I'm not asking you to do anything I haven't done myself."

Cooper looked at the length of metal doubtfully. He put it against the cage, and it looked like he planned to drop it onto the power cable.

"That's not going to work!" Harris boomed at him.

Harris walked up, shoved the strut into the cage, and it immediately flared into a hot burning mess. The metal was melting, releasing a screaming sound. This seemed odd, as the spinning light looked cool enough from the outside—but somehow he'd interrupted the field that contained all that power.

"Whoa!" Harris shouted, lifting his hands from the strut. He backed away a step. "Okay, bunny. Now all you have to do is connect these two, quick-like."

"Is that an order?"

"Damn straight it is! Move your—!"

Cooper was quick, agile and mean. That's why he'd become a scout in the first place. Sweeping a foot low, he hooked Harris' ankle. His hand pushed on a balancing point, and Harris pitched backward.

I saw right off what his plan was. He'd figured out that a lot a weight was needed to bend that strut down to touch the cable on the floor. The weight of a large man would do the job nicely.

Harris wasn't an easy man to take down, however. You could trick him, but you might just pay a price for it.

The adjunct's long arm shot out, grabbed Cooper and dragged him down too. They fell together on the strut, which then levered down to touch the cable.

There, they did a little dance until they burst into flames. Cooper looked surprised, which was only to be expected.

But Harris? To be honest, he looked determined. He had Cooper wrapped up in a bear-hug. There was no escaping death for either of them.

After that, the lights went out. My men in the tunnels wandered out.

"Those aliens, the humanoid types, they were coming at us, but they stopped."

"What do you mean they stopped?" I asked.

The specialist shrugged. "They just stopped, sir. They keeled over and stopped moving. I'm not sure if they're really dead or just playing opossum, but I'll take it."

"All right, go back and man your post."

"McGill!" Leeson said a moment later, "you did it!"

"I would give Harris the credit, actually."

The two men who'd given their all, Cooper and Harris, were no longer with us. Their bodies were, in fact, still on fire.

"No, no," Leeson told me. "I mean our tappers are live again. We're on the grid!"

Glancing down, I saw he was right. I immediately contacted Graves.

"McGill?" he asked. "Is that really you? I had you marked down for dead hours ago."

"No way sir, I'm harder to kill than a swamp rat."

"Excellent. The dome is down—I've got a confirmation of that coming in now. How'd you pull that off?"

"Well sir, we found one of those whirly-gig generators, like the one I came across back on Dark World. We killed that, and the power went out for the force field."

"Upload that vid, will you? And push all your survivor engrams, just to be sure."

I frowned, but I worked my tapper to do as he asked. "What's up now, sir? What's the big picture like? We've been cut off for so long, I don't—"

"No time now, McGill. I'll brief you back at Central. You've earned that—well done."

I opened my big mouth to talk to him further, but I closed it again with a frown. The channel had closed.

"So what's the story?" Leeson asked. "Can they spare a lifter for the crew of heroes we've got here?"

My eyes came up from my tapper. They met Leeson's. He saw the truth there, the dark suspicion that I couldn't get out of my head now that it had come inside to roost.

"Aw... are you shitting me?" Leeson asked. "After all this?"

"Let's go outside and talk to those bird-things for a second."

"A blaze of glory, huh? Why not? I swear, I should quit Varus and become a hog."

"That's an awful thing to say, Adjunct."

We walked outside with our weapons ready. A dozen surviving troops followed us. They were all wary and ready to shoot—but there was nothing much going on outside.

"Huh..." Leeson said. "Do you think they've run off?"

"Maybe when we killed the queen and their power supply, they got orders to move and defend another target."

"They are machine-like. An organic critter would have probably stuck around for revenge."

Whatever the case, the plaza had been transformed. It was light now, the dawn having lit up the sky with a pink glare.

I have a vague memory of the following moments, but its ragged and incomplete. It seemed to me later that I looked up at that sky, that the other fighters I'd led all night came out into the open and whooped in celebration.

And why shouldn't they? The enemy was nowhere in sight, and the sun had come out. The dome of force that had enveloped us, shutting out the rest of the planet, was gone.

But there was something. A roar, perhaps. An aircraft? Flying so far overhead it was invisible to my eye from the ground? That was my impression, but as I say, it's all hazy now.

What happened after that moment? I'm not sure. But I stopped existing, as did everyone else within the township formerly known as Hammonton.

We'd been nuked.

-20-

The next time I was revived, I was a little peeved. Graves wasn't even there to preside over my rebirth. That was disappointing. He'd been super happy to see me the last time, after we'd blown the jawbone off the invading ship. Maybe he felt differently today.

"Score?"

"Seven point five. Make that an eight—he's tuning in."

It was true. My mind, my senses, they were all beginning to operate again.

"I'll take an eight. Get off my table, McGill." It was the voice of some bio technician who I didn't recognize.

"Where am I?" I whispered. "Is this Central?"

"No such luck, Centurion. You're aboard *Legate*. Head for Gold Deck. They're waiting for you upstairs."

The steamy chamber smelled like piss and blood and hot chemicals. I slipped off the table while blinking, clawing at my eyes and trying not to breathe too deeply. Doing stretching exercises, I got my eyes and fingers working—at least well enough to pull on some clothes. Dressing sloppily in a uniform, I stumbled out of the stinking chamber.

The bio people didn't even give me a second glance. They were already reviving someone else. I got the feeling they'd been working for long hours, functioning as slaves to their alien machine.

That was the first inkling I got that something was wrong. Not *desperately* wrong, mind you, but this was certainly not the hero's welcome I'd been expecting.

Shrugging it all off, I straightened and walked tall. My confidence was increasing with every step. By the time I reached Gold Deck, my spine was rigid, and I was standing two meters tall again. Even my sandy blond hair had begun to dry out.

Finding the main conference room, I barged inside. No one stopped me.

Six people looked up from the star map displayed in three dimensions on the table between them. Turov, Graves and Winslade were all there. For the most part, that wasn't surprising, as this was clearly a meeting of Varus officers.

But why Winslade? I almost opened my mouth to ask, but I caught myself and sat down at the seat Graves indicated with an impatient wave.

"Please join us, Centurion," Graves said. "We thought you might be able to enlighten us with what you found under that dome."

"Didn't you get the vids?" I asked.

He shook his head. "Not all of them. Just the last few you pushed. What we got was confusing… walking machines with leg muscles? Are they robots or not?"

"Not exactly. They're cyborgs. Half metal and electronics, mixed with meat and nerves."

Galina gave a tiny shudder.

"What about the power supply?" Winslade asked. "Are you sure it matched the design of the unit you destroyed on Dark World?"

"Sure did. You could have just brought up the reports and checked those manually."

"Not actually," Winslade said. "We're far from Earth now, and a lot of things didn't survive."

"We're flying then—after the aliens."

"Yes, we're in pursuit."

My mind was trying to catch up. I hadn't expected to die during an attack from the ground, then wake up in mid-flight, chasing after our alien attackers.

113

"You said something about survival, sir?" I asked as a feeling of coldness came over me. " What exactly was there to survive back on Earth?"

They paused and looked down. Galina was the one who answered me. "James… when we repelled their landing, the aliens didn't take it lightly. They destroyed a large portion of Central City with missiles."

"Nuclear missiles?" I asked, feeling sick all of a sudden.

She nodded.

My mind leapt suddenly to Etta and Della. "What about Central itself? Was it destroyed?"

"No," she said. "We set up defensive batteries and a shield—but the city around it…"

"I understand," I said.

I felt a surge of relief which was quickly followed by guilt at having experienced a good sensation in the face of so many tragedies. "What happened next?"

"The ship turned and ran," Graves said. "It left the Solar System. The damage you did to their main hatch—they didn't seem to be able to fix it immediately."

"But they might do it out in deep space somewhere," I said in alarm. "They might come back and dust off our whole planet."

Galina nodded, leaning toward me. "Now you see the nature of our mission. It is urgent and essential. We're aboard *Legate*, and we're following the enemy vessel."

I let this sink in for a few moments. "Good."

Graves smiled slightly. He liked it when I got into a killing mood. I wasn't sure if that was because he felt I was good at it, or if he just liked killing on principle. I suspected it was a little of both.

My head jerked toward Winslade. "What's the hog doing aboard?"

Winslade looked me up and down and pulled his neck back a ways, like he was a cat that had smelled a dog.

"I'm here at the request of the praetor," he told me stiffly.

"Drusus sent you?" I said, then I grinned. "Let me guess: He told you it was an honor. That you were his best man, and

114

you had experience with Varus, so he figured you were perfect for the job."

Winslade narrowed those already narrow eyes of his. "Something like that."

I laughed. "You've been turfed, Winslade! Wrapped up with a bow on top and dumped on the nearest unsuspecting dupe."

"James," Turov said, "you're being disrespectful."

"Sorry, sir."

"As I was saying, we're aboard *Legate* in pursuit of the enemy ship," she continued, "the battle on Earth to knock out the enemy base killed sixty percent of our legionnaires. As a consequence, we're reviving our people as we go. Another transport is nearby in space, carrying Solstice. Both ships have an accompanying near-human legion with them, of course. There's also an escort of nearly a hundred naval vessels."

Winslade snorted. "Not that the navy can do much against this sphere of death we're chasing."

Despite Winslade's cynicism, I was encouraged. Solstice and Varus—we might not be the most prestigious outfits, but two experienced legions were better than one. All the other big-name legions were stationed on various other planets as garrisons.

I was also glad to hear we were to be supported by Blood Worlders—zoo legions, as less charitable people called them. Altogether, that put our combat strength at around fifty thousand ground troops.

"Do we actually have a fix on the enemy ship?" I asked. "Or are we flying blind?"

She shook her head. "We have better technology these days. We can track them—even in warp."

This was news to me. My eyes widened, and I nodded appreciatively. "Those nerds slaving away under Central have paid off, is that it?"

"Exactly."

"Okay, great. I'm down for this fight. But... why am I at this meeting in the first place, sirs?"

"An excellent question," Winslade said in a snotty tone.

"Because of something Graves mentioned in his report," Galina said. She looked at me intensely. "I know you have a tendency to exaggerate, to stretch the truth at times in imaginative ways..."

"Aw now, that's not a fair statement, Tribune!"

"No," Winslade agreed. "It would be more accurate to say you're a consummate liar."

I glared at him, and he returned the expression.

"Gentlemen, this is your second warning," Galina said. "Stop bickering. I'm not in the mood. Earth has suffered a hard kick in the teeth, and we're out here to make sure it doesn't happen again."

Turning away from Winslade, I faced the tribune again. "My apologies."

"Accepted. Now James, can you confirm that the generator you saw in the center of the alien nest was from Rigel?"

I frowned in thought. "Which vids did you get from the Hammonton expedition?"

"We got what you sent up when you were outside in the center of town," Graves said. "We saw that... uh... flesh-factory. But we didn't see the inside of it."

"You bombed them out too soon, didn't you Graves?" Winslade asked. "Not that I blame you, McGill can bring out the urge to act with deadly force in anyone."

Graves ignored Winslade's barbs. "The system always uploads the older vids first. Consequently, we've only seen the outside of the complex."

"Well," I said, "I can tell you that it was the same *kind* of reactor I ran into on Dark World. Does that mean it was manufactured on Rigel maybe?"

They nodded their heads.

"That is most likely," Graves said.

"Good enough," Turov said. "You're dismissed, Centurion."

I stood up and left. The higher ranked officers would meet all day, probably. Not for the first time I found myself thanking my lucky stars that I was only a centurion. I hated long meetings, and the more you went up in rank, the more of those you got.

As I hit the doors, another primus walked in. He looked me up and down in surprise. Clearly, in his mind I wasn't supposed to be here.

Worse, I saw he had wet hair. He had to be a fresh revive. Knowing they'd revived a centurion before him—that wasn't a sweet taste for any primus.

I touched my cap in salute, and I gave him a smile and a nod. He frowned back, and he watched me swagger out of the place with disgust.

-21-

The flight took weeks, which was a good thing to my mind. First off, it let us get our people revived. It would have been a sad result if we'd caught up to the aliens and gone into combat with only a handful of troops to throw at them.

"This is a game," Carlos told me. "I've seen it before, and I'll see it again—if I don't get permed this time."

"What are you on about now, Specialist?" I asked.

We were having lunch, and I was eating with my unit instead of in the officers' mess. I usually did that when we were deploying to some hell-hole planet or another.

"We aren't catching these aliens," Carlos said, "but we aren't being outrun, either. I mean, what are the odds that our ships and their ship have exactly the same maximum speeds?"

Thinking that over, I blinked twice. "Hmm... doesn't seem very likely."

"It's basically impossible."

"Yeah..." I said, turning it over in my mind. "If the aliens were faster, they'd just pull away and escape. The odds that all our ships fly at the same speed—no way, too big of a coincidence. So, why are we going slow and tailing them?"

"The only reasonable conclusion is that our brass has decided to pace them. To follow them home hoping they don't know we're here. Then we'll jump them and deliver our counterpunch."

I nodded slowly. I couldn't find a flaw in his logic. "And here I was thinking you were a dumb-ass all these years."

Carlos snorted, but he also seemed oddly pleased. Compliments were few and far between in Legion Varus. Even the backhanded kind was always welcome.

Standing up suddenly, I left my unit's module. I wanted to go talk to the people in charge.

These days, I wasn't a total pariah on Gold Deck. Sure, everyone who had a permanent office up there was a primus or worked for one as a staffer. It was an easy way to climb ranks, so many centurions and even some adjuncts did their damnedest to get out of the modules and as close to the brass as possible. That had been Winslade's path to promotion, back in the day.

I'd never had much interest in all that. If I'd wanted to push numbers around and make appointments all day, I'd have been an accountant.

Deciding not to ruffle feathers, I hammered on Primus Graves' office door first.

An adjunct appeared behind me. "Excuse me?" he said. "Can I help you... Centurion?"

I pivoted and stared at the guy. "Who are you?"

"I'm Primus Graves' assistant. You must be McGill?"

Glowering briefly, I gave my head a shake. It was a strange thing to learn Graves had a staffer of his own. He'd always hated that sort of thing.

"I am," I said. "When can I see Graves?"

"There *is* an appointment schedule. Let me see... Next Thursday he's open from 9:15 to 9:30."

"Really? What's he doing right now?"

The adjunct frowned. "He's on Green Deck, I believe."

Green Deck was our exercise chamber in the day and our city park at night. It was full of half-fake trees and entirely fake rocks and waterfalls.

"What's he doing up there?" I asked.

"I believe he's planning an exercise. Listen Centurion, I've been given special instructions regarding your unscheduled appearance. If you would care to—"

"Yeah, yeah," I said, walking out. I straight-armed the door and left.

Green Deck was several floors below. I made the trip, but I didn't enter through the main doors which opened onto nature-trail-looking paths among the lush, fake trees. Instead, I took a tube that only officers had access to and walked a catwalk to a central pod.

There, hanging from the ceiling like a spider, was the officers' observation platform. Being a centurion these days, the computer opened the door at my touch, and I barged right inside.

"McGill?" Winslade asked, sneering. "What are you doing here? I'd accuse you of schmoozing, but I know you're unfamiliar with the concept."

Winslade was there with Graves and several other primus-ranked people. To my surprise there was a single tribune there as well—Armel.

I fixated on him and approached with a big smile.

"Hey, Maurice!" I boomed, offering him a hand to shake. "Good to see you escaped Storm World. How'd you manage that?"

Reluctantly, Armel stood and shook my hand. We'd worked out a minimally functional relationship back on Storm World. I wouldn't say we were in love or anything like that, but we'd learned to tolerate one another.

"I was... transferred," Armel said in his snotty Parisian accent.

"And now you're here planning a human vs. near-human blood bath for training, is that it?"

"No, McGill," Graves said, speaking up for the first time. "We're discussing how we can avoid exactly that sort of disaster."

"A good goal, sir," I said. "You can't let the boys get out of hand in these trainings. Never know what kind of accident might happen."

"Weren't you involved in a nightmare event last year, McGill?" Armel asked in a falsely innocent tone. "Where so many of our near-human brothers were permed?"

"It's the God's-honest truth that I was. At the time, no one had understood that near-human troops weren't going to be revived like the human troops. As a result, well, let's just say the exercise got a little out of hand."

"There were nearly five hundred permings that day, as I recall," Winslade said.

"Like I said, a little out of hand."

They all looked at me like I smelled bad, but I grinned back.

"Anything going on I should know about?" I asked. "I'd love to see another battle royale like we used to have in the old days."

"We're not doing that again, McGill," Graves told me.

"Aw... too bad. Well then, when are we going to catch that ship ahead of us and run her to ground?"

This question left them blinking quizzically because I'd switched topics. I kept a harmless smile on my face. I'd finally steered the conversation to the subject that I wanted information about. You don't want to go at such things too suddenly, it will spook people.

Armel was the first to recover from my change of topic. "What makes you think that we aren't doing our best to catch up to them now?"

I quickly laid out Carlos' idea, but without mentioning him by name. If they'd known it came from a specialist, they would have scoffed. After all, most officers thought they were a different class of human being when compared to the rank and file.

"Hmm..." Armel said. "You have touched upon a sensitive point. I've been wondering the same thing myself."

He was probably lying, trying to sound smart. But I let him do it, as it increased the odds I'd get an answer from the others.

Graves finally spoke up. "It's true. We're not trying to catch them. The navy escort with us is no match for that big sphere. We can't even be sure the door is still open for an attack by teleportation—and while we're in a warp bubble, we can't attack anyway. It's been decided that our best option is to follow them until they come out of warp and jump them when they do."

121

"Another humiliation heaped upon me," Armel complained. He was getting a little red in the face. "You, a primus, were aware of all this while I of superior rank knew nothing? The situation is absurd."

Graves looked at him with a flat expression. "Perhaps you'd like to take that up with the praetor. He's flying with Solstice, in the other ship."

Armel straightened out in hurry. He didn't like to tangle with Praetor Drusus, who'd exiled him to Storm World in the first place and might well do it again. "That will not be necessary. Please proceed with the discussion."

Graves turned back to the tactical map. "The cone of possibilities is narrowing as we go. We're down to a destination somewhere in the Pegasus region."

I sucked in a surprised breath. They glanced at me. Graves looked annoyed. "You've got something to say, McGill?"

"Just two words: artificial intelligence. Pegasus is where all the smart AI programs come from!"

"That's true," Graves admitted, "but that doesn't mean there's a connection."

"Which star in the Pegasus region is the home world of the Pegs?" I asked.

Graves frowned. "51 Pegasi, right here," he said, showing a spot in the cone of probable targets. "It's a yellow main sequence star, rather like our sun. It's about fifty lightyears from Earth."

We all studied the map. Most of the officers were frowning.

"It doesn't make sense," Armel said. "Certainly, the world of the Pegs is known for creating excellent AI. But they are part of the Empire, not a subject of Rigel. In fact, they're not all that close to the frontier. No, I reject this notion of yours, McGill."

Graves stared at the map for a time. "We have two points of reference so far: the AI connection and the direction of travel the enemy sphere has taken. I'm not convinced, but I will admit it's possible. I'll report the concept to the praetor's group. Our orders don't involve figuring out where we're going, anyway. We're the secondary command group."

"Secondary?" I asked. "What's our mission then?"

"To come up with a way to penetrate that ship's defenses."

I stood up and clapped my hands together twice. That made the smaller men present wince. "In that case, I'm your man, sir! I've managed to get inside before. I can do it again."

"They will not fall for the same cheap trick twice in a row," Armel assured me.

"Well then," I said, sitting back down. "You must have a Grade-A plan of your own. Can you tell me about it, Tribune?"

Armel looked annoyed. He obviously had nothing. "You don't even belong at this table. I'll tell you nothing."

Graves turned to look at me. "McGill, I'm sending you over to the praetor's office on Solstice's transport. Throw your idea about the Pegs being involved at him. See what he thinks."

"Uh..." I said. "How am I going to get there, sir? I'm... kind of hoping it won't involve a killing and a revive."

"No, no, we don't need to waste resources like that. We're still reviving legionnaires that died back in New Jersey. We've set up jump-posts between our ships. Go to engineering and tell them I sent you."

"Huh... okay."

I got up and walked out of the place. I wasn't really all that happy with the orders I'd gotten, but I had heard a lot of good information. I had an idea where we were headed and where we might end up.

Unfortunately, the situation wasn't clear. We didn't even know who our enemy was. If the Pegs had sent a monster ship to Earth to attack us... that wasn't good at all. On the other hand, if it come from Rigel, at least that was an enemy we already had on our radar.

-22-

After a bit of arguing with the engineering people, I was allowed to walk between two gateway posts and teleport over to *Legate's* sister ship, *Aeternum*.

The Solstice legionnaires on guard duty were pretty bored when I stepped through. There were two of them, and they were playing cards on their tappers.

When I showed up, they stood and raised snap-rifles to aim at my face.

Solstice boys were a pretty rough lot—almost as rough as Varus people. I respected them the way I could never respect an Earthbound hog soldier. They were known for their willingness to die to complete any mission. Fortunately, I wasn't a target today.

One of the veterans spotted my legion emblem, and he relaxed immediately. Solstice troops wore the emblem of the rising sun. Varus people wore the wolfshead. The man who'd recognized me pushed the other man's gun barrel down toward the deck.

"Varus?" he said. "What do you want, Centurion?"

"Sorry to spook you ladies," I said. "I'm here with a message for the praetor."

They took my comments good-naturedly. Solstice and Varus had always gotten along pretty well. We were both at the bottom end of the totem pole of legion hierarchy. As a consequence, we cut each other breaks whenever we could, keeping all our bad feelings bottled up for the snooty top-rated legions—and the hogs.

They directed me toward Gold Deck, and I marched through the ship like I owned it.

Aeternum wasn't anything special. It was, in fact, identical to *Legate*. I found Gold Deck without a problem and after a few more checks made it to the biggest office at the end of the hall.

Tapping on the door, I found it didn't open right away. As a result, I formed a fist with my fingers and started hammering. I just wasn't certain if the staffers inside had heard me.

To my surprise, when the door popped open it wasn't some secretary kiss-up frowning at me—it was Drusus himself.

"McGill...?" he said, then he looked down at his tapper. "Ah, yes. I see a note here from Graves. Why are you interrupting me today?"

"Uh..." I said. "Sorry sir. I was sent straight here to present a theory from our team's side of the fence."

"A theory about what?"

"The origin of our attackers, sir."

Drusus squinted at me. He didn't like things to get out of place. That was a source of tension between us, because I never stayed in any kind of box when placed there.

"All right, come on in."

I followed Drusus, half-expecting to see a meeting in progress—but the office was empty. There was no one around—not even a single staffer. That was very odd, as Drusus was a hard-working man that never let an hour of office time go by.

Then I caught a scent. Was that perfume? I thought that it might just be. What's more, I thought I knew that scent, vaguely. It wasn't Galina's, fortunately. I knew everything she had in her makeup kit intimately.

No... but it *was* familiar.

"Where is everybody?" I asked loudly.

"I've given them leave to take a late lunch," Drusus said. "Now, come over here, to this conference room."

He crooked a finger and walked through a doorway, indicating I should follow.

But the scent seemed to be coming from the opposite direction. The door down at the end... was that a suite inside there? Was I glimpsing Drusus' adjoining quarters?

The door down there at the end slammed suddenly. Possibly, someone inside had noted my scrutiny.

Shrugging, I turned the other way and followed Drusus to the conference room. We sat down, and I laid out my thoughts about 51 Pegasi—the AI and all the rest of it. Drusus listened politely.

"You'll have to go back to *Legate* and offer my thanks to the officers there," he said. "But there's nothing to worry about."

"I sure will. But... what do you think of the theory?"

"That the Pegs are behind this attack? Not much. We considered them and rejected them right from the outset. By all accounts, they're loyal subjects of the Empire."

"But... they make the best AI in the province, right?"

"That's undeniably true."

"And we're flying directly toward them—correct?"

He looked a little annoyed. "Centurion, we've checked out this lead—"

"Like that fancy auto-driving air car of yours back on Earth. The Pegs programmed that."

He made a wry face, and I realized I'd made a mistake bringing up his air car. I'd had a little trouble with it and inflicted some cosmetic damage to the bodywork. Perhaps he hadn't entirely forgiven me yet.

"They program all the auto-pilot AI," he said. "But we would have heard about it if they were fomenting a rebellion. Think, James: They don't even have a battle fleet. Not a single ship. How could they build something like a warship the size of a moon with collapsed stardust for a hull?"

"Huh... I don't know."

"Exactly. It makes no sense to us, either. Now, since you've explained your concerns, it's time for you to be on your way."

He seemed to be in a powerful hurry to get me out of his office. I got an inkling then that he wanted to be alone.

Could he have a lady-friend in the office with him? That wasn't like Drusus. In fact, in all the long years I'd known him, he'd only been intimately involved with one person.

Suddenly, I knew where I'd smelled that perfume before.

"Golden China!" I said loudly.

He blinked at me. "What?"

"That's the name of that fragrance! Golden China. Tribune Deech used to wear it all the time!"

Drusus sighed. "Thanks for the insights, McGill. Now, get off my ship before I send you back in a box."

"Uh... okay, sir. Sorry, sir!"

I left in a hurry after that, but I kept casting glances down that hall to the door at the far end as I crossed his empty staff area. Was Deech lurking in there? It was my impression that she was.

Hmm... if Drusus and Deech were back together, well, that was a bad piece of luck. They'd had a thing going years ago, and the praetor's famously good judgment had gone out the window.

Deech had ended up pulling garrison duty on Machine World—a punishment post. I'd kind of figured that was the end of it.

But maybe not. Maybe she'd gotten out of that purgatory somehow, the same way Armel had managed to escape Storm World with his zoo legion.

Sometimes, I wished the most annoying people in my life would just stay put.

After popping back over to *Legate*, I reported my findings to Primus Graves. He didn't look happy to hear about Deech.

"Are you *sure* it was Deech?" he asked me again.

"Well, I didn't see her in the buff, or nothing like that. But I know that woman's perfume. It was all over the place in her office when she was running Varus."

"Hmm... I knew she was back, but I'd hoped she would keep her distance from Praetor Drusus."

"Sir... just how, exactly, did she get away from her duties on Machine World?"

"Well, a post like that is far from ideal. Ambitious officers usually find their way out after a few years. In her case, she

127

agreed to take over a near-human legion in order to get reassigned back to Earth."

"Huh… wow. A zoo legion? That's even worse than Teutoburg."

"Yeah, maybe. But at least she's not freezing in a methane-ice storm every night."

Machine World was a strange planet populated by large indigenous artificial life. They lived by mining metals to eat— and we humans had decided to exploit their tunnels, making mines out of them. Titanium was particularly common and particularly valuable. It was Machine World's prime export.

"Are we going to do anything about this… situation?" I asked Graves.

He looked at me sharply and glowered. "That's not an appropriate question, McGill. It's not our place to do anything about our superior officers, especially not when it involves their personal lives."

Graves was a rules-stickler, whereas I was more of a rules-dodger. Accordingly, I nodded and gave him a reassuring smile.

"Shouldn't have brought it up, sir. Just a passing, impure thought in my wandering mind."

"Make sure it stays in there," he grunted, getting to his feet. "You're dismissed, McGill. Don't forget the contest tomorrow."

I blinked at that. "Huh? What contest, Primus?"

"Oh… right. You left the meeting early. It was decided that we should do something new this deployment. Last time it was too costly in irreplaceable near-human lives. This time out it will be officers-only."

"Really?" I said, brightening.

Graves laughed. "You really do have the blood-lust in you, don't you McGill?"

"The more I think about the idea, the more I like it," I said. "After all, the new recruits have never had a chance to watch one of these bouts, and we don't always get a chance to participate. This way, everyone gets a new experience."

"The most important thing is that all the participating officers will be human," Graves said. "Everyone who dies will

128

catch a revive that way. We can't afford to lose troops permanently—I have a feeling we're going to need every last one of them when we catch up to this enemy."

"Agreed."

I took my leave and headed for the showers. After all, I was still sticky from my latest revive.

It was there, in the warm waters, that a familiar face showed up to greet me. It was Kivi.

"Hey, girl," I said, "I haven't laid eyes on your since we got trash-canned back on Earth."

As I spoke, my eyes ran over her body appreciatively. Kivi was a curvy woman—and she wasn't shy in the least.

"Don't remind me," she said. "I was dead for a week. It's not even slightly fair the way they choose who comes out of those machines first."

We talked, and I filled her in on recent events—not all of them, mind you, just the important ones. I told her what kind of monsters we were up against, the fact we were heading toward the Pegasus constellation, and a few more things.

It wasn't until I got to the topic of Deech and Drusus that her eyes lit up with interest. She'd always enjoyed a scrap of gossip.

"Are you sure about that?" she said. "There are plenty of women aboard these ships who would love to bag our top officer."

"I'm sure there are," I said, thinking of Kivi herself. "But Deech seems to have managed it first, last, and only."

"So odd... She's such an unappealing woman."

"Aw well, I don't know about that."

She twisted her lips up in disgust. "You would go for anything."

"That's not true. I have high standards... like you, for example."

Kivi hesitated. I knew she was weighing her options, but she didn't answer my unspoken offer right away.

"Hey," I said, "did you know the officers are going to have a contest tomorrow. Last man standing, as I understand it."

"Or woman."

"Or woman."

Kivi squinted at me. "So… you high-ranked bastards are going to die in some scenario on Green Deck instead of us?"

"That's it."

She smiled at last. "I like that idea. I just came alive an hour ago. I'd be pissed to die again tomorrow in some pointless training."

"It's not going to happen."

She looked at me again with a different light in her eyes. "Is this McGill still a virgin?"

"I sure-as-shit am."

Kivi reached out her index finger and ran it down my arm, tracing the water from the shower.

"Are you done washing?"

"I don't get any cleaner."

The truth was, I was almost pruned up. I'd been about to leave when she'd shown up, changing my mind. I found I was enjoying the company.

"All right," she said. "I know a place. Follow me."

I did, and she was right. She *did* know a place.

Of all the girls on the ship, Kivi was the only one I knew of who tended to seek out and locate private spots to have intimate moments. As a tech, she had a big advantage. She could tap into the surveillance system and check to make sure no cameras were watching.

We went to a maintenance closet, still wet under our clothes. The room was hot and noisy. It was right under the ship's automated laundry.

But I didn't care. This McGill really needed breaking in, and a freshly reborn Kivi was just the thing for that.

-23-

The next morning's contest came far too soon. I rolled out of bed early and suited up. We had a few fresh recruits, and Moller was busy kicking their tails onto the floor.

Without warning, I banged open the door that led to what we called "the freshman dorm". Moller was in there, dragging people out of bed with her thick-fingered hands.

"Officer on the deck!" she shouted.

Half-dressed noobs stood up in a panic. They scrambled to pull on their kits, realized it was hopeless, then just stood at the end of their bunks in two rows. I walked down the middle, wearing armor and magnetic boots that clanged with every step.

"The sorriest excuses for legionnaires I can recall," I said.

"That they are, Centurion," Moller said, slapping down a wad of squirming smart-cloth one of the recruits was holding.

Barton appeared in the doorway behind me. Someone had alerted her, and her sides were heaving, but she acted like everything was cool. These were her charges, as she was in command of the light platoon.

"Are these your people, Barton?" I asked without looking at her.

"They are indeed," she said. "I apologize in advance, Centurion."

"They all need a good killing in my opinion," I said. "Better to do it today than later on in the face of the worst enemy Earth's ever encountered."

"Damn straight they do," Moller said.

The recruits looked like they were going to puke. It was 0500 hours, and many of them had died under the dome back at Hammonton. Some had only gotten a few hours rest since then.

Normally, that would have made me cut them a break—but not today.

"Listen up, people," I said. "Some of you are very green. I would like to apologize for everything that's happened to you in the service of Earth and Legion Varus so far—but I never apologize. That's a luxury in these dark days. You've joined an elite legion to serve Earth, and this is her hour of need."

Walking the other way between the ranks, I was pleased to see that none of them met my eye. They stared straight ahead and kept quiet. I'd half-expected a few snorts when I called Varus elite—but I heard nothing of the kind.

Could it be that our rep was improving? That the list of deeds we'd accomplished had finally helped us rise above our sordid past?

It was my impression that Varus was regarded more favorably than it had been in years past. Perhaps just as important, these troops all knew that Earth had been invaded and almost taken out. The stakes were high, and everyone knew it.

I nodded as these thoughts ran through my mind.

"Normally," I boomed, "we would hold a traditional celebration in honor of all you noobs today."

A few of them frowned in confusion for a second, but no one dared meet my eye.

"By celebration, I mean butchery. Legion Varus normally kills every recruit at least once in training—often two or three times. This is done to toughen up new soldiers. To get them used to the idea of fighting and dying. To shake loose all of that nonsense it tends to trigger in a weak mind."

At this point, there were definitely some widening eyes. Several of them dared to flick their eyes to me, then back to the wall dead ahead again.

132

"But you're in luck. I almost reversed my decision when I saw the sorry state of this barracks... but no, I'm sticking with the plan. Today, you'll be witnesses to a deadly struggle, rather than participating yourselves."

A noticeable wave of relief ran through the room. I thought one or two of the skinny ones might pass out—but they didn't.

"That's right," I said. "You've all had the privilege of dying in actual combat already. No matter how green you were before, I count that as a mark of distinction. Normally, new recruits undergo at least a few months of intensive training before they meet their first aliens in combat. This group, however, has been run over by trams with arms hanging out the windows. You've been eaten by things that look like storks and--worse. Accordingly, I'm inviting all of you to witness a new exercise—officer on officer, to the death."

You could have heard a pin drop. To signal them I was finished and wanting approval, I raised my gauntleted fist high and grinned.

"Blood and honor, people! Your centurion and his adjuncts are representing 3rd unit today!"

Moller and Barton clapped, and the troops joined in. Slowly at first, then with more enthusiasm, they began to clap and cheer. Some had a stray tear run out of their eyes—I pretended not to notice that. They were green, after all, and many had just suffered their first death and revival.

Marching out of that bunker, I was a hero with an extremely happy entourage behind me. They struggled into their kits and followed as fast as they could, hopping on one foot to pull on boots, helping each other with gear and straps.

Leading the way down to the mess deck, we found hundreds of others there, eating and catcalling at us. They were rowdy, but they were all in a good mood. How could anyone be unhappy about skipping a solid death?

"A good day to die, McGill," Leeson said when we'd left them behind and headed back to officer's mess.

"It sure as hell is," I told him.

We sat with our cohort. All around us hundreds of officers, from primus down to adjunct, sat on benches and ate slightly better chow than the troops below got.

The mood was significantly less bubbly up here. In fact, it was positively sour.

Determined to make my table stand out as an exception, I told jokes about Winslade. I detailed various illnesses he was no doubt faking today to get out of this particular duty.

"You just know he's got a doctor's note from Blue Deck," I said.

For several reasons, everyone in my cohort thought this was tremendously funny. First off, no one really liked Winslade. He'd done countless shifty things in his long career, and he was the kind of officer that sought advancement through association, rather than competence or valor.

To clarify, he wasn't *completely* without honor. At times, we'd worked well together. But when he'd become a hog to keep his rank of primus, he'd pretty much turned all the Varus people against him. We had contempt for hogs—mostly because they were failed legionnaires.

"What's so funny, Centurion?" a familiar sneering voice asked behind me.

Craning my neck around, I grinned. "Why, there you are, sir!" I clapped Harris on the back since he was sitting next to me. "Harris here's been telling us funny stories about you cooking bacon in the kitchens, sir."

The humor died on Harris' face. He glowered at me, then glowered at Winslade. "Leave me out of this, McGill."

"Such insubordination," Winslade said in a severe tone, shaking his head and crossing his skinny arms. "I'm not sure which of you I'll enjoy killing most today."

I snorted a gulp of milk. "What makes you think that might be in the cards, Primus?"

Winslade smiled. It was a wicked thing to see. Right off, I knew he had an angle. Winslade always had an angle.

"Haven't you heard the good news?" he asked. "No, I see you haven't. Well then, it might be said that while you were visiting Drusus, I helped formulate some of the rules for today's event."

Everyone at my table had stopped laughing. We frowned in confusion. This was exactly the kind of underhanded behavior we'd come to expect from this primus. It was exactly why he wasn't very well-liked.

"Rules like what?" Leeson asked.

Winslade's smile split his face even more broadly. "Oh... could it be that you don't know? Hasn't Graves explained the rules yet?"

"Just tell us how we're screwed, Primus," Harris said.

"Very well, although I hate spoiling surprises. The event will pit the upper ranks against the lower ranks. Primus and Tribune levels against the Centurions and adjuncts."

We nodded suspiciously, we'd heard that much.

"However," Winslade continued, "this arrangement is problematic."

"How so?" I asked.

"Simply put, I pointed out that there was a basic unfairness to this event. Our upper-tier officers are physically much older, man for man, the higher they go up in rank. More importantly, there are far fewer of us than there are of the riff-raff classes."

I didn't know where he was going with this, but I was already frowning. I knew I didn't like where he was headed.

Winslade began to grin. Before, his lips had been curving in a tight line—but now, they split open and showed his gray-white teeth.

"So?" Harris asked, unable to contain himself. "So what's the deal?"

"So the suggestion was made that superior weaponry would be given to the higher level officers to even the odds."

"The suggestion was made?" Leeson snorted. "By you?"

"I might have had some input on the details," Winslade admitted. "But the officers as a whole made the decision. In any case, I'm looking forward to the event. See you on Green Deck."

He walked away, and my boys fell to muttering. Even Barton looked irritated, and she was normally a straight-arrow.

Winslade was a master at pissing people off.

"He's gonna cheat," Harris complained. "He'll come out wearing power armor and give us sticks to fight with. You watch."

No one argued with him. We'd all begun to suspect the worst.

-24-

When we assembled on Green Deck, we learned the rules of today's very special contest. Tribune Armel appeared on the walls of every ready-room adjacent to the large chamber we called Green Deck.

"Officers of Varus," he said with his French accent on full display, "as your legion's officers are in today's battle, I've been awarded the honor of playing referee."

Armel seemed very happy with his role. He had a thin, twitchy mustache and a drink that looked like iced tea in his hands. Being familiar with his habits, I suspected there was something stronger in that glass.

"Today's exercise will pit the lower ranked officers against those of higher rank. Essentially, the adjuncts and centurions will face your tribune and everyone of primus rank."

At face value, this sounded like a good deal. After all, there were way more centurions and adjuncts than there were upper ranks. I heard snorts and scoffs from other unit officers—but not from my group. We were sour-faced. We all waited to hear how Winslade had "weighted" these rules in his own favor.

"Naturally, as the lower ranks badly outnumber the upper ranks, such a contest is inherently unfair. To remedy that situation, we've given the smaller team superior weapons."

He took a moment to slurp his drink and smile at us. "Now, as to the rules: they are simplicity itself. Whichever side kills the other in its entirety wins. And—one last note. Put on a good show, everyone. Every enlisted person on this ship is watching the proceedings with avid interest."

He threw down the rest of his drink and pushed a button on his desk. The scene rolled away, as did the door in front of us.

Suddenly our tappers went dead. Men cursed on both sides. Apparently, we weren't going to be allowed to have any outside help from spies, or even radio communications among ourselves. Not this time out.

Each of the ten cohorts entered from a different door, with about forty officers in each group. My group was from 3rd cohort.

In a rush, every junior officer I knew trotted into the room. We couldn't see the other groups, however. They were a few hundred meters away in various directions.

None of us had been issued weapons or armor before we walked onto Green Deck. That was normal for this kind of exercise, but it always left a man feeling vulnerable and almost naked at the start. Accordingly, when we found racks waiting immediately inside, we rushed to grab the new gear.

Unfortunately, the pickings were very slim indeed.

"Say what?" Harris demanded. "I get the jump suit I came in with... and a knife? Is this some kind of joke?"

"A bad one, I'd say," Barton said.

I glanced her way. Her face was bitter as she picked up her combat knife and checked its balance. Her attitude surprised me as she wasn't usually a complainer. Perhaps Winslade had managed to trigger a sense of injustice even in Barton—he had that kind of effect on people.

On the forward rack, those of us who were of centurion rank stepped up and took our slightly better gear.

"...fucking kidding me...?" Manfred complained. "This is balls, McGill."

"Yep. But don't piss yourself yet. We'll win."

He snorted, and together we pulled on breastplates and snap-rifles. That was it. We didn't even get combat knives to put on our empty belts.

"No grav grenades?" Harris complained. "No spears, even? This is bullshit. Us adjuncts are jokes even compared to you half-naked centurions. I might as well slice my own gonads off right now with this pig-sticker."

He waved his knife around in disgust, and I couldn't blame him. I had armor and a snap-rifle. That wasn't much—but it was a hell of a lot better than a knife and a thin cloth jumper.

"Okay," I said, "how do we decide who leads?"

There were ten centurions. One of them spoke up immediately. "Let's operate as squads," she said. "Each centurion will lead their adjuncts as a team."

The other centurions nodded in agreement.

"That idea sucks," I said. "Let's vote for one commander."

"I second the motion," Manfred said. "I vote for McGill."

"I agree," Harris said, "I say we all—"

"Excuse me," the first centurion said. "Adjuncts don't get a vote. This is a military hierarchy—not a democracy."

Looking her over, I saw her name was Venner. I didn't know her well, but I didn't have any reason to dislike her.

"Look, Venner," I said, "are you suggesting just the centurions should vote?"

"We should get a move on," Manfred complained. "We don't know what's out there."

Venner scoffed. "There are only about twenty primus-ranked people on this entire ship. No matter what weapons they have, they can't kill us all so quickly."

About then, I heard the crump of explosives. Everyone hit the deck and crawled for cover. The chatter of distant snap-rifle fire began a moment later.

"Barton, scout for me," I ordered. "Venner, I'll vote for you if you like—we need a single leader."

She thought about that for a second, but she shook her head. "What's wrong with operating as a set of tight teams? Maybe when we see what we're up against—"

"Off to the east," Barton called back. She was crouching in the brush to our right flank. "There's action over there. Do we advance to support?"

"I say no," Venner said stubbornly. "That's 6th cohort. Let them dull the blade for us."

Harris, Leeson and I exchanged glances. My adjuncts were frowning, but they didn't have the rank to argue.

Accordingly, I stood tall. "I'm moving to support 6th cohort. Do you really think Winslade set this up so forty guys with pig-stickers can kill all twenty of them? If we let them take us out one cohort at a time, we're doomed."

Manfred stood with me—he was a rare friend of mine among officers of any rank. "I'm with McGill."

Without looking back at the rest of them, we advanced. It was six of us against God-knew-what, but I would be damned if I'd sit on my hands while forty comrades got torn up.

As we got closer to the action, we began moving from cover to cover. Our centurions with rifles calling overwatch as the next man advanced. To my surprise, I saw people joining us—it was Centurion Venner and the rest of the 3rd cohort officers.

"You just *had* to start something, didn't you McGill?" Venner asked me.

She was hiding behind the same tree I was, and I thought about a few choice comebacks—but I passed on them. She'd come around and joined me, after all.

"That's my approach to life," I admitted. "I'd like to think 6th cohort would come to our aid if we were in a bad way."

Venner snorted and rushed ahead. I followed a moment later.

There were only bodies left when we arrived at the entry door. Centurions with snap-rifles, adjuncts with knifes... they were all as dead as yesterday.

"Holy shit..." Harris breathed. "This was a slaughter!"

"What's it been?" I asked. "Five minutes?"

"About that, yeah," Leeson said. "Since the first shots were fired."

Green Deck was big—but not as big as it seemed. Aboard *Legate*, it occupied about a square kilometer of space. It felt bigger than that due to the thickly overgrown trees and the holographic walls that projected grand, false vistas.

My mind ran through those numbers, and I didn't like the answers. This entire group had been butchered fast. That meant the enemy had overwhelming firepower.

Now, I'd been under no illusions that this would be in any way a fair fight. First off, Winslade was in charge of the arrangements. Secondly, there was no way the higher ranks could win when outnumbered twenty to one unless they had some pretty big advantages.

"They have grav-grenades?" Venner said. "Heavy armor with morph-rifles—at least that."

I nodded in agreement.

Harris threw his knife down in disgust. Just when I turned to demand his "resignation" which meant I would execute him on the spot, he picked up a snap-rifle and breastplate from a dead centurion. Strapping on his knife again, he gave me a grin, and blood dripped from him.

I grinned back. "You're better equipped than I am now."

Venner scowled, then ordered her adjuncts to grab up better gear. Everyone got something, even if it was only a second knife.

Slightly better equipped, we moved on, heading west again.

Another group approached, and we went to ground. After a few moments of tense drama, we realized it was the officers from 9th cohort. We greeted one another like we were blood-brothers.

Eighty strong now, we decided to move to the center of the field. That was sheer balls, but we could already hear fighting in that direction. The brass had caught up with another company of ours somewhere in the woods.

"There's no time to lose," I said. "We have to hit them all at once, or we're doomed."

No one could find much fault with my logic, not even Venner. We hustled to the mid-field, where a strange scene was in progress.

The middle of Green Deck generally contained a quickly fabricated fortification. Today was no exception. A series of low steel shields, just the right height to fire over, had been erected to form loose walls. There were two rings of these shields, forming a very basic fort.

The two barriers encircled an empty spot at the very center of Green Deck. The whole thing wasn't much to write home about, each shield in the rings being a meter high and twice as wide, but they were better than nothing. They were built of heavy metal with supporting pylons.

141

Circled up inside this primitive fort were at least three of our cohorts, over a hundred men in all. They were pointing guns in every direction, and they looked nervous.

"We can't go in there," Venner whispered to me. "Every good firing position has been taken."

"Agreed. Let's stay in the trees and act as reinforcements."

We didn't have long to wait. A few minutes later one of the upper ranked officers strode out of the trees onto the field. He wore heavy armor, as I expected. But it wasn't just a regular suit, he was in a full battlesuit, the heaviest stuff reserved for our weaponeers. It was the kind of armor I'd worn back in the day, or that Sargon often wore today.

In that thick plate armor he might survive a strike from a light artillery piece.

"Damnation," Harris breathed. "That's not fair at all."

"I think that's Graves," I said, squinting, "and they've targeted him."

The three teams in the center of the field had been sorting themselves out, taking up defensive positions as best they could. Now, they all shouted and directed a storm of fire against Graves. He bounded back into the trees, chased by countless streams of snap-rifle rounds.

"Those sped-up BBs are never going to penetrate that armor," Harris said.

"They might get a lucky hit on his faceplate," Leeson said.

"Not when he's got his ass pointed their way."

Frowning, I swept my gaze toward the opposite side of the field. Barton was already looking that way, and she pointed.

The main attacking force emerged. There were ten more primus-ranks in full heavy armor—and something else walked behind them. It was a dragon. A walking, fighting machine that stood three meters tall.

Riding inside, I saw a face I knew all too well. Tribune Galina Turov was at the helm.

-25-

Long ago, when I'd encountered my first dragon, Galina had been driving it. She'd gotten it on Tech World, and she'd kept it aboard our ship for emergencies.

Striding through our transport *Corvus*, she'd been enraged with yours truly that day. She'd made Carlos her first kill, and I was her second.

I almost shivered to see her in the cockpit, grinning and driving the dragon like a woman possessed.

The central groups had spotted the approaching enemy by now. They were turning and scrambling on all fours behind their squatty walls to fire at the small charging group of armored men.

Galina tilted up her shoulder-mounts and unloaded smart-grenades. These lobbed into the midst of the unarmored troops and popped with air-shivering reports. Picking up any debris, even flying bullets, the grav-grenades tossed them in random directions, shredding the men inside the fort.

"That defensive position is a death trap!" Harris shouted. "All they have to do is sit back and bomb them!"

But Galina didn't. After showering maybe four glowing blue balls into their midst, she let the primus-ranks rush in to finish the job.

"They aren't firing," Venner said. "Why not?"

"No morph-rifles," Leeson said. "Graves and his crew aren't entirely unfair. They're going into hand-to-hand with force-blades only."

It all made sense. They couldn't give us garbage and give the higher ranks unlimited ammo. Galina probably had a limited number of grav grenades. The others had armor, but no guns.

Fair? Far from it. But at least it wasn't going to be a hopeless slaughter. Butchery, sure—but there was a dull gleam of hope.

"Let's pull around behind them and hit them in the ass," I said. "Come on!"

Manfred followed me immediately. Venner gritted her teeth, but then she sprinted in our wake, cursing.

It's hard to commit yourself to a charge that will probably end up with you being torn apart. Even knowing that you'll catch a revive isn't enough. Just try stabbing your hand with a knife because you know you'll heal, and there's nu-skin spray in the cupboard.

You still won't want to do it.

But we had no choice. Over half our number was in this fight already. If we didn't win right here, right now, the rest of us were going to be hunted down and butchered. It was as simple as that.

Galina advanced in her dragon while we circled around. Graves had come back onto the scene as well. He led the rest of the primus-ranked knights, and they quickly reached the barricade on the other side. There was no escape for the doomed men inside their precious fort.

Snap-rifles hammered, aiming at faceplates, but it took dozens of rounds to penetrate. We saw two of the higher officers falter and tumble—their ballistic glass punctured at last.

The group in the middle released a ragged cheer. It was more of a growl of group defiance, really. They couldn't hope to win. They'd lost half their number and only taken down two of their attackers. But for all of that, they were game.

Staying inside the treeline, we ran around behind Galina's dragon then charged in from the flank.

We almost took her by surprise. She was sidestepping her dragon eagerly, shouting orders to the armored men struggling in the fort.

Galina spotted our rush at the last moment. She made a squawking sound of surprise and hopped backward to escape—but we were in too close.

She released two more of her precious grav-grenades. Leeson ate one, Venner ate another. A dozen other adjuncts, looking pathetic with their knives out, died as well.

Fortunately, I knew a few things about dragons. I'd practically lived inside one for months back on Machine World.

One of their many idiosyncrasies was their tails. They weren't just for show. Running around on two legs was difficult for a robot, and they used their tails for balance. The tails were, in fact, fully automated constructs, like segmented metal snakes that whipped and curled as needed.

Hopping on top of her tail, I caused the machine to wobble as it tried to balance. The tail lashed, but I hung on for dear life. Not knowing what was wrong, Galina backed up. It was a natural response—but it was the wrong one.

When she was off-balance already, I leapt off the tail and shoved it upward. The machine, trying to compensate, pitched forward. I thought I heard her squeak inside, but it could easily have been my imagination.

Now, it should be said here that I didn't want to kill Galina. I was kind of sweet on her, if the truth was to be told. We'd had an on-again, off-again relationship going for years. Call it a fatal attraction, or inappropriate romance—it was all of that and more.

Whatever the case, I will forever be able to claim that I didn't bring about her demise on that grim day. What happened—and this is the God's-honest truth, I swear—is she panicked, just a little, and released two more grav-grenades.

Normally, that wouldn't have been a problem. In fact, it might have saved her. After all, our people were all in close, stabbing at every cable and joint with knifes, firing streams of snap-rifle rounds point-blank at her cupola. In that situation, a well-placed grenade might have taken out most of us.

Unfortunately for Galina, when she released her grenades I'd just gotten done messing with her tail, upsetting the machine's balancing algorithm. The dragon did a face-plant—and in that precise instant, the grenades burped out of the chest cannons, right into the churned up mud under the machine.

They went off right under the machine's belly. The dragon did a hop and smoked. It was dead, and so was our beloved tribune.

"That was *magnificent*!" Barton said, limping up to me and clapping me on the back.

I nodded, panting and hurting from a few slivers of shrapnel that had escaped the explosion. "Please don't tell Turov who did it," I said. "Okay?"

Barton blinked, but then she nodded and shook her head bemusedly.

Harris came up and pulled me to my feet. "Manfred's dead. Turov snipped his head clean off, that witch. No offense…"

"None taken. Let's help with the rest."

We waded into the steel barricades then. Half the primus heavies were down—but our side was running out of troops, too.

None of us were pleased to see that Graves was still in the fight.

"Damn!" Harris breathed. "Look at that mother! He's poetry in motion!"

Harris wasn't exaggerating. I'd only tangled with Graves on a few occasions, but believe me, when you went into a fight with that man, you damn-well better mean business.

He stood in the midst of several of the steel shields, and men rushed him with knives from every direction. His stance was so practiced, so effortless. No matter how they hit him—tackling low or high—they couldn't seem to take him down.

In the meantime, his two blades hummed and slashed. They thrust through guts, sliced through ribcages and always seemed to be directly in the path of every attacker that dared to charge in.

His faceplate was a glittering tangle of glass. Round after round had been fired into it, shattering every inch. The face inside looked barely human—but for all that, he was still on his feet, fighting.

"Your commander is down, Graves!" I roared through cupped hands. "Give it up!"

He seemed not to hear me, or maybe he didn't care. I hadn't expected he would.

"You're wasting your time, boy," Harris said. "I've fought with Graves for a long time. He's not giving up while he's still breathing."

Watching him, I saw Harris screw an extension onto the snap-rifle he'd taken off a dead centurion somewhere. He quickly and expertly converted his weapon into a single-shot sniper rifle.

Taking careful aim, he waved to me. "Get him to look this way!"

Trotting up, I shouted at him. "Graves!"

He turned to see me. I waggled a knife in each hand, issuing a clear challenge. I gave him a feral grin.

"Two blades against two blades!" I said.

He nodded. He seemed beyond speech—then I saw how injured he was. Some rounds had penetrated his faceplate. It looked like his jaw was hanging down, useless and flapping. Blood was everywhere inside his helmet, and a lot of it had to be his.

I charged, but before we could meet, a rifle cracked. Graves flew onto his back, stone dead.

"Ah well..." I said. "It would have been a fine fight."

A general round of catcalls went up from the group around us. They didn't like how we'd suckered Graves.

"Shut the shit up," Harris snarled at them, no matter what their rank. "McGill did his part, and Graves is down. Any recruit that did that would be given a medal."

They still grumbled. Looking around for more upper ranks, we realized that Graves appeared to be the last of the enemy. We'd won.

There was some ragged cheering, but not much. Most of us were hurt, and all of us were bone-tired.

"We need to get out of here," Harris said. "Are the doors still locked?"

147

"Yep, they sure are."

"This is bullshit," he complained. "It must be Armel up there in the ops booth. He's probably drunk. That man is as useless as a pecker on a pope."

There was scattered laughter and agreement on that point.

Barton walked over to me, and she laid a hand on my shoulder. I thought for a second she was going to admonish me over Graves' death—but she didn't.

"Hey," she said, pointing. "You see that pile of bodies over there?"

I looked. "Yeah?"

"Winslade went down right there, but I didn't see anyone actually kill him."

Barton and I glanced at one another, and we both grinned.

"This is ours—all ours," I said.

"Agreed. How are we going to do it?" she asked me, whispering.

After a few minutes, we organized search parties to head into the woods. Ostensibly, this was just in case there was another primus hiding in the trees someplace, like that last Easter egg with the ten credit piece in it no kid seems to be able to find.

In the meantime, Barton and I took our combat knives and we went to work on the belly plates of the dragon. They were warped and jammed, but we got one open eventually. Reaching my hand way up into the magazines, I managed to pull out one last grenade.

We walked over to where Winslade was napping under a grisly pile of death.

"Looks like everyone's left," I said loudly. "Kind of weird how they don't want to let us out."

"Right," Barton said with equal volume. "How about that lamer Winslade? He went down in the first thirty seconds, didn't he?"

"Sure did. I killed him myself."

"No you didn't, sir! I killed him. He ate it like a hog right at the start!"

148

About then, the pile of bodies stirred. They slid aside, and something gory and metallic stood up in their midst. Inside that blood-smeared faceplate, a triumphant Winslade sneered at us.

"You're both liars!" he shouted, and he began to wade toward us. His force-blades sprouted and began to hum.

That was our cue. Barton and I hit the deck. We'd been standing near the barricades, and we made sure the thick shields were between us and the flash of blue-white plasma that ignited the area a moment later.

We'd booby-trapped the bodies Winslade had been hiding under. His suit was blown open.

Unfortunately, Harris hadn't gotten wind of our plot. He charged Winslade from behind, and he blew up with him.

Barton and I stood up when the smoke cleared, grinning at each other.

"See that?" I asked. "You've made an honest man out of me, Barton. I now can prove I had an undeniable hand in killing old Winslade."

"No charge, Centurion. No charge."

Moments later, a voice like that of the Almighty spoke. It rumbled across the vast chamber that was Green Deck. It took me a second to realize it was Armel. His words had been amplified, and they were ear-splittingly loud.

"The last of the better men has fallen. The lower ranks have won this dark day. Congratulations, peasants. You have thrown down your masters. This contest is finished."

Then, and only then, did the massive doors of Green Deck roll away and allow the survivors to exit.

149

-26-

It had been a grim slaughter. By the end, three quarters of the officers who'd participated had died. Despite that, the enlisted types seemed jubilant.

"Blowing up Winslade," Carlos said, clapping me hard on the back. "That was the coolest thing I've ever seen you do, McGill. We were all watching, and when Graves led that charge into the center—well, we thought all you guys wearing your undies out there were finished."

"It was a close thing," I agreed. "It would have helped if all the cohorts had decided to jump in."

"Yeah, the 2nd and the 5th… I don't know how they can look themselves in the mirror after that embarrassment."

"They pissed themselves and shivered in the woods," I said loudly, giving an eye to a few centurions who were in earshot.

They showed me their middle fingers and hunkered over their gear. They couldn't fool me—they were feeling ashamed.

Graves entered the mess deck then, and we gave him a cheer. He saluted us in return.

"I'm here on the part of your superiors," he said. "We would like to congratulate the lower ranks of Varus on a job well done. There are no hard feelings, and we'd like every centurion to join us for a banquet on Gold Deck tomorrow night. By then, the revival queues are scheduled to be empty."

Another cheer went up, and he marched back out again.

"That's totally cool of him," Carlos said. "Graves is a class act."

"Would have been cooler if he'd invited the adjuncts," Harris grumbled.

"Not enough ballroom," Carlos said.

"What's that, Ortiz?"

"That's just what I've heard, sir. Gold Deck can't squeeze hundreds into their banquet chamber."

"Let me tell you a little story, Ortiz…" Harris said. "You're an idiot."

Carlos laughed, but Harris glowered and poked at his food. He'd died in the exercise, and he somehow seemed to blame me for it. From my perspective, that was just sour grapes. Harris was always in a bad mood after dying. Always.

I searched for Kivi that night, but she was otherwise engaged. That's how it went with her. You couldn't get attached, or you were sure to get your dick shortened.

My mind considered the idea of wandering up to Gold Deck and trying my luck with Galina—but I passed on that. She and I had a long-term, simmering relationship. But when we were on deployment, we rarely got together. It never seemed to work out when we were under the stresses of a military campaign. On top of all that, I'd just ganged up with twenty other guys to kill her. She was unlikely to be in a receptive mood.

So, I returned alone to my quarters. I was surprised to find someone waiting there for me. It was Adjunct Erin Barton.

Now, let me get things straight right here, I'd always played the game strictly by the rulebook with Barton. I hadn't even hinted around with her, as she was my immediate subordinate.

She'd come to Varus out of Victrix, under somewhat mysterious circumstances. Her shoulders were broad, her face was sharp. She wasn't an ugly woman, far from it—just… kind of mean-looking.

Tonight, she looked different somehow. More feminine and inviting. I thought it was her smile and her eyes. They seemed to glow at me.

Uh-oh.

She'd been through a lot today, and I'd somehow struck her fancy. I'd have to step carefully tonight.

"Good evening, Adjunct," I said. "You did some excellent killing today."

"I could say the same, sir. I especially liked tripping up Winslade at the end. Is it wrong to feel vindictive like that?"

Blinking for a second, I could tell by her smile that she was joking. I laughed and opened my door.

"It sure isn't," I said. "Not where he comes from. Winslade is like a snake lurking under your porch swing. He's always fair game."

I stepped inside my quarters, and I half expected her to say goodnight and walk off—but she didn't. She just kind of lingered there, canting her hips so they leaned against my doorway.

"Uh…" I said. "You want to come in? We could have a drink or something."

It was the wrong thing to say. I knew it the second those words were out of my mouth, but it was already too late by then. She slammed the door behind her, and she sat on my bunk. I made us a couple of drinks in disposable cups, and we both downed them.

"You know what?" she asked. "I think I'm finally feeling at home here—with Varus, I mean. I owe a lot of that to you, sir."

"You don't say?"

"That's right. From the start, any normal centurion would want to know how a girl like me got herself kicked out of Victrix, demoted to adjunct, and sent down to Varus. But you didn't pry."

There was an insult or two buried in her statements, but I let that slide. A man who gets offended easily rarely gets any tail—not that I was angling for that tonight. It was just reflexive for me to let a lady speak her mind.

We had another shot each, and she heaved a deep sigh. I'd rarely seen her drink. She'd always been a tightly wound creature from day one.

"I'll admit," she said, "I considered Varus a worse fate than perma-death. There are so many stories, so much sneering…"

"Uh… how about now?"

152

"I feel differently about things. I spent that first year, back on Storm World, trying to be an exemplary officer."

"And you achieved your goal, by the way."

"Thank you... but it didn't work. I didn't get a reprieve. All my requests to return to Victrix went unanswered."

That surprised me. I hadn't known she'd been working hard to transfer out. Normally, when an officer wanted a transfer, they were supposed to inform their direct commander.

But I knew what she meant. She wasn't making formal written requests. She was feeling the waters back home, testing the ears of whatever friends she had back there. Apparently, Victrix had taken a pass.

"Their loss and our gain," I said firmly.

She gestured with her cup. I hesitated, then poured her another.

"Well sir," she said. "I'll say goodnight if you want me to."

She wasn't looking up. She was studying her hands, eyes downcast. That wasn't the norm for her. She usually met any gaze with her own steely blues—but not tonight.

For some reason, this caused a surge of attraction to grip me. She was making it clear she was interested—but it was all up to me.

Damn.

I knew I shouldn't, mind you. I'm not the young savage I was thirty years before. Oh, sure, I still felt all those old emotions. Hell, my body was at least thirty years younger than my mind at the moment. But the passions and hormones of a young healthy male were definitely affecting me tonight.

Reaching out a hand, I touched her arm. It was a chaste thing, a comforting thing—but it garnered the expected reactions.

She jumped my bones. Right then and there. That single touch... I guess she'd taken it as a sign I was interested— which I was.

But I hadn't been expecting her to come on strong after looking so demure. Whatever was going on in her mind, the whole situation was beyond control about ten seconds later.

We made love like a couple of animals. Damn, she was kind of hot. Passionate. She clawed at me, even.

153

Sometimes the reserved ones... I don't know, they're bottling it up.

When we were finished, she sprang off me and started pulling her clothes on. I raised myself on my elbows and watched.

"Uh..." I said. "You in a hurry, Erin?"

That was probably the first time since we'd met that I'd used her first name. She paused and softened.

"I... I think I made a mistake. I'm sorry, sir."

"Aw, come on. I wasn't that bad, was I?"

She laughed at that. She shook her head. "It's not that. This just isn't appropriate."

"You mean the part about jumping on your centurion by surprise? No... that sure as hell wasn't," I agreed. "But it happens. Don't freak out about it. This is Varus, not Victrix."

Erin nodded and took a deep breath. She found her cup and waggled it at me. I poured her one more, and we kissed for a while.

"I really should go now," she said. "I can't spend the night or anything—the troops will know by morning."

I didn't have the heart to tell her they were most likely playing buzzer vids of the action right now in the recruits' bunkroom. Varus officers weren't the only ones who broke the rules a lot in this legion.

"All right," I said, giving her one more kiss. "Don't be a stranger."

She took a step toward the door, but she paused. Those eyes of hers were downcast again. Calm and demure all of a sudden—damn, this girl could switch moods like a rainstorm.

"You want to know why I got kicked out of Victrix?"

"Uh... sure, if you want to tell me."

"I slept with a primus. The tribune found out—and that was it. I was demoted and out on my ass."

I laughed. "Don't worry about that happening again. Not here. Hell, if they kicked you out of Varus, where would they send you? Even hog-heaven back at Central would be a promotion. There's nowhere to go from here but up, girl."

Erin smiled, and she left.

After that, I stretched out on my bunk until my feet hung over the sides, and I slept like a baby.

-27-

The next evening I attended the banquet on Gold Deck. The room was crowded with officers, but I didn't care. The food was top-notch.

Two plates sat in front of me. One was for the light stuff: potato salad, chicken, black olives and peeled shrimp. The second was stacked with three steaks, each as thick as my thumb.

My mouth was watering, and I could barely listen to the speeches. *Damnation*, why did people always like to talk so much before they ate? That was bass-ackwards in my book. I couldn't even *think* with all that food staring up at me.

"51 Pegasi is home to a strange, friendly species that is famous for their AI creations," Drusus said calmly. "I'm here today to tell you about it, as we'll soon reach that famous star system."

Galina walked by and eyed me from across the table. Her gaze was frosty, to say the least.

"Don't hunch, McGill," she said. "Show these people you are an officer and a gentleman—not a professional ape-impersonator."

Nodding, I tried to look at Drusus, and I pasted on a smile for everyone to see. Galina walked away to join the top table, which was occupied by Tribunes Armel, Deech and Francisco, who commanded Legion Solstice. Drusus was standing over them all, making his endless speech.

156

Out of the corner of my eye, I watched more people up at the buffet, filling plates and yakking. Soon, they would all filter down to the tables, shut up, and the signal would be given for us to dig in.

That was Deech's rule, mostly, but I thought Drusus and Turov liked it too. We didn't say grace in Legion Varus, but we waited until everyone got their food so we could all eat at once.

It was senseless decorum to me. The kind of thing that damned-near drove me crazy at times.

"From my understanding," Drusus continued, "the Pegs are not flying horses at all."

There were a few twittering laughs. Drusus was bad at jokes, and he'd dropped another bomb as far as I could tell.

"They are, in fact, enterprising creatures that resemble six-legged felines. They can run on all six, or they can rear up and manipulate objects with their front two appendages."

He displayed pictures, and people oohed over them.

The Pegs looked like freaks to me. Short-furred, with the head of a lynx, maybe. They had some extra legs with creepy-looking black hands at the end. I didn't like the look of them right off.

"So cute," Galina said.

"Cute...?" Drusus asked. "Not really, they're apex predators. They weigh around six hundred kilograms on average—and that's with a slightly lower gravity index on their home world."

The image shifted to show the 51 Pegasi star system. My stomach rumbled mournfully.

"Exoplanets that could support life were discovered in this star system by Earth astronomers as early as 1995. It turned out later, when these discoveries could be verified, that life would be comfortable for Earthlings on the Peg home world. Even their star is quite similar to our own sun."

Up until this point Drusus had been rather upbeat, but now he frowned and looked serious.

"We've been trying to communicate with 51 Pegasi since the... incident on Earth. We've had no luck. They either aren't answering, or they're not able to answer."

He paused for a moment to let that sink in.

157

"That fact, coupled with the knowledge that the enemy ship is heading directly toward 51 Peg has led scientists to believe a disaster has occurred on this planet."

"What kind of disaster?" Armel asked, speaking slightly out of turn. "Have they decided to rebel? To create monsters and strike at their local enforcers?"

"That's unlikely," Drusus said. "It's a mystery, really. We just don't know what's going on. We'll arrive in a few days, and we'll get our answers then."

Armel's mustaches drooped. He swirled a glass of brown liquid, and ice cubes spun with the movement. Then, he tilted back his head and gulped it down.

"Our fear is that the situation is worse than a mundane rebellion," Drusus continued.

He had my attention now, despite the nearness of food. Everyone else fell quiet too. We all wanted to know what the hell was going on.

"We're considering the possibility... that they may have taken their skills with artificial intelligence too far. They may have created something smarter than themselves. Something which has gained sentience and decided to take over their planet."

You could have heard a pin drop for the next several seconds. Not liking uncomfortable silences just on principle, I whistled. The sound was low, long, and loud.

Drusus glanced my way, then looked back at the star charts that glowed on the wall behind him. "That scenario only fits some of the facts. For instance, it explains why the invader was full of strange cyborgs with electronic minds. It also explains why the ship and its alien crew might want to return to Pegasi after being injured by our defensive efforts. It does not, however, explain how these creatures could have built such an advanced ship so quickly."

I raised my hand and wiggled my fingers in the air. Drusus reluctantly called on me.

"The situation seems obvious to me, sir. The Pegs are dead and gone. Maybe they have been gone for a while. The AI knew it couldn't take us all at once, so it kept up appearances. Shipping AI toys out for trade, for instance. Now that it's ready, it went for Earth next, as we're the only planet in the area with a fleet to oppose them."

Drusus stared me with squinting eyes. He nodded at last. "We've thought of that. We're seriously hoping it's not the case."

Something wonderful happened right about then. The last centurion—it was Venner, of all people—finally sat her ass down with a plate of food.

Not waiting for the okay, I dug in and started to eat. The food was just as delicious as it looked. In fact, I was the first man to return to the buffet for a third helping.

Eating is serious business for me. I think that's true for anyone who's two meters in height and over one hundred twenty lean kilos of bone and muscle.

As a result of my natural hunger, I didn't hear the rest of the speeching. It was just as well in the end, because no one knew what we were going to meet up with when we got to 51 Peg, anyway. Not really. They were just talking at the problem so everyone felt better.

Oh, they had their theories and plans—but none of them meant diddly-squat. Not until we came nose-to-nose with the enemy, took his measure, and devised a plan to destroy him.

And if we failed...? Well, it wouldn't be first time a race of machines took out a biotic species.

Not by a longshot.

-28-

51 Pegasi was a pleasant looking star. When we first arrived, it was pretty much indistinguishable from old Sol back home.

That impression shifted when the klaxons began to wail and *Legate*'s PA system began making alarming announcements.

"Enemy craft detected. Enemy craft detected. All hands to battle stations. Follow your deployment arrows immediately."

"Frig it," I said, deciding to stay and finish the leak I'd been taking in my module's tiny officer's head.

The problem with shipboard emergencies is they didn't mean much to ground-pounders. Unless they boarded us, we were as useless as tits on a boar.

Just as I was zipping up, a pounding began at the door.

"I'll be right out!" I called. "Get the troops to gear up!"

"Yes sir," Moller said, her voice coming through the door in a muffled state.

I shook my head. It was always Moller. She was built like a fireplug, twice as tough, and a very focused woman.

The ship trembled just as I was stepping out of the closet-sized facilities. We were maneuvering. I threw an arm wide to catch myself, then glanced down at the arrows on the floor.

The red arrows were for ground troops. They led out into the main passages.

"Shit..." I muttered to myself.

I'd dared to hope we'd sit this one out in our cubicles, but that wasn't going to happen. We were being directed to defensive positions.

Could the enemy really be thinking of boarding a transport carrying two active legions? They had some balloon-sized gonads on them, if they were.

Two minutes later I was trotting at the head of a column of troops. Most of them were fiddling with their straps and smart-ties, trying to get their armor and other gear to stop banging them in the back of their knees.

Tuning into command chat, I listened to a lot of confusion.

"We've got a bogey on the port bow. Solution plotted, no impact unless it changes course."

"We should leave it alone," a female said, I thought it was Galina.

"We should shoot it down," Armel suggested.

"Armel's right," Drusus said, "free the port cannons. Take it down the moment it's in range."

The situation concerned me. Our top commanders normally let the ship's captain fly *Legate*—but with a praetor on board, anyone else could be overruled. Drusus was like a four-star general from the old days.

We followed our red arrows until they led to a circle—a stopping point. To my surprise, the spot was the primary lift lobby. From here, the various traffic between the decks came and went continuously.

"Well..." Harris said, "at least we aren't sitting out in the crawlspace between the hulls."

He was talking about Death World, I realized. Back then, we'd been placed inside the outermost defensive region, an airless void between the inner and outer hull of the transport. We'd seen plenty of action that day, I recalled.

"Leeson," I said, "you're in charge. I'm going up to Gold Deck to see what's what."

My adjuncts all looked at me in surprise and concern. Adjunct Barton dared to take a half-step toward me.

"Are you sure that's a good idea, Centurion?" she asked.

Right off, I was sorry I'd slept with her. It was a grand mistake by any measure, but I'd hoped some more time would pass before it bit me in the ass.

No such luck.

"Uh…" I said, thinking of an angle. Harris and Leeson were already exchanging surprised glances. "I'm full of bad ideas so—fingers crossed!" I said this with a smile, deciding to take the whole thing lightheartedly.

Slapping the elevator call button, I stepped inside the first car that showed up.

"Ten minutes, tops," I told my officers. "If anyone calls or something happens, message me immediately."

Erin took another step toward me, but she halted and didn't say anymore. Maybe she'd sensed the heightened interest of her colleagues.

Behind her, Leeson made a heart symbol with his fingers. He put it over his chest and broke it apart with a sad shake of the head.

Damn. They knew something was up already.

Ignoring them all, I rode the lift to Gold Deck. The mood was chaotic. I tried to stay out of the way, but Graves spotted me.

"Centurion!" he shouted. "What's wrong?"

"Uh… Nothing special, sir. I was wondering—"

Graves' expression downshifted from concern to anger.

"Were you wondering why centurions get demoted to adjunct over and over? Well, a common reason is desertion of assigned posts."

"Sorry sir. I'll head right back down to the elevator lobby—but, you see, I was worried that something was going off up here."

Graves squinted his already squinty eyes at me. I could see he was full of mistrust, curiosity and bedevilment. I'd seen that look before on my superior officers faces countless times.

The truth was I'd often been a misunderstood individual. As a consequence of my naturally helpful attitude and cheerful disposition, I'd been enlisted in any number of off-color escapades by other officers. Due to this checkered history, some of them had come to distrust me when I showed up at odd times.

"You know something, don't you?" Graves asked, demonstrating exactly the kind of paranoia I'd lived with for decades.

"Huh…?"

"You know why those Peg ships are coming at us, is that it?"

I blinked twice. My mouth must have hung open. Graves hated that dumb-ass expression, despite the fact I couldn't help it. He'd come to see it as some kind of dodge—the trouble was, this time it was indicative of nothing more than honest confusion on my part.

"Sir, I'm completely ignorant about any ships coming from—did you say they were Peg ships, sir?"

"That's right, as if you didn't know. They're coming up from their home world. Now, I want you to confess to me: this is some kind of special op you cooked up with Claver, isn't it?"

Claver. That was a name I hadn't heard in a while. He was the most infamous space traveler in province 921.

"If I ever see Claver again, sir, I plan to kill him."

Graves gave me a few more seconds of his evil eye before he shook his head and walked off.

"Get off this deck, McGill. Confine yourself to your station, or I'll have you confined elsewhere."

"Got it, sir."

Doing an about-face, I headed back down to my unit again. But I wasn't happy.

"What did you find out, Centurion?" Leeson asked me.

"Not much… but there are ships on the way up here—from 51 Peg."

They blinked at me uncomprehendingly.

"Yeah, you heard me. Ships are coming at *Legate*—right now. But not from that giant cue-ball out there. They're coming from the planet."

"Holy shit," Leeson said. "That's not good. Are they talking? Are they—?"

"I don't know," I interrupted. "If you want more info, you can go up and sniff around on Gold Deck yourself."

163

"Wait a minute," Erin said, putting her hand on my bicep. Her hand lingered there, and she looked in my eyes. "So, we're not talking about that giant spherical ship—we're talking about other ships? Coming toward us? That indicates 51 Peg is compromised."

I blinked at her. It obviously did mean that, but I hadn't had a chance to absorb it fully.

Erin took her hand off my arm now—but it was way too late. People had seen it.

No other adjunct or veteran in my unit would have left that lingering hand on me so long. No way—and they all knew it.

It was high time for a distraction.

"Natasha!" I boomed, and she came running.

"Centurion?"

"Hook me up, girl. I need a feed from outside."

She glanced around at the adjuncts, who were all curious. She nodded.

"Give me a minute." She walked away and began hacking.

One sought-after resource for every serious officer in Varus was a tech with solid hacking skills. Having such a person on your staff made the difference between knowing the score and only knowing what the brass wanted you to know.

Barton looked at me, and she shook her head. "This outfit is so different than Victrix."

"Took two years to figure that out, did it?" Harris laughed.

Barton smiled back, and I was glad to see it. She was fitting in better this year. On our previous campaign, she'd never been one of the gang—not really. She'd been like some kind of snooty exchange student from a better place.

Leaving them to plan what defensive actions we could take in what amounted to a wide corridor, I followed Natasha.

She'd found a source of power, hooked up her satchel-based computer, and she was already making it hum.

"Decryption algorithm," she said. "It helps that I already have all the keys—I just have to figure out which one they're using right now."

I nodded, letting her work. It didn't take long.

"I've got something," she said about a minute later. "It's an external feed from a repair drone. They left it out there to weld, and it auto-shutdown. Now, I'm waking it up... adjusting the camera angle..."

A few moments later, she relayed the results to my tapper.

There was a moon nearby, and a planet that looked much smaller in the distance—but wait. That wasn't a moon. That had to be the alien ship.

"No sign of the smaller ships coming up toward us?" I asked.

"No... not with this. The drone welder doesn't have long-range lidar, or anything like that. But, James... that big ship, it's not moving. It's just sitting there."

"Why would it do that? Why not fly over to 51 Peg and get fixed, or destroy the planet, or whatever those crazy aliens have in mind?"

She looked at me, and her tongue slipped out to touch her lips.

"I don't know—but I can make some guesses. The ship was damaged. It flew in warp a long way with that door open."

"Can you confirm that it's still unable to close?"

Natasha nodded. "It looks that way. I'm getting scraps from other reports..."

Looking over her shoulder, I smiled. She was reading Galina's email—probably before the tribune herself had gotten around to it.

"Hmm..." I said. "The ship might have suffered internal damage. If you go into warp with the window open... All that radiation can't be good for the skin."

"No. No it can't."

She ran some numbers, some calculations. "I've got it. The ships coming from 51 Peg aren't headed toward *Legate*. That's clear now. They're headed to that giant ship."

We locked eyes.

"James," she said, "I'm pretty sure they're moving to repair the super-ship. That scenario matches all the data points. Their ship is damaged, the ships coming out aren't warships, they're civilian vessels."

"What do we do about that?"

She shrugged helplessly. "I don't know. I'm not an admiral or a praetor. Ask them."

165

"You know, I think I might just do that."

-29-

A rush of small ships moved to cluster around the big spherical invader we'd chased all the way from Earth. Once the brass aboard our two transports was convinced these ships weren't going to attack us immediately, they rotated my unit off "hall monitor duty" as Leeson was fond of calling it.

As we were wrapping it up and handing the post over to another unit, a team of primus-level officers stepped out of the elevator. Winslade was among them.

"Ah!" he said. "If it isn't our legion's most intrepid crew of ruffians. You've been busy today, haven't you McGill?"

I tossed a glance at Natasha, wondering if Winslade had somehow figured out that we'd been hacking officer accounts all day. She looked scared, but she wasn't speaking up.

"Uh…" I said. "That's right, sir. We're ready for the Pegs, no matter how many arms and legs they may have hanging out of their cyborgs when they invade this ship."

Winslade squinted at me. People did that to me all the time. Usually it meant they were dreaming up a secondary, more sinister meaning to every statement I made.

One of his stick-like fingers came up and wagged at me. "You're far too glib about this. First, you somehow managed to get yourself assigned to this critical juncture. Then you proceeded to visit Gold Deck uninvited and unannounced. None of this smells right. I'm going to have to report your activities to the praetor."

"Please do, sir. 3rd Unit can always use some well-deserved praise from the higher-ups."

Winslade made a pffing sound of dismissal and tapped at his arm for a moment. He appeared to be sending out a message. I did my best to look like a moron throughout this process.

At last, he lowered his arm and gave me a nasty, self-satisfied smile.

"There. All fixed, McGill. Good luck!"

Frowning at his back, I watched him walk to the elevators. He boarded the first one to respond to his call and was whisked away by it.

Harris came to join me then. "Seems like your fan-club has increased by one overgrown rodent today."

"Looks that way."

Harris eyed me sidelong. "I don't think he liked the way you tricked him on Green Deck yesterday."

I shrugged, not caring at all. "Nah... Winslade's not like that. He's not petty, or vindictive... He barely cares about who kills who on the field of honor."

Harris laughed and marched his platoon away. I was about to move out myself when my tapper began buzzing.

With a sigh, I answered it.

"McGill?"

It was Tribune Galina Turov. She didn't sound happy.

"Yes sir! McGill on station, reporting in!"

"Get up here to Gold Deck. I want to discuss some things with you."

About then, I noticed Adjunct Erin Barton was watching me closely. Natasha and Kivi were eyeing me as well.

They were all subtle, but I knew how women kept a man under surveillance. They liked to turn their heads away but still study the innocent male with their peripheral vision. Sometimes, like in the case of Natasha right now, they'd slide their eyes to one side tightly—staring without seeming to stare. Using a variety of methods, no less than three women were spying on me at the moment.

Now, that might be nine kinds of a coincidence—or even a delusion of grandeur on my part—but I didn't think so. Two of

168

the three had been intimate with me over recent nights. As for Natasha... well, she kind of had a permanent thing for me that never seemed to fade away completely.

"Uh... sure, Tribune," I told my tapper. "I'll be right up there."

Avoiding the critical eyes of all three curious ladies, I headed to the elevators. I stepped inside and pressed the button that would whisk me away to Gold Deck.

At the last moment I stopped the car by reaching out a hand to keep the doors from sliding shut.

"Adjunct Barton?" I called out to Erin, as if I'd just had an afterthought.

"Sir?"

"Take everyone that's still lingering here back to our module. Await further orders there. We're off active duty, but we're still on alert."

"Got it, Centurion."

Then the elevator door shut, and I escaped from all those prying eyes.

Gold Deck had never looked so busy. People were bustling everywhere. There were even a few squids in evidence, sub-centurions from Armel's zoo legion.

One of these tentacle-types approached me. I didn't recognize him, as squids all looked alike to me, but I caught sight of his nameplate.

"Bubbles!" I said, throwing my hands wide in greeting.

Sub-Centurion Bubble was fussy, even for a squid. He turned to look at me in confusion. "Is there a reason why you are addressing me, Centurion McGill?"

"Damn straight there is. I thought you might have died back on Storm World, but here you are, safe and sound."

"I did die, actually. Twice. But on each occasion, Tribune Armel saw my value and committed resources to revive me."

"Doesn't that beat all? Wow, I didn't think he would revive anything less useful than a giant with that expensive rig of his..."

"Your statement is both inaccurate and somewhat insulting."

"Now, now, when your tribune assigns you a relative value, you can't go around saying his judgment is poor. You'll never get a promotion with that kind of attitude."

"I was not suggesting that the tribune—"

"Hey," I said, taking an aggressive step toward him.

The big squid shifted his bulk uncomfortably, but he did stand his ground without inking himself.

That was one of the many strange things about Cephalopods. They could be cowed if you acted tough enough. The fact this stack of raw calamari was powerful enough to rip my limbs off like rose petals didn't change that reality: Bubbles was a scaredy-squid.

"Hey, how about you tell me what these Peg bastards are up to? Surely you know the real score."

Bubbles looked confused, which squids expressed by wriggling their tentacles around aimlessly.

"I don't understand your request, Centurion."

"Are they in cahoots with that big invasion ship or not?"

"Cahoots...? A colloquialism suggesting a temporary alliance? No, Centurion McGill. I am not 'in cahoots' with anyone else on this ship."

I frowned at him for a second. Had his translation box goofed up? I'd asked him about the ships outside—not about old Bubbles himself. Maybe my use of a new term had confused him. I decided to let old Bubbles slide on it.

"So," I said, rewording my question, "you have no idea who these attackers are, or what they might want?"

"That is essentially correct."

"Hmm..." I said, beginning to wonder about him. Squids were never trustworthy, not unless you had a gun aimed at each eyeball—and they had a lot of eyeballs. "What are those Peg ships doing out there, then?"

"McGill!" Tribune Turov interrupted.

I turned to see her standing with her fists on the nice swell of her hips. She looked annoyed.

"There you are, sir," I said. "I've been looking all over for you."

"I've been waiting in my office since I called you. Get in here."

"Right away, sir. If you'd just—"

I turned, expecting to see Bubbles standing around—but I didn't. He'd made off down the nearest passageway. Strange behavior—even for him.

"Uh..." I said, pivoting back to Galina. "Lead the way, sir. I'm right on your tail."

She gave me a sour glance with twisted lips and marched away.

I'd vaguely hoped she'd been planning to meet with me alone. Possibly, this could lead to a little private moment—but it was not to be.

Winslade was there, sitting at a small table. At his side sat Armel. Together these three made up a big percentage of all the brass aboard *Legate*.

Surprised, I stood at attention and let my face shift toward hardcore ignorance.

"Sirs! McGill reporting as ordered!"

"You took an incredible span of time getting here, McGill," Armel complained.

"Sorry sir. I met up with an old friend who wanted to wish me well."

"You mean Sub-Centurion Bubble?" he asked. "I had no idea you two were so close."

My eyes flicked down in surprise, then back up again. I stared fixedly at the forward bulkhead like it owed me money.

"Uh..." I said. "Bubbles and I go way back. Way back, sir."

"I'm sure you do, but in any case, there's been a complaint lodged against you."

"Really? What might the nature of the charge be, sir?"

Armel leaned forward. "You've been accused of having rigged the exercise on Green Deck yesterday, Centurion. Knowing your reputation and the highly unlikely outcome that resulted during the contest, I'm likely to agree with your accusers."

I got it now. Winslade had tattled to Armel, who'd been judging the contest. Galina had joined in, doubtlessly with hurt feelings over the abuse her dragon's tail had suffered at my hands.

171

Sometimes, I wished people could just suck it up when they died badly and soldier on. This group had clearly decided to form a court of inquiry instead.

"Now that the accused and the injured parties are all present, we can continue," Armel said. "Winslade, state your case."

Winslade adopted an air of formality. "Yesterday, during a routine exercise, there was a surprise upset. The higher ranked officers were supposed to win—but they did not."

"Wait... The brass was supposed to win?" I asked suddenly. "I didn't get that feeling at all."

"Possibly," Armel said, "it wasn't spelled out."

"Nonsense!" Winslade objected. "The situation was obvious from the start. That's why the primus-level officers received vastly better equipment."

"Yeah," I said, "but we outnumbered you twenty to one. Sir, don't you think it would be better to just accept your ass-whooping? It would set a better example for the troops."

"I will *not*. I was cheated. No one could have imagined what was about to take place!"

"I sure did!" I argued.

Armel smirked at that and Galina frowned—but Winslade... he was fuming.

"All right, Winslade," Galina said, "you called this lynch party. What do you propose should be done about it?"

"He killed you as well, Tribune. Try to remember that."

"My memory is excellent," Galina snapped, giving him a threatening glance.

Over the years, Winslade had been involved in any number of wrongful actions. The span of his crimes covered quite a range, from assassination to treason, dereliction of duty, and so much more.

Winslade turned back to me. "One more chance to confess before I show much greater crimes than this, McGill."

That alarmed me a bit. After all, I was no boy scout.

"Uh... I can't confess to something that never happened, sir. Sorry."

"Very well."

Winslade picked up an instrument. It looked like a writing stylus. He waved it over the table we encircled, and an odd vid began to play.

It took me a few seconds to get the perspective—but then I had it. Natasha and I were in the foreground, huddled-up and working on her computer. For a moment, the scene swooped and dived sickeningly.

"You put a drone on me?" I asked.

Winslade shrugged. "Absurd paranoia. I merely scan Gold Deck's defenses with regularity. It's one of my duty assignments."

We watched for several more moments, and soon it became evident that Natasha and I were hacking officer tappers—in addition to *Legate's* data core.

"Um…" I said, and they looked at me. "We were bored. We were just trying to figure out what was going on out there in space."

Winslade looked like a kitten getting ready to pounce. "And you expect us to believe you did nothing like this to find out about the strategies and equipment involved in the Green Deck exercise?"

"Stand down, Primus!" Armel said suddenly.

Surprised, Winslade withdrew and sat down. He did maintain a smug expression of insufferable self-satisfaction, however.

Armel studied me coldly. "James McGill… at it again, I see. Insubordination, dangerous sharing of intelligence—the list seems endless."

"I would like to see the record of this event swept clean," Winslade said. "McGill didn't win that contest. He cheated. He—"

"Silence, Primus Winslade," Armel said. "You're embarrassing yourself. This is much bigger than some exercise. I will report this to Drusus. McGill should be executed and expelled back to Earth for a proper court martial when we have time. Optionally, we could just leave him dead and save ourselves the trouble."

Both Galina and Winslade were frowning now. I could see they'd been looking for some petty revenge—at least Winslade was, and Galina had gone along for the ride to teach me a lesson.

But talk of perming me? That wasn't how they'd thought this would end up.

They argued for a moment about what should be done. I stood there, imitating a bag of hammers.

"All right," Turov said at last. "As McGill's CO, he's my responsibility. I'll bring the matter up to Drusus when it's appropriate to do so."

Armel twisted up his lips at her. "Appropriate, eh? That's a curious word to use."

She glared back at him. He was obviously referring to our personal conduct.

The meeting ended with no one being fully satisfied, least of all me. Winslade and Armel left, but I lingered hoping Galina would soften.

I was sorely disappointed.

"All right McGill," she said. "You've embarrassed me again. I placed you at the gates of Gold Deck, as safe and easy a post as I could imagine, but you still managed to fuck it up."

"Huh... you did?"

"Who runs Legion Varus?"

"You do."

"So, who do you think assigned 3rd unit to that hallway?"

"Um... you, sir?"

"Exactly. Get your head out of your ass, McGill. Now I have no option but to give you hazardous duty. That will get these two morons to leave me alone."

"Leave *you* alone? Don't you mean to leave *me* alone?"

She rolled her eyes at me. Girls did that a lot.

"Didn't you hear those barbs coming from Armel about our relationship? He wanted to make me save you, to embarrass me. His gambit won't succeed."

"Well... maybe you could give me a kiss to remember you by, if I'm going on a dangerous assignment."

"Don't," she said, and I got nowhere.

Kicked out of her office, I found myself heading back to my module. There were plenty of mysteries in my near future, but I didn't let any of that bother me. I took it in stride and made passes at Adjunct Barton, Kivi and Natasha in that order.

I flamed out all three times. Unfortunately, they'd all noticed each other. They'd all seen other women watching me with interest in the elevator lobby—and they knew what that meant.

Not for the first time, I spent the night alone.

-30-

The next morning we were called to arms. At roll call, we got a televised briefing on the day's operations. The most interesting part concerned the intel we'd gathered so far.

"51 Pegasi is a peaceful star system," Drusus said, "or it was, until today. We've never been hired as mercenaries to come here, nor have Earth's legions been deployed in our official capacity as local enforcers of Galactic Law."

He gestured, and a sweeping map of the planetary system came into focus. Our two ships were far from the central star and the single inhabited planet. We were hanging around the moon-sized invasion ship that had threatened Earth.

"So far," Drusus continued, "the enemy has ignored our presence. They are focused on repairing the damage we did to their ship. The local space traffic we expected to see is nonexistent. As well, there's almost no radio communications going on down below, on the planet itself."

The praetor paused to let that sink in.

Carlos took that moment to sidle up to me.

"Where's Turov?" he asked. "I like it better when she does the briefing."

"Same here—shut up."

"We aren't sure what's happening down there on the Peg planet." Drusus droned on. "It could be everyone is dead, but we're not seeing any signs of mass destruction, nor of a poisoned atmosphere. There is some particle radiation... but not enough to kill the population. Our best guess is they've suffered a massive EMP attack. Perhaps a series of fusion weapons were set off in the upper atmosphere. Such an attack could cause an EMP blast that would fry unprotected electronics."

He motioned with his fingers, making a spreading movement. The camera zoomed in sickeningly. "We're going to insert a squad here, at one of the largest population centers. Their mission will be to scout the location, seeking evidence of an EMP blast and looking for survivors. Tribune Turov? Please take over."

Turov strode onto the stage at last.

"About damned time…" Carlos said.

I thought about giving him a kick in the pants, but I couldn't muster the anger to do it. After all, Galina was dressed up again, wearing her uniform an extra size too small and tight. Was she doing that just to tease me? Or was her natural desire to look attractive in front of a crowd coming out? It could have been anything, but the effects were obvious. Every male in my unit was squirming, and every female was whispering.

"Hey McGill," Carlos asked me. "Is that a camel-toe or a—"

That was as far as he got. Moller had spotted him and come up from behind, waiting for him to speak out of turn again. As a commanding officer, it really was beneath my rank to discipline the enlisted types personally—although it still happened now and then. I had a couple of veterans who were built like apes to handle that kind of thing now.

Moller landed a boot in Carlos' ass that dropped him to one knee. Cursing, he got back up slowly.

"Eyes-front, mouth-closed, Specialist," she whispered to him in an unusually sweet voice, and she moved on down the line.

Grumbling briefly, Carlos finally shut up.

"…and so you can see, a small team at the communications hub right *here* should be able to determine the nature of the situation on the ground. Of all my beloved troops, there is one cohort that has shouldered more of these special missions than all the rest combined. That would be 3rd Cohort, under the expert command of Primus Graves."

A few groans went up. Every experienced infantryman knew that doing impressive things only led to more difficult assignments. That had been true throughout history, so Legion Varus people weren't the type to show off unless it was by accident. Clearly, my unit had failed to escape notice when it came to successful teleport missions.

"Over the last two decades," Galina continued, "Earth has developed our teleport technology. It's no longer a curiosity, it's now a vital tool in our arsenal. We also have gateway technology, but that's quite different in function. The teleport suits—or teleporting harnesses for bombs, as the case may be—allow a small mass to be moved to a variety of locations with adjustments. They work once or twice on battery power, but after that they must be recharged. This allows great flexibility."

People around me shuffled their feet a little. They already knew all this, and they were worried Turov's speech might end on a bad note for us. Everyone wanted her to get to the point—but I knew this woman well, and that wasn't going to happen anytime soon. She liked the sound of her own voice even more than most high-ranking officers did.

"Gateway technology can only go between two points, but it connects them on a more permanent basis. Effectively, with enough power and time, an army can be marched between any two equipped stations. We're planning to use both these varieties of transportation technology in new ways starting with today's mission. I'll now defer to Primus Graves for a special announcement."

"Thank you, Tribune," Graves said, stepping forward. "My cohort has been elevated in importance—let me explain why. We're now the first official jump-troop cohort in Earth's legions. Eventually, there will be a jump-troop unit in every legion, but to start with—it's just us."

The imagery on the display began to swoop, zoom and pan. We saw the spherical ship, which had been hanging around in far orbit over the Peg planet for days now. We saw the great door I'd damaged too, hanging open like a sleeping giant's mouth.

On the planet, we saw strange cities that were oddly quiet. There was little in the way of traffic or radio signals.

"They aren't *all* dead," Turov said, looking things over. "We're getting some life readings, but they aren't transmitting much. Maybe radio emissions attract the aliens. Maybe they've all gone into hiding—or maybe all their transmitting devices have been silenced. We just don't know."

The display showed empty roads and oddly shaped puff-crete buildings that were seen from a great height. We had to have spy drones down there to get that kind of intel.

"Since the enemy is ignoring us," she continued, "we've decided not to provoke them until we must. We'll send a team to the planet. They will then be in a position to have a direct path to the open door on the alien ship. Right now, it's turned away from us—we believe the aliens have positioned their ship that way purposefully."

All of these things were rapidly displayed in a series of images on the screen. We saw the quiet Peg cities, and then the new moon with the toothless mouth in their sky.

"The plan is to send our team to the Peg planet first," she said, "if possible, we'll then jump from there into the gap again—"

A few gasps and a general buzzing of conversation went up around me. Moller and Sargon stomped around, shouting "shut up!" at all of them.

My eyes and ears were glued to the big screen. Were they seriously talking about sending us up there into that ship again? The last time, we'd all died and nearly been permed.

"Teleportation won't work to invade the ship if we don't have a clear line-of-sight through that gap," Turov continued. "Eventually, the enemy will repair it. Then what?"

The briefing continued, explaining how we would scout several locations on Pegasi, most of them communications and military sites. I didn't give a shit about that and neither did anyone else in my unit. We'd heard enough.

"We'll do this all at once," Graves said as he stepped onto the stage to sum things up. "We'll use coordinated attacks by

179

small groups in teleport suits. With luck, our recon teams will land, investigate, and teleport back here before the enemy knows what's happening."

Some of my people were hanging their heads. They knew 3rd Unit was likely to be picked for this "special duty" nightmare. We were, after all, every officer's personal whipping boy.

The briefing went on, but I'd heard enough. I tuned out and began coming up with a roster and a plan.

When it was over I got the call from Graves. I was more than ready to suck it up and serve legion Varus and Earth by that time.

My troops were shell-shocked, however. They were crying to each other and anyone else who might listen.

"McGill," Carlos implored me, "you've got to do something, man. They're going to perm us for sure this time. They can't even teleport through that hull. What makes anyone think that we can do it with a gateway if we can't do it with a suit? That's crazy."

He had a point there, but I wasn't qualified to judge the validity of his complaints.

"Turov just said the technology is different," I told him.

"No... no way, I'm not buying that. We got the teleport equipment *and* the gateway systems from the Rogue World people. They both move people around over long distances. How can they *not* be related?"

"I don't know," I admitted, "but neither do you. It takes a certain amount of trust just to put on one of those crazy suits and blink away to another distant point in the cosmos, doesn't it?"

Shaking his head sadly, he wandered away.

Drusus was speaking again on the big screen, so I shouted for everyone to hush up so I could hear him.

"...one final thing," he said, "we've discovered that the biomass that was used to build the hybrid creatures back on Earth wasn't all human."

He paused to let that sink in. "In fact, some of the—for lack of a better term—*meat* the aliens used wasn't from Earth at all. We've traced it down using the Galactic data core and found a genetic match here, in the Pegasi system. We believe it came from the Pegs themselves."

Carlos finally spoke up again. He looked horrified. "Is he saying that we're fighting some kind of stitched-up monsters built with spare parts from all over the place?"

Moller came to discipline him again, but I waved her off. Carlos looked truly disturbed.

"Some of those things we fought—they didn't look remotely human, did they?" I asked him.

He shook his head, shuddered in disgust, and we turned back to the presentation.

"These aliens..." Drusus said, "they're something new. They aren't a single homogenous species. They are more of a disease—a scourge that consumes anything it finds and builds an army with the spare parts. We believe it came from somewhere outside Province 921."

"No shit..." Harris whispered quietly.

"—and the invasion ship arrived at 51 Pegasi first. This world is optimal for their purposes, containing a biotic species that's famous for their development of artificially intelligent hardware and software. After feasting here, they built an army to invade Earth."

"And we beat them!" I shouted, deciding to get a little positive morale going. My people were looking pretty glum.

A few of my troops cheered, but it was without much enthusiasm.

"After being repelled," Drusus said, "they've returned here to rebuild and—probably—to try to take Earth again. They must be stopped. Do better than your best, troops. Dismissed."

The screen darkened, and I was left with a hard job. Even Moller, Sargon, Harris... they all looked kind of sick.

Smashing my hands together and grinning, I walked among them, giving them the hard sell.

"We're going to finish them right here," I said firmly. "We kicked their butts back on Earth, they've run back here to lick their wounds—but they won't get any rest. We're going to finish the job."

There were smiles, nods and a few quiet high-fives, but mostly, people looked kind of sick.

-31-

After his first dozen solid deaths, no legionnaire worth his salt was terrified about getting killed. That was just part of the job, an unpleasant thing that happened to everyone now and then.

But... the prospect of going back inside a super-dense shell of matter was something else entirely. The invasion ship prevented all signals—even teleportation—from working. That meant there was no escape, no way of reporting a death. It was a perming scenario, and we all knew it.

Worse, we in the 3rd Unit, 3rd Cohort knew that we had the most experience with teleportation attacks. That meant we were destined to be Graves' first-line commandoes with all the grim realities that went with that job.

"This is going to be the shit-show to end all shit-shows," Harris said glumly in the officers meeting after the briefing. "You mark my words."

"I can't argue your point, Harris," Leeson said. "We're as good as permed already. There's no winning this. If we screw up, we're permed. If we nail it, they'll just keep sending us first until we're permed anyway."

"All you can think about is getting out of doing this?" Barton asked incredulously.

"Damned straight!" Harris said. "If I thought there was a way out, I'd take it in a flash. The odds are high we'll get our asses permed. Does that make you happy or something?"

"Of course not," Barton replied. "But we're the best shot Earth has to stop this menace."

They eyed her coldly. "Playing the goody-goody to the hilt, eh, lady?" Leeson said. "You won't last forever with that attitude."

She returned their stare with an angry look of her own. She crossed her arms over her breasts and turned to me.

"These men are going to ruin morale, sir."

"Yes…" I said, "and no. This is Legion Varus. We don't like to lie to ourselves. Let them get all the bitching out of their bellies. In the end they'll come around and do their jobs."

Harris and Leeson continued to grumble. We drained a whirring, gurgling coffee-bot and reviewed every frame of the briefing. About an hour later they finally got off their asses and got moving.

They still weren't happy, mind you. Not by a long-shot—but they'd go, and they'd fight, and that was the most I could ask from hardened men that knew the stink of a bad mission when they smelled one.

We thought at first they'd give us the day to prep and gear up—but that didn't happen. Right after lunch, the first launch was announced—and yours truly was leading it.

"McGill, your unit is on point," Graves said. "Remember, you're on radio silence on this trip. You'll jump down to the planet surface, sniff around and jump back—that's it. Pick your order of battle. I'm leaving the details up to you but remember to move quickly. We can't take the chance the enemy will detect what we're doing and take steps to stop us."

"Roger that, sir. We'll hit Gray Deck in thirty minutes."

"Make it twenty. See you there."

Graves closed the connection, and I had to hit the ground running. I'd been half-joking about thirty minutes—but he'd called my bluff.

Twenty-five minutes later we were all on Gray Deck, which was a new region down in the laboratories for things like teleport-attack launches. An army of techs worked the place. They outnumbered my entire unit.

I didn't know them all, but I knew a few. There was one little adjunct tech that I recognized right off.

"Lisa?" I called out. "Is that really *you*, girl? When did you sign up with Legion Varus?"

Tech Adjunct Lisa Smith approached, moving almost shyly. A few unfriendly glances were tossed her way as I had plenty of women I'd known intimately in Legion Varus over the years. Most of them didn't like each other.

She reached up, pushing a lock of hair out of her eyes. Her gaze met mine briefly, then she dropped it and blushed.

"I'm surprised you remember me, Centurion," Lisa said. "It's been years."

"Of course I remember you, girl!" I boomed. "We defended the Home World together, just you and I. We made this whole teleporting racket famous!"

"Infamous, more like," she said. "Anyway, I'm not part of Varus. I'm still Hegemony. But they sent me along as a T-port expert."

"That you are," I said, "that you are…"

We had quite a history. Back when teleporting was a new thing, we'd killed dozens—no, *hundreds* of sad-sack hogs in the suits while we worked out the bugs. They'd fried in the suits, mostly. Cooked in a high-powered metallic skin that didn't jump a single meter.

But then I'd come along and helped out with the Galactic Key. It was a small, incredibly illegal device that broke security on anything made by Imperial planets. It was the security systems that had been frying the hogs, and Lisa and I had broken that tech roadblock together.

"We're going to do it again," I said to her softly.

Her eyes flashed up to meet mine. She was a bit older than the last time we'd met, some ten years earlier, but she was still one of the cutest girls in the room. As something of an authority on the topic, I should know.

"Do what?" she asked.

"Make history. Kill aliens. Save Earth—all that stuff."

She smiled, but she also seemed slightly disappointed. "Oh yeah, all that."

We suited up, and we stood on raised circular pedestals with wires hooked to our suits. Right before launch, they would break away and fall to the floor, having charged our harnesses as fully as possible.

These new, lighter rigs were more efficient for small jumps, but they couldn't teleport you lightyears away to another star system. For our purposes, they were perfect.

Lisa came to check on me before launch. I found it hard to believe that was an accident.

She fluffed my collar a bit, just like the old days. Back then, she'd been using the Galactic Key to bypass the suit's security and send me on my way. These rigs didn't need that anymore of course, but it was nostalgic to see her make the move.

"Remember this?" she asked.

"I sure do!"

So saying, I grabbed her up and kissed her. Everyone looked shocked—and I do mean everyone. I think most of the people in that chamber were watching us.

"Let's go, people!" I shouted as I let her back down to the floor. "First squad, port out! Second squad, stay here until you get the go-signal."

We'd planned the attack carefully. The first squad would hit the ground, recon, then signal back whether the rest of the operation was a go or a bust.

As was my usual style, I went with the first squad. In the old days that would have been considered reckless behavior on the part of a unit commander. After all, if the top officer got killed right off the bat, the rest of the operation may be compromised.

My thinking was different these days. Sure, I might die in the next few seconds, but then again I might gain valuable intel. Nothing beat seeing the situation on the ground with your own two eyes.

And what if I did die? Well, they'd print out a new McGill an hour or so later, and he'd take another shot.

That was life—and death—in the legions.

There was a blur in the air, a ripple in space. A moment later I winked out with a dozen others. When I opened my eyes again, I was in a different place.

Teleporting was far easier on the mind and body when you traveled a relatively short distance. Long trips, like from star to star, took several minutes in perceived time. That was pretty harrowing.

You felt like you were dying, breaking apart—dissolving in a thousand threads and coming back together again like twisting tendrils of smoke.

But none of that really struck me this time. We were pretty close to 51 Peg, and it seemed like a blink of the eye between Gray Deck on *Legate* and the wide open vistas of the planetary surface.

Sure, I was a little disoriented. You always stumbled a bit and landed off balance when you suddenly hit with a slightly different cant to the ground, or a different gravitational tug. Even the air pressure felt wrong, making my ears pop.

I was wearing combat armor and a teleport harness—but I hadn't bothered to close my visor. After all, 51 Peg had a breathable atmosphere.

It was night, but it was pretty warm out. A puff of warm wet air gusted into my face, and into my suit, and I was taken aback.

"Damn, that's a funny smell! You smell that, Carlos?"

"Nope, I'm not a moron. I've got my faceplate closed and sealed, Centurion. Just the way it's supposed to be."

I cast a dark glance his way. Damn if that boy hadn't constantly begged for a beating from the very first time I'd met him all the way up to today. Some people never seemed to change.

The smell wasn't unpleasant... it was just kind of... Earthy. Like something you find in a farmer's field. An enchanting mixture of green growth, blossoms and manure—all of that, mixed up with a fresh, bell-peppery scent.

"Smells like home to me," I said, stepping forward through some tall grass and putting my gauntlets on my hips.

We were on a hilltop outside a major city. We'd decided not to land in town directly, as according to the habits of these invaders, they liked to make towns into flesh-factories.

I could see the town lights, what few of them still burned. Our intel from the Galactic data core said the Pegs liked it dark

186

as they had excellent night vision—but the sight of their city so nearly blacked out didn't give me a confident feeling.

"Squad, spread out and recon the area. Stay within a hundred-meter radius for now. See if you can find anything we haven't already spotted from space."

Moller was the noncom I'd chosen to go on this flight, and she trudged off, tossing out orders. The squad fanned out, weapons at the ready. They were all heavies, with a few specialists like Carlos thrown in.

"Kivi, what have you got on your buzzers?"

"Nothing," she said. "We're in the Peg equivalent of the boondocks, as far as I can tell."

Overhead, I scanned the skies. Our ships were too far off to be visible, but I saw something big hanging up there. The sunlight from 51 Pegasi glared on its side in a crescent shape. The enemy ship was the only moon in sight.

"If there are any Pegs alive to see this, they must be freaking out," Carlos commented. "They only have two small moons, like Mars. This big new bastard, playing the part of the scary intruder—I bet they scat themselves every time they see it."

"I couldn't blame them," I said, twiddling the controls on my helmet's visor. I had put it down now so it could amplify my vision. The screen inside zoomed and focused—then I frowned.

"Uh…" I said. "Isn't there supposed to be a hole on the side of that ship? Facing the planet?"

Kivi came close and dug out an optical instrument. "It's still there…" she said.

I sighed with relief. "Good. I'll report in to *Legate*. This looks like—"

She put her hand on my arm, and she tugged hard. She was still gazing up at the big moon-sized ship.

"McGill, call them fast. The door—the one we broke—it's closing! I can see it. they must have fixed it. The damned thing must be halfway rolled up already."

A chill ran through me. I glanced over to the gateway posts a team of two techs were setting up in the wind-blown grass. The posts glowed with an odd, electrical pulsation.

"Is that thing operable yet?" I asked the techs that were fooling with it.

"Yes sir, Centurion. Just let us align the—"

Without warning, I marched toward them. They scattered back.

Then I stepped through the portal and vanished.

Walking onto Gray Deck again, I felt a bit woozy. Maybe the techs had been trying to tell me something—but I didn't care. I had to talk to Graves.

"Sir! Primus, sir!"

Graves spun around on one heel. He strode toward me purposefully, leaving a team of techs in his wake.

"McGill? What the hell are you doing back here—what's the matter, man? Are you hit?"

"I…" I said. I stumbled and fell. My hand went out, but it only partially broke my fall.

"Medic!" Graves called out.

I felt rough hands on me. I expected to be helped onto my feet, but that wasn't Graves' way. Instead, he flipped me over on my back, grunting with the effort.

"I don't see any injuries. Did you breathe the air?"

"I did, sir—"

"Poison, then. Where's that damned bio—?"

My hand shot up and gripped his arm. I pulled him back around to face me.

"Sir… it's the ship. I saw it. The alien ship—they fixed the door. It's closing, right now."

His eyes widened. "Are you sure?"

"Positive, sir. Visual confirmation."

"Right… and you were on radio silence, so you walked back to report. I get it—but I don't know what we can do about it."

"Maybe send in another commando team of jumpers. Right now, with a bomb. Maybe they can do it again."

"Don't you think they'll be prepared for that this time?"

"Maybe, sir, but we have to—"

"What's wrong with you anyway, McGill? Your voice is weakening. You're going pale."

A bio specialist finally wandered up and began to work on me.

"Blood loss. Nothing visible… it must be internal. I'm reading several ruptured organs. Did you fall off a building, Centurion?"

"Not lately," I said. "It's probably because the gateway wasn't calibrated yet."

The bio pulled out a syringe and prepped it.

"What's that?" I asked.

"It's a cure-all," she said, giving me smirk.

Now, I wasn't born yesterday. I knew what she was up to. She was just as lazy as your average bio. They'd all rather stuff a man into the recycling blades than work up a sweat trying to save him.

"Sir! Graves, sir!"

"What is it, McGill? I'm trying to figure out a course of action."

"This woman is trying to off me, Primus. I just thought you might like to know."

Graves stepped toward us. He frowned at me, then at the bio. He shook his head. "I can't use a man who's crippled. Not now—not ever," he said coldly. "Kill him."

I didn't put up a fight. That was mostly because I was too weak to do so. I could barely catch my breath.

A moment later, I felt a sting.

My heart beat seven more times after that, then I died.

189

-32-

Awakening with a growl, I pushed people away with rubbery fingers. They backed off while saying soothing things.

I didn't listen. I got my feet off the gurney and almost did a facer right there—but I caught myself. This wasn't my first rodeo.

"Centurion? Let me check you out first, please."

Squinting at brilliant lights that stabbed into my skull, I let her fool around—but only until I was strong enough to brush her aside. I got into the shower and dressed.

"What's my score?" I asked her.

"I don't know," she huffed. "You wouldn't let me finish all the routine tests."

She sounded pissed off, but I didn't care. I wasn't looking for a date—not today.

Staggering down the ship's passages, each step I took became more purposeful. Soon, my eyes worked well enough to read the time on my tapper.

I'd only been dead for twenty-nine minutes. That made me grin.

Dead for less than half an hour? I thought that might be a personal record. There must not have been anyone else lingering in the death-queue.

But I was pretty familiar with hostile planets. I figured that state of affairs wouldn't last long.

Graves was busy on Gray Deck when I caught up with him again.

"McGill, reporting for duty, sir!"

He glanced at me, then turned back to the unit he was marching through a set of gateway posts. Centurion Manfred passed by in the lead. I gave him a wave, and he gave me the finger.

When the unit was off, Graves turned back to me.

"Feeling better, McGill?"

"Right as rain, sir."

"No hard feelings this time?"

I looked startled. "What? About offing me just half an hour ago? Hell no, sir. You had to do it. I was messed up pretty badly."

He nodded. "That's the right attitude. I don't want any whiners in my outfit. Now, get your ass back down there. Things are heating up. Your unit is in action, and they've got no centurion."

"Uh…" I said, dumbfounded. "Has there been a change of plan? My recon team did all they could. Shouldn't we pull out and—"

"And what? Sit on *Legate*? In case you haven't heard, McGill, Legion Varus is a ground force. The enemy has shut that door you opened up, so we can't board her. We're going to take 51 Peg back instead."

"Okay… Full deployment?"

"It's already underway. We used your beachhead as a starting point. Varus, Solstice, and our supporting near-human legions—they're all deploying as fast as they can. We'll see what they throw at us, we'll kill it all, and then it will be their move after that."

"You make it sound pretty easy, sir."

Graves gave me a reproachful look. "Well? What are you waiting for? There are enemy vehicles of some kind approaching your troops right now. Walking armored units."

"Armored, huh? All right. See you down there."

Taking advantage of a break in the endless stream of men and material, I marched through the posts and transferred my existence down to the planet surface.

It was kind of like walking into a giant bug-zapper. You felt like you'd been blasted apart, burnt away to dust, and knitted back into a whole piece again someplace else. The sensation was enough to make a man wince, I don't mind telling you.

Marching out at the far end of the gateway, I was startled to see how many troops had appeared. There were thousands already, with at least four gateway posts working continuously.

In the night air, I could hear that zapping sound every few seconds. Even the wind didn't completely carry away the stink of burnt hair and ozone that those strange devices always left behind.

"McGill!" Manfred called out. He came trotting up toward me. Built like a barrel, the man walked with a swaying step. "When I saw you up there talking to Graves, I thought you were chicken-shit or something."

"No such luck," I told him. "You're going to have to share your medals with me tonight."

Manfred smiled, but then quickly became business-like. He pointed to the corner of the night that was slightly brighter than the rest of it. "They're coming from the Peg city. Thousands of them. Half-metal, half-meat. An army of walking dead things."

"Who is in charge of setting up our defensive lines?" I asked.

Manfred winced. "Turov."

I gave him an apologetic nod. No matter our personal lives, everybody knew she wasn't the best choice for a field commander. In fact, she was pretty bad.

"She's building a bunker in those trees for herself," he said, pointing south. "We've been ordered to take high ground and dig trenches with the pigs. Choose your unit's position on the line and set up camp. It's going to be an all-out firefight by dawn."

I gazed upward then, looking at the warm sky. The only moon in sight was the invasion ship.

The land surrounding us was comprised of rolling hills with standing groves of weird-looking trees. There were dark clumps of them in every lower fold. The higher ground was grassy and wind-blown.

"Over there," I said. My finger aimed at the highest bald hump in the land. "I'll set up there."

Manfred looked and laughed. "Perfect. You won't miss a thing. I'll set up on your west flank where there's plenty of cover."

Meeting with my unit, I directed them to move out toward our new hilltop. While they gathered their gear Harris approached me.

"Uh... sir?" he asked. "Wouldn't it be more prudent to stay in the center of the formation where we'd be less exposed?"

"Maybe so, Adjunct," I told him. "Just one thing, though: I'm no sissy. I *like* a challenge."

Leeson laughed at Harris, and he glared at both of us.

We soon set up on the west flank of the legion. Downhill from our spot was a dense growth of trees. Manfred set up down there.

"Those trees are freaky," Adjunct Barton said staring downhill. "Those hanging growths—they must be fruit or something, right sir?"

I glanced at the trees. They *were* odd... it looked like dead monkeys hung from the branches.

"Just the local flora, Barton," I told her.

Lifting my rifle, I fired into the closest tree, nailing one of the odd-looking pods.

To my surprise, the pod-like thing opened leathery wings and shrieked, flapping awkwardly away. After about a hundred meters of flapping, it dropped like a stone.

"You killed it, sir," Barton said reproachfully.

"Huh... Well, at least we know they're harmless."

Pigs were employed to dig trenches in minutes. We set up in the trenches and formed a rude defensive line. Kivi put out drones, auto-turrets and pop-up bombs. By dawn, we had a fairly functional fortification.

In front of us, downslope, a near-human cohort set up a more primitive position. The heavy infantry were too big to be completely covered by a standard-depth trench, but nobody seemed to care, not even the big men who hunkered there.

Lastly, we set up 88s on the highest spots. Back behind the hill others deployed star-falls.

193

"That's heavy artillery, that is," Leeson observed, coming to visit my part of the trench. "You think the enemy has seen anything like a star-fall yet?"

"Maybe not here on Peg 51," I admitted. "The Pegs wouldn't have had much in the way of defensive ground forces."

"According to one of those briefings you ignored, they have police robots and whatnot. That's about it."

I glanced at him, but he didn't meet my eye. I didn't complain about his implicit suggestion indicating I hadn't studied this enemy. We all knew each other pretty well by now, and Leeson was right, I hadn't bothered.

Less than a minute later, the sky lit up. We all ducked until we realized it was our side that had fired first.

The star-falls sent bolts of energy in glimmering arcs that moved at a surprisingly low speed. This kind of artillery was supposed to be able to penetrate the various types of protective force-shielding that protected modern armies from missiles and aerial assaults.

Like meteors crashing in slow-motion, the salvoes rose high before falling to the ground again, smashing everything they landed on. In the distance to the south, where the Peg city lay, brilliant flashes glared. Each impact lit up the night down there as if it was broad daylight.

I knew from long experience the dirt would be fused into glass and radioactivity levels would spike at ground-zero. Anything within a hundred meters, shielded or not, would be vaporized.

The battle had begun.

-33-

51 Pegasi didn't have any roads to speak of. There were clearings, paths through trees, and even simple bridges of a sort. But there were no actual roads for ground vehicles.

I'd learned enough after repeated briefings to know that the Pegs usually flew in automated air cars, or used gravity-repelling ground vehicles, or simply walked on foot. So they didn't really need what we called "roads" for travel.

Accordingly, the enemy advance didn't follow any obvious approach. They came toward us in a sweeping rush, more like a migratory herd on the run or a cavalry charge.

As the alien sun rose, looking very like our own yellow-white star, the bright light flashed and gleamed from their armored bodies. I imagined that in centuries past the Earth's legionaries had faced similar charges by armored horsemen or war elephants.

The approaching wave of creatures was more like the latter. They were huge, and they ran with an odd, loping gait. It wasn't a gallop exactly, it was more violent and surging than that. You could sense the powerful muscles under those metal plates and the swiveling turrets that rode their backs.

These armored monsters had both cameras and fleshly eyes. The guns on their spinal ridges were guided by eyeballs, while camera lenses examined their surroundings and chose their best path.

As they got closer, I saw broad, pounding feet encased in more metal. It was like being charged by a horde of steel-clad rhinos.

Behind that first, massive wave worse things marched toward us. Two-legged walkers like the ones we'd seen at Hammonton strode quickly, there beam-cannons looking like beaks. I noticed they were tall enough—and I didn't think it was an accident—to shoot right over the backs of their rhino-like front line.

"Permission to fire, sir!" Sargon called out.

"Hold!" Leeson shouted back.

Leeson knew his shit when it came to timing a light artillery barrage, so I didn't interfere. I turned to Harris, who had ordered his men to switch over their morph-rifles to long range mode.

"Don't," I told him. "Stay with medium ranged assault."

He looked at me, and I could see his eyes were bloodshot. He hadn't gotten much sleep since yesterday—no one had, unless you counted my twenty-nine minutes of nonexistence.

"We've got a double-line of heavy troopers at the base of this hill," Harris told me. "You really think they're going to get past that?"

"Yep."

Harris rubbed at his jaw for a few seconds, jutting it out in thought. I knew he was thinking about arguing with me. But then he roared at his men to switch their rifles back to assault mode. Confused, they hastened to comply.

Forward of the trenches, lying on their bellies, my light troopers were steadily sniping now. Barton was running them smoothly, as usual. She had turned a rabble of recruits into functional soldiers on the way out here aboard *Legate*. Someday when I had the time, I'd have to study her training methods...

"Barton!" I called out. "Fire at those bird things in back!"

"On it, Centurion."

The snap-rifles paused, then began to crack and flash again.

Zooming in with my helmet's HUD, I started marking targets. Red triangles appeared on the heads of individuals I'd spotted that seemed particularly vulnerable. The troops

196

naturally concentrated their fire on the marked enemy, and they began to go down.

The star-falls were still sending beautiful arcs of death toward the approaching line—but they weren't striking the rhino-things, or the storks—they were landing far away, over the folds of the nearest hills.

"What in the hell are those blind fools aiming at?" Harris demanded. "The enemy is right here!"

"Maybe there's something else out there," I said, "still inbound. Watch your own targets. They're coming into range."

Leeson gave the word to fire at the same moment, and both our unit's 88s sang their song of death together. A flood of radiation saturated the air over our heads. It was a glaring, sickly green and seemed to turn the air it passed through into a rippling mirage.

The beams swept horizontally, consuming whatever they touched. The rhino front line was set ablaze—but they kept charging. They came at us exactly as if they *weren't* roasting to death in their metal shells.

Leeson shouted again, his voice cracking. The beams reversed and swept back the other way, igniting more of the aliens.

Only after a second stroke of intense radiation did any of them stagger and tumble. Even when down, they kicked and struggled to fight on. I saw exposed bones in their feet and flapping skin that had half-turned to ash.

The first two ranks were destroyed, but the rest made it to the croaking line of near-humans who stood their ground stalwartly in front of us. I felt proud to see their bravery.

Sure, others might call them morons, twisted genetic freaks and worse—but I called them brothers. A century back, before all the intensive breeding programs of their Cephalopod masters, their ancestors had been born on Earth, the same as mine had.

Lifting cannon-like gunpowder weapons, the heavy troopers released a volley of fire. The results were surprising— they inflicted nearly as much damage as our 88s had done.

The explosive pellets they fired penetrated armor and blew apart the internal organs of the charging enemy—or maybe

197

their circuitry, it was hard to tell. Hundreds of the enemy dropped and tumbled, but for every one that went down another leapt over the fallen gracefully, continuing the press right up to our foremost trench line.

It was then, at that very moment, that the attackers drew close enough for me to recognize them. These aliens... they were the altered bodies of Peg civilians. They had to be.

The original images I'd seen of the cat-like natives of this world, with arms in front and powerfully-built bodies behind... It had to be their bodies the aliens had bastardized with strange surgery. These rhinos weren't rhinos at all, they were hybrids. Mixtures of machines and meat. Flesh and blood creatures that had been torn apart and reassembled in a new form with electronic brains connected to their nervous systems.

My lip curled up. All of these monstrosities had to be destroyed. All of them.

The rhino-like things had lost half their number by the time they hit the heavy-trooper trenches. I dared to hope they wouldn't break through.

Thousands of struggling forms met in the clash of battle. Swinging swords, the heavy troopers had dropped their rifles and drawn thick-bladed cutlasses. They didn't fence with these weapons, they used them the way a madman might use a cleaver. They hacked without finesse, with berserk power driving their blades.

Our troops were smaller and less armored than the enemy, but many of the rhinos were injured. It was a ghastly fight. A cloud of dust and smoke arose, soon obscuring the field.

Sucking in a breath, I stood up in the trench and roared at my men.

"Heavy platoon! Advance!"

With that command, I climbed out of my safe hole in the ground and marched downhill. Startled, Harris fell in behind me. We marched to support the near-humans in their trenches, as we could no longer see well enough to shoot into the tangled mess below our position.

"This is crazy, McGill!" Harris shouted. "Fucking crazy!"

Graves buzzed in my ear a moment later. Had Harris complained to him? I hoped not, but I wouldn't have put it past him.

"McGill, why are you out of position? No one gave you the order to die—not yet."

"I get that, sir," I shouted back. "But we can't support the Blood Worlder troops with fire from the hilltop. We're advancing to stop the enemy charge now, with everything we've got."

Graves was quiet for a moment. I knew he was examining the situation from my perspective using remote cameras and battle computers.

"Carry on," he said at last, and the connection dropped.

I waved to Harris, who rushed over to me, sweating and breathing hard.

"Are we pulling back, sir?" he asked.

I pointed toward the lines of legionnaires on our flanks. We saw hundreds of other heavy Varus troops joining our charge, moving rapidly downslope to the meet the enemy.

"Not quite. Press the attack."

Harris nodded dejectedly and faced the dust and smoke ahead. He took in a deep breath of his own, and then we plunged onward. A platoon of our Legion's finest followed in our wake.

-34-

When we reached the Blood Worlder front lines, they were in a bad way. Blue-white smoke drifted everywhere accented by orange flame. A blacker smoke billowed up from some of the destroyed aliens that lay sizzling.

That had to be the weirdest thing I'd seen yet on this planet, this world of armored beings. The alien constructs sometimes caught on fire, the way any damaged machine might do.

But the strange part was what happened to the meat fused inside these evil machines. It began to cook, to sizzle, to smoke like a barbecue gone horribly wrong.

Harris paused when we got to the trench line and flipped open his visor. He reached inside to mop his sweating face— but that was a mistake. One whiff of that frying alien meat, and he retched.

"Pull it together, Adjunct!" I said, gripping his armored shoulder and giving him a shake.

He gave me an unhappy glance, but he nodded. He slammed his visor shut again, and we marched on, plunging into the flowing smoke.

The fighting was just ahead. As soon as we reached the forward trench line, we saw struggling figures. Most were grievously wounded. Heavy footmen from Blood World had hacked with their swords and fired point-blank into the bleeding, smoldering monsters that sought to tear them apart.

These front line troops weren't sophisticated. I guess they were akin to the converted citizens we'd had to blast to fragments back on Earth. But these guys were a lot bigger. The average Peg citizen was around eight hundred kilos in weight without any electronics or armor attached.

My platoon of heavies waded into the fight. When we found living enemy constructs, we switched our morph-rifles into close-assault mode. We used grenade-launchers and plasma torches liberally. Often, it was hard to fire because the Blood Worlders were in the way, tackling the enemy hand-to-hand.

In such cases, we extended our force-blades and killed the armored creatures with thrusts and cuts. There were cracks in the enemy armor, and we drove our weapons home to strike the muscles, electronics and soft vitals.

"Centurion!" Harris shouted, grabbing me and turning me around.

I almost slashed him—but I stopped myself.

"McGill! Something else is coming!"

There was a hint of fear in his eyes. I didn't usually see that. Harris had witnessed things far more gruesome than these cyborg freaks.

Following his gestures, I first heard rather than saw what he was talking about. A deep rumble shook the ground we were walking on.

As a precaution, we both slid down into a trench. It was deep, dug for men a meter taller than we were.

"You think that could be those bird-things?" Harris asked. "You think they're charging us behind all that smoke?"

I climbed up to get a view, grunting and working my elbows in the blood-soaked mud. Wiping at my faceplate, I scanned the battlefield.

"I don't see any bird-things," I said. "I don't see much movement at all except for those trees... Something is knocking the trees down... Over there, see?"

The smoke had cleared somewhat. A few distant cheers went up as my men retook the trenches. The army of rhino-type creatures had been defeated.

Blood Worlders who'd survived the onslaught were filling the trenches around us. They dragged behind them any of their brothers who were too wounded to walk, but they offered them no other aid. In their culture if you couldn't recover on your own, you should die.

They blinked at us in confusion, as if wondering what we were doing in their foxholes—but they didn't ask any questions. They almost never did.

In the meantime, the rumbling sounds only grew. The thick liquids puddled up in the trenches and shook like jelly due to the vibrations.

Beginning to worry, I tried to contact Kivi first, to see what her drones had spotted. There was no response—her name was blinking red in my HUD. She'd caught a stray round at some point.

Next, I reached out to Graves with my tapper. He was my immediate superior, and he should have a better perspective than I did. After a few tries, he finally answered my call.

"McGill? Have they hit you yet?"

"Uh... has what hit us, sir?"

"Those giant tanks. They're mowing right through the trees like grass. It's too late to run now, just hunker down and let them roll over you. The stork-things following them should be easier game for infantry."

Alarmed, I relayed the message up and down the trench. As the Blood Worlders didn't seem to respond, and I didn't see their squid sub-centurion, I flipped up my visor and roared at them, using my voice.

Choking smoke rolled into my face, but I didn't care.

"Get down! Everyone, get down in the trenches as flat as you can!"

A few did it. I don't know how many. My own troops were more with it, so they laid down first. Then, the grunting heavy footmen followed suit with bewildered expressions.

That's about when the rush of tanks hit us. They didn't fire, they simply rolled their treads right over our positions. Each tank was bigger than a diesel truck and twice as wide.

Big, steel arms like crane booms swung overhead of each treaded vehicle. The tanks had three arms each, and these limbs moved independently. Picking up soldiers, both human and near-human, they began a grim, methodical slaughter.

Often, they simply plucked limbs and heads from the struggling forms. In other cases, they raised the victim into the air. That invariably resulted in a storm of beams firing, lancing through the body from a dozen angles. The stork-like things were right behind the tanks, and they were excitedly beaming any human they could get a bead on.

In my case, a tank rolled up and over my trench. A Blood Worlder was crushed, his ribs crackling and his skull popping like a melon. He was too big, too badly placed to survive the weight of those massive metal treads.

Harris was on my right, and he didn't fare any better. He tried to scramble away, he even made it a dozen meters before one of those long, segmented arms with a three-clawed hand at the end caught him.

Up into the air he went, and the stork-things burned him greedily, marching around in clacking circles as they struggled and competed to get a shot.

There I was, on my back, pinned by mud and bodies, all of which was being compressed by the terrific weight of the enemy vehicle.

As I couldn't do much while lying on my back, and I was pretty certain there was no surviving this particular situation, I lit up one of my force-blades. One arm was free, and I saw the tank's metallic belly overhead. Here and there hairs sprouted out of it—but it was mostly metal.

Thrusting my force-blade deeply into the enemy, I was pleased when a gush of—*something*—splattered my faceplate. Was it piss? Blood? Something worse?

I couldn't tell, but a yellowy, thick liquid was running down out of the tank's gashed belly. I was reminded of corn oil, or olive oil...

The tank lurched away from my trench after that. I got the feeling it had sensed the damage to its undercarriage and decided to move on. The huge shadow retreated, and smoky daylight swept over me. Struggling up into a sitting position, I was quickly surrounded by the bird-machines.

I'd never been this close-up to so many of these freaks. They were animal-like, curious. They walked around, staring down at me with camera eyes and those deadly, plasma-tubes that resembled giant beaks.

They didn't fire right off. That was their mistake. Maybe they were hoping I'd get up and try to run. Maybe that made the game more fun for them—but running had never been my plan.

Each man in Legion Varus is issued a single grav-grenade. I used mine now, arming it and throwing it directly upward.

The storks tracked the glowing object curiously, their long snouts rising to follow it. A few beams slashed the air—but they missed.

Then, the grenade went off. I was blasted flat on my back again. I was hurt bad. As a man who's been on a first name basis with the angel of death for decades, I could tell I was a goner.

But the half-dozen stork-things that had been hunting me weren't in good shape either. They staggered, falling into one another. They were blinded, it seemed.

A crowd of others were attracted to this anomaly. These didn't fool around. Maybe they didn't want to know what I'd done to their stunned brothers.

They beamed me from a dozen angles, burning me alive in my armor at the bottom of that stinking trench. I was struck three times, then six more, and I was glad when it was finally over.

-35-

"Score?" a clipped, high-pitched male voice asked.

"He's a seven-point-nine."

"I'll call it an eight. Get him off my table."

Hands roughly hustled me into a sitting position.

Sometimes when I woke up in the morning, I felt refreshed and full of life—but today wasn't one of those times.

Groaning, I rolled onto my feet and almost slipped and fell onto the floor. Catching myself with wide-flung arms, my wobbly legs barely held me.

"What the hell?" I croaked. "Did you guys use spoiled meat to print me out?"

"Recycled cells are as good as fresh ones," the bio told me without a glance. "Don't go offing yourself just because you find out you've got a bad back, Centurion. This is the best you're going to get today—we have a long backlog."

I remembered the battle then, in a rush.

"What happened down there? Did we wipe?"

"Not exactly. The lifters pulled out half the legion."

"Varus? Half of Varus?"

"That's what I said."

"What about the Blood Worlder legion?"

The bio looked at me crossly. "I don't know about those apes. Ask Tribune Armel."

Becoming angry myself, I told him I would do just that. Then I put on some clothes and staggered out onto Blue Deck.

Orderlies watched me, stopping their private conversations to stare. It was their job to make sure I got out of their universe—which we called Blue Deck on every ship—without causing any undue trouble.

I might have messed with them, but I figured the snotty bio was right. I wasn't going to get any better materials if I got myself killed again. When fresh supplies were running low, complaining about it wasn't going to change anything.

Making my way to the elevators, I was faced with a choice. I could go down to the modules and check in on my troops— but most of them were still dead. I could see their status on my tapper.

The other option was to take a little field trip up to Gold Deck. I chose the latter direction and controlled the elevator with a flick of one finger.

Up I went. When I reached the end of the line, I was on Gold Deck.

"Centurion?" asked an inquisitive guard. "Do you have business up here, sir?"

"I sure do. I'm going to see Tribune Armel."

He eyed me for a moment, then consulted his tapper.

"His office is right down the hall, sir—in the back."

I walked off, slightly surprised. The guard hadn't demanded anything special—like orders. Maybe that was because I hadn't demanded to see Graves, or Turov. Legionnaires with murder on their minds tended to go straight up the chain of command.

Likewise, I was a centurion now. We had free run of the place most of the time. Hell, if I ever made primus, I'd end up flying a desk on Gold Deck myself, just like old Winslade did on every campaign.

Getting past Armel's secretary wasn't difficult. She was Centurion Leeza, a longtime confident of Armel's. She didn't really like me, but we did go way back together, having first met on Tech World.

"My how the years do look good on you, Centurion!" I told her with a grin.

She twisted her lips into a frown in return.

"I was killed this morning," she said sourly. "What do you want, McGill?"

"Why, to see your lovely face again, that's all!"

Leeza wasn't an idiot. She narrowed her eyes in my direction. "Just go in—he'll see you now. But if you shoot him or something, I'll kill you myself."

"I'll take that as a promise."

Figuring I should take the invitation I'd been offered without negotiating, I walked into Armel's office and found him stripped to the waist and toweling off.

"Uh... hello, Tribune."

"Ah, McGill! Do you know why I let you come in here?"

"Uh... no sir."

"Because it's been ages since we last met and planned a disastrous military operation together. I simply had to hear whatever cock-and-bull story you wished to annoy me with today."

"Glad to see you, too. Listen... about that battle. We lost, right?"

"Heh... *quel idiot*! Did you seriously come here to request a briefing? What is the matter with pestering Graves? Does he blame you in some way? I would not be amazed to learn this was the truth."

"No, no sir. That's not it at all. I—I just wanted to know what happened to the Blood Worlders. To your legion, sir."

He blinked twice in surprise.

"They did exactly what they were supposed to do: they died face down in the mud, that's what."

"Really sir? No survivors?"

He shrugged. "There might have been a cohort of stragglers that managed to shove themselves aboard the lifters before they took off. Don't worry about it. We're getting more troops from Earth right now. Thousands of fresh apes are marching through the gateway posts onto this ship as we speak. Not even an army of bio specialists with revival machines churning night and day can replace human troops that fast."

"Well... that's not very encouraging. They fought hard down there. They fought and died hard. They deserve a burial, or something."

Armel snorted. "A ceremony? For the dead? What century is this, McGill?"

"One where Blood Worlder troops get permed all the time. Do you really think we can keep on getting them slaughtered while we recycle our own lives right in front of them?"

Armel laughed and opened a cupboard. He pulled out a crystal bottle and two glasses. "Come, McGill, you must drink with me now."

"Why's that?"

"Because you've made me happy on this dark day. I can't believe I've found a fool who's more worried about my own lost troops than I am."

It wasn't much to drink over, but I accepted his expensive brandy and gulped while he sipped. He watched me over the rim of his glass.

"You died in the trenches, correct?" he asked.

"Yup. Right under a flock of those stork-things."

"Ah then... " he said. "You never encountered the true enemy, just the underlings that came first to skirmish."

My mouth fell open and hung there. I hate when it does that.

"Uh... the real enemy? You mean those armored rhino-things and the storks with beamers for beaks—they weren't the worst?"

Armel laughed. "Not at all. They were merely an *hors d'oeuvre*. The true enemy came after that wave. A battalion of vast tanks. Vehicles so large and deadly they swept away our legions without a care."

He looked away, as if haunted by imagery.

"Actually, I did see a few of them. They overran us at the end. I cut the belly of one of them open."

"Did you now! Well done."

Curious, I reached to his desk. He had an open after-action report on the desktop. I made a spinning motion with my finger and a video began to play.

"I'll be damned..." I said, watching in horror and fascination.

The vids were taken by a flying drone, that much was clear. The battle looked a lot different when you could see the whole thing.

As I watched, a column of vast vehicles swept down over the hills. The tanks were so big their treads took down trees the way a mower takes down a field of weeds. At the first trench line, where I'd so recently died in the mud, they overran the battleground. They crushed humans, near-humans and converted Pegs with equal disdain.

Pressing toward the Varus lines higher up the hill, they shrugged off blasts from our 88s, but when a star-fall hit one it was destroyed.

Each tank had small missiles on its back that launched now and then, destroying artillery pieces and clumps of our troops. Turrets swiveled and blasted our trench lines, destroying our troops and causing a mass retreat. In the end, the tanks overran our lines, and the lifters began to flee.

"You see?" Armel said. "Complete disaster. They should not have bothered with the smaller troops first. Perhaps they were testing us—or perhaps they didn't want to commit their tanks until they realized they needed them. It hardly matters. We were driven from the field in disgrace."

"We didn't stand a chance..." I finished, closing the vid file and pouring some more of his brandy into my glass.

He nodded and put his glass on his desk. "My analysis is essentially the same. It is often this way when an armored enemy meets a force comprised of infantry. We need heavier weapons that can penetrate their vehicles from a distance."

"Can't we just blow them up with mines—or use star-falls?"

Armel wagged a finger at me. "If you watched closely, the star-falls were firing as the enemy approached. But hitting a fast-moving target with slow-firing artillery is never easy."

"What about the city? Can't we take that down?"

Armel waved his hand dismissively. "They've domed off the city where they make these abominations. Such odd creatures."

"Creatures? Don't you mean machines?"

I told him about the general theory my techs had that these beings were ruled by artificial minds, but they moved using biologically grown muscles.

"Even more strange..." he said. "But where are their masters? That's what I want to know. I've dealt with any number of machines, McGill. There's always an intelligent creature behind them somewhere, pulling the strings."

"Maybe they killed their parent race of biotics," I suggested.

Armel looked thoughtful. "That is probably true. Seems odd, doesn't it, that aliens clever enough to create intelligent machines would be dumb enough to allow them free reign? In any case, there must be a thinking being of some kind behind this rabble, a creature that's directing these nightmares. They can't have sprung upon the universe whole and ready to run amok. They're not natural."

Thinking about it, I had to agree with him on that last idea. *Something* had made these strange constructs. Something that was smarter than they were.

"Who would send these things here?" I asked.

Armel scratched under his chin like a languid cat. "I do not know... but it's likely that whoever created these monsters directed them to come and harass us."

"An enemy of Earth, then?" I asked.

"Or at least an enemy of the Mogwa."

I thought about the possibilities, but the list of suspects seemed prohibitively long.

"Well, if I get any more information, I'll relay it. I assume we're attacking again tomorrow?"

"Yes... after a fashion. We have a new plan. You'll learn about it in the morning. Go get a good night's sleep."

I wondered what that meant, but he didn't seem to want to tell me. Shrugging, I let the matter go.

I figured I'd find out what my fate would be in the morning.

-36-

No one bothered to brief me about the new operation the next day. I thought that was rather strange, but at least they didn't give my troops much time to worry about it.

We were scrambled out of the mess hall at 0600 and hustled toward Red Deck—that was where they launched lifters and dropped drop-pods.

I arrived on Red Deck fully kitted in heavy armor. Turov and Armel were both there, and Graves arrived moments later.

Turov put up a hand to stop my unit and frowned at Graves.

"Didn't someone tell them how to dress for this? I said light tunics only."

Graves slid his eyes toward Armel. Graves didn't look all that happy, but he was outranked by both of them, so he kept quiet.

Armel made sad little sucking sounds with his mouth. "It was an oversight," he said. "They will learn the details soon enough. Their small part is rather simple to play, after all…"

"All right, whatever," Turov said. "McGill, get your men out of that expensive gear. Everyone is going down in a light trooper suit—nothing else."

"What? Are you kidding? Can't we at least take snap-rifles?"

I was joking, but she seemed to honestly consider it. "Yes… I think that would be for the best. Strip down, take a snap-rifle and board the lifter."

She walked away, and Armel went with her. I was too confused to even stare at her butt. I thought about going after her and demanding an explanation, but it would have been noticed by everyone. Generally speaking, she wasn't my girlfriend when we went on campaigns. It just didn't work given the rank differences and all.

I relayed the order to my baffled troops, and to more units as they came on down to board the lifter. Everyone was confused and annoyed.

"This is bullshit," Leeson said. "Mark my words, I'm smelling a gigantic French rat here."

Graves had a word with me after I'd stripped down to my skivvies. I felt naked going into battle like nothing but a spacer's suit. It was airtight, but it provided no protection against anything more dangerous than a bee sting.

"What are we supposed to do, sir?" I asked. "These aliens are tough. It's not time to try and save on the equipment bill today."

"I hear you McGill. For what it's worth, I didn't come up with this cockamamie plan—but it just might work."

I blinked twice. "What might work? I don't even know what we're supposed to do!"

"Land, scramble out the door and hide in the trees. If the enemy comes, engage and skirmish. You'll do fine."

I watched as unit after unit boarded the lifter. There was one from each cohort. That was odd, as we usually traveled together as a cohesive force. The lifters were designed to hold a full cohort.

"How are we supposed to coordinate...?" I began, but Graves cut me off.

"Board, drop, land, fight," he repeated quickly. "You'll do fine."

Graves wasn't a man who liked to listen to complaints. I sighed and grabbed a snap-rifle off a rack. Pigs were carrying our discarded gear away.

I boarded the lifter and sat near another centurion from the 9th Cohort. She was kind of cute, and she eyed me with mild curiosity for a moment. But then she saw my nametag.

"Wait... You're Centurion McGill? Um... no thanks."

"What?"

"You're McGill, right?"

"Yeah…" I said.

"In that case, I'm not interested."

"Huh? Oh… no, no, I'm not hitting on you. I'm here to ask if you know why the hell we're going on a hot-drop in our underpants."

She shrugged. "No clue. The enemy city is shielded. Maybe we can't get through the shield with heavy gear."

I jutted out my jaw and nodded. It sounded logical—sort of—but it wasn't. I'd been under one of the enemy force domes back on Earth. We'd walked through in heavy armor without a hitch then.

When I opened my mouth to voice this objection, the ship lurched. We'd been dropped into free-fall. With my guts coming up into my mouth, I endured the next eight rough minutes.

When a lifter enters a hostile atmosphere, the pilot takes his ship down at top speed. No one wanted to linger and make a target out of themselves. As a result, the noise was deafening and the cabin began to heat up. I was forced to seal my suit and wait it out.

We landed with a crushing reverse thrust to slow us down, followed by a jarring thump. It was a good thing lifters were as tough as nails.

"Nothing fired at us," I told the centurion next to me.

She looked relieved and started shouting at her troops. I did the same with mine.

"Say, uh…" I said, checking her out a little. "I've been noticing you for a long time now. Let's say we both survive the day. You got plans tonight?"

She shook her head and slapped her hand over her nametag. "What's my name?" she asked.

"Uh…" I said, straining my brain. "Centurion Mills!" I shouted, half-guessing. There were only three female centurions in my cohort, and my odds were pretty good.

She nodded appreciatively. "Not bad… First name?"

"Uh…" I was a total blank. But that never stopped a man like me. I squinted, trying to remember.

213

"Come on," she said, pointing over my shoulder. "The ramp is going down. We're deploying in ninety seconds."

By this time, there were a few of her officers and mine watching and nudging one another. They were making bets—but I didn't care.

"Jennie?" I asked.

"Oooo," she said. "So close. It's Sheryl."

"Dammit!"

She turned and trotted away from me then, shouting for her unit to deploy. They rushed out into the open, and my unit was up next.

Leeson caught up with me when we hit the ramp and fanned out.

"Don't tell me you were hitting on Mills!" he said.

I ignored him.

"Make for the trees!" I shouted, and we rushed out into the sunshine.

It looked a lot like Earth, except for those dead-monkey things in the forest. Damn, there were a lot of those flapping monsters around.

Leeson was huffing, but he managed to keep up with my long strides. I considered outrunning him, as he had shorter legs than I did, but I thought it would be bad for morale to have my unit watch me dodge my own adjunct.

"Centurion Jennie Mills," Leeson said, laughing. "I'm surprised it took you so long to take a shot at her. Every guy in the legion has to put his helmet in his lap when he thinks about her. She's new, and she's—"

Whirling around, I grabbed up a big wad of his tunic.

He looked up at me in comic surprise. He figured I was about to beat his ass—but that wasn't what I was planning at all.

"Are you telling me her name *is* Jennie?" I demanded.

"That's what I said…"

I let go of him, and I walked under the trees laughing. That girl had got me good—but it didn't seem fair.

"Jesus…" Leeson muttered, straightening out his kit.

Harris ran up next, looking everywhere at once. "Where are the bunkers, McGill?"

214

I pointed downslope. There, in the distance, we could see the shimmering force dome.

"Down there in the Peg city—if there were any Pegs left alive in it, which I doubt."

"Say what?" he asked, craning his neck. "What kind of a shit-show is this? We're sitting ducks out here!"

Right about then, we heard a roar. Turning back the way we'd come, we saw the lifter rise up on a plume of fire. It took off, full thrust, and shot over the horizon.

"He's hugging the treetops," Leeson said with a long whistle, "heading due south, away from the city. You think he knows something we don't know?"

Harris raged. He took off his helmet and slammed it on the ground. "This is so fucked up! No armor, no heavy weapons— and we're even closer to the city than we were last time. It's obvious to me that those monsters are going to just roll right up here and take us all out. How can they not know that?"

"Are you going to tell him?" Leeson asked. "Or do you want me to?"

Harris glowered at both of us. "Tell me what?"

About then, after she got each of her troops hidden behind the trunk of his own individual tree, Barton came up and crouched nearby.

"Sir," she said, "the men are placed. How long do we have to wait?"

"Depends," I said, "on how long it takes the freaks to notice us and mount another counterattack."

"That was..." Barton said, frowning, "about ten hours last time. I'd say we've got less than six at this distance."

"Agreed."

All this time, Harris was frowning at me and Leeson. "Sir, you were going to tell me...?"

I plucked a grass stalk, put it in my mouth, and chewed on it.

"Hey, that could be toxic you know," Barton said.

I smiled. "Doesn't matter."

Leeson cackled then. He had an annoying laugh, and he let it out now. Full-force.

215

Harris gave him an odd glance, then he turned to me slowly. I stared back.

"Oh no…" he said. "You're shitting me, right McGill? Tell me you're shitting me!"

"Wish I could."

Harris flopped down on his back and shaded his eyes with one hand. "Just wake me up when it's over."

Barton looked around at the three of us. Leeson was grinning, Harris seemed depressed, but I was looking stoic—maybe a little bored.

"What's going on, sir?" she asked. "I don't get this kind of op. Legion Varus officers… are they all crazy? We've got no chance out here on this hilltop."

"That's right," I said. "No chance at all—but that's the plan. We're the rabbits this time."

She looked startled. Being "the rabbit" was never a good thing in the legions. Usually, it meant you were cannon fodder used to bait the enemy.

All of a sudden, she caught on and closed her eyes in defeat.

"We're bait," she said. "They want those armored… *things*, to come out of their dome and swarm us. Then what? Will they drop a bomb on this hill? Wipe the place clean?"

Leeson went into another bout of annoying laughter. "You got it, girl! Welcome to getting screwed over by the brass!"

"Welcome to Varus, you mean," Harris muttered. "Such bullshit…"

Barton looked at me. Her eyes were big.

"It's true then? The tribunes… they're going to wipe us?"

"One unit from each cohort," I told her. "No good weapons, no armor… you do the math. Where I come from, the answer isn't good."

She gazed out toward the domed city.

"So… are we going to just sit out here and wait to die?"

Something about her statement bothered me. She was right, we'd all given up.

Standing up, I threw back my shoulders.

"Uh-oh," Leeson said.

"Maybe not," I said. "Maybe not…"

A plan—no, that was too big of a word for it—a *thought* was forming in my mind.

-37-

It was kind of a mixed blessing when the enemy showed up early. On one hand, it was always tough waiting for certain death. On the other, the day was kind of pleasant—up until the monsters arrived and ruined it with violence and battle.

The enemy was led again by a wave of those bounding, armored, animal-like things. They seemed to move faster than the other creatures, so maybe that was why they tended to arrive first.

There had to be a thousand of them. Like fools, my fellows began to fire snap-rifles at them as soon as they appeared. A few went down, but hundreds more turned, like a herd of buffalo, and charged toward the trees where we'd taken cover.

"Aw, shit!" Leeson said, getting to his feet. "Fall back!"

I frowned at him for a moment—but then I realized he was right. We couldn't take these things on with our low numbers. And without a single primus to command us, the force as a whole was doomed to behave in a random and unorganized way.

"Fall back!" I echoed, and our men withdrew into the cool gloom of the forest.

"Isn't this desertion, Centurion?" Barton asked. "I mean, I understand why we might do it, but—"

"Not at all," I said. "Our orders were to distract and engage. To keep the enemy's attention. We can't do that for longer than ten minutes if we go toe-to-toe with them."

"That's the ticket," Leeson said. "We're skirmishing. Shoot and run!"

So we ran. Sure, I was feeling a little guilty, so I contacted Centurion Jennie Mills. She answered, and I heard the sounds of battle in the background.

"McGill? This had better be good!"

"We're falling back into the trees, Jennie. I thought I'd tell you. We have no overall commander."

She didn't talk for a moment, but I could hear gunfire in the background and an occasional roar as one of the monsters made it up the slope to the plunge into the trees and the Varus lines.

"You're running out?" she demanded.

"No, I'm lasting longer. We're supposed to keep the enemy busy as long as we can. That's why we're here. If we wipe in ten minutes—we failed."

"You're right... Mills out."

Soon, many of the units were pulling back. We headed into a denser line of trees, into a zone where the elephant-sized creatures couldn't follow us without shouldering their way between tree trunks.

We went downhill, then up again. Pausing when we found more open ground, we crouched undercover.

"Something's on our tail, sir!" Harris shouted.

He waved his platoon forward, and they knelt behind trees. The bush was moving behind us.

"Hold your fire!" Barton called out.

It was Centurion Mills with her surviving troops. They straggled up and fell to the ground around us, gasping for air.

"Head count?" I asked her.

"Fifty-seven..."

Half of them were dead. We'd lost a dozen ourselves.

I gazed out over the forest. It wasn't quite like an earthly forest, it was denser, more like a jungle in a colder clime. Maybe that was due to the different atmosphere. I'd read the land was very fertile.

Mills sat beside me.

"What's your plan?" she asked.

219

"Plan? To last a few more hours. That's about it—unless we get lucky."

"Lucky?"

"Yeah... Natasha!"

It took a few minutes, but my best tech finally showed up. She was the best in my unit, the best in our cohort—and probably the best in Legion Varus.

Her eyes darted to look at Jennie, then swept back to me. "What is it, Centurion?"

That was an insolent way to address a superior, but I let it slide. Natasha had always had a thing for me. What I needed now was her brain, not her jealously and snappy attitude. But bringing that up now wouldn't help anything.

I explained why we were here, what we were expected to do, and what I needed from her.

Natasha sat her ass down hard on the ground. She put her rifle down and rested her chin on her knees.

"They really ditched us here?" she asked. "They really did that? Just to get a clean ground-zero on these freaks?"

"Yeah, looks like it. But listen, we might get a chance to change things up a bit."

I explained about the tanks that were certain to come after the rhino creatures, especially if we hadn't been wiped out yet.

Natasha looked fearful. "What the hell are we supposed to do in this situation, sir?"

"Die," I said, shrugging. "But maybe we can do more than that. I've been thinking about these vehicles—the big ones, I mean. The living tanks."

We talked, and we plotted. Soon, we got the chance to put our plans into action.

The first thing we did was leave the rest of the cohort behind. We had to draw the enemy into a region that was apart from the others in order to have a chance. Accordingly, we sprinted across some open ground, then entered another wooded hilly area to the east. Behind us, there was a lot of firing and now and then a faint, echoing scream.

"I'm having real trouble with this, situation McGill," Adjunct Barton told me.

"How's that? You hurt?"

"No… no, that's not what I meant. I'm talking about the fact we ran out on the others."

I shrugged. "We're destined to die out here today, Erin. I'm good with that, but I'm going to take as long as possible to do it. Therefore, I'm following orders."

She still looked troubled, but I didn't care. As far as I was concerned, we were doing our jobs better than the rest.

We waited in the new hiding spot for about twenty minutes before a trio of hunting stork-things came along. They were clearly looking for survivors.

"Ambush them," I ordered.

We waited until they were close, then rushed out and gunned them all down. Not a single trooper died.

After that, morale improved. It really shouldn't have, but men always like fighting and winning more than they like running away.

We went back into the trees and hid.

"Um…" Leeson said. "Maybe we should move on, sir? To another position? They'll have us zeroed soon."

"Yep. That's the point. We're trying to attract a bigger group."

The adjuncts looked at each other nervously, but they didn't say anything.

A few minutes later, my tapper began to buzz. It was Graves. My face soured, and I silenced it.

Centurion Mills came looking for me about ninety seconds after that.

"The primus wants to talk to you, McGill."

With a grunt, I answered the call.

"Primus Graves, sir!" I said loudly. "I just want to thank you for this fine vacation you arranged for me and my deserving men. I can't imagine why no one of primus rank accompanied us. We're all down here having the best shore-leave of our—what's that, sir?"

"I said shut up, McGill. Why are you so far out of position?"

"Uh… I'm following your orders, sir. We're still alive, we just killed an enemy patrol, and we're—"

"McGill, you're going to start listening to me, or I'll turn you into an adjunct the next time you come out of the oven on Blue Deck."

That made me wince a little. Due to various misunderstandings and injustices of the past, I'd been demoted from time to time. I had no desire to experience the process again.

"Right sir. Tell me what you need."

"I need you to get your asses closer to the LZ. There's a formation of their largest armored vehicles coming out from the city right now. Those vehicles are our primary targets. I want them all in one spot for easy disposal. We can't bomb the whole area without using nukes, and we're trying to avoid that for environmental reasons."

Confused, I scratched at my face through the open visor. "Did I hear that right, sir? You're trying not to blow down too many of the flowers out here?"

"That's right. We're visitors on 51 Pegasi. This is, in fact, the first time Earthers have landed on this planet. If we blow everything up—well, it might not leave the best diplomatic impression."

"I guess I can see that. All right, we'll return to the LZ. McGill out."

Glumly, I closed the connection. I told Centurion Mills what he'd said. She looked sick.

"You mean he wants us to march toward the enemy? Right into the targeted area?"

"Yeah. He wants them tightly circled up, I guess. A saturation bombing with conventional smart-bombs is coming our way, if I had to guess."

"After all this our reward is to be blown apart? It seems so pointless…"

"Not at all. With luck, we'll kill a shit-load of their best armor. We can't bomb our way through that dome from space—not easily. And I wouldn't want to march an infantry formation inside there to dig them out if they still have their tanks. This way, we're drawing them out and destroying their best cyborgs with minimal loss."

Jennie shook her head, but I honestly thought it was just sour grapes on her part. After all, dying face down in the mud was just another Sunday afternoon in Legion Varus.

-38-

Another alien patrol found us soon thereafter. It was made up of both storks and rhinos.

As we had a decent amount of firepower on hand, and they weren't able to close with us fast enough. We put them all down at range.

"Three rhinos and five storks so far!" I shouted, beaming.

My positive attitude uplifted the troops, and I wasn't even putting on an act. I really *did* enjoy killing these alien bastards. They were as ugly as sin by any measure, and they all deserved killing just on principle.

One of the creatures must have reported in to their main army. We knew they had radios in their bodies and worked them like speech organs. They bleeped and blipped, and they ratted us out.

Shortly after the firefight, we soon heard a rumble that grew into a roar. The sounds separated into the rattle and squeal of spinning treads.

"Come on!"

I took off at a dead run, and as people tended to do, they followed me.

I don't rightly know what the tank that burst out of the tree line had expected to see with its roving cameras, but I'm pretty sure it wasn't a hundred and fifty lightly-armed humans.

We rushed it like a herd of ostriches. Anti-personnel weapons budded up on the sides of the tank, and they began tracking and firing. Some troops were blown to fragments on my left, so I jogged right.

"Encircle it!" I shouted. "Throw grav-grenades into the treads!"

The running troops did as I suggested. Mostly, Jennie's people ran to the left side, and my people followed me to the right.

Nasty things began to happen. The tank surged forward and ran over about thirty of us—but then the grenades blew its treads off, and it ground to a halt.

The tank seemed like a huge, complex thing with lots of mechanical parts. There wasn't so much flesh involved on this monster but there was lots more metal.

Then I spotted the arms and the eyes. Actual organic eyes roved over the turrets, aiming them with muscles that bulged with the effort to swing the barrels into line. We were too close, too small—

Boom!

Surprised, I found myself flying ass-over-teakettle into the air. It was a shockwave, not a direct hit. I was hurt and shocked, but I wasn't torn apart.

The world went blank for a moment, but then it came back again. I was pretty sure I wasn't dead... Not yet.

My ears were ringing with tinnitus. I rolled up into a crouch, coughing. I felt for busted ribs and shrapnel wounds—there were a few, but not enough to stop me immediately. Taking a nap in the shadow of a raging house-sized tank was never a good idea.

Forcing myself to stand, I felt a strong arm loop around my bicep and haul me up. It was Sargon. He was shouting something, but my bell was rung and I didn't even answer.

Pointing. He was pointing. I looked at the tip of his dirty, gauntleted finger and followed in that direction with fuzzy vision.

Someone was waving. Women. Two of them, one was Natasha, the other was Centurion Jennie Mills.

Breaking into a trot with Sargon half-dragging me, I moved toward those beckoning girls. Maybe, in this rare instance, my natural drive to mate helped me out.

225

They all hauled me into a close, tight space. A door made of metal and meat closed behind us.

Natasha ripped my helmet off.

"James! James, can you hear me? James?"

"What's the fuss about?" I asked in a drunk's voice. I was coming around, getting a grip, but I wasn't all there yet.

"We're inside the tank. There are compartments and things like that."

"What about... where's my unit?"

They exchanged glances.

"They're mostly dead, sir," Sargon said. "We wrecked this tank pretty good, it can't move, but it tore up our men. We found this door when we were down to about ten percent effectives and climbed inside. Centurion Mills noticed you were moving again, so we decided to haul you in with us."

I blinked and squinted at them stupidly. "I was out?"

"You sure as hell were. I thought you were stone cold dead three minutes back—before things went to Hell."

"Right... Status?"

They looked at each other, and that kind of pissed me off. I was functional. I was still in command.

Taking a deep breath and a stim, I gave my head a shake.

That was a bad idea. I closed my eyes and groaned in pain.

"Okay," I said. "I take it we're all that's left except for a few other stragglers. What are we going to do now?"

Opening my eyes again, I saw them all staring at me and one another. They didn't have a clue.

"Since you're in bad shape, McGill," Centurion Mills said, "I'll take over. You're senior to me, but I'm definitely in possession of all my faculties."

"Uh... what? Oh... okay, sure. Take your best shot."

Slumping on my back, I closed my eyes again. But I still listened in.

"What are we going to do?" Natasha asked. "Those things will find us. We can't sit in an ammo compartment for days."

"Don't panic," Mills insisted. "We'll be fine if we keep our wits."

"That's not our mission," Sargon said.

"What?"

"We're supposed to attract attention, round up all the machines we can and let *Legate* blow them away. Sitting here and not panicking—that's against orders."

My eyes fluttered open. I sat up. "Sargon is right. We're getting out of here."

Heaving myself up again, I headed for the strange door. It seemed to have tufts of fur on it… disgusting.

I reached out for the bony release that opened it, but Mills put her hand over mine.

"McGill," she said in a soft tone. "The missiles already came down. We saw the flashes in the distance. That's partly why—why we decided to take shelter in here. There's a fallout cloud outside, and God knows what else."

My mouth sagged low. I looked at her in disbelief, but after I saw the expression there, I was convinced.

They'd nuked the aliens after all? Graves had said he was trying to avoid that… but worse our small group had been so far out of position he'd missed us anyway.

"I get it now…" Mills said. "That was why Graves ordered us to head back into danger, back toward the LZ. He wanted to make a clean sweep of things."

"Yes," I said. "That's what he told me."

"That prick…"

I didn't argue. I looked back at the others instead. They had haunted eyes. I especially felt for Natasha. Once, long ago, she'd been exiled from Earth because they'd made a copy of her by accident. Unable to go home for fear of execution, she'd stayed on Dust World for a decade.

Now, we were in a similar situation. If they revived us back on *Legate*, then there would be two copies of all of us. We'd all be twins. On the other hand, if they didn't have confirmation of our deaths, they'd let us rot down here.

If we got killed now—well, that might mean we were permed.

"This sucks," Sargon said suddenly, and with feeling.

I had to agree with his sentiment.

-39-

It didn't take long before I made a crucial decision. Normally, Centurion Mills might have been expected to take over, as I was in bad shape—but she had a few decades less experience than I did.

Painfully, I dragged myself to my feet again and went outside.

Behind me, the others were calling out. I could tell they'd just as soon sit in this dark, gross hole and hope for rescue—but I wasn't interested.

The tank-creature was dying around us. It had given up running on its broken treads. The eyeballs on the turrets and the eyes that moved them still operated, after a fashion. They swiveled and tried to track me as I exited the machine-hybrid, but they couldn't get a good shot.

I imagined the tank would normally have slid around and run over any impudent weasel like myself. If the tank had been healthy, daring to get in so close the guns couldn't target me would have meant certain death—but this tank wasn't doing any fancy maneuvers today.

Lighting up my tapper, I beamed a note to Graves. It wasn't much, just a coordinate ping and a basic sitrep.

After that, I turned to go back into the tank. There were worried faces looking out at me.

"You'll be seen," Natasha said. "Get back in here, McGill."

"He doesn't care if he's seen," Sargon said, stepping out into the open. He blinked and flipped his visor open—but after getting a whiff of the stinking machine we were hugging up against, he changed his mind in a hurry and flipped it closed again. A mild coughing fit ensued.

"What a horrible smell," he complained.

"McGill?" Mills said sharply. "Did you... did you send a message?"

"Sure did."

"My tapper is lighting up," Natasha said.

"Mine too," Sargon said.

They were all getting a message.

"It says: 'hold your position. Help on the way.'"

"Hmm..." I said, not liking the sound of that. "Natasha, give me your kit. I need more power to uplink to *Legate* from here."

Biting her lip, she came outside and hooked me up. I used her tech specialist's more powerful computer and power supply to reach out to orbit.

"McGill?" Graves asked, coming online. My tapper was cracked, but it still worked.

"Yes sir. McGill here, reporting in. We've made a very significant find. You'll want to—"

"Just hold tight. Don't move from those coordinates. Bird is in-bound."

"Uh..." I said, knowing exactly what that meant.

Often, officers found it expedient to kill troops who were stragglers rather than commit resources to a rescue mission.

"That might not be the best plan, sir. Take a look at what we've captured."

Using my tapper's camera, I panned around, showing the tank.

"Is that one of the enemy armor units?" Graves asked.

"That's right, sir. Disabled, but still alive. We could study it—it sure would be nice to know what we're up against..."

Graves seemed to think it over. "Dammit... all right. This better not be bullshit, McGill. I'm dispatching a lifter. Be ready to board with your prize and deliver the briefing of your life when you haul it back up to *Legate*. Graves out."

I whistled long and low through cracked lips. "Kids, you all owe me your lives today. We're getting a first-class rescue."

"A lifter?" Sargon said doubtfully. "Sir, that's nice and all, but I'm not sure it's such a good idea. This robot, here... he might put a hole in the lifter when it lands."

"Oh God," Mills said. "He's right. You aren't thinking right, Centurion."

"He's thinking just fine," Sargon muttered. "The problem isn't brain-damage. He's just dumb."

Centurion Mills shot him a dark glance. She didn't like enlisted men talking shit about their officers, I could tell that right off.

The thing was, however, Sargon was correct in this case. I hadn't thought my plan through completely. In fact, calling my little scheme a 'plan' at all was kind of extreme.

"Hmm..." I said, then I looked at Natasha. "Can we disable these guns somehow? Without killing the tank?"

"I'm not sure."

She got down on her back and slid under the treads. She vanished underneath the monster a moment later.

"What's she doing?" Mills asked.

"Don't worry!" I told her. "If a broken machine can be fixed, Natasha can do it. She'll patch it, muzzle it, and spay it by morning."

"We haven't got until morning," Sargon pointed out. "We've got maybe thirty-five minutes."

In the end, that turned out to be cutting things pretty close. When the lifter landed, the eyeballs still sighted and the arms still aimed—but the guns didn't fire. She'd severed the nerve to the guns that carried the critical impulse.

Dragging her out from under the vehicle by her feet, we stood her up and marched her aboard the lifter. A pack of wary techs came the other way, staring at my prize with huge eyes.

"Now, don't go and mark up my pet!" I admonished them. "He's not house-trained, but he's worth a lot to the brass."

Nervously, the techs circled the monster and applied grav-clamps to lift it from the mud. Soon, they began to guide it toward the lifter's cargo ramp.

Right about then, the tank must have figured out it was being captured. It spun broken treads. The turrets swung wildly, and those eyeballs—they were peeled back to the whites.

But despite all this, we got the thing aboard and lifted off into space. I took a prime window seat on the top deck, where the brass normally hung out. With a grateful sigh, I sunk into a seat with some actual padding on it.

Other than crewmen, there weren't any officers aboard. Just me and Centurion Jennie Mills. I didn't waste any time hitting on her.

"Hey," I said. "Where do you want to go tonight?"

She blinked at me uncomprehendingly.

"Um… I was daydreaming about a hot meal and a hot shower, actually."

My eyebrows shot up and I grinned. "That's pretty direct—but I like it! We can—"

"Wait a second, McGill," she said sternly, having caught onto my meaning. "That wasn't an invitation."

"No? Oh… I thought we had a deal. I guessed your name right when I first met you, didn't I?"

"Well… yes." She looked down a little sheepishly.

"Well then, I'm asking you out. Point-blank. Yes or no, Centurion?"

She seemed to think about it. Then she sighed. "All right. If you don't die from internal injuries tonight… we can go on a date."

"Always hedging your bets, huh? Come on, have a drink with me. I know they keep liquor in the officer's lounge for special occasions."

"That cabinet is locked, McGill."

There was a popping sound. "All fixed," I said, and I poured us each a foam cup full of sherry. It tasted like it'd been in the cupboard a long time, but I didn't care.

Jennie didn't seem to care much, either. We had a few, and we were smiling by the time the lifter reached *Legate*.

When we docked, Centurion Mills was leaning against me and giggling. My cracked ribs were crying about that, but I didn't let on. Whining about the pain would have ruined the mood.

The seals on the lounge door cracked open, gaining our attention. Jennie straightened up, causing me to wince again.

A suited figure entered the chamber. It was Primus Winslade.

"Hey, Winslade," I said. "Care to join us for a celebration?"

"What's this?" he asked. "Are you drunk on duty, McGill? Again?"

"Not at all, sir. I'm off-duty. I'm overdue for some Blue Deck patching-up and a little R&R."

Winslade laughed. It was a nasty sound.

"Dream on, McGill. We're in trouble. Haven't you been following all the briefings and bulletins flowing from the ship's network onto your tapper?"

"Certainly sir, every word of it."

"Of course you haven't. Turn your tapper back on, switch off the mute button, and pay attention. We have company. Grand Admiral Sateekas is here in-system. He has an entire task force, actually, and he's moving to engage that giant cue-ball out there."

"Really? That *is* big news."

I got up and rushed out of the place. To my surprise, Centurion Mills looked kind of disappointed.

That was just like Winslade. The man was a force of nature when it came to cock-blocking others. He was cold rain on every parade in town.

-40-

Winslade turned out to be right. Sateekas *was* in the Pegasi system, and he had a new fleet of ships with him.

His new fleet was small and not too impressive. Compared to our province's mighty Battle Fleet 921, this collection of aging cruisers was almost an embarrassment—but it was better than nothing.

"There you are, McGill," Graves said when I arrived on Gold Deck. "You've been incognito as usual, right when we need you most."

"Those are some mighty kind words, sir," I told him. "What seems to be the emergency?"

Graves gestured toward the battle-planning room. I wasn't normally allowed into that vaunted chamber, but this was an exception.

Following him inside, I saw all the brass was there. Armel, Turov, even Praetor Drusus was there—but he was just a hologram transmitted over from the second transport ship.

"Ah, McGill shows up at last," Drusus said. "Wait—are you injured? Can you stand and think, McGill?"

"I'm right as rain, sir," I said, trying not to sway on my feet. Fortunately, the sherry I'd drunk had taken the edge off my pounding headache and grinding ribs.

"Excellent. We'll contact Sateekas, then."

"Um…" Turov said, eyeing me critically. "Perhaps we should wait until McGill has been checked out by a bio—or at least briefed."

"There's no need. Communications, patch the channel through."

The screen flared up between us and the most god-awful looking lump of flesh I'd seen all day squatted there. It was a hologram of Grand Admiral Sateekas.

Now, all of us knew his real title was Province Governor, or Chief Inspector—something mundane like that. But we dared not use those words. Sateekas had been demoted from the admiralty and reassigned to a civilian post, but he didn't want anyone to remind him of these unpleasant realities.

"Grand Admiral!" I boomed. "Great to see you again, Your Highness!"

Sateekas was facing away from me, but he shuffled his bulk around to gaze down in my direction.

That frontal exposure made me wince—he sure wasn't getting any prettier.

Like all Mogwa, Sateekas had a spidery body with a central thorax, a thin-skulled head, and six limbs that could operate as arms or legs depending on the task at hand. But what was shocking about him was his age.

Sateekas was *old*. Humans aged pretty badly, in my opinion, but this Mogwa put us to shame in that department. He had flappy jowls, a thorax that had changed from a sleek black to a mottled white, and a dozen other disgusting signs of advanced years.

"Is it…?" he asked, peering my way. "Yes! The McGill-creature! It has been a long time. You are a favorite slaveling, and you have doubtlessly pined away for me during my absence."

"I sure did, sir. All Humanity has spent loads of idle time waiting for you to return. We've been muddling along, doing our best to enforce the will of the Galactics in this frontier province."

Sateekas flapped his limbs for a moment before answering. "It seems that in this instance, you have failed your Empire. These intruders must be removed."

234

"Uh…" I said, glancing around at Turov and Armel.

They both looked a little bit sick, and it occurred to me that maybe I shouldn't haven't opened my big mouth and engaged our haughty governor immediately—but that couldn't be fixed now. He was staring right at me, expecting me to say something meaningful.

"Is that why you brought this new battle fleet here, Grand Admiral? Have you come to drive these aliens away?"

Sateekas worked his limbs idly and eyed me. "This is hardly a battle fleet. I have twelve ships, not twelve hundred. True, they are new ships, not broken down rust buckets, but still…"

"Perhaps if we combine our forces?" I suggested.

"McGill!" Turov hissed at me. "Shut up!"

Sateekas drew himself up proudly. "The Empire doesn't require a militia fleet to maintain her borders, McGill. We shall… we shall remove this intruder ourselves!"

Everyone looked astonished at this announcement. That included the humans, the Mogwa officers behind Sateekas, and even the Nairbs I saw on the cruiser's bridge. They were trying to pretend they weren't listening in—but they all turned and stared when Sateekas committed them to battle.

"That's the spirit, sir!" I boomed.

"What means have you employed in previous encounters?" the Mogwa asked me.

Turov made a frantic waggling motion with her hands, and I returned her wave with a friendly gesture of my own.

"Well sir, it went like this…"

I proceeded to spill my guts. I held nothing back, telling all about our t-bomb attacks, our teleport suit commando mission—the works.

The situation was Turov's fault, to my way of thinking. After all, she'd insisted I come right up to Gold Deck without letting me stop off at Blue Deck where I really belonged. The truth was, my brain hadn't been operating at a hundred percent of its admittedly limited capacity since I'd experienced a concussion the day before.

Sateekas listened and took it all in while the rest of them squirmed.

"Hmm…" he said. "I… I have a suspicion. A dark suspicion… I'd assumed all along this ship was from the frontier, something those squalid little bear-people from Rigel might build."

"We thought the same, Grand Admiral."

"But now, I doubt my presumptions. The technology you describe is quite advanced. To my knowledge, no species out here on the galactic rim should be capable of producing such a ship. Collapsed matter formed into a hull the size of a planetoid? That is truly unprecedented outside the Core Systems. No, we would have heard of such a threat rising on the fringe of the Galaxy…"

"But you're still going to kick their asses, aren't you?" I demanded.

"Grand Admiral!" Turov burst out, unable to keep her peace any longer. "Don't listen to McGill. He's injured. He's on… medications. We don't believe your force is sufficient to defeat the intruder."

Sateekas looked at me, and then he eyed Turov in turn. "Sometimes a sacrifice is required for the good of the Empire. Today, I'm willing to make that sacrifice. I will transmit a message to Trantor first, and to your ship as well for safekeeping. Wish us well, slaves."

"Farewell, Grand Admiral," Turov said in a defeated tone.

"Kick their asses, Sateekas!" I shouted.

The channel closed, and Turov came at me immediately. Now, I'm not so good at reading a woman's mood. But those little fists, down at her side and trembling, gave me a hint. Her face was red and kind of twisted up, too…

"You shouldn't make expressions like that, Galina," I said. "What if your face stayed like that?"

"You *asshole!*" she shouted. "Why couldn't you keep quiet?"

Turov whirled around toward Drusus, Graves and Armel. "And you three—what a lot of help you were. You were three mutes while McGill went full-retard and talked Sateekas into a suicidal attack!"

Graves spoke first. "It wasn't my place to interfere."

"It wasn't McGill's either," Turov snapped back.

"Galina..." Drusus said—or rather his quiet hologram spoke for him, "we were in a difficult position. When we talk to the Mogwa, it's Earth policy to allow lower-level individuals to engage in actual conversation."

"Yes, yes, yes," she said disgustedly. "Plausible deniability, I know. You can always execute McGill and call him a renegade officer. And I know that if his words came out of your mouth, Drusus any insult might cause our entire species to be blamed, as you are a top Earth official. I know the theory, but the stakes were too high this time."

"How so?" Armel asked in a mild tone. "These hysterics are... if I dare... unbecoming for a tribune. So what if the Mogwa dies? Another governor will be sent from Trantor eventually. It is no great loss for Earth."

Galina approached him and put a finger in his face. "Wrong, Armel. First of all, you were only thinking of yourself when you kept quiet. What's the old saying? Mutes are never permed first?"

"Something like that..." he admitted.

"The difference here is that Sateekas is in the middle of reconstructing Battle Fleet 921. He dearly wants to be an admiral again—our defensive admiral. He's pulled together a handful of shiny new ships, but what is the likelihood of him getting full funding if he's dead—and he's lost all his ships *again*?"

Armel tilted his head and gave her a sneering shrug. "I will admit that situation may be difficult to recover from."

"Right..." She stalked away.

While she'd been yelling at the other brass, I'd begun to feel a little funny. I'd found a seat to collapse into.

Someone sent a bio around to check on me eventually, but by that time, I'd passed out.

-41-

"You've got to be kidding me," I croaked when I awoke to bright lights and strange sounds an unknowable time later.

I'd been recycled and reborn. Take it from someone who knew every sight and sound of the process—that's what they'd done.

Groaning, I climbed off the gurney and struggled to dress. They shoved me in a shower stall first, and I washed off.

It was a good idea, on one level. I felt better when I got out of the shower and managed to get my uniform on right.

But then on another level, it kind of pissed me off. These bio people could have patched me up.

"Hey," I said to the specialist who'd presided over my birth. "Why the recycle? Couldn't I have been given a shot of bone-grow and nu-skin?"

She shrugged. "Probably. But your tribune ordered a fresh start. She was very clear on that point. She said you had to have all your brain cells switched on the next time she met you."

"That's what I thought. Spite. Petty revenge... Dammit."

When I marched out, I was in a bad mood all over again. Working my tapper, I managed to get Galina to answer. That was a surprise all by itself.

"Hey," I began, "why did you—?"

"McGill? You're back in the game? Good. Get up here to Gold Deck immediately."

238

The connection closed. I was left in an irritable state.

With a sigh and a shrug, I began a shambling trot toward the elevators. By the time I reached them, I could almost run straight.

There was something in Galina's voice. A note of real worry—of fear. That feeling had come through loud and clear. Despite all my anger, I put my emotions on hold and decided to play the part of a dedicated supporting officer for now.

When I arrived on Gold Deck, I was challenged by noncom guards. They let me through a moment later.

Up on the bridge and the tactical CNC next to it, the chambers were crammed with officers.

They were all looking up, craning their necks. In their midst was a central holographic image. It was so high-resolution it was as if the fleets outside had been shrunken down and placed near the lofty ceiling for our viewing pleasure.

Center-stage was a big grayish-white cue ball I knew too well. It was the alien invasion ship. This time, it had no visible damage other than a few scorch marks. You couldn't even tell where that big roll-away door was. They'd repaired it completely.

That's what they'd been doing all this time, I realized. The ship hadn't even moved. It had just sat up there, fixing itself with the help of the Peg automated repair vessels. In the meantime, we'd destroyed a lot of their machines down on the planet's surface—but this big bastard hadn't even reacted.

So strange… I knew a lot of aliens, but these folks were a different breed. They didn't operate like living things. They didn't have the same normal responses to injured allies. It was as if the ship were only interested in itself, not the invasion forces it seeded on planets.

Sateekas was on an attack vector from on high. He'd swung around 51 Pegasi, coming at the strange vessel from an oblique angle. From our point of view, he appeared to be above it.

Turov spotted me at this point. She worked her way through the crowd easily. Her rank, more than her bulk, caused people to step out of her way.

"I hope you're happy," she said. "You're about to watch Sateekas die for his honor."

"Honor?"

"That's right. Don't tell me you don't know what you did to him. You embarrassed him. You declared your willingness to die, and you explained how you'd already done it twice. Then you asked if he had the balls to do the same. He's just vain enough to fall for that kind of twaddle."

"Twaddle...?"

She didn't answer me. She was standing at my side, gazing up at the fleet action again.

Normally, when one group of ships in a system attacked another, they came in fast and hard—but not old Sateekas. Maybe he knew a thing or two about dealing with fully-automated enemy ships. He was edging closer, keeping every ship at exactly the same range. When the enemy finally took notice and responded—that's when he'd fire. Not a moment earlier.

"What if they're baiting him in closer?" I asked aloud.

Galina pinched my arm then.

"Hey!"

She glared up at me. "You think about that while you watch good crews die today."

I rubbed the spot she'd pinched absently. My mom did the exact same thing to my dad when she was pissed at him. I found the thought disturbing. Were we a couple? Sometimes, that was a very hard question to answer.

The fireworks began at a range of about sixty thousand kilometers. That was pretty close by our standards. A big ship couldn't light a match with a laser at more than two million kilometers—but sixty thousand? That was point-blank.

The big ship didn't open its doors, but it did begin to slowly rotate. I corrected myself even as I had this thought. It was so fast that the motion only appeared to be slow. In actuality, it was turning very rapidly.

Sateekas didn't wait around for the enemy guns to get into optimal firing positions. He unloaded.

Right off, I was impressed. Beams lanced out, scorching long furrows on the spinning sphere. An ass-load of missiles came out of every Mogwa ship. They were all heavy cruisers, and they sent a screaming barrage toward the enemy mass.

For several minutes, all this abuse went unanswered. The big ship was just turning, like a giant who's finally noticed a buzzing swarm of gnats overhead.

Finally, the big ship returned fire. A gush of fire leapt out without warning, catching one of the cruisers and incinerating it on the spot.

I whistled long and low.

"Damn!" I said. "That was quite a shot."

Galina punched my arm, but I didn't really feel it.

The big ship had stopped rotating. After firing a concentrated barrage at one ship, I got the feeling it was charging up to do it again.

The Mogwa ships started to dance, then. It was something I hadn't seen since the Rogue World ship had done it years back.

"Hey!" I shouted. "They've got a program of little random teleports going! Just like Floramel's gang did way back."

There was some mild cheering as the second barrage reached out from the invading ship—and missed. The Mogwa ships were popping around every few seconds, making targeting almost impossible.

"You see?" I demanded, flicking my fingers at Galina. "These Mogwa crews aren't losers. They've got new, state of the art ships from the Core Worlds."

"This ship they're facing isn't primitive either, James," she said eyeing me.

I frowned. She knew something. She knew more about this ship than she should have known. That worried me more than anything else.

Back in the day, Galina had been quite the schemer. She'd tried to take over Earth on several occasions among other, darker crimes.

The battle, such as it was, continued. The big ship fired several more times, about once every minute, while the Mogwa ships kept dodging and stabbing burn-holes into the monster that stalked them. They weren't doing much damage, but they weren't dying—until everything shifted again.

"Dammit..." Graves said under his breath.

241

The rest of us collectively gasped. Another of the heavy cruisers was caught and embroiled in flame. It wasn't a clean, direct hit, but it was enough to send them into a spin.

"They're venting," Winslade said. "That ship is a goner."

"How did they figure out the algorithm so fast?" Winslade asked. "The Mogwa jump-pattern appears to be completely random."

"It never is," Galina said tightly. "Not really. Random to a computer is predicable—if you figure out the software."

"That fast?" Winslade asked. "How could they…?"

Galina shrugged. "The enemy isn't natural AI. It is… advanced."

Graves gave her a long squinty-eyed stare after that exchange. He was beginning to suspect her, too. I could tell.

"The Mogwa missiles have reached the hull!" someone shouted.

That surprised me. It had been quite a while since they'd first been fired, but then again, it takes a missile a lot longer to travel sixty thousand kilometers than it takes a beam of light.

The strikes were impressive. Those warheads…

"Antimatter?" I asked aloud.

"It must be," Winslade said, his tone hushed.

We were all overawed, because these warheads were something else again. It wasn't the fact of their composition, it was their yield that made a hushed silence fall over the audience while we watched.

"Gigatons…" Graves said. "A lot of gigatons."

The whole face of the moon-like ship was ablaze now—in fact, it was pushed back some. I couldn't believe it, but the raining impacts were actually *pushing* the moon-sized giant away from the attacking fleet. The amount of energy released was fantastic to behold.

"We're totally outclassed…" Drusus said. He was back, in hologram form. He looked like a ghost, and he sounded like one too. "Nothing in our fleet could stand up for five minutes against either of these forces."

No one argued with him. We were glued to the projections.

"They could have shredded Earth at any moment," I said. "Why didn't they?"

"That's not what they came out here to do," Turov told me.

The giant, armored sphere finally seemed concerned at last. That missile barrage had gotten their full attention. Moving away and spinning to present a fresh side to the attacking fleet, the monster ship didn't retreat—but they did put some distance between themselves and the Mogwa ships.

"Things are going to get ugly now..." Galina said.

She gripped my arm. That was a surprise, and I almost pulled away, fearing another vicious pinch—but it didn't come. It might be an unconscious reaction, but she seemed to want some physical contact. I reflected on the fact our relationship had always been a damned strange one.

Moments later, a bad thing *did* happen.

Three of the Mogwa ships blew up in rapid succession.

"T-bombs!" Winslade said. "It has to be. Inserted right into their guts, right through their shields and their dodging... remarkable."

The Mogwa ships all vanished a moment later.

"Where'd they go?" I demanded. "Are they running? Did they blow up?"

"No..." Winslade said, working the console. "They appear to have teleported farther than I would have given them credit for. In fact... there they are. We've picked them up again on our sensors."

The ships reappeared on the hologram projection a moment later—and they were all around us.

Galina yelped. That was the only word I had to describe it. She sounded like a small dog when you step on it.

She ripped her hands off of my bicep, and I don't mind telling you her nails left a few curvy lines behind.

"Drusus!" she called out. "Get us out of here! Withdraw, flank speed!"

"Are they attacking us?" Winslade asked.

"No, but the invader is fully engaged now. It's guilt by association. We're about to be destroyed, trust me!"

Drusus' hologram turned toward Galina. "Helm, withdraw in good order. Take us to the far side of the planet."

"No, no," Galina said. "You have to warp out, right now!"

Drusus' wavering form regarded her. "There's something you're not telling me, Tribune. Would you care to explain your intimate knowledge of—"

"There's no time!" she screamed.

Just then, a strange brilliance lit up the bridge. It was from space, I could tell that. A light so bright it shone right through the portholes and maybe the hull itself.

Drusus' image blinked out.

"*Aeternum* has been destroyed..." Winslade said in a shocked voice. "She's gone. Legion Solstice is gone... Drusus is gone. There's nothing but radiation and—"

"Shut up!" Turov shouted. "Crew, as the most senior officer left alive in this expedition, I order you to go to warp— *now!*"

Armel looked as shocked as anyone else. He was a tribune as well, but he wasn't as senior as Turov was. He nodded.

"I concur. Helm, get us the hell out of here."

Legate heeled over and began to flee. We nosed toward open space and home, hopefully.

A few seconds later, before they could engage the warp bubble, a glare lit up the bridge again.

Were we hit? It was all I could think of.

What a way to get myself permed...

-42-

Fortunately, although we'd all gotten a nice dose of hard gamma rays, we were still alive.

"Sateekas..." Winslade said. "His flagship has blown up."

He sounded stunned. For him, that was an unusual tone. He normally didn't give a rat's ass if anyone died—other than himself.

"Get us into warp—now!" Turov ordered.

Within ninety seconds, *Legate* generated a warp bubble and slid away into space. We felt mildly safe for the first time in days.

Everyone felt safe, that is, except for me.

Turov's eyes had turned into slits. She rounded on me, and she might have landed a fist on my cheek if I hadn't reached up a hand to block her.

That was a mistake, because she hurt her wrist on my hand, and then she got *really* pissed. She pulled out a pistol.

"Aw now, come on," I said. "I just got out of Blue Deck ten minutes ago."

"And you've earned your way back there already!"

"Tribune," Armel said. "I know how you feel—believe me, I do. You are in command... but I'm not sure if executing McGill now is the best choice."

She turned to look at him, and I thought for a second she would gun him down instead. But then, with a roar of anger, she spun on her heel and shoved her pistol back into its holster. She marched away into the main passage.

Armel approached me with a grin floating under that thin mustache.

"I think that you missed your calling in life, McGill," he said. "You should have been born a court jester. A fool who lives at the sufferance of those he mocks."

"Yeah...?" I said, turning his words over in my mind once, then twice. I was pretty sure I'd been insulted, but I wasn't clear on how, exactly.

"Thanks for speaking up, Armel," I told him.

"Think nothing of it. Right now, she is a woman in a rage. If she were to kill you, nothing would be solved. Worse, she would be forced to identify a new target for her frustrations."

"Oh..." I said, catching on. "You intervened so she could kick me around again later—instead of you?"

"It was a risk, I admit," he agreed. "But what I said is true. Come, we should get down to Blue Deck."

"Huh...? why?"

"Because our new leader should be coming out shortly. Check with your contacts—I know you keep them at every critical station."

I frowned at him, not exactly sure what he was talking about. I did, however, have plenty of friends on Blue Deck. Mostly, they were women I'd hit on repeatedly, a few I'd dated...

Sending out several quick texts, I got a response from a gossipy bio on Blue Deck. She liked to tell people who was being revived—if it was someone important.

"An alien?" I said aloud.

Armel tossed me a knowing smile over his shoulder. He must have people down there too—people he'd bribed, or threatened. He didn't have any friends to the best of my knowledge.

"I thought you meant Drusus was coming out," I said. "He should be the next in line since *Aeternum* blew up."

Armel made tsking sounds and shook his head, like I was some new and advanced variety of moron. He did that a lot.

246

"Such a lack of imagination," he said. "First of all, it should be obvious that Drusus would never be popping back out of the oven so quickly. Turov seems quite worked up about recent events, and she's very recently inherited command. Surely, you can see that she isn't eager to remove herself from that lofty position so soon."

"Uh... okay. But if it's not Drusus, who is it? You said 'our new leader' I don't miss a trick when it comes to something like that."

"No, you certainly don't. Let's use a bit of logic, shall we?"

"Logic?"

"Yes. Try it, McGill. Do your best. I wish to be amused— or possibly amazed."

"Uh... well, let's see... there are other officers back on Earth that might be considered a new leader. Various imperators and equestrians... But they wouldn't be coming out on Blue Deck, they'd come to Gray Deck, using the gateway posts."

Armel made that annoying tsking sound again. "Failure. Not even an amusing failure. You've disappointed me, McGill. Too bad the game is finished, as we are here at the very gates of Blue Deck."

Eyeing the sealed pressure doors and the unsmiling bio guards who watched our approach, I was suddenly struck with an idea. I stopped dead in my tracks.

"You don't mean... You didn't revive Sateekas, did you?"

Armel turned toward me with a shitty grin. "Ah-ha! You have redeemed yourself!"

"That file he sent... he was talking about his own body-scans, his engrams, right? But can we print out a new Mogwa? I thought these machines were charged with materials for human organics."

Armel waved off the two bio guards, who reluctantly retreated. They knew not to mess with a tribune.

"Such things can be fixed in desperate times," he said, "and recent events have proven desperate indeed, have they not?"

Not sure what Armel's game was, I began to grow suspicious. He was the kind of tricky officer who couldn't be trusted. Galina was the same way, but she always had lofty goals. Armel's were usually... personal.

Reaching down to my tapper, I muted the speaker and cranked up the microphone. Then, I tapped the record button.

"So," I said loudly, "let me get this straight, you tricky old bastard!"

He paused in the hallway, frowning. I'd stopped walking and grinned at him hugely.

"You pulled this whole thing off, didn't you?" I demanded.

"Do not be absurd."

"Aw, come on. You're just being shy. I stand impressed! You just brought me along to witness to your masterful maneuvers, isn't that right?"

Armel looked slightly proud. He loved praise. "Well... yes. Come now, let's be going. Sateekas is due to be reborn—"

"Hold on, hold on," I said, laughing and touching his shoulder briefly.

His eyes glanced at my hand with extreme disapproval, and I dropped it immediately. My grin was as wide as I could make it.

"Why'd you do it?" I asked in a hissing whisper. My tapper was up high, as if I was holding my hands up between us in a gesture of supplication. In reality I was trying to make sure I caught every word he said.

"Don't you want to see our Mogwa overlord live again?" Armel asked. "He's our governor, and he seems to be your personal friend, McGill."

Having heard enough, I tapped the stop recording button on my tapper, then hit transmit. The file went straight to Galina.

Unfortunately, Armel had quick eyes and a quick mind. He hadn't missed my move, and he knew what it meant. I'd ratted him out.

"What's this? You sent my confession to Turov?"

"Sure did. She's on her way here, right now."

"Treachery!" he said, hissing like a stomped snake. "I should never have brought you along."

"I guess not," I told him.

Unexpectedly, Armel's frown faded away. He reversed his expression, and in moments he was smiling again. I realized then that his rage had been fake.

"Uh... what's going on?" I asked.

"You have been most helpful," he said. "I thought you'd have to see the Mogwa's feet sticking out before you caught on. But no, you followed my clues and came to the conclusion I needed you to reach."

"What the hell?" I asked. "Are you telling me you wanted me to tattle on you? Why?"

"Because," he said, "I knew that if I asked Turov to come here with me, she'd suspect something and hesitate. But not with you serving as her spy. She trusts you, in an odd way."

I opened my mouth to ask another question, but I never got it out.

Armel must have had a needler in the palm of his hand. He shot me dead without warning.

-43-

It's my firm belief that there comes a moment in every man's life when enough is enough. When I groaned awake sometime later, I felt I'd reached that delicate tipping point.

Long familiarity with the revival process helped me out. I couldn't see, but I could hear them talking. I couldn't move fast or accurately, but I knew my surroundings very well. I'd memorized the layout of your typical revival room by this time in my endless parade of existences.

Under the table I was on, for instance, I knew there was a drawer. It had a stainless steel pull-handle, and it was full of interesting things.

One of them was a scalpel. Another was a pair of razor-sharp surgical scissors. These instruments could be used for lots of things, but they were generally employed to cut the umbilical on a fresh grow.

My fumbling fingers discovered the drawer was ajar. I reasoned that umbilical-severing step of the operation had already been performed by the bio people who stood over me.

My hand slid inside the drawer, and I closed it on the scissors. I didn't have much of a grip, but I didn't need strength now—I needed the element of surprise.

"What kind of numbers do we have?" a female bio asked.

"It doesn't matter," said a familiar, French-accented male voice. "This man is standing trial. He's about to be found guilty and executed."

"I'm sorry, sir," the bio said coldly. "But no matter what your plans are, I have to enter an Apgar score on every birth."

The Frenchman sighed. "Very well, proceed with your formalities."

Armel. That was definitely his voice—I hadn't recognized it at first because my mind was still floating, just a little.

A blinding light shined in my eyes. It was painful.

"He's a nine. Maybe a nine and a half. An excellent grow."

Armel clucked his tongue. "A pity, then. You did your best work to no purpose."

I needed him to come close, so I stashed the scissors under my butt, then reached into the drawer again. I rattled it, making sure it made some noise.

"What's this?" Armel demanded.

Three quick steps. He crossed the room, and I could feel the heat of him, standing over my nude, sticky body.

"Sir, if you would please—"

"No, I will not! He is attempting to arm himself. Such incompetence! I should have—"

I never found out what Armel should have done, because about then he made a funny choking sound.

"Oh God!" the bio screeched.

Equipment clattered to the floor, and she ran. I could hear her steps and her cries for help.

In the meantime, I opened my bleary eyes and sat up. I couldn't see Armel very well, but I figured he could see me. He was on his knees next to the table, with a pair of scissors sticking out of his neck.

"Damnation!" I said, grinning down at him. "I'm mighty sorry about that, sir. You just can't go sneaking up on a Varus legionnaire. Safety first, I always say."

Armel's hand was still moving around. I figured he might have been digging for his needler, so I kicked him a hard one. He went over on his back, and he didn't get back up.

Standing and stretching, I reached down and pulled his hand out of his pocket. Sure enough, he had a needler secreted in his palm.

About a minute later, something like eight orderlies rushed me. They pushed me up against the wall, but as I was unarmed

251

and buck naked, they gave me a second to explain. I pointed out the needler, and the fact that Armel had recently killed Galina Turov.

"Look," I argued, "I was just revived. You boys don't think I came back to life with that needler stuck up my ass, now do you?"

They hemmed and hawed after that. I'd guessed rightly that Galina was dead. After I demanded loudly that they bring Graves down to sort things out, they finally relented and did exactly that.

I watched them all closely even after Graves arrived. Bio people can be snakes of the worst variety, and I still didn't know who exactly was in on this conspiracy.

"McGill?" Graves asked me in a tired voice. "Why have I been pulled down here only to find you standing over a superior officer's corpse—again?"

"He's a scoundrel, Primus! He killed Turov, and he tried to off me again the moment I caught a revive."

That was enough for Graves to launch an investigation. He liked the rule book, and he always followed it—always.

Naturally, I wasn't given my freedom during this time. For hours on end, I was left in one of those smocks that leave your ass hanging in the breeze.

When Graves finally returned to the Blue Deck holding cell for mental cases, he eyed me like he still thought I belonged in that particular cage.

"Primus? I was right, wasn't I?"

"You were... it seems that the moment *Aeternum* was destroyed, Armel decided to mutiny. I'm not sure why, he's been a talented officer for decades."

"Maybe we should revive him and beat the truth out of him."

"I suggest the same plan for you," Graves said coldly, "but I know it wouldn't work. Come on!"

I walked after him out the door, and he did a double-take.

"Put some clothes on first, Centurion," he ordered.

Happy to get out of my medical prison, I kitted myself out in dress blues, complete with a beret—but no sidearm. Graves

252

wasn't sure what was what yet, and he didn't trust me for some reason.

That was the problem with developing a certain reputation over time. A man might be mistaken for a criminal just because he had had questionable associations in his past. It was purely unfair.

Following Graves, I couldn't help but notice the four noncoms that fell into step behind me.

"A lack of trust in your top supporting officers is a terrible thing, sir," I complained.

"You're alive, aren't you? Stop bitching."

Graves wasn't a warm man. He was fair—usually—but never warm. I guess I had to take the good with the bad.

We went to Gold Deck, and I had the rare treat of attending a trial where I wasn't the defendant. Instead, Armel sat in chains.

They'd done everything but nail him down to a steel chair. There were even a few lumps on his face. I know it's not polite to gloat, but I couldn't help giving him a smile, a nod, and touch of the cap as I took my seat among the other officers present.

I noticed Galina wasn't there. Neither was Deech or Drusus.

Hmm… Armel outranked Graves. The old primus must be in a pretty paranoid state to run a trial solo.

"McGill, let's hear your testimony," Graves said.

"This is a charade," Armel said before I could do more than open my big mouth. "You bring in a star witness that hates me? What will this prove?"

I started talking anyway, and I blathered on for a time, I detailed what I'd seen, and when I'd seen it. Fortunately, there were body cams and the like to back me up. Graves had been thorough in gathering evidence.

"I never thought you would go down this path, Graves," Armel said when I'd finished. "At least have the decency to admit you're trying to rebel against Earth."

"Look Tribune, let's cut the bullshit," Graves said. "We've got the evidence. You went off the rails, and when I get Drusus to look at the data, he'll agree with me."

"But by that time, I'll already be permed, is that it?" Armel laughed. A few flecks of blood flew from his lips.

"That depends entirely on your—"

"A confession? Is that what you expect? Very well, yes, I did move against the leadership of this doomed expedition. I can say this without fear of repercussions, because all of you are as good as dead."

Graves watched him with a hooded gaze. "And why's that?"

"Because that ship out there isn't going to let any of us go. None of us. Don't you realize what it is? What power it possesses?"

"Enlighten me."

"Very well. It is a Galactic ship. A vessel from another species from the Core Worlds. It was not built by Mogwa, but rather by their greatest enemies. It will take over this Province in time. Already, it has defeated the paltry Mogwa ships they threw against its impenetrable hull. I suggest we all take our own measure, and we each adjust our minds. We are still part of the Empire. We still serve the Galactics—but we serve a different faction from the center of the galaxy from this day forward."

After this speech, my mouth hung open so low I could scarcely credit it.

"Is that true?" I asked, turning toward Graves. "Are we being annexed?"

Graves was squinting at Armel. He always did that when he looked at something he disliked.

"It might be…" he said at last.

Winslade spoke up then. He'd been sitting in the back and up until now he'd kept quiet.

"Sirs…" he said. "I think Armel is probably correct. We've gone back over the battle, the cryptic statements made by Sateekas and everything else we've got… That was no normal ship. We also know that at least two of the species who are among the upper crust of the Core Worlds are dominated by machine intelligences."

"But if it's so powerful," I demanded, "how did we drive that monster ship from Earth in the first place?"

254

"We did manage to surprise it," Armel said. "A natural response might have been to destroy our planet, but our new masters demonstrated restraint. They recognized we're a warrior species that might serve them well after annexation. Accordingly, they withdrew to make repairs and to try again. This particular species of robot is very methodical and patient, you see. They will own us eventually, if it takes them a century to complete the process."

"Won't the Mogwa fight?" I demanded.

Armel made a dismissive gesture. His chains rattled on his wrists.

"Of course they will. But you've already witnessed the likely result: total catastrophe. They threw everything they had in the province against this monstrous vessel, and they died like pigs. They will be unwilling to discard more ships to keep possession of such a distant, low-value region such as ours."

I thought all of that over, and I have to admit, I was horrified.

Graves spoke next. "I'm bringing in a greater authority," he said. "One I'm certain will be able to shed light on this situation."

Armel laughed again. "Drusus? He's a brilliant strategist, but he's weak. He'll never—"

"I didn't say it was Drusus," Graves said. "Now, Armel, tell me why you did it? Why you broke the chain of command?"

Drusus thrust his hands toward me accusingly. "You dare accuse me of this while a serial mutineer sits at your side?"

"McGill is disobedient, but he never tries to overthrow a legitimate authority. He put you down because you were breaking ranks, not him."

Armel shook his head patiently, like teacher talking to a dull student.

"You aren't getting it," he said. "The Mogwa conquered us a century ago. Today, we stand at the brink of being conquered again by their enemies. I'm not a mutineer, I'm merely foreseeing the future."

Graves snorted. "Here's what I think: you're bitter. You used to run Germanica, but they took that top legion away and saddled you with a pack of Blood Worlders. Then, they ditched you on Storm World after that campaign. You were left to rot as a garrison commander, and I think that stung your pride."

"And why shouldn't I be bitter?" Armel demanded. "Hegemony's decision was insanity—but that doesn't change the realities we're faced with today. You saw those Mogwa ships explode one after another, Graves. Open your eyes, man! We have been conquered—again."

Graves looked troubled, but then his tapper beeped. He looked up at us after reading a message.

"He's here. Open the chamber doors."

The doors swung wide, and a very odd individual entered.

To me, he looked like Chief Inspector Xlur. He was a youngish Mogwa in the prime of his life. But then, I caught sight of the insignia.

I knew Mogwa ranks, and I could usually recognize their symbols.

"Grand Admiral Sateekas?" I asked in an incredulous tone. "But... you look so *young*, sir!"

It was true. The Mogwa who strode among us with six limbs churning with a characteristically odd gait was no oldster. Gone were all the discolored wattles and drooping limbs. His body was sleek and so black it shined.

Sateekas had been revived at last, and he'd chosen to make himself young again.

-44-

"Ah, if it isn't my favorite slave," Sateekas said warmly. "It's good to see you clearly again, McGill-creature. One such as myself can look past the natural bestial appearance of your species, and today I feel no urge to wretch while in your presence."

I knew I'd just been complimented in the backhanded manner of the Mogwa.

"That's a mighty fine thing to say, sir!"

Armel rolled his eyes and blew out a puff of air as if disgusted. "So pathetic. Why don't you just lick his genitals and get it over with, McGill?"

While I gaped at Armel's rudeness, the Mogwa ambled closer to him.

"Ah... the traitor, correct?"

"Yes," Graves said. "We were interrogating him, but without much success."

"No? Perhaps I can be of some aid in this matter..."

Sateekas circled Armel, looking at him sternly.

Armel, for the perhaps the first time since we'd caught him, looked concerned.

"I'm afraid I don't know anything other than the items I've already put forth," he said. "I think your portion of the Empire is crumbling, Sateekas. Only a fool wouldn't see it—but that's only an idle opinion on my part."

257

"This beast needs to be tamed," Sateekas said, and he circled Armel one more time.

The tribune frowned in concern.

Right then, watching his behavior, I thought I might be witnessing a darker side to old Sateekas. He had a predatory cast to his features. He wasn't just an old, washed-up admiral anymore. Today he was a younger version of himself, sharp, cool and determined. He was no longer fussy and prone to pointless rages.

Finally, while he walked behind the prisoner, a quick foot-hand lashed out to slap him on the back of the knees. Armel's legs wobbled, but he didn't fall.

"I'm intrigued," Sateekas announced. "We accept this challenge. We will find out all he knows."

"We?" Graves asked.

"Yes. I ordered all your revival machines to switch over to Mogwa reproduction. My retinue is being revived now. We will require a small space, no more than a hundred meters to enjoy ourselves within. Can this be provided?"

"Um..." Graves said. "I think so."

"Graves!" Armel said. "What are you saying, man? Execute me cleanly, and I'll be on my way. I have an appointment prearranged."

Graves appeared to consider his options. "I don't have the authority to allow you to torture one of our top officers aboard an Earth ship, Sateekas, as much as he deserves it. There is no legal precedent, and it would be bad for morale."

Sateekas eyed Graves for a moment. "Uncreative, but dedicated. I shall take no offense at this rebuke. I will instead offer a compromise: Place us in one of your modules, outside your ship. No one need witness the proceedings."

Graves chewed that over, tapping on his chin with one finger.

"Graves!" Armel shouted, becoming alarmed.

"I agree," he said at last, "but under protest. I wouldn't allow such a thing if the stakes weren't so high." He waved his hand dismissively. "Take him away."

"Graves! You are a Judas! A traitor to your species! A creature of low—"

The guards hustled him out, and the door slammed. Sateekas followed into the passages.

I stepped up to the door and put my hand on the touch-lock.

"Where are you going, McGill?" Graves asked sharply.

"Oh, I thought maybe I'd listen in some…"

Graves stared at me for a moment. He knew me pretty well, and I figured he probably knew what was in my head right then.

At last, he sighed and nodded. "All right. But don't make any moves unless they get too messy with Armel, all right?"

"I promise," I said, and I went after Armel and his entourage.

When I caught up, I found Armel walking sullenly. His eyes were downcast, but they were also darting around, searching for some means of escape. By escape, I mean any handy way to inflict a quick death.

Being a resourceful man, he soon found what he was looking for.

Armel made his move when we got to the torture chamber—or "private module" as Graves had described it.

There were more Mogwa waiting there. This was the critical moment, because the human guards turned to go back to Gold Deck. They were assuming that six Mogwa crewmen plus Sateekas himself could handle one man with his wrists grav-clamped together.

I could have told them it was a mistake—but no one was asking me anything.

"The genitals are key," Sateekas was saying to Armel in a conversational tone, "it's my experience that reproductive organs are unusually sensitive in most species across the cosmos. Why? I can only conjecture, being neither a xenologist nor a student of evolutionary causation."

The item Armel had fixated upon was a simple one: a wrench attached to the bulkhead near the entrance to the module. It wasn't a huge thing, being no longer than a man's forearm and perhaps as thick as two fingers—but it was enough.

The Mogwa crewmen surrounded Armel, pushing him into the module with an air of excitement. No doubt they had

259

serious plans for the human who'd mouthed off to them so openly.

Sateekas, for his part, was still speeching about the coming torments. He was oblivious to the danger he was placing himself in.

"Flaying away the skin and musculature while being careful to clamp off blood vessels—that's essential to keeping the subject alive—allows the exposure of white filaments you call nerves. At that point, the application of trauma becomes unnecessary. The slightest contact with these fibers is overwhelming."

I made a mistake as the group reached the door and passed through: I underestimated Armel.

With a causal move, he reached up and plucked the repair wrench from the wall. The Mogwa hustled him inside, and they slammed the door.

Running up to it, I hammered on the portal, but no one opened it.

"Graves!" I shouted into my tapper. "Open the module door!"

"Now McGill, I know why you followed them. You can't let your emotions get the better of you so quickly. Has Armel even screamed yet?"

"No, no, sir! You don't understand—Armel will kill them all!"

Graves hesitated. I liked to think I'm one of the few people in the galaxy who could manage to get such a response out of such a driven man, and under different circumstances, I might even have grinned.

"All right, McGill," he said. "But you better not be full of shit this time. If you are, I'll have your rank—no scratch that, I'll make you serve under Winslade. As his personal valet."

The chance of such a horrific fate almost made me change my mind about saving the Mogwa—but I just couldn't let Armel have a free hand.

The tribune had already proven he was a traitor. I'd be damned if he was going to get to enjoy himself on his way out of the legions.

"Primus! Sir! The override, please!"

The door hissed and popped open. I stepped inside.

There was a heinous scene in the main chamber. Four of the seven Mogwa were stone dead, their thin skulls crushed in by the dripping tool in Armel's hand. Two other Mogwa had fled, probably hiding in one of the bunkrooms.

But poor Sateekas was still alive and still in the room. He hadn't fared well. Armel had cracked three of his six kneecaps. Crawling around in a circle, the Mogwa stared up at Armel balefully.

"You're weak," Armel told him. "Full of yourselves until you have no technology to rely upon."

Armel flipped the wrench in the air and caught it without looking. He was a master swordsman and highly dexterous.

"The torment will be indescribable…" Sateekas wheezed.

"It already is, from the look of it!" Armel laughed.

Flicking out with his wrench, he snapped a shin-bone. Sateekas hissed.

That was enough for me, I marched toward him, drawing my pistol. Armel put up a hand and cautioned me to halt. I did so, but took careful aim at him.

"Now…" Armel said to the Mogwa, walking around the crippled alien in a threatening manner. "Ask me whatever questions you wish answered. I'm in a much better mood now. McGill is here, and he will no doubt enjoy hearing my answers as well."

My instinct was to shoot Armel—but then I would never hear what he had to say. If he killed Sateekas, well, we'd just print out a fresh one. This model was pretty banged up in any case.

"I want to know what your price was," Sateekas said.

"Really? You don't want to know who these beings are? Who you faced and failed to defeat in battle?"

"I know they are the Skay," Sateekas said. "They're Galactics that are part machine and part biotic—a hybrid species. But that is unimportant. What matters is the nature of the deal they made when coming here."

"Hmm…" Armel said, frowning. He tapped his cheek with the gory head of the wrench, which was crusty and dark indigo in color. "I will answer you: our price was the end of the Mogwa regime."

Even Sateekas blinked at this unexpected response. "Impossible. You've been sold a fantasy."

"Not at all. It is said that there exists an antidote for every poison. We have that antidote. You, creature, are the poison."

"Even if true, you are only trading one master for another. Do you think us heartless? Think again—nothing is more heartless than the mind of a machine."

Armel furrowed his brow. He seemed to doubt himself for a moment.

But then he lifted his wrench high for a killing blow.

"Hold it!" I said, aiming at him with my pistol and taking two quick steps forward.

Armel turned to me, his arm still raised. "Don't be a fool, McGill. Squanto approached me at Blood World, but I resisted. Again at Dark World, he made his offer—but still, I refused. It was not until Hegemony abandoned me with an army of stinking apes on Storm World that I accepted his offer."

"Keep talking," I said. "What was the offer?"

He laughed. "I just stated it! Relief for all humanity! The removal of these vile overlords. You know about the bio-terminator. You know these Mogwa are weak, you've even seen their home world. So vulnerable…"

Armel was talking about the fact that the vast majority of Mogwa citizens lived on Trantor, a planet covered by a single city. If that single planet were poisoned—they would all perish.

Sateekas had big eyes now. They roved between me, Armel and that dripping wrench.

"Thanks for being honest," I told Armel.

Then, I shot him.

-45-

Sateekas wasn't really grateful for my efforts, at least not openly. He was too proud for that.

"We had no weapons..." he complained and then went into a coughing fit. When that subsided, he spoke again. "Our ship was destroyed only an hour ago. What could be expected? I barely know how to operate something as primitive as a snap-rifle. It's a slave weapon—the very idea is offensive."

I happened to know the Mogwa did have advanced small arms. Once, a Mogwa named Xlur had tried to disintegrate me with a pretty cool little weapon. That hadn't worked out too good for him, but the technology was still impressive.

"You guys really should be careful when you're up-close and personal with aliens from higher gravity worlds," I suggested. "Humans are killers, after all. That's why you made us your enforcers."

Sateekas eyed me in obvious pain and rancor. I'd long since summoned the medical people—but Blue Deck was moving slowly today.

"Yes... Killers. A less forgiving master would order you all expunged."

As he made this statement, one of the chicken Mogwa who had run off returned to the center stage. He poked at his dead comrades and inspected Sateekas.

"These injuries are debilitating," he said.

"Yes, obviously. I'm planning on another revival. It's shameful."

The scaredy Mogwa turned his head to regard me. "This one did nothing."

"Untrue. He killed the rebel."

The other stared at me coldly. "Only after talking to it at length in a most familiar manner. I think we should destroy it."

Crossing my arms, I couldn't help but feel a twinge of irritation. After all, I saved their shiny butts just moments earlier. But that's how it was with the Mogwa—nothing was ever their fault. If anything went wrong, someone else had to die for inconveniencing them.

"Listen, Mr. Mogwa, sir," I said.

"I am Captain Akuma," the alien replied sternly. "We're all captains—and your tone is a rude one, human."

"You don't say? Well, welcome aboard our ship. Maybe you can tell me why all you captains ran off when Armel started smacking people?"

Captain Akuma rotated his body, cross-stepping with his many feet, so he could face me fully. "Offensive! Impertinent!"

"Yes, he is," Sateekas coughed. "But he's a killer—a true master of the art. Compared to him, this scrap of meat on the floor was an amateur."

Captain Akuma eyed the dead figure of Armel. His eyes then flicked toward my pistol—and he backed away quietly.

Could Sateekas actually be signaling his captain to cool it? To settle the hell down and be polite for one moment? That would be a first if it was true.

"McGill," Sateekas rasped at me. "I'm dying from injuries—but don't worry about it. I will return. What I want from you now is some clarification."

"Uh... about what, sir?"

"About the conversation you had with the traitor. Is it my understanding that you know what he was blathering about? Poison? Trantor?"

"Uh... Oh, yeah! I think I heard-tell something of that. Sheer nonsense, of course. No one could create a genetically perfect Mogwa-poison. Even if they did, how would they deliver it to your home planet?"

"How indeed…?"

"What I want to know," Captain Akuma asked, scuttling forward again out of the shadows, "is how you visited Mogwa Prime in the past. That is most unusual."

"Well sir, I've got an even better answer for you in that instance: I never did. That story from Armel was pure horseshit."

"Large animal excrement?" Akuma asked. "Has my translator failed me?"

"No sir, that's exactly right. You see, Armel was just throwing up dust with his words, trying to get me in trouble. He hates me, you see. He's tried many times to palm-off his own crimes on some useful stand-in such as myself."

Akuma's eyes flicked down to Armel's motionless form, then back up to my face.

"So… if he is so unreliable, why was he your superior officer?"

"He wasn't—not really. He commanded a Blood Worlder legion. That's a lower-status formation of near-human troops. That's why he was pissed off, actually. Just like a Mogwa who's banished from the home world forever, he went a little crazy in the head."

They both murmured in understanding. All Mogwa overlords who served out here at Province 921 hated being so far from home. For them, a remote assignment like Earth was an insult, a punishment.

It stood to reason that every Mogwa out here was a pariah of one sort or another. Maybe that was why they were always in such a bad mood.

Right about then, the rescue team showed up. Armed guards rushed in and arrested me. They cuffed Armel, too, even though he was stone dead. They liked to be thorough.

The team of medics came in second, and they fawned over every injured Mogwa like they'd found run-over kids in a cul-de-sac.

Graves brought up the rear of the team, and his fists were planted on his hips. He eyed me with fantastic distrust.

"Fancy seeing you here, McGill—in a room full of the dead and dying."

"It's a wild coincidence, Primus," I said with conviction. "But at least it was a *happy* coincidence this time. I was able to step in and stop this madman Armel from further dishonoring Earth's good name."

Graves looked at the scene, and he seemed to recognize Sateekas for the first time. That could be forgiven on his part, as the Mogwa wasn't in the best state of health.

"Good Lord... Grand Admiral Sateekas? What happened to…?"

Graves glanced at me again with murder in his eyes, but fortunately, Sateekas spoke up.

"The McGill-creature must have sensed the renegade's intent. We thought we could handle one bound, unarmed human—but I've been informed he's a master of personal combat."

Graves looked at me sharply, and I gave him a tiny, urgent nod.

"That's right," he said unhappily. He hated to lie to people, but he could see that Earth couldn't afford to take the blame on this one. It was too bloody. "You outnumbered him so significantly we thought—well, please accept my apologies in this matter, sir."

Sateekas breathed a few raspy puffs but didn't say anything. I thought maybe he'd bought the farm—but then he spoke up again.

"We will do so. Now, if you don't mind, I'm going to allow myself to expire. We'll continue our discussion when I've been revived."

"Yes sir—thank you, sir."

Weirdly enough, Sateekas relaxed, and his eyes glazed over in death on the spot.

"Wow," I said. 'That's really weird! Did you see him off himself like that? Just by sheer willpower alone!"

Captain Akuma shuffled closer to me after Sateekas willed himself to die. He seemed braver now that I was handcuffed.

"I remain a skeptic," he said sternly.

"About what in particular, Captain?" I asked.

"About your involvement, creature. Even your superior officer blames you, and I doubt he's wrong. Don't think I've

266

forgotten your discussion with the renegade of genocidal poisons and scouting visits to my home planet. There will be an investigation—mark my words."

"There should be!" I insisted loudly. "Get to the bottom of it, sir. Don't let that criminal rest in peace! If you want, we could revive him under more controlled circumstances for a round of torture and a good perming."

Captain Akuma kept eyeing me. I wasn't sure if he was buying any of my bullshit, but I was pretty sure Graves wasn't.

After a while, Graves led me out in chains. They hauled away Armel's corpse as well, like a sack of grain.

When we were out in the passages and out of earshot of the aliens, Graves turned on me.

"How could you do that?" he demanded.

"Uh… do what, Primus?"

"Let the Mogwa know about the poison—and your trip to their home world. That information is *beyond* classified, McGill!"

"Don't I know it, sir—but Armel told them. That's God's honest truth."

To prove my point, I played back a vid on my tapper. I'd hit the record button during the encounter, suspecting it might be critical later on. Graves often did the same. Body-cams could be used as great tools to cover one's ass—or to incriminate another.

In this case, I had proof, so I was believed.

"Uncuff him," Graves growled at my guards. Then he marched off toward Gold Deck.

I followed along, matching his stride easily. "What are we going to do now, sir?" I asked. "Go home to Earth?"

He stopped and stared at me in surprise. "Whatever gave you that idea?"

"Well Primus," I said, ticking off what I considered to be salient points on my fingers. "For one thing, we just lost one of two transports. We can't hope to beat the Skay, and we're two and a half legions down, sir."

Graves looked unhappy with my accounting, but he didn't argue the point.

"I'm reviving Drusus," he said. "He'll decide what we're going to do next. If you're lucky, you'll keep breathing yourself."

"Is that an offer to testify in my defense? If so, that's mighty kind of you, Primus!"

He was already marching away again. I was talking to his back.

-46-

Drusus reviewed all the information, and he heard testimony for about three hours. It was an extremely boring time for me, let me tell you. I'd heard it all twice by now.

"So... let me get this straight," the praetor said. "Armel and Turov were involved in some kind of conspiracy?"

"That's not confirmed," Graves said. "Armel has publicly confessed—that's all that's known so far."

"But you still saw fit to revive none of your superior officers during this crisis?"

Graves looked uncomfortable. Drusus was asking a tough question, after all. When major strategic decisions were to be made, the natural thing to do was revive the brass and let them sort it out. Instead, Graves had decided to use his own judgment and keep everyone else on ice.

"There was a crisis of leadership," Graves said. "Since we had escaped immediate danger, and I didn't know who was involved in what, I decided to investigate while no one could interfere."

"By implication, your list of suspects included me as well?" Drusus asked.

"I knew one thing: I wasn't involved. I chose not to alter the command structure until I felt certain it could be done safely."

Drusus seemed to chew this over. It had to be annoying that Graves had suspected even him—but that was Graves. He

269

wasn't interested in personal loyalties and favors. He went by the book even if it hurt.

At last, Drusus came to grips with the situation and nodded slowly. "All right. I accept your explanation. This mess has been of unusual proportions. I can understand extreme caution on your part, Graves."

He turned to me then, at long last. I stifled a yawn and straightened up.

"McGill, you must know more than you're letting on. It's time to speak openly."

"Huh?"

Drusus compressed his lips. "Did you, or did you not, materially participate in this mutiny?"

"What...? No sir! I helped put it to rest, in fact."

"That's one possible interpretation..." he said, frowning as he replayed vids of the Mogwa slaughter.

By this time, they'd pulled the security files on everything. We'd watched Armel cracking skulls and kneecaps ten times from ten different angles.

"If we live through this, it will be a miracle," Drusus said. "You see how polite the Mogwa are behaving after this disaster? It's my impression that Sateekas was just playing for time, hoping he can get off our ship before we kill him—does that match your theory, McGill?"

It was my turn to frown. "Uh... kill him, sir?"

"Of course. He and all his ships were destroyed. We revived him once, but we have the power to rectify that error at any moment."

"By... killing him?"

"Exactly. After that, we could just leave him permed and stay quiet. That would be the easiest thing. But we still might need the Mogwa to help us against the Skay... So, I lean toward reporting the destruction of Sateekas' fleet—leaving out the part where we revived him. Then, they could do whatever they wanted."

"But he's alive right now, sir!" I objected. "You're talking about him like he's already dead."

270

Drusus cocked his head and stared at me. "You are an odd one, McGill. I've never seen anyone so quick to kill a foe and equally quick to defend a comrade."

"Thank you, sir," I said, deciding to take his words in the best possible light. "I just don't like treachery under fire. Sateekas plowed his cruisers into that Skay ship, partly with my urging. He did his best to protect us—to protect the province. I wouldn't want to see him permed after that due to our chicanery."

Drusus looked mildly troubled by my words. "You do realize we can't simply allow him to relay what Armel did, don't you? That other Mogwa—Captain Akuma—he's already announced he plans to investigate you. He wants to investigate all of us."

"Sir," Graves said. "I agree with your assessment. In fact, I've already made arrangements."

"What kind of arrangements?" Drusus asked, swiveling his chair toward Graves.

"We've got a small quantity of a... certain toxic substance aboard. We'll pump it into their module, and down into Blue Deck where two of them are convalescing. No one else will be affected. No one else will even know why they died."

"Now, hold on just a second!" I said, standing tall. "If we do that... well, we're no damned better than Armel!"

"Not true," Drusus said. "Armel was acting out of self-interest. We're acting out of caution. We have every life on Earth hanging in the balance. If we don't exercise caution, extinction could result."

He was right about that. The Mogwa were partly to blame for the situation. They had such strict policies and punishments that they forced underlings like us to consider extremes matching their threats.

"But..." I argued, "what if the poison lingers? What if it can be traced years later? Some nosy Nairb will find out eventually if we use it now."

Drusus frowned. "You could be right. I have a new idea: We'll get them all into that module they're camped in. After the deed is done, we'll jettison the whole thing into hyperspace.

271

The radiation and friction involved in reentering normal space will vaporize it."

"That's just plain wicked!"

Graves looked toward Drusus. "Is that a firm order, sir?"

Drusus thought it over. At last, he nodded tiredly. "Do it. Just don't make any mistakes."

"But sirs! Those aliens fought on our behalf. A dozen Mogwa crews died battling the Skay. We can't just—"

"McGill," Drusus said, "I understand your outrage, but the stakes are too high. We must—in this instance—reroll."

"You mean we're going to revive them again? With some editing of memory engrams?"

He blinked at the idea. "That's... possible."

"But dangerous," Graves said. "If anyone slips up, or if they find out somehow, we'd be dooming our species."

Drusus nodded. "We'll figure all that out later. Primus, oversee the matter personally."

Graves got up and walked out. The determined look on his face told me the story: there would be no mercy in his heart tonight.

I followed him, even though I knew I shouldn't. Sateekas hadn't come out of the oven yet downstairs on Blue Deck. Graves went there first.

When he ordered the bio people to abort Sateekas and the other dead Mogwa, they looked ashen.

"Sir, I'm not sure we have enough of the right proteins to mix up if we—"

"Dump the machine's contents. *Now.* You can recycle the materials in case we need to do another grow for some reason."

The bio blinked at us in confusion. I felt for her. She had a nasty job, but her kind were usually involved in the re-creation of life, not the premature ending of it. Getting these orders now must come as a shock.

She turned away and called to her staff. To my surprise, I recognized one of them: it was none other than Raash, a saurian from Steel World.

Raash and I had never been buddies. When we'd met in the past we'd always hissed and spat. Occasionally, we killed each other.

"So…" he said, eyeing me. "The butcher McGill comes to salivate over this injustice. I have no words for the overwhelming disgust I feel."

"Funny," I said, "that's exactly what I heard from Floramel about you the last time I took her on a date."

Raash was a hundred and fifty kilos of alien lizard-monster in his prime. His teeth, muscle and scales made him more than a match for any human—even me.

But I didn't care. I was ready to throw down with him any day of the week.

"Centurion, Specialist," Graves said. "Now is not the time. Arrange to meet each other on Green Deck the next time you're both off-duty."

"We aren't having a date, sir," I said.

"Nor are you two going to fight a duel right now on Blue Deck. Get over it."

Grumbling, we separated. Raash went to the big machine and dumped out a slimy lump of meat. It was disgusting in appearance, smell and texture.

"Damn, Mogwa corpses smell bad," I commented while watching.

They stuffed the half-grown body into the recyclers, which hummed and buzzed in protest. I saluted it as it went down the chute.

Graves noticed this and shook his head at me.

"That alien has threatened to kill Earth on many occasions, McGill."

"Yeah… but he died a hero's death this time around. I won't forget him, even if we just permed another Mogwa."

Graves narrowed his eyes at me. "Another Mogwa? What are you talking about?"

I realized I'd just let the cat out of the bag. Graves had known about my trip to Mogwa Prime during the Storm World campaign—but he hadn't been privy to all the sordid details.

On that trip, our last governor Xlur had ended up permed.

"Well sir… it's kind of hard to explain…" I said.

Graves thought that over for a few seconds.

"Never mind," he said at last. "Just… don't tell me anything. I don't want to know."

273

"You got it, Primus."

Graves kept casting me glances after that as the recyclers buzzed, but I said nothing.

That was for the best, really.

-47-

After mulching the half-grown version of Sateekas, I wanted out. Graves was now carrying a tank with yellow and black warning signs all over it, but I never saw the actual application of the poison.

I refused to watch the Mogwa die. Sure, that Captain Akuma fellow was a first-class asshole, but he'd fought well, and he was our guest.

When it was all over, the ship shuddered a little. I knew Graves must have jettisoned the module, causing it to fall out of the warp-bubble and disintegrate.

"What was that?" Harris asked, peering around at the walls suspiciously. After having endured several battles with overpowered opponents, he seemed to be more paranoid than usual.

"It's a ghost, Adjunct," I told him with a smile.

He peered at me next. "I know that smile. You're holding something back. Thirty years of service with you... I know you, McGill."

That troubled me almost as much as killing the Mogwa had. If Harris had learned to penetrate my lies due to over-exposure, well, he'd be a lot harder to deal with on a daily basis.

"Now, that's just crazy-talk, Harris," I said. "You know I'm a straight-shooter."

He snorted. "I know no such thing... sir."

"Excellent!" I said, clapping my hands together. I made a loud popping sound by cupping my hands a bit, and slamming them hard.

He jumped, just a little.

"What's excellent?"

"I accept your generous offer, Harris. And I appreciate it. As you've probably figured out by now, there have been some investigations and… uh… trials aboard ship lately."

"What?" he said in alarm.

"You know I've been lurking on Gold Deck, right? You also know that some of our Mogwa guests met with untimely ends. What I need today is a character-witness. A man who's known me for over thirty years should do the trick nicely."

I reached out to put my arm around his shoulders, but you would have thought I was trying to slip a rope around his neck.

"Whoa! Hold on right there, McGill! I want nothing to do with your alibis or distracting side-stories."

"But… you just said…"

His big flat hand came up between us. "Forget what I said. Erase it from your mind. You're on your own."

He stalked off then, and I smiled. I could still pull a move or two on him. Harris hated commitment to a cause—especially if it met sticking his neck out for someone else.

Whistling a tune, I headed down to see if I could get the attention of a lady-friend. I had several aboard ship at this moment, as it so happened. Since events were finally in a state of relative stability, I thought I might look one of them up.

Deciding to go to Green Deck, where people on break were congregating this time of the evening, I headed for the elevators.

Alas, romance wasn't in the cards for old James McGill tonight. I didn't make it twenty steps toward Green Deck before the entire ship rocked under my feet.

Now, I'm no expert at flying starships, but I'd only felt something like the sensation I'd just experienced once before.

"What the hell—?" I asked no one, reaching out and clutching at a bulkhead. It was as if I'd been struck by vertigo.

Then it happened again. The ship rocked, and the lights flickered.

Power loss?

When it passed, I did a U-turn and ran for engineering. Could something be extremely wrong down there with the Alcubierre drive? That's what if felt like to me.

Long ago, when we'd been traveling about three hundred lightyears out to Blood World, our journey had been interrupted. On that occasion, a ship full of Gremlins had disrupted our warp bubble, causing us to fall out of warp and into normal space.

This felt like that time.

"McGill to Graves," I called into my tapper. "McGill to Graves, I think there's something wrong with the drive, sir."

A moment later Graves spoke from my tapper. "You're right—but it isn't what you think. We didn't run into anything, instead, we've been hit by force-beams."

"Huh?"

"Force-beams. Gravitational influencers that cause an object—even one in warp—to be tugged at and slowed down. The nerds down on the Lab decks explained it to us."

"We gotta run then, sir!" I shouted, stopping and breathing hard. "If they force us out of warp, we'll be destroyed."

"The odds are high," he admitted. "But that decision isn't my call."

Drusus, I thought to myself.

I cut the call with Graves, and I tried to get through to Drusus next—but it was already too late.

All around me, I heard the moaning wind-down sound of the warp drive dying. They were dropping the warp-bubble, and I had no idea where we were. I doubted Drusus knew, either.

A few minutes later, the walls began displaying an external view. I'm not sure what I expected to see—maybe that some Mogwa vessel had found the module full of their dead officers and run us down—but no... It wasn't a Mogwa ship. I was quite surprised when the truth was revealed.

"The Skay..." I said, looking at the walls in disbelief. I glanced at my tapper, but the same vid was playing everywhere.

277

Behind our admittedly large ship was a *huge* one. The giant scarred-up sphere lurked close, right off our stern.

In comparison to *Legate*, the Skay Invader was massive. You could only realize its true scale when it moved up-close and personal like this. A thousand of our vessels would have fit inside it.

I began trotting, then running, for Gold Deck. A few minutes later I reached *Legate's* circle of commanders and barged right in.

No one ordered me out, or even challenged me. They seemed mesmerized.

"We've been caught," Winslade complained. "Like fleeing rats. I can't believe their tech is so advanced. They ran us down while we were inside a warp bubble—how do you go about explaining the physics of that?"

"Shut up, Primus," Drusus said in a hushed, defeated tone. "We've been captured. We can't resist such a ship. Contact the Skay—tell them we surrender."

"No!" I shouted, and everyone in the place swiveled their heads to look at me in shock.

"McGill!" Graves boomed. "Get off this deck!"

"I'm sorry sir, but—"

"Let him speak," Drusus said in a tired voice. "Are you about to scold us for having killed the Mogwa, McGill? Is this our comeuppance?"

"No sir, not exactly. But I do think jettisoning the Mogwa pod was a mistake. Think about the trail it must have left as it disintegrated into particles—like a flare in space."

They stared at me for a moment. One of the techs on the crew cleared her throat. "Ah… he could be right, sir. Dropping a large object out of warp causes a comet the speed of light to appear. Of course, we had no idea we were being pursued…"

"Of course we didn't," Drusus said. "Their tech is so superior to ours, it's like witchcraft."

"But don't surrender, sir," I advised. "That's the wrong move."

"Why not? These are Galactics, McGill. They've caught up to us fair-and-square. There's no breaking away from their force-beams. Firing at them now is pointless."

"Firing at them?" I laughed. "No sir, that wouldn't be a good idea either. These creatures are like the Mogwa, but worse. They are a species based on machine intelligence. If you don't give them a good reason to let you live... well sir, there's not much hope."

"Go on."

"I've been to the Core Worlds, sir. I've walked the slideways of Mogwa Prime. I saw other Galactic species come and go back then. To them, rebels are useless—but slaves can be valuable. We have to convince them we're valuable."

Drusus blinked at me, and Graves took an angry step in my direction. "Are you suggesting we should offer ourselves up as servants to this new master? That's the same kind of crap that Armel was peddling."

"Noooo, Primus," I said. "Not that. Not exactly. We have to make them curious. We have to make them uncertain."

"And how, exactly, do you suggest we do that?" Drusus asked.

"Well sir, it's kind of hard to describe. If you could see fit to putting me into contact with them, however..."

"That's out of the question, McGill," Graves snorted.

Drusus was quiet. Graves looked at him with a deep frown. "Don't tell me, sir..."

"We'll intrigue them," Drusus said at last. "Send no messages. Fire no weapons. Allow ourselves to be drawn toward their ship."

"That's good," I said, smiling.

"Sir, we have to fight or flee," Graves said.

Drusus looked at him. "McGill is right. We can't do either."

After that, the force-beams got a really good grip on us. Slowly, we were drawn closer and closer to the giant ship.

"We're going to crash into that thing," Winslade complained.

"Steady as she goes..." Drusus said.

Right before the gravitational tug of the bigger ship should have taken over and crashed us into the planet-sized mass, a massive dark line appeared on the face of the vessel.

This black line quickly widened into a slit, then a mouth—and finally, a yawning doorway.

We were being dragged inside the heavily fortified planetoid. Techs read off distances and velocities, but no one spoke among the top commanders.

I got the feeling they didn't know what the hell they should do.

-48-

Of everyone on that bridge, only I had been inside the monster before. I felt like an unlucky Jonah, once again being swallowed by the same damned whale.

"They must have been following us all the way out from 51 Pegasi," Drusus said. "I just can't believe it."

Winslade tapped at a screen and shook his head, sighing deeply. "Although it pains me to say it: McGill was right. The techs have confirmed it. We left a trail in space by jettisoning that module full of dead Mogwa. Instead of covering for our crimes, it lit us up like a spotlight."

"Told you," I said.

Graves hung his head. I could have told him it wasn't his fault, not really—but I didn't have time for babysitting. Besides, he wouldn't have listened to me anyway.

"McGill," Drusus said, "you've been in the belly of this beast before. What's our best course of action?"

"Uh... probably to warp out again."

"Don't you think we might have already tried that, hmm?" Winslade asked. "They've got some kind of warp-dampening field. We can't generate the bubble. We're being dragged inside their ship, probably to be dismantled and probed."

"Or turned into some of those armored monsters," I suggested.

They all looked alarmed at that, as if the thought hadn't occurred to them before. That seemed odd to me, but then I hadn't been floating around on *Legate* in relative luxury during these engagements like they had. To me, the conversion process these hybrid aliens could put a man through was very real.

"What's our second best option?" Drusus asked, looking around at his team.

Graves spoke up after a pregnant silence. "I think we've all come to the same conclusion: there's only one option."

"And that is?" Drusus asked.

"We self-destruct *Legate* once we're inside, naturally." Graves looked honestly surprised at the rest of us, as if this drastic move was glaringly clear to him.

"That sounds… extreme," Winslade said. "How will we escape?"

Graves snorted. "We don't. Come on, Primus. Sew your balls on. It's better than being ground into hamburger and stuffed into one of their machines."

"There's no way we can get a signal out to Earth from here," Drusus said, tapping at the controls. "That machine is casting too much interference to use any normal transmitter, and *Legate* doesn't have an onboard deep-link."

"We've got gateway posts," Winslade said. "We could set them up and send a messenger… I would even be willing to volunteer for the duty."

Drusus and Graves looked at him sourly, but Drusus nodded. "All right, run down to Gray Deck and try to port home. Carry our roster of dead and living with you. They can assume we all need a revival if they don't hear from us in a year or so. Hurry though, once we get into that ship the posts may not work."

He was already talking to Winslade's back. Damn, that boy could scoot when a nasty death was right on his tail.

"So," I said conversationally, "are we going to blow ourselves up?"

"We don't have any A-bombs left," Graves said thoughtfully. "We've got a few low-yield fusion warheads on our missiles—it will have to do."

"See to it," Drusus ordered, "but don't blow us up just for the hell of it. Wait until I give the order."

Graves looked like he disapproved, but he was too good of a soldier to argue with a superior officer. He marched off the deck with sharp, steady steps.

Drusus turned to me next. I could tell by the look in his eyes he had something unpleasant in mind.

"I'll do it, sir!" I said loudly.

"I haven't described your mission yet."

"Doesn't matter. I'm your man. It's time to push all the chips in the middle right now."

"True..." he said, thinking hard. "I'm going to organize an attack on their bridge."

"Uh... does anyone have the slightest idea where that might be located?"

"No," Drusus admitted. "This vessel dwarfs anything we've ever seen. All of Battle Fleet 921—the original fleet—would have been outclassed by this monster."

I'd actually laid eyes on old Battle Fleet 921 on a few occasions, prior to its destruction in the Core Systems. *That* fleet had been powerful—but I had to agree with Drusus. This monstrosity would have taken down all twelve hundred of those ships.

"Maybe, sir," I said, "we could concentrate all our guns on the hinges again. We could leave the Skay ship's mouth hanging open, just like I did last time."

"That's a reasonable suggestion, McGill," Drusus said. "But I don't think that trick will work twice. The enemy has force beams locked on our ship. Even if the door is left hanging open, we can't escape. Worse, what do you think the enemy response would be to such an action?"

"Hmm... They'd probably blow us away."

"Exactly. And we know they can repair the door. All we would do in that scenario is inconvenience the enemy and get ourselves killed. I want more than that, if I can get it."

This concerned me, as I was of the mind that just hurting this monster would be pretty impressive at this point.

"Here's how I want to play this," Drusus told the staff. "Assuming they don't just blow our ship apart, I'm going to deploy our ground forces on their inside hull, prepped for battle."

283

"Really?" I asked. "You think that's going to work out?"

"Maybe not... but we'll do it anyway. From everything we've learned, these Skay like to capture people and convert them into their servants. I think that's why they're dragging us into their ship right now. Capturing is always harder than killing. It gives us a chance to strike back."

"Speaking of capturing..." I said, pointing at the displays.

The universe outside went dark. All the stars vanished as we were swallowed by the bigger ship. The massive door began to roll downward ominously the moment we were inside.

"We've got some weapons, don't we?" I asked.

"We do—but we don't know where to aim them. That's where you come in—not just you, I'm sending out dozens of deep scouting patrols."

"Uh..."

"I know it doesn't sound promising, but we've got no other plays. Get out there with a hand-picked squad. Scout for me, locate a vital target. We'll fire on it when you do."

"What will you guys be doing back here in the meantime?"

"We'll take improvisational action. We'll distract the enemy. We'll put up a lively fight and let them capture some of us. That way, you'll get time to locate targets."

This was sounding worse by the minute to me. I didn't know my ass from a hole in the ground when it came to taking down a vessel this big—but I knew for sure there was no way these aliens were going to let me run wild inside their ship for long.

"Hmm..." I said doubtfully. "How do we get past their initial troop formations? They'll probably send those flying robot-things and lots of runners out to surround us..."

"No doubt they will. In fact, I'm counting on it. I've got a plan this time, you see. It's so crazy, you might have come up with it."

"You're using one of *my* plans?"

He gave me a grin, but I didn't feel cheered up. Not one bit.

-49-

Less than an hour later, I found myself in an unfortunate position: upside down and ass-backwards inside a drop-pod chute. The tubes all around me were occupied by my most loyal regulars and some other good folks, too.

Now, if you're anything like me, you might be wondering what the hell I was doing inside a deployment device built to fire a man down from orbit onto a planetary body. And if you did think that, I'd be first to congratulate you on pinpointing the logical fallacy in my current predicament.

In fact, I'd pointed out this flaw to any number of disinterested persons ever since I'd heard of Drusus' brilliant scheme.

Sure, it was true that we were inside a ship that was so big it was like a small planet—but there were limits. Once you exceeded those limits, in any chosen direction, a man in a drop-pod would be just so much spam in a can to that harder-than-stone outer hull.

Wriggling a bit, I shifted inside my tiny, tomb-like pod and waited for the action to begin outside.

The only method I had of witnessing events was through my tapper, which had been connected up to a screen in front of my nose. That screen displayed numbers, mostly. Pressure readings, troop readiness levels, all kinds of crap like that.

I didn't care about any of it. I just kept straining my fingers and my eyes, panning around the camera view to see if the enemy Skay-critters had arrived yet.

Strangely, they seemed to be taking their time. At last, Drusus lost his patience and decided to make the first move.

A full cohort marched out of the ass-end of *Legate*. That was a first to my knowledge. The ship was built so it could land on a dockyard asteroid or even a planet, but that wasn't its usual mode of operation.

The cohort was full of light troops. Almost all of them were unarmored. Only the officers and weaponeers had been issued a powersuit to wear.

Drusus had a sense of humor, I saw—or maybe it was just pride. Every unit was marching in formation, with a red and gold Varus banner overhead. Due to the thin atmosphere inside the big ship, the banners didn't flutter, they sort of drooped—but they were glorious to behold all the same.

Each pennant was carried by the senior noncom in every unit. They all bore the wolfshead of Legion Varus, along with a unit number.

The cohort reached the open deck and spread out, looking warily for attackers—but there weren't any. Not yet, anyway.

Each unit formed a square and placed itself in position around the ship. I had to smile, they were bait, and they probably knew it.

About five full minutes passed. The enemy didn't do a damned thing. Apparently, we hadn't triggered them yet.

Finally, my radio crackled.

"This isn't working, McGill," Drusus said. "How did you piss off the enemy and get them to attack last time?"

"Well sir, we shot up some stuff. That got their attention."

"All right..."

The channel went dead. I was surprised Drusus had called me at all. He must be feeling nervous.

I saw motion on my tiny screen then—a turret was swiveling.

A stream of shells fired. A rippling series of cracking sounds reached me, even buried inside the ship, carried by the thin air and the hull.

Trying to follow the trajectory of the shot, I saw it was headed up toward a protruding nodule of metal and glass far and away above us. It looked like the super-structure of a ship—perhaps it was.

The nodule was destroyed. The turret swiveled and fired again.

This went on for maybe two minutes—then something happened.

An army of... things boiled up out of the hull. It was weird to watch. The thick hull of the ship was rounded like the inside of a cannonball. It was so dense that we stuck to that surface, tugged toward its mass with something like the gravitation force of the moon.

The whole ship was a big round hollow thing, and we had landed *Legate* on the inside wall of this sphere. The troops surrounding the ship looked like ants crawling on the side of an empty bottle.

The aliens were now boiling up all over the place, surrounding the ship. The gun turrets swiveled, aiming at the growing, approaching horde. They hammered out shells and beams. The ranks wilted—but thousands more rushed closer.

The hapless troops surrounding our ship were joined by a second cohort—then a third. Graves was deploying them now, before all was lost.

It looked hopeless to me, but I still wished I was out there on the front line, fighting with the rest of my legion.

"McGill," Graves said in my ear. "We're sending your squad off now. Bend your knees."

I barely had time to fold my legs a fraction before the capsule was shot out of *Legate*. Usually, drop-pods fired downward out of the ship's belly. But this version of Red Deck was different, it could aim in a variety of angles.

The sensation was terrifying and exhilarating at the same time. I could see the ship disappearing behind me, and up ahead there was a gloomy, misty darkness. The atmosphere inside the great ship was thin, but it wasn't clean. It was sooty and full of floating particles. These formed burning streaks around me as my pod hurtled through them.

287

How far did I go? A thousand kilometers? Something like that.

But finally, the pod began to arc downward again. It was falling, toward the curved wall of the ship.

Even that, though, might be a false impression. An illusion. When you were inside a sphere, and you shot at an angle across it, the curving interior wall soon came back at you again. It appeared, in fact, as if I was slanting down into the ground.

The pod flipped, and the retros fired, ramming against my boots. I was coming in for a harsh landing—but where?

There was no escape, no exit from this artificial world. The single great door we knew of had closed.

Trapped and desperate, I was going God-knows-where to battle God-knows-what.

-50-

When I plunged into something solid again, I blacked out for a moment—or maybe a minute.

"Sir? Centurion McGill?" asked a youngish voice. He sounded like a recruit.

Someone was shaking me. I groaned awake.

"He's alive!"

"Get him out of that pod," someone more familiar said. "Form a perimeter. Chop-chop!"

That last voice... it was Leeson. Someone had handed him a pitchfork and invited him to Hell with me.

I was hauled to my feet, but I stumbled. Putting a gauntlet on the steaming wreck that had been my pod, I steadied myself. My drooping eyes examined the pod briefly. It looked like someone had bent it over and done wrong-minded things to it.

"Damn," I said, "it's a good thing they build these things tough."

"They build Varus troops tough too, sir," Leeson said. "Can you walk? Are you with us, man?"

"I am."

"Good—then you're back in command."

With a painful effort, I straightened and looked around. I had an awful crick in my neck. A blinking red medical light indicated I had a cracked vertebra.

There wasn't much I could do about that right now, so I thumbed off the warning light on my tapper. It would only freak out the rest of the squad.

"What's our situation?" I asked Leeson.

"We lost three on landing. Two are walking-wounded, like you."

"I'm good. Take me off your list."

Leeson shrugged and tapped at his arm. "Okay. You're fit as a fiddle now."

"Where the hell are we?" I asked, looking around at our LZ curiously.

It wasn't what I'd been expecting. I'd envisioned an industrial location—but this looked more like a crystalline bug-hive. There was slimy stuff, frozen-looking resins everywhere. Clinging strands of liquid flowed like wax from above.

"We crashed into some kind of a wasp's nest," Leeson told me. "At least, that's the best I can figure out. Who knows why ops thought this garden-spot was perfect for a commando mission, but here we are."

"Right..." I said, checking my gear. My armor and weapons were all in better shape than I was. "Send Cooper up to scout on the roof. The rest of you, fan out and search the hive."

Cooper grumbled, but he crawled up the wall and onto the roof like a fly. That trick was easily done in the low gravity. Then he went into stealth mode and vanished as he slipped out of a hole one of our pods had made while punching down into this odd organic structure.

"Report!" I urged all the scouts.

"Nothing up here," Cooper said. "Just a few of those buzzing things, but they're pretty far off."

"How far?"

"Uh... the lidar says two kilometers."

The rest reported in as well. It appeared we'd landed in a nest made for flying creatures, the type we'd encountered when we'd first invaded this ship.

I summoned them all back to the central chamber, and we huddled up.

"All right," I said, "we could wreck this place, but I don't think anyone would care. There must be thousands of these nests inside this huge ship."

"Maybe this really *isn't* a ship," Cooper said. "I mean... maybe it's more like a world."

"Clarify that, and quickly," I told him.

"That's the feeling I get, sir. These creatures live here—but they don't serve like a crew. They waited until *Legate* fired shells to come against us. I mean, it *is* a ship, but it's also an inside-out planet. A place where things live. They might not even know they're inside a ship at all."

I thought that over. It was a weird idea, but it did fit the facts. This ship... this *world*... was capable of sustaining life inside it, and was so vast it wasn't organized in a strict hierarchy. It was more like an island that could travel independently through space.

"But there must be a crew, a captain," Leeson insisted. "Somebody controls that door, the force beams that dragged us in here, and the weapons outside."

"You're both right," I said. "This place functions as both a ship and a habitat. That makes things easier in a way. They don't have a crew of millions to hunt us down. They have hives and colonies, maybe. What we have to do is find the bridge, where they control the flight capacities and the weapons."

"None of that is here in this place," Cooper pointed out.

"No..." I said, standing. "Cooper, come with me. We're going out onto the roof."

"I told you, there's nothing—"

"Cooper!"

I was already climbing up to the holes in the ceiling, using my hands to pull myself up off the ground. It was harder in armor, but not impossible. It was kind of like doing a chin-up with someone pushing on your feet. The low gravity really helped.

"Sir, yes sir!" Cooper shouted, scuttling after me.

When we got to the roof, I had him throw a fold of his stealth suit over me. It hadn't really worked back on Earth, but I figured it couldn't hurt. We both looked out at the inside of this strange new World from behind the woven veil that hid us.

291

"It's different…" I said. "The inside of the hull looks more like natural ground out here. There are plants, even. There's a glow coming from somewhere, too."

"No plants without a light source," Cooper agreed. "I haven't been able to pinpoint an artificial sun or anything like that. I think the light is ambient—like maybe the hull glows in patches. I don't know."

"That is interesting… What else have you noticed, scout?"

"Well, I think the area around the big door that leads to space is kind of a dead zone," Cooper said. "When they open that thing up, it lets in cold and sucks out some air. Even with a force field in place to prevent that loss of gasses, it must happen."

"Right, we're farther inland now, away from that single entrance. That must be like a dead-zone for the native creatures."

I couldn't believe I was thinking of all the strange monsters we'd encountered as inhabitants of this 'world' but that's the way I now saw it.

Using my helmet optics, I finally spotted something interesting. It was pretty far off, but it was the only target I could see that might be worth investigating.

"You see that thing? That tower, or mound, or whatever it is?"

"Sure do, it must be about as high as Mt. Everest."

He was right. In fact, I thought I saw frost on its upper regions. Like everything in this world, it was strangely shaped. It appeared to be partially organic and partially manufactured.

"Well, it's the biggest structure in sight. Maybe it's a lighthouse, or a latrine-making factory. It doesn't really matter because it's the only lead we've got. We're going there."

"Roger that," Cooper sighed. "Cooper in ghost mode, moving out."

The stealth suit swept away from me, and Cooper ran off. He was in stealth mode, but I could still follow the impressions his boots were making in the papery surface of the hive for his first dozen steps. After that, I lost him. I hoped the aliens here couldn't see through his little trick as easily as they had back on Earth. I guessed we'd find out soon enough.

"Squad! Saddle up!" I called down to them.

"Where are we going?" Leeson demanded.

"I see a nice diner down on the main floor. It's only about twenty kilometers away. Let's get going!"

Taking the lead—except for the invisible Cooper—I marched out into the open. Every few seconds, I cast a glance over my shoulder, which gave me a sharp pain in the neck.

But I couldn't help it. I was looking out for those flapping things, hoping they weren't done with *Legate* and now searching for any escaped morsels like us.

-51-

We marched for hours. Now and then, we ran into some freak or another. Often, they ignored us. Once in a while, they took notice and attacked. We responded appropriately when necessary and blasted them down quickly.

"It's like we're on the Serengeti Plains," Leeson said. "There's some kind of freaky water-buffalo every hundred meters."

"At least they all seem surprised," I said. "As long as we keep moving, they don't seem to be gathering up against us."

"Hey, Centurion," Carlos called, trotting to move up the line and catch me. "Seems like we've been on this pointless deep-patrol long enough, doesn't it?"

Leeson and I glanced at him.

"What did you have in mind, Specialist?" Leeson asked. He'd never liked how I let Carlos talk to me on an equal footing. "Do you have some important advice to give our centurion about leadership?"

Discretion actually seemed to penetrate his thick, smart-assed skull, and Carlos changed his expression. "Take it easy, sir." Falling into step behind us, he lowered his voice a little.

"Hey, let's get real, shall we? We have killed more than a few creatures."

"That's 'cause we were fired into some empty wasps' nest!" Leeson insisted.

"Exactly. Not our fault—but regardless, we're good and screwed. *Legate* is probably scrap metal by now, and the rest of the legion is being run through sausage-grinders to power one of these walking rickshaws."

Leeson frowned fiercely, but he didn't order Carlos to shut up—probably because I was there.

"Have you got a constructive suggestion, Specialist?" I asked.

"Only that we should call in—to find out what happened."

I stopped marching and stared at him.

"These things *hear* radio signals," I said. "You got that after the first time we went around, right? They'll come humping over here and take us out."

"Maybe. Or maybe Graves is holding them off. If he is, we can try to go back. If he's dead and gone, we're screwed anyway. We're just prolonging the inevitable."

"I *like* prolonging the inevitable," I told him, "especially when the inevitable is a heinous death."

"Look—" Carlos said. "I don't want to be shredded down to meat and stuffed into some monster's jock strap any more than the next guy."

Leeson released a dirty laugh. "You sure about that, boy?"

Carlos ignored him. "My point is," he said, "we're never going to capture some distant mountain that's about as tall as Mons Olympus. We're just not."

I didn't like what I was hearing. It was defeatist talk. But I couldn't help thinking Carlos had a strong argument. If we called in now, we'd either get rescued, or we would have a new goal—or we'd die quick.

After thinking it over for a few minutes, I shook my head. "We're marching. Keep up and don't prattle so much."

Dejected, Carlos retreated and marched with the single-file patrol again.

We continued for several hours. We had plenty of power, air and water, because we could leach and recycle most of that stuff from our environment—but we didn't have limitless food. That would be the thing that got us in the end. Unless we wanted to try to eat the muscle fibers out of one of these abominations, we would eventually starve.

295

Stopping for a rest, I got an idea. I took it to Kivi and discussed it, as she was our tech.

"Yeah," she said. "I can do it. Let me work on scripting a buzzer."

After our rest, we continued on. There was no night or day inside Armor World, so we just took rests and ate when we felt like it.

The landscape was bleak, but increasingly natural-looking. It was like crossing a desert. There were some spiny, dry plants, rocks and bones—lots of bones. Over time, we came to realize that the animal parts of these aliens died and were left to rot, fueling the rest of the eco-system, such as it was.

"Ew," Carlos complained. "We're walking on dirt that's really just rotted meat and shit ground down to dust."

"Shut up," Leeson told him. "Oceans are made of fish-piss, and every inch of soil on a farm came out of an animal at one time or another. You're a frigging bio—you should know this."

Carlos shut up.

"Okay, Kivi," I said when we'd traveled for another hour. "Is it time?"

"Yeah, the buzzer will be going off any minute. I'll hook-up."

We gathered around and plugged our suits together. This allowed us to share power, data and also see the vid on Kivi's tapper play on everyone's screen.

The buzzer woke up and began to fly. It lifted off, headed for *Legate* and began broadcasting.

There was no reaction at first. But after a time, something came through. It was Graves' face.

"This is an unauthorized signal," he said. "Radio silence is paramount for all patrols."

My squad whooped. We weren't alone and trapped inside this rock.

While we watched his image and listened, Graves looked down—nodding and frowning. It had taken him a minute to realize we weren't complete idiots, and we'd programmed the buzzer to send a short message a distance away from our location.

"McGill's squad… I might have known. We're still alive here, but it was a close thing. The initial attack was driven off, but our xeno people say they'll gather a bigger force and hit us again within twenty hours."

He looked down again for a moment. Then, he sighed. "If you want to press ahead, you can. If you want to return, you can do that too. We're not getting any positive reports. We're attacking a planet-sized enemy. With one legion, it's like trying to kill a dinosaur with a pin. We're only pissing it off. Godspeed, Graves out."

"Damn!" Carlos said loudly. "That has to be the most beaten and piss-poor state of mind I've seen on old Graves. He knows we're dead. He *knows* it."

Leeson got up and kicked him. I wished Moller was here, but she'd died on the drop. She'd know how to get him to stay quiet.

Cooper came up to me next. "What's the plan, Centurion?" he asked.

I looked at him, and he looked back at me.

"It's pretty bleak," I admitted. "I'll put it to a vote: we keep marching to the mountain, or we go back to die with the rest of the legion at *Legate*."

Everyone got out their thumbs. By tradition, as old as Rome itself, we all stuck out one thumb, either up or down depending on our desires.

Only I didn't vote.

When the thumbs shifted, I was honestly surprised. About two-thirds voted to return.

I stood up and loomed over them. "Two things," I said loudly. "I'm disappointed that so many of you are still cowardly after all these years. What's a bad death to a Varus man? Nothing!"

"What's the second thing, Centurion?" Cooper asked.

"This isn't a democracy. Only one man here gets a vote. That's me, your commander. Get up, we're marching to that frigging mountain over there."

"That's what I figured…" Cooper said.

The man next to him handed over some cash. Cooper knew me pretty well, and he'd bet on the outcome.

Grumbling, they all got up and followed me. They were good men, but they needed a swift kick in the ass now and then to be reminded of it.

-52-

We didn't make it all the way to the mountain. We tried, we really did, but they caught up to us somehow and sent a force we couldn't deal with.

"Tanks, sir!" Cooper screamed.

I saw footprints sprinting down from a ridge. We'd stuck to the lowlands for hours, making ourselves less visible, walking in trenches and streams that were usually as dry as grave dust.

Looking back the way our trail of footprints led, I spotted the enemy soon enough.

Tanks. Big-ass tanks. These were possibly even larger vehicles than the ones we'd dealt with back on 51 Pegasi.

"Stop running!" I ordered. "We can't outrun those tanks. They're doing fifty kilometers an hour, easy. Take up positions on the ridge!"

The squad reversed direction and trotted up to the ridgeline. Once up there, they got a good look at what was coming our way.

"Dude..." Carlos said. "We're dead. We are so, so, freaking dead. It's not even funny."

No one argued with him.

"Weaponeers," I said, "choose your ground carefully. It's all up to you. Shoot for the eyeballs that aim those turrets. When they get in range, give them a dose of rads that will blind anything inside about a five meter radius."

299

It helped that I'd once been a weaponeer myself. I understood their weapons, and what they could do. Belchers weren't easy weapons to handle, but they were very flexible in their application.

Cranking their apertures open, our two weaponeers did as I commanded. I felt a moment of pride to be commanding such troops. No one ran, no one threw down their weapon and started crying—they just prepped for battle like pros. It was good to see.

We were well and truly fucked this time, and we all knew it, but my squad was game anyway.

The sand splashed next to me on the ridge, but no one was there.

"Good to see you didn't run off, Cooper."

"I've got nowhere better to be, sir."

The tanks were spreading out now. There were seven of them, and they were six meters tall each, by my HUD's best guess.

"You think they see us?" Cooper asked.

"Yep."

"It's over then, right?"

"Looks that way."

The rumble grew louder and louder. The treads were churning, kicking up looping spirals of dust behind each vehicle. Those eyeballs that guided the many turrets—I could see them now on extreme magnification. They never seemed to blink. I hadn't noticed that before.

"It's been good serving with you, McGill," Cooper said. "And I've always wanted to apologize for what a dick I was back in the beginning."

"You mean at the Mustering Hall?"

"That, and everything else."

I laughed. "We're more than even, kid," I said. "Remember, I talked you into joining Varus."

He was quiet for a second, then he spoke again. "That's right... you did. Why am I apologizing to you?"

"Because you're a dumb-ass. Now, get your head in the game. Start sniping on some eyeballs."

Everyone with a snap-rifle was plinking away soon after that. We were still a kilometer out and shooting at moving targets the size of cantaloupes, but you could always get lucky.

A few of them pulped red, but not many.

At around 800 meters, the belchers began to sing. They smoked whole areas, blinding turrets on good hits.

That changed things. The enemy swerved, sending two tanks directly at us. The rest lined up behind them. We couldn't hit the ones in the back.

We gave the front two hell, however. They didn't have an organ left on their forward sloping armored region by the time they reached us.

"Why aren't they firing back?" Cooper asked.

"Don't ask, and keep shooting."

When they got close, they ran right up the ridge and sent us scattering like rabbits.

"Overrun!" I shouted. "Get low, don't fall under those treads!"

It was a useless order. Three of my men were crushed, including Carlos.

The rest of the tanks rolled up, encircling my team and aiming their guns down at us.

My men had pluck, I had to give them that. They keep shooting out eyeballs. Sure, we were about to be turned into spam, but we were dishing out a little pain first.

"...cease..." a voice said.

It was a loud voice. The voice of the Almighty himself.

But it wasn't God, it was the tanks. They all spoke with one voice, at one time.

"...cease the damage..."

We looked at one another.

"What do we do, Centurion?" Leeson called to me.

"Uh..."

Most of my men stopped rattling snap-rifles and screaming, but one of my weaponeers didn't. He burned a cluster of eyeballs into curling black stalks.

A single cannon fired in response. It was so loud, so close, the dirt spanged off my armor. The weaponeer was gone. There was nothing left but a crater in the dirt.

301

"Ceasefire!" I shouted.

"They just want to eat us or something," Leeson complained.

"Probably. Cease firing!"

When the shooting had stopped, we were left crouching, hugging dirt and staring up at machines that dwarfed us. The tanks were terrifying in every way. So alien, so powerful, so without pity or reaction to pain.

"What do you want?" I called out, cupping my hands. "You want to talk?"

"You must not damage me further. You are bad-stuff. You are a mistake."

"Uh…" I said. "Am I talking to a Skay commander?"

The tanks were quiet for a bit, then they answered all at once again. "All Skay are commanders. All Skay rule their environments. You are disrupting my digestive processes without purpose."

"Huh…" I said, chewing that over.

I lowered my rifle and looked at Leeson.

"Don't ask me," he said. "Romancing aliens is your job, McGill. Ask it if it's male or female. Maybe if you get lucky, you can be the girl this time."

Finding his suggestion unhelpful, I turned back to the grotesque monstrosities that encircled us.

"Take us to your leader," I said, belting out the words. "Take us to the captain of this great ship. I have a gift for him."

"Your words barely comport meaning. You are failed-things. You will stop your actions and comply."

"Sounds like a typical Galactic asshole all right," Leeson muttered.

That gave me an idea.

"Skay," I said. "We are indeed irritants. We are powerful fighters, don't you admit? We serve the Empire. We are enforcers for the Mogwa, but maybe we can serve you."

"What the fuck?" Leeson said. "McGill…?"

I waved a hand for him to be quiet.

The tanks didn't answer for a few moments.

"You are not good slaves if you would so willingly switch masters."

"Not so!" I shouted. "We serve the *Empire*. If this province is legitimately owned by the Skay, then we serve the Skay. That's not treachery. It is not even a choice."

The tanks cogitated a bit more. I have to admit, I was feeling a trickle of sweat inside my suit. That often happened whenever I stepped over a new line of conduct I'd never even considered stepping over before.

My troops were looking at one another, gripping and regripping their rifles in confusion—but I didn't care. This was do-or-die now.

"You have little to offer. You could not crack one Skay. There are thousands of us in the Core."

"I'm sure that's true, but wouldn't it be nice not to have to come out here and patrol all the time? Look at the Mogwa, they had only a handful of ships stationed here. We are the true militia of Province 921, we garrison this province for them. We serve our owners with distinction, no matter who our rightful lords might be."

Again, the Skay were silent. I wondered if they were slow-thinkers, or they were conversing among themselves, or if their translation device was imperfect.

During the pause, I had time to consider some of the things the Skay had said. *You could not crack one Skay.* That was confusing. Was Skay their name for their great ships?

The tanks began to move all of a sudden. They encircled us fully now, and they aimed their guns at us from every angle. Some of those turrets had no eyes left—lots of them didn't— but they still aimed very well.

I realized then that they probably were networked. A few eyes in the group could be shared by all. We'd worked hard to blind them, but we'd been outclassed from the start.

"I have considered your words. You are not useless, but you would revert to supporting the Mogwa should they send a fleet here to retake this province. That makes you too unreliable to serve the powerful Skay."

"Wait!" I shouted. "We have another gift, something much more valuable to give you!"

The tanks paused, and we sweated. I truly didn't know if I was living through my last few seconds of life or not.

To die here, inside the belly of this Skay ship, that would surely mean a perming. No one would ever find me, or think to revive me. Hell, Humanity was likely to die soon after we did.

-53-

This time, the Skay gave it a long, long think before it replied to my offer of a gift. Leeson just about lost his mind during this period of waiting.

"McGill!" he hissed at me.

"Shut up."

"Centurion, sir? Have you considered what it's thinking of doing to us? Better to be blown up right now!"

I looked at him. He might be right, after all.

"It was stalking us right from the start," he said. "Planning to harvest us to make new troops or something. Maybe your balls will end up serving as shock-absorbers inside one of these tanks!"

"Shut up," I repeated, and he finally fell silent.

At last, the tanks spoke again.

"We are curious about your offer. This is an interesting behavioral test. Are you simple creatures of desperation and deceit—or possibly something more useful...?"

The Skay was talking faster and more clearly now. I realized it seemed to get better at speech every time it talked to me. Was it learning English that fast? If so, the AI was more than impressive. It wasn't just smart, it was scary-smart.

"I assure you, Mr. Skay sir," I said carefully, "that we humans are very useful. We've served under the Mogwa for a long time. We know secrets about your rivals."

"Show me this secret instantly."

"Uh... it's not here, sir. It's back at our ship."

Another quiet ten seconds passed. Leeson looked like he was doing the potty-dance.

"We will move to that location. You must stop them from firing at my children. I have not yet calculated a way to subdue them without substantial loss. Perhaps you can help with that."

"I sure will!"

The tanks backed away and turned. They began to rumble off in the direction of *Legate*. We trotted after them, but we were soon falling behind. One of the tanks returned to us to complain.

"Are you attempting to delay? To make your existence last as long as possible?"

"Uh... yes sir, but we're not moving slowly on purpose, if that's what you mean. Humans without technological vehicles don't move very fast."

"Disappointing. This experiment is now nine percent more likely to fail."

"I've got an idea, why don't you let us crawl on your backs, or into an ammo compartment? Then you can race at top speed."

Another delay ensued.

"You're sick, McGill," Cooper complained. "I don't want to climb into the guts of one of these things!"

I didn't glance at him, but it was obvious Cooper was stealthed and standing nearby.

"You may not enter the bodies of my children," the voice said at last. "You may, however, ride on their backs."

The tanks sat there, motionless. Sucking in a breath, I knew I had to make the first move. I climbed up the armored side of the lead tank. In between its armor plates I could see hairy, leathery, lumpy places—but I didn't shiver in horror.

Standing tall on the top of it, I called down to my troops, ordering them to do the same. There was a lot of grumbling and cursing, but we all managed to get up on the slanting armor and find a handhold.

"You're a fucking genius, McGill," Cooper whispered. "We're going to ride these big retards right back to *Legate*, then we'll tear them up, right? Color me impressed."

I didn't answer. I didn't want to blow his cover, and I didn't want the tank to doubt me in case it was listening.

We rumbled away. The initial lurch sent one team member sprawling on the dusty ground. He was quickly run over by the next tank in the column.

Shrugging, I turned my attention forward again. This whole thing was a gamble. There was no sense crying over one soldier. Either my plan would work, or it wouldn't. In the latter case we were all as good as dead any way.

"Hold on tighter," I told the rest. They didn't seem to need more encouragement. They were clamped on like kittens on a curtain.

The trip took maybe ten long minutes. At last, the tanks stopped.

"*Legate* is a few kilometers farther," I said.

"They will fire on us if we get closer."

"Why didn't you just destroy our ship?" I asked.

"You question me? You are indeed a troublesome slave."

"Ah," I said, "I understand. You're afraid. You feel pain. One tiny injury drives your kind away. Good to know."

A turret and its associated cluster of eyeballs aimed at me. I wasn't sure if it was checking me out or taking careful aim.

"There is no form of cowardice possible in the mind of a Skay. We calculate, and we proceed down optimal routes of logic."

"Yep. That's the kind of thing chickens say back home, too. Why'd you even come out here to Province 921 if you were afraid of an injury? Did you think you could kill us all without getting hurt?"

"Holy shit, McGill..." Cooper hissed beside me. "Cool it down!"

I ignored him.

The tank didn't answer right off. At last, when it spoke, the answer surprised me.

"You are correct. I expected no injuries. Your weaponry was unexpectedly advanced. The Mogwa must be mad to arm frontier militia with teleport weapons."

"They didn't," I told the Skay. "We figured them out ourselves."

"That shifts the blame for this violation from them to you—but the guilt is shared, as you are under their dominance."

"Listen," I said, figuring it was time to change the topic. "I'll communicate with my ship, but you've been jamming our radio transmissions. Turn that off, and we'll communicate."

"You will deceive us. You will use the signal to home in missiles on this location."

"Well, normally that would be a good tactic," I admitted. "But the trouble is we can't get out of this place, and we can't kill all your tanks and other creatures. So, we need to deal in order to escape."

"Nothing that enters the mouth of a Skay exits again unaltered."

I blinked twice at that statement. The thing was referring to that giant door, calling it a mouth... *the mouth of a Skay.*

All of a sudden, an obvious thought struck me. Most of my troops had probably figured it out already as they listened into our talk, but the idea was brand new to me.

This thing, this giant ship... I now realized it *was* a Skay. All of it. The whole thing was a planet, a living world... and a single, artificially intelligent being.

"I didn't realize any of the Galactic races were as big as you are," I said, seeking confirmation on my hunch. "Can you feel pain when we fire missiles at your outer hull? Are you alive, or just a numb ball of star dust?"

"Your questions are absurd. Star dust feels no pain. My mind triggers regret software when events go in an unfortunate direction, but that is all. Now, human, contact your ship. I grow tired of this process."

Tapping at my tapper, I contacted *Legate*. It took about twenty seconds to get Graves on the line. He looked annoyed.

"McGill? What did I tell you about transmitting in the clear? You're supposed to be on radio silence, and any..."

He trailed off, having apparently noticed the turrets, cannon barrels and eyeballs behind me.

"What the hell...?"

"Primus, may I introduce you to a child of our host Skay. Our new Galactic friend is interested in talking to us personally. Can we approach without being fired upon?"

"McGill... you have to be the craziest rodent I've ever laid eyes on. You want me to stand down and let you roll an alien tank right up to *Legate* without us firing a shot?"

"That's exactly right. Here's how I see things, sir: We're trapped inside the belly of this Skay-thing. But I've been making friends, and I think we can make a deal with this Galactic, the same way we've made deals with the Mogwa in the past."

Graves didn't answer right off. His screen went dark. I thought he was conferring with Drusus or something. I began sweating again, even though it wasn't that hot out.

"I grow impatient," the Skay complained. "The digesters on these vehicles will now transform you. Please climb down and stand near the orifice."

"Uh..." I said, hearing some awful sounds from lower down on the tank. It was shifting around, opening armor plates and no doubt revealing a nasty maw of some kind that was interested in eating us.

"Graves!" I shouted at my tapper. "We're wasting Mr. Skay's time here, sir!"

He finally came back on the screen. He looked annoyed.

"Roll your friends down here. If they fire at *Legate*, we'll incinerate the lot of you."

"That sounds mighty friendly of you, sir," I lied. "Downright hospitable!"

The tanks began to roll, and we traveled over a hill. *Legate* appeared in the distance. Each kilometer we traveled, I found myself swallowing harder.

This bit of diplomacy was going to take all my skills—and all my luck—to pull off.

309

-54-

The tanks rolled us closer to the squatting transport. Every gun on *Legate* tracked the tanks, and the tanks returned the favor with obvious paranoia.

I seriously considered telling Graves to open fire. It would be a coup if I could get *Legate*'s gunners to destroy these tanks without taking much damage, but I passed on the idea. Battling with a few vehicles now was pointless. Armor World was full of Skay minions. A handful of destroyed mega-tanks meant nothing to the enemy. Eventually, they'd wear us down.

So, I kept my bargain instead. I climbed down off the lead tank and headed for the nearest ramp. There wasn't a human in sight.

Behind me, my troops began to dismount as well, but I raised my hand to stop them.

"Hold on, you're staying here with the tanks. You're all hostages."

Glumly, what was left of my squad stood under the watchful alien eyes.

Nearer at hand, as I climbed the ramp, Cooper released a dirty laugh. "You're such a bastard, McGill. Are you going to dust them all off together?"

"Negative," I said, and I considered ordering him to take his stealthing ass back down there to face the music—but I didn't. He wasn't hurting anything by making good on his escape.

When we reached the top of the ramp, Graves and Drusus were waiting. They looked tense and annoyed. Graves had an arm missing just above the elbow—but I didn't ask about it. Injuries were temporary in the legions.

"McGill..." Drusus said. "I'd welcome you back, but I'm not sure that's appropriate. Why'd you bring a squad of Skay tanks with you?"

"These aren't the Skay, sir," I said. "Not exactly. You see, this entire inside-out planet is what's called a single Skay."

"You're talking about the ship?"

"That's right. You see, the Skay are one of the Galactics that are machine intelligences, rather than biotics. They're a race of giant ships, or planets, or moons—whatever you want to call this thing we're trapped inside of."

Drusus looked surprised, but he appeared to get it. "I see... that does clarify some things. There's got to be a computer somewhere instructing these tanks. Have you spoken with it?"

"Yes, in a manner of speaking. I've talked to it through the tanks themselves. I suspect we could have talked to the Skay at any point through one of its abominations, if it had felt like talking."

"Why did it talk to you?" Graves asked, narrowing his eyes. He moved as if to cross his arms, but failed due to the missing limb.

"That's a plain mystery to me," I admitted. "But I think it's because we were irritating it and it wanted to get on with the business of consuming us. You see, this weird species—if you can call a race of cyborgs that—likes to tear down biotics like us and add some metal, maybe a few computer chips, and make new, obedient soldiers out of us."

Graves looked me over as if suspecting I'd been compromised in some way. Knowing my only hope for reason was going to come from the praetor, I turned to Drusus.

"I made a deal with it. I told the Skay if it brought us back to *Legate* and let our ship go, I'd give it a gift of great power."

Drusus laughed politely. "That sounds like classic McGill. The only trouble is I can't imagine anything we have that would interest this monster, other than allowing it to devour our flesh. I'm not interested in such a trade."

311

"Hold on," I said. "We *do* have something to trade. I told the Skay we had a weapon—a powerful weapon it could use against the Mogwa. That's why it's out here in the first place, see. This Skay wants to horn in on Province 921, which it regards as unguarded Mogwa territory."

They both squinted at me in confusion for a moment, but Graves figured it out first.

"A weapon against the Mogwa?" Graves asked, shaking his head. "Forget it, McGill. We're not going there. We'll blast our way out first."

"Haven't you tried that already, sirs?" I asked, glancing over my shoulder toward the distant coiled spring.

We'd bombed out that tower-like coiled spiral structure the first time we'd come to Armor World to pay the Skay a visit. We'd successfully broken a huge spring and caused the door to sag open and require repairs.

"Looks like the mouth over there is pretty scarred up, but the door is still shut," I remarked.

"The 'mouth?'" Drusus asked.

"That's what the Skay calls that cargo door—its mouth."

"That's cute. But yes, we shot it up as best we could. We couldn't damage it because it has shielding now. The Skay not only repaired itself, it made improvements."

"Why not use an A-bomb?" I asked.

"We're too close," Graves said. "*Legate* would be destroyed at this range. Besides, we've been holding onto the last big weapons in our arsenal in case one of you scouts located a better target."

I looked back at them. "Like the Skay's brain-pan?"

"Exactly."

"Any luck finding it?"

"No," Graves admitted. "That's what you're supposed to be doing, and in fact, most of the patrols we sent out are all dead."

"It was a good effort," Drusus told him. "A desperate move that never had much chance of working, but a good effort nonetheless."

Graves looked sour. To him, any failure was a failure. Nothing more.

"Well?" I asked. "Are we going to hand it over? It's our only way out."

Drusus narrowed his eyes. "Hand it over… now I get it. You must be talking about the Mogwa bio-terminator. Can that possibly be your plan, McGill? Seriously?"

"Of course, sir. It's the only bargaining chip we have. The Skay are at war with the Mogwa. If we give this thing a weapon, it will see us as allies."

"There you go, negotiating diplomatic deals again," Graves said, shaking his head. "Praetor, I urge you to ignore this insanity. Fight well. Die well. After that we can be remembered honorably."

"Yeah, the honorable dead," I said. "All ten billion humans, maybe a few other local species can go out with honor, too."

"You think this Skay will exterminate Earth?" Drusus asked.

"I do. This thing is a heartless machine. It has no capacity for empathy. No kindness. No soul."

Drusus rubbed at his chin. He had bristles there, a testament to his stressed state of mind. Drusus never looked like he needed a shave unless it was a very bad day indeed.

"It appears that this Skay visited 51 Pegasi first," he said. "After subduing that planet and colonizing it with a processing plant under a dome, it moved on to Earth."

"Obviously, it planned to do the same to us," I said. "We have to make a deal with it if we can't destroy it. We won't be able to trick it so easily again by teleporting into the mouth. It knows that move, and it's taking steps even now to stop such attacks in the future."

"Yes, it learns…" Drusus said. "It's a smart robot." He looked conflicted.

Graves looked disgusted. I waited while they mulled it over.

Suddenly, however, there were pounding footsteps behind me. I turned to gaze down the ramp.

It was Kivi, running for her life. She had a desperate look on her face. A pleading expression.

Boom!

313

A deafening report sounded. There was nothing left but a single boot and a puff of gray smoke. The ramp itself was damaged, with a crater blasted into it.

"Seems like our guests are getting impatient," I told the others.

Turning around, I walked down the ramp toward the tanks. "If you change your mind, sirs, send somebody out with a barrel of Mogwa poison. I'm going to go talk to it some more and stall in the meantime."

"We're not going to make the slightest effort to miss you when we blow those things away, McGill!" Graves called after me.

I gave him an unconcerned wave over my shoulder and trudged outside.

The cyborgs were in quite a mood. They were rolling around on their treads impatiently. My troops, white-faced, clung to the backs of the tanks. They were close to bolting as Kivi had done. Only the instant death she'd faced had kept them from making a run for it.

When they saw me, the lead tank seemed to recognize me. How? Who knew?

"It is the speaking ape," the tank said. "Why have you delayed me? Is this how humans reward their new masters? With long waits and treachery?"

"Not at all, sir!" I said loudly. "I had to get my superiors to agree to the exchange, that's all."

"You have not even explained the nature of this offer. I'm growing weary of your nonsense. Stand still so that I may cleanly expunge you from my presence."

At that point I noticed one of the turrets was tracking me closely. It couldn't miss at this range.

"Don't you want to hear how you're going to defeat the Mogwa first?" I asked.

"You trouble me, creature... but speak. I will listen for a few moments more."

Smiling big, I began to make my offer. It caught on pretty quickly—but unfortunately, it seemed unimpressed.

"A bio-terminator? That's it? I'm overcome with disappointment. We've already purchased that formula. It's nearby in Province 929, waiting to be picked up."

My brain clicked inside my head. I swear it did.

Province 929 was a lost frontier land bordering ours. Rigel was out there, about five hundred lightyears away.

"That rat-bastard little bear…" I said to myself, then I raised my voice. "Uh… Mr. Skay? You wouldn't have had any dealings with a fellow about yay-high, would you?" I placed my hand about a meter above the ground. "All hairy and ugly? Goes by the name of Squanto?"

"You describe the creature accurately. How would you know this?"

I laughed. "Because I'm his supplier! You see, Earth made the stuff, and Squanto wants to buy it from us. I guess he planned to turn around and sell it you afterward."

The Skay tank froze again, thinking.

"What you say is possible," it said at last. "But you must prove it. Hand over the formula now, or die."

The turrets whined and shifted, lining up not just on me, but on several critical areas of *Legate's* belly.

I wondered if these frigging tanks could destroy *Legate* with a surprise attack. I couldn't rule it out.

My reading of the situation was bleak. Unless I missed my guess, this whole powwow was about to go tits-up and turn into a firefight. I would be the first to admit that I was starting to feel the heat. The tanks were all acting up, and I knew our own gunners were just *itching* to lay destruction down upon them as well.

Worst of all, poor old James McGill was standing at ground zero, waiting to become a smear of charred meat on the field of honor.

"Hold on!" I said, waving my hands over my head.

This gesture seemed to work a little too well, and I gained a few extra turrets swinging in my direction. They tracked me with eerie precision.

"I'll do you one better than the formula—I'll give you a working sample. A dose strong enough to dust off a Mogwa city!"

315

The tanks reversed their massive treads. Two of them surged up to loom over me like giants.

"The Mogwa only possess one city," the voice said, and it sounded like it was hungry.

"Uh... Oh yeah. Well, that was hyperbole on my part. Earth cities are much smaller. But it will be an impressive amount, I assure you."

"Excellent. Present your gift quickly."

"But we haven't talked about what we're getting out of the bargain," I said.

"You are gaining your continued existence."

"Right, great. That goes for all humanity, right? Not just me? Not just our one ship?"

The tank thought about it. "If the product works as described, then yes. You will have proven yourself worthy slaves."

"Fantastic! Let me just go up this ramp and get the sample. I'll be right back!"

Trotting up the ramp, I soon vanished into the ship's interior. Drusus and Graves were still up there, but if it can be imagined, they looked even less happy than they had the first time we'd spoken.

"You offered them not only the formula—but our stock of the poison?" Drusus asked. "What authority did you have in making such an offer?"

"Well sir, I'm as human as the next fellow. I want to keep breathing—and I wanted to keep everyone on Earth breathing, too. In short, I've got a stake in the outcome of this situation."

"But why did you offer them more than Rigel did?" Graves demanded. "If you'd given them the formula alone, it would be much harder to trace where it came from. The organic chemistry... there might be signatures, if you know where to look."

"Sirs, if there is one thing I know well, it's horse-trading. I couldn't offer to match Squanto—I had to beat him. I had to one-up him in a clear and concise fashion."

The two officers glanced at one another. They looked pretty uncomfortable.

"Well?" I asked. "The tanks are going to get anxious again soon. Is it a go?"

Drusus blasted out a deep sigh, closed his eyes and let his chin sink to his chest in defeat.

"Graves... go get the items. Give them to McGill—and do it on the double."

Cursing under his breath, Graves trotted away from us. Drusus stayed in his pose of distress.

"Aw now," I said, "don't worry so much, Praetor. This will all work out."

"This is what Turov wanted, you know," he said, keeping his head down. "You've turned, James. You've become her creature."

"Uh... how's that?"

"Didn't you wonder why she's being kept in the revival queue for so long? Why she and Armel were out here pulling a deal together?"

I squinted at him. "Are you saying that Galina and Armel hatched a plan to sell out the Mogwa? To the Skay?"

"Yes. That's what's been going on. We've been investigating everything while you were out on patrol. We found out that they wanted to switch masters—they've always wanted to switch masters and ditch the Mogwa because they were too weak. Remember the Cephalopods?"

"Oh yeah... Galina did want to go rebel then, didn't she?"

"That's right. Now, today, you've come back to me with an ultimatum of the same general nature. Here I am, going along with it. Earth is a rebel state now, in the eyes of the Mogwa. Worse, we're cooperating with the enemy, arming them..."

It was true, of course. Every word of it.

"But this is different," I argued. "We're not rebelling against the Empire itself. We're just accepting a new lord from the same Core World powers. We can't be blamed for that. It's a matter between the Mogwa and the Skay."

Drusus snorted. "I'll have you explain that carefully to the Mogwa if they return one fateful day in the future."

"That might not go so well..."

"No, it won't—and that's why I'm really going with your plan. If you're going to do a dirty deed, McGill, you have to go all the way. If you take a shot at the King—you'd better make damned sure you kill him."

Graves showed up then, and he was puffing. He shoved a yellow barrel at me with a data chip on top.

"Do your worst," he said.

Turning around, I ran down the ramp and greeted the Skay tanks, which were restlessly rolling around on their man-high treads.

-55-

The Skay tanks rolled away without a word of thanks. They carried the deadly cargo I'd given them, and I had to wonder if they'd really kill the Mogwa with it.

Walking back to the ship, I whistled a cheerful tune. As far as I was concerned, I was a clear hero. I'd saved the day and then some.

I did feel a pang though, a real pang, when I considered old Sateekas. He was almost a friend. Sure, he was an arrogant gas-bag who would as soon torch-off the Earth as stub one of his thirty-odd toes, but I still had lingering feelings of admiration for him.

Legate was freed within the hour. The big door began to rumble, and we all stowed our gear for takeoff.

"Say Primus?" I asked when we were all strapping in on Gold Deck.

"What is it, McGill?" Graves asked. "You do realize you're only been allowed up here in case the Skay contact us. I'd also remind you of your promise to keep quiet."

"Got all that, sir. I was just wondering what we're going to do about Sateekas. Has anyone reported his status to Mogwa Prime yet?"

"No, *Legate* doesn't have a deep-link system. All of his ships were lost, so we'll have to report the matter when we return to Earth."

"Hmm..." I said.

319

Legate lifted off then, rumbling and shivering under our butts. The big door—make that mouth—of our Skay host had cracked open far enough to let us out.

A glowing field had formed, much like the ones we used to keep air pressure on fighter hangars. It wasn't perfect, however, judging by the thin cold atmosphere inside the Skay and the dead zone around the only entrance.

Everyone was working instruments and watching screens tensely, but I wasn't worried. If the Skay changed its mind and wanted us dead, it could shoot us down at any moment. Worrying about it wasn't going to fix anything.

"You know what I never thought to do?" I asked loudly.

Graves shot me an irritated glance. Something seemed to be bothering him.

Drusus spoke up. "What did you forget, Centurion?"

"I forgot to ask this Skay's name. Can you believe that? He must have an identifying label, don't you figure? How will we tell if the next one we meet is the same guy or not?"

Drusus squinted at me. "Did the Skay say anything about returning?"

"No, not specifically. I was just assuming he would. After all, we've sworn our undying allegiance to him."

Graves finally lost it. "Has it occurred to you that the Mogwa also assume our loyalty? That they will return in force someday soon to claim what they consider to be their province? That you, James McGill, have single-handedly brought the civil war of the Core Systems home to our lonely corner of the galaxy?"

That was quite a speech for Graves. He must have been stewing over there for a long time.

"You think so?" I asked. "You really think the Skay and the Mogwa will fight over this patch of stars? As far as I can tell, they both think it's a turd-water province, not worth a damn to anyone."

"It'll be a matter of pride," Drusus said, looking at the screens.

We exited the Skay's mouth and glided out into open space. Everyone on the bridge breathed easier after that.

320

"Go to warp as soon as we can," Drusus ordered, and then he turned back to me and Graves. "A matter of pride..." he repeated. "Countless are the empires that have ground themselves to dust over worthless patches of territory."

"The important thing," Graves said, "is their tendency to scorch the planets of anyone who has the misfortune of getting in their way. McGill, do you recall what Magnate Xlur told you about the last Civil War they experienced in the Core Systems?"

"Yeah, sure. He said twenty thousand worlds were destroyed," I said, and I scratched my ear for a moment. "That does seem like an awful lot..."

"No shit," Graves said, and he turned back to watching the screens.

I knew he didn't like it when I overstepped my boundaries, but it was just something that happened now and then. I didn't go out of my way to get into trouble. In fact, the most infamous disasters I'd triggered had happened while I was actively trying to avoid such complications.

"Should we have died back there, Primus?" I asked seriously. "Because if you really want to go for it, we might be able to pull a U-turn right now, go back into that thing's mouth, and unload every nuke we've got."

Graves turned back to face me. "What the hell good would that do?"

"It might destroy the Skay tanks—and the Mogwa poison."

Graves thought about it, but he shook his head. "It won't help. The Mogwa will come back here anyway. They know this Skay invaded their territory. They'll want revenge no matter what we do now."

"Bingo!" I boomed at him. "It doesn't matter one frigging finger what we do now. But at least this way, we're alive and breathing, delivering the news to Earth. We've got options— and we aren't dead yet."

Graves sighed. "I guess I'm just regretting the situation we're in."

"There you go! That's right where you should be, with all due respect, sir. When you feel like that, like all the universe is

321

crouching on your shoulders, that's when you call in James McGill to fix the unfixable."

Graves stared at me for a moment, and I grinned back. He turned away at last, shaking his head.

Drusus had watched this exchange with mild interest. He sucked in a breath and faced me.

"Once again, we're in your debt, McGill. I don't know how we could have gotten out of that monster's belly without you."

"You couldn't have," I said with certainty. "There was no hope at all."

"Why's that?" he asked, slightly amused.

"Because sir, you fellows think in straight lines, see. I never do that, and I never have. My mind is all loops and swirls, spins and twists... There isn't a straight line in my skull. Not a damned one of them."

Drusus turned away with a half-smile, and he began giving orders. Soon, the screens went white, and *Legate* slipped away in a warp-bubble.

We'd escaped the first Skay humanity had ever met, but I couldn't help wondering what would happen next out in the Core Worlds.

-56-

On the long way home, I met up with a woman I'd meant to spend time with, but never had: Centurion Jennie Mills.

It happened at an award ceremony where they were giving out promotions to recruits who'd made it to the status of 'regular'. That wasn't a big deal to anyone other than the recruits, but they didn't know that. To them, it was the biggest day of their lives.

After distributing insignia, better uniforms and even outfitting some of them in heavy armor, I managed to sidle away from my unit and over closer to Jennie's.

"Hey Mills!" I said, tipping a squeeze-bottle of beer in her direction. "I haven't seen you since 51 Pegasi."

She looked around, spotted me, and then she let her face soften. She didn't look super-happy to see me. It was more like she was amused.

That was okay. As long as a woman didn't greet me with the stone-face of death, I knew I had a chance.

Grinning, I scooted around some excited new regulars and headed toward her. She waited, tilting her head a little. She didn't even say anything.

"Damn, was that a fight inside Armor World or what?" I offered.

She shuddered a little. "That death ship wasn't to my liking. No sun. No natural ecosystem. So alien... so evil."

"It was that," I admitted. "Say, you want to have a beer with me? I've felt bad for a while now about how we were separated and never had a chance to meet up again."

Jennie looked at me speculatively. I knew that look. She was making her decision, right then and there, whether I had a chance in hell with her or not.

Looking as clueless and friendly as possible, I stood there, waiting for her to make her decision. Sometimes, a man had to know when it wasn't time to push.

"All right," she said at last.

We got two fresh beers—my first one was empty by now—and took a seat.

We were on Green Deck. We enjoyed the fake sky, the fake trees, the fake grass, and the very real company.

Jennie didn't make me wait around. I'll say that for her. Lots of girls—even hard-bitten Varus veterans, would make a man wait for a week or so. But not her. We went to her module, went into her cabin, and made sweet love.

Then, an hour later, I snorted awake.

It was my honest opinion that she'd kicked me. But that couldn't be…

"What's up, girl?"

"Get out," she said.

"Uh… is something wrong? Did I snore, or something?"

She flipped on the lights. She was standing over me, buck-naked and looking great. She was one of those girls who had big hips, a narrow waist, and squared-off shoulders. Her hair hung around her face, and she had that dark-circle look, like when a girl's makeup melts around her eyes.

One finger extended toward my tapper. It was lit up with a message.

The message was from Adjunct Barton. There was only one visible word, on the subject line. The word was *tonight?*

I think it was the question mark at the end of that single word that had screwed me. The implications were all too clear.

"Oh…" I said, thinking as fast as my blurry, half-asleep mind could carry me. It didn't do all that well, as things turned out. "Hey," I said. "She just wants to talk about our exercise we're planning in the morning. One of those crack-of-dawn surprises for the troops."

"Really?" Jennie said, crossing her arms over her tight breasts. I was sorry to see them go. "That's seriously the lie you're going with, McGill? I'd heard you were good at making up shit to tell women."

"Huh…" I said, scratching at my ribs and dressing. "She's not like my girlfriend or anything. Neither are you. I like you a lot, Jennie. I didn't figure you were the possessive type on the first date."

"This is our third date, and you are screwing your own adjunct. That's unacceptable."

Grumbling, I got myself kicked out into the passages. On the way to the elevators, I thought I might have heard a few snickers from passersby, but it could have been my imagination.

Returning to my own module, I stretched out on my bunk and sighed.

It felt pretty good to sleep alone and uninterrupted. Unfortunately, I didn't make it all the way until morning. There was a tapping at my door sometime after three a.m.

Getting up and yawning, I opened it.

Erin Barton stood there. She looked kind of hurt, and kind of pissed, too.

Damnation. Had these two women talked already? That was downright unfair. They always teamed up on a man like me.

"Good morning," I said in as cheery a voice as I could muster.

"You never answered me," she said.

She was sullen, staring down at the deck.

"Huh…? Oh… right. Sorry about that, girl. I must have been asleep."

Those eyes flicked up at me, then down to the deck again.

"I came by before and after the text. You weren't here."

I sighed. "Look, Erin. I've been thinking."

"Stop," she said, putting up a hand. "I know. It's wrong. We have to cut this off right now. It's not good for the troops. Not good for morale."

She stood on her tiptoes, and as she was a tall girl, she was able to brush her lips against my stubbly cheek.

My hand touched the spot, which went cold with the lingering kiss.

"All right then," I said. "We had fun, and it's over. Are you okay?"

She nodded, and she walked away. I could tell she wasn't okay. Not entirely. But at least she'd never found out about Jennie, and I hoped she never would.

-57-

On the way home, they revived a lot of our dead. Not all of them mind you, but most of them.

Legion Varus people were prioritized to go first. This was because only our transport ship had survived. The Solstice people would have to stay on ice until we got home.

Right at the head of the queue was someone I hadn't seen in a long while—Tribune Galina Turov.

She came out kicking and hissing—at least, that's what the Blue Deck rumor-mill said. For my own part, I believed them. She'd never liked dying much.

When I heard about it, the news came from Carlos. He was happy to tell me. Too happy.

"She's looking for you, McGill. You know that, don't you?"

"How do you figure?"

"Are you kidding me? You're her white knight! The boy-toy who never fails to rescue her shapely ass. That is until now, when you went and left her on ice for weeks while you chased every piece of tail in the legion—and no, don't think she doesn't know about that. Everyone does."

Ever since I'd met Carlos, many decades ago, I'd felt like clocking him on a regular basis. This was just one more checkmark on that long list of special occasions.

"Everyone should keep their noses out of my business," I told him and stomped off.

Experimentally, I sent Galina a text when I was alone in my office. *"Hey! I hear you're back with us again. Great to hear Graves finally approved your revival. I've been worried sick."*

The middle part was intended to shift blame, and the last part was a bald-faced lie. Of course, Galina would know that instantly. The way I figure though, it never hurt to make a show of caring, even if both sides knew it was a pretense.

There was no answer. After about three minutes went by, I stopped looking at my tapper and shrugged. If she was in a bad mood, well, it was for the best that she not talk to me until she got over it.

Going back to work, I drilled my troops. Everyone was lazy and half-assed about it, and it was hard to blame them. We were on the way home to Earth, and once we got there we'd probably be demobilized.

My men stood in a sloppy imitation of troops at attention. I walked the line and praised them for their performance back on Armor World.

"That was a hairball planet, wasn't it?" I asked. "The word 'nasty' now has a new meaning in my book. Think about it: we were really inside the living guts of an intelligent machine the size of a planet. According to our xeno people, that's how these Skay things all operate. They build cyborgs in their bodies that operate like enzymes, or white blood cells. Those freaky meat-and-machine constructs digest incoming matter, clean up the place, even defend and heal the greater host."

Suddenly, I became aware of a shift in attitude among my men. They were standing tall, becoming alert and aiming their eyes front. No longer was their previous slouching, hooded-eye stare the norm.

On a hunch, I glanced over my shoulder. Sure enough, the tribune was behind me.

"Tribune on the deck!" Harris shouted, having figured out we were being observed at the same moment I had.

Turov eyed us all coldly. Was her hair matted, sticky and curly? I thought that it just might be. She was fresh out of the revival machines, and she'd come straight here. What did that mean? I wasn't sure, but I was certain it wasn't good.

"At ease," she said at last. "Carry on, Centurion. Tell us what you've learned. Some of us have been out of the loop for a long time..."

"Uh... yes sir."

Turning back to my assembled unit, I noticed they were looking a trifle freaked out. It wasn't every day the brass left Gold Deck and came down here to slum around in the modules with the common soldier. In fact, as far as I could remember, this had *never* happened before.

"As I was saying," I continued, "the Skay are not only real-deal Galactics, they're probably the strangest race we've encountered yet among the stars. They build sub-creatures out of flesh and metal, but their brains are always electronic. Fortunately, this gives them a certain inflexibility of the mind which we were able to take advantage of."

I heard a tiny snort from behind me then. That was the tribune—it had to be. I took her rudeness good-naturedly, refusing to allow it to put me off my game.

"Are there any questions, troops?" I asked.

Cooper appeared suddenly and raised his hand. I rolled my eyes and pointed to him.

"What is it, ghost-man?"

"What happened to the Mogwa?" he asked, touching upon a sore point. "Where are they? I saw them waddling around Gold Deck, but by the time we reached that big bastard Skay planetoid, they were all gone. Did we sell them out to these new Galactics or something?"

I blinked. It was a tell, and a bad move for bluffers like me in general. I'd done it in a moment of weakness.

"Huh... that is a good question," I said, rubbing at my chin in simulated thought. "How did you get a peek at them, by the way?"

Cooper released a little puff of air. "A Ghost is supposed to watch things, sir. I was watching."

"Up on Gold Deck? You're not authorized to go up there..."

"Even if one of our tribunes is about to mutiny?" he asked.

A stunned silence fell over the group. Everyone looked at Turov, assuming he had meant her.

329

"That's a damned lie, Cooper," I announced. "I thought everyone aboard knew that Armel ditched Solstice and damned near sank *Legate* as well."

There were a few gasps. Not all my people were in the dirty loop of talk that existed on the ship.

"In any case," I said, "back to your original question. Earth is one hundred percent loyal to the Mogwa. If we were to switch our allegiance to a new Galactic species, surely we'd have been officially told about it."

Cooper pursed his lips and nodded. He already knew I was bullshitting. In case the rest of them were still in the dark, I pressed onward. I briefed them all on the voyage home, our expected deactivation, and what to do if they needed some special problem fixed.

After they'd all asked a few questions and been dismissed, Galina stepped closer.

Cooper vanished—but he didn't do it quickly enough. I kicked out to my left and hooked his ankle. He went sprawling on the deck and cursed while I pretended to be concerned for his well-being.

"You've got to watch that stealthing nonsense Cooper," I told him. "Accidents happen all the time to Ghosts who overuse it."

"Thanks for the tip, Centurion," he said sourly from the deck.

Galina stepped up to my side. We watched my unit file out of the main chamber together.

"Great to see you back with us, sir!" I gushed. "What can I do you for?"

"You're not doing *anyone*, McGill," she said in a low tone. "Not today."

"Huh?"

"Drop the stupid act. I find it intensely annoying right now. Just tell me how you did it? Just tell me how you manipulated everyone into thinking you're some kind of hero while they're looking at me like I'm a streak of shit."

She was angry. I knew all the tell-tale signs, and Galina didn't hold back on the best of occasions.

"Maybe we should go for a little walk, sir? To somewhere people aren't listening?"

I gestured with a tilt of my head toward the various trolls who were watching us surreptitiously.

Fuming, she marched away. Pasting on a smile, I walked after her.

-58-

Out in the passages, Galina went full alley-cat on me.

"So, it's true," she said. "You left me dead for more than a month, so you could chase tail all over the ship. I don't know what I ever saw in you."

"What? Hey! I wasn't the one who made the decision to leave you dead."

"You certainly didn't try to revive me. Do you know how many times I've pulled strings to breathe life back into your worthless corpse again?"

I mulled that over. It did seem like she'd made such efforts on several occasions. On the other hand, she'd also tried to get me killed more than once in the past. We didn't have what you might call an ideal relationship.

"Listen," I said, "I'm only a centurion. I don't have a budget and political contacts. I shoot things for a living—that's about it."

"What bullshit. You do whatever you damned-well please. I wouldn't feel so betrayed if you'd been romancing bio women to try to get me back—but no! Nothing of the kind— and yes, I checked."

"Huh…" I said.

"That's it? That's the entirety of your eloquent self-defense?"

I leaned against the wall of the passage and put on a smile again. I gazed at her thoughtfully for a moment. "Well, I am glad you're back, even if you're busting my balls right off the mark."

Galina turned aside in frustration, walking quickly away. I watched her go, wondering if I should follow.

I'd never been the puppy-dog type. Generally, if a woman wanted to walk out on me, well, I just went and found another one.

But watching this particular woman's hindquarters always had a certain effect on me. It made me want to follow after her, if you know what I mean. None of the other women I'd been around lately could compare.

Heaving a sigh and suspecting I'd regret it, I began taking long strikes in her wake.

She walked faster, but it was damn-near hopeless. Unless she wanted to pick up and run, she wasn't going to stay ahead of me. My legs had to be half-again as long as hers were.

"Where are we going?" I asked when I'd pulled up next to her.

"I'm facing a court of inquiry," she said. "I'm going to meet my lawyer-bot and plan my deposition. Do you still want to come along?"

"Uh…" I said, chewing that over. "All right. Maybe I can help."

She looked honestly surprised. "Help with what?"

"Details. Remember, I know things no one else does. I talked to the Skay. I talked to Armel and Sateekas during their final moments."

She stopped at the elevators, slapped at the buttons and waited irritably.

"You don't know anything I don't know. I've read your reports, seen your body-cam files."

"Uh-huh… That's right, those things tell all. They never miss a trick."

I was freaking her out on purpose, and it was working. She let me into the elevator, which sped off sideways to Gold Deck. All the while she was studying me intently.

Putting on an affable smile, I let her stew until we got to our destination and walked to her office, which also doubled as her quarters on *Legate*.

A few hog-like guards watched us enter with raised eyebrows. I ignored their stares, just like I ignored the dismay on the face of her boy-toy secretary. He'd probably thought he was rid of old McGill for good after listening to the tribune rant about me.

"Tribune?" he asked as we whizzed by his desk. "There's a lot of correspondence to catch up with, and a raft of requisitions to sign. You'll find them—"

Swish, the door closed in his face.

"Drink?" I asked her.

"No way. You don't fool me. Tell me something I don't know, or I'll kick you out of here right now."

"About what?" I asked, playing hard-to-get. I walked over to her tiny bar and helped myself.

"About Sateekas or these Skay things you've sold your soul to."

I looked at her then. "So… you don't want to work with them? You don't want to swear allegiance to a new race of Galactics?"

"I want to survive, James. I want to stop Rigel and keep Earth from getting caught up in the new civil war breaking out in the Core Systems."

"They're up to that again, huh?" I asked. "You know what Xlur told me? That the Empire needed an emperor. That's the real problem, according to the Mogwa. There's no designated ruler. How can you have an Empire if you don't have a ruler at the top?"

She blinked at me. She hadn't heard that before, I didn't figure.

When you thought about it, the problem seemed obvious. Not all figurehead despots were good guys, but a system built from the ground up to be ruled by a single individual couldn't stand long with an empty throne.

"That's what they're fighting about? Succession?"

"Yes. Thousands of worlds burned. Decades of conflict. The stakes are high, there are too many players, and they can't agree who should ascend the throne."

She studied the wall, but she wasn't really seeing it.

"The war is finally leaking out to us, James," she said quietly. "We're becoming participants. Everything we think is important pales in significance compared to a single battle in the Core Systems—all our squabbles, our petty struggles for dominance out here on the frontier... "

"That's no way to think about it," I said, pressing a drink into her hand. She took it with numb fingers. "Look, to a fly, all he cares about is that one fly-swatter. He doesn't care if a city is dusted off in another sector."

"We're the fly, huh?" she asked, sipping her drink. "Is that what you're saying?"

"If the shoe fits."

"Right... now, tell me what really happened with Armel and Sateekas. The reports cleaned it all up. It was written to calm nerves back at Central."

I gave her the rundown. I included everything, even the part with Armel using a simple tool to cave in the thin skulls of several Mogwa.

"That isn't like him," she said. "He's checking out. He must be."

"Checking out?"

"Yes—a cover-up. Leaving Earth. Getting himself 'permed' as far as we're concerned, but living on somewhere else."

"Oh... you mean the way Claver does it? But who would want to revive old Maurice Armel? He was an irritating prick on a good day."

She looked at me expectantly, tilting her head and sipping her drink. She said nothing.

I stared at her for a second. She must think I should know the answer to my own question, but...

"It can't be Rigel," I said. "Those bears are so arrogant they'd want nothing to do with a human officer."

"Very true," Galina said.

"Well then... who else is there? The Mogwa sure as heck don't... wait a second. You don't mean Claver did it, do you?"

"You mentioned that name yourself."

"Sure, Claver is the human wizard of illegal revives," I admitted. "He even revived me a few times to talk to me, out there on his weird clone planet."

"And why do you think he did that? What do you think he hoped to get from that?"

I stared at her. "A new follower? A man like me?"

She pointed a finger at me. The nail was unpainted, but I knew that wouldn't last long. She was the kind of woman who only had unpainted nails after a fresh revive. "Claver needs a military man," she said. "Isn't that obvious? Armel wasn't afraid to die, even to be permed—you said yourself he was anxious for you to get on with his execution."

"That's right... he said he had other places to be. Could he have meant Claver-world?"

She pointed that finger at me again. "Yes. Claver has begun to gather a following. Just living with his own clones, dumbing them down—such a society would be highly limited, don't you think?"

"You've been out there," I said in a hushed tone. "You and Armel both."

"Of course I have," she said, shrugging. "Did you really think that Claver only used his revival machine as a special favor to you? That you were the only one he'd met with that way? You are naïve. Others have been revived there, and they have spoken with him. The only difference is the rest of us were smart enough to keep our mouths shut about it."

Chewing that over, I found I didn't like the taste.

"Galina," I said, "maybe you shouldn't tell me any more. If you want me as a supporting witness at your trial, you shouldn't admit things that border on treason."

She laughed and downed her drink. "Are you kidding? First of all, I'd never ask for your testimony. I'd have to be insane. And don't forget, my overgrown boy scout, any talk of Claver's illegal revival machines might get us both permed."

"Okay..." I said, pouring us both another drink. "Where does that leave us?"

She stared at me thoughtfully. "It's going to leave you with your ass kicked out of here. You still haven't given me any useful information."

That surprised me. I'd figured after a lot of talk and a drink, she'd forget about that requirement.

I thought hard for a moment, then I shook my head. "I'm not sure…"

She downed her drink and turned away, heading to her bathroom. "I'm going to take a shower, I'm sticky after that last revive. And no, you're not invited in with me. If you can't come up with something impressive, get out of my quarters before I'm finished."

Leaving me there with a drink in my hand, she began stripping down before she stepped into her bathroom. In a cruel twist, she left her door ajar. I was haunted by the sounds of her undressing and climbing into one of those water-sucking, tube-like shower stalls they have on all spaceships.

My first instinct was to down my drink and walk out with the bottle. I almost did it, too, but then I recalled something that had been bothering me.

Snapping my fingers and grinning, I sipped and I poured her a fresh glass.

A few minutes later, she came back out. Her hair-drying robot had done a good job. Her hair was straight and glossy down her back. The only surprise was that she'd forgotten to put her uniform back on.

Now, I wasn't born yesterday. Galina was an ambitious woman, and she was very uninhibited. She liked to use every gift the Good Lord had seen to bestow upon her for her own advancement in life. Today was no exception, and she was clearly offering up a mind-fogging view of herself to get me talking.

And if I stayed quiet, or I was just plain clueless? Well, she liked tormenting the sad likes of me anyway. The truth was, she couldn't lose in this situation, and she knew it.

"Well?" she asked, standing with her fists planted on her hips.

"I remembered something," I said. "It must have been the mist from your shower that awakened my mind."

She laughed. "Right… Now talk or get out."

"You remember back on Dark World, when I brought down that orbital factory?"

337

Her face darkened. "Why, in a million lifetimes, would you bring that up? Do you want me to call the MPs and tell them you won't leave?"

"No sir!" I said, sitting up straight. "I'm talking about the generator. There was a strange device on that orbital platform that powered the whole thing—or at least part of it. When I shorted it out, the whole structure ended up crashing down into the planet's ocean."

Her eyes narrowed. "I remember. What about it?"

"Did you read my report from the action under the alien dome at Hammonton? We found another generator just like it—on Earth."

She nodded thoughtfully. She pulled out a robe and slid it over her skin. I watched regretfully as she covered up.

"All right, I'm listening," she said. "You found two of the same alien generators. That's interesting, but—"

"One of them was at Dark World," I said. "The second one was on Earth, and it had to have come from the Skay."

"That stands to reason, but I'm not impressed. Seriously, James, is that all you've—"

"Think about it," I said. "Where did that orbital platform come from? Do you think the Vulbites built it?"

"No... that seems unlikely. They aren't very creative or intelligent. They worked on the factory, but they didn't build it."

"Who built it then?" I asked.

She shrugged. "The Cephalopods, probably—or Rigel."

"That's what I thought at first, but now, I'm not so sure. Do you know that our province isn't really the frontier? That the Empire used to be bigger? That they've already abandoned some of the fringes?"

She nodded, staring at me and frowning now. She didn't know where I was going with this, but she was intrigued.

"The next province over was called 929. We're 921. A century or so ago, before Earth was even annexed by the Mogwa, they abandoned Province 929."

"Okay, all very interesting, but how does this involve these generators?"

"Here's my theory: The Skay told me that his kind once ruled over 929. It was the Skay, therefore, that built that orbital shipyard at Dark World. They still use the same kind of power-generators today." I nodded with a self-satisfied smile on my face.

She stood up and began to pace. I sat low in my chair, sipped my drink and enjoyed the spectacle.

"I'm beginning to see where you're going with this..." she said. "The Skay once owned neighboring property along the frontier with the Mogwa in this region. Perhaps they wish to again. It's too bad the damned Galactics don't bother to teach us about these things directly."

"Knowledge is power," I said. "Historically, many empires with a slave class made it a crime to teach slaves to read."

"Hmm..." she said thoughtfully. "I can use this information at my trial. I thought of it—all of it. Is that understood?"

"What?" I said, pretending to be outraged. "I planned out a college lecture circuit on this topic."

"Sure you did," she said, sitting in my lap all of a sudden. "Are we in agreement?"

"Yup."

We made love then, and she complained that I was too enthusiastic for her freshly regrown body—but it had been quite a while since I'd been with her. It was like going home again.

-59-

Legate made planetfall over Earth about a month later. We were immediately summoned to Central, the biggest building on the continent. I was invited to join Drusus, Graves and Turov as we exited *Legate*. We took a lifter down to the spaceport, then hopped a military sky-train going to Central. I thought it was kind of cool that the top officers had brought me on a VIP trip directly to Earth's military headquarters.

We were the only passengers on the sky-train, which was kind of weird to me. I wasn't used to traveling like royalty.

Looking out the window as we came down out of the clouds, I spotted Central right away. The black puff-crete and ballistic-glass structure was more or less pyramid-shaped. It was an impressive building, squatting like some kind of gigantic sacrificial altar in the middle of Central City.

"Holy shit..." I said, sucking in a breath of air, "look at the city!"

No one else spoke. They were all looking, and they were all glum.

Central City was a mess. There was a circular region immediately around Central that had been blown flat. Only stumps of buildings still stood, like the ground-down teeth of an old dog. Farther out, toward the harbor district, things looked pretty normal. You could tell the Skay had done a number on the city immediately adjacent to Central.

I'd never seen this damage, naturally, as I'd been dead after the Hammonton operation ended.

"But..." I said, still staring, "if the Skay ship retreated before we nuked Hammonton, who did this exactly?"

"Some of their assault ships survived our nuke," Graves told me. "They returned the favor by firing missiles from New Jersey before we could take them all out."

"Such firepower..." I marveled. "I guess the war could have gone a lot worse for us. That robot-minded Skay was just toying with us all along. It wanted raw materials and compliant subjects, not a full-blown war."

"I think that's correct, McGill," Praetor Drusus said from the row of seats behind mine. "It's actually not an uncommon pattern when dealing with Imperial powers. When a given Empire faces a minor power, they often possesses superior forces, but they're unwilling to take serious injury when subjugating much weaker nations. It's just not worth it to them. On the other hand, we'll fight to death to defy them. That's how guerilla wars can be successful."

"It's a matter of commitment," Graves said.

Looking down at the flattened streets, I figured we must have lost a half-million human civilians right there. That demonstrated a serious level of commitment on Earth's part, if you asked me.

We passed through a force-shield and landed on the roof of Central. It was surreal, being on a whole and undamaged building in the midst of such destruction.

"There were a lot of good restaurants and bars down there in those streets," I lamented.

"Don't worry," Drusus said. "They've already begun to rebuild."

We went downstairs using the roof entrance and got into an elevator together. That was when something unexpected happened.

I figured out later that certain members of our foursome had planned something, but they hadn't included me in on their designs. That was their prerogative, of course. They all outranked me—but it was bad policy anyway.

341

Drusus made the first move. He turned toward Graves and nodded his head.

I noticed this, but I didn't think much of it until Graves took a step forward and reached for Galina's sidearm.

Now, I shouldn't have done anything. A thinking man probably wouldn't have moved a muscle—but I'm not always a thinker. I'm more of a doer.

I believe I was triggered by pure instinct. Galina was standing there, minding her own business and tapping at her tapper the way most women did night and day. She looked pretty innocent and unaware.

Seeing Graves grab at her from behind like that… I guess it was more than the animal side of my brain could handle. After all, she and I had been in a half-assed, on-again-off-again love affair for years. In short, I felt an immediate urge to defend her, and I did so without hesitation.

Graves found his own wrist clamped by my bigger hand. He made a fast move to break my grip, being no less of a combat-trained individual than I was.

Of course, I'd anticipated this, so I swept his feet out from under him with one of my oversized boots. He landed hard on his can, cracking his skull on the elevator floor.

If I'd hurt him, it didn't show any. He bounced up like some kind of a ninja and squared off with me. Both of us were crouching and in a combat stance.

About this time, Galina turned around to see what was happening. She had her pistol in her hand.

Drusus had his gun out by now, too. It was a real-life Mexican standoff if I'd ever seen one.

"All right, all right," Drusus said. "Let's calm down a moment."

"What is this, Drusus?" Galina demanded. "Assassination?"

"A praetor doesn't assassinate tribunes," Graves said, never taking his eyes off me. "He rightfully executes them."

"Is that what this is, sirs?" I asked. "An execution?"

"No," Drusus said firmly. "It's an arrest. I apologize for the clumsy handling, but it is legitimate."

At this, Galina looked at me appraisingly. "You saw them move on me, and you attacked them?"

I shrugged, beginning to relax and stand straight again. Graves did the same, but he never took his eyes off me. He never even blinked.

"Uh… yeah," I admitted. "I didn't know what was going on."

Galina nodded and squinted at the other two. "Am I really so threatening you thought you should do this in an elevator? I feel proud to know I fill you with such fear."

Drusus and Graves looked annoyed. Drusus put his gun away first.

"That's a mistake, sir," Graves said, but Drusus waved for silence.

"Tribune Galina Turov, we're arresting you on suspicion of treason."

Galina's head tilted to one side. "Oh really? Treason to whom?"

"To Earth. To Hegemony… to all humanity if you like."

By this time, my eyes were pretty wide. If they were arresting Galina, there was probably a good reason for it. She always had been the shadiest girlfriend I'd ever known.

"Very well," she said. "I submit to your arrest."

She handed her gun to Graves, who took the weapon and cuffed her with gravity-clamps. Only when she was safely in custody did Drusus seem to relax.

Graves aimed a finger at me.

"What about McGill? Is he under arrest as well, sir?"

The elevator door finally dinged and opened. We'd moved several hundred floors by this time.

The group stepped out while Drusus considered his options.

"No," he said. "McGill was just playing watchdog. We've got no reason to arrest him."

Graves shook his head. I could tell he thought Drusus was too lenient. I restrained my natural urge to give him a quick victory smile. He was, after all, still my immediate superior.

As we walked down the passage toward Drusus' office suite, I began to wonder about Turov herself. She seemed far

343

too quiet. When she was caught off-guard she normally hissed like an alley cat.

Further, I noticed that her hands were rubbing at her wrists… no, that's wrong. She was tapping on her tapper. I'd seen her do that before under extreme circumstances.

Alarmed, I began looking this way and that. It wouldn't have surprised me if a team of commando squids jumped us right then and there.

But they didn't. We made it all the way to Drusus' office, where the door swung open at our approach. Drusus stopped before walking inside. He was frowning at his tapper.

"What is it, Praetor?" Galina asked in an innocent tone of voice.

We were all immediately suspicious.

Drusus did a rare thing. He reached out a hand and gripped Galina's shoulder. He gave her a little shake.

"What have you done?" he demanded.

"I've done nothing!" she insisted, but her eyes were glittering dangerously.

Drusus pushed past her, he pushed past us all and rushed into his office. Soon, he broke into a trot.

Over the top of his central battle table a hologram had appeared.

I knew in an instant what and who was calling us.

It was a Mogwa. An individual known to me as the Governor of Province 921, Sateekas himself.

-60-

Drusus reached out and touched the mute button. He'd put Sateekas on hold.

Breathing hard, he turned to face us. Galina was sauntering up, hips swaggering just a little. Graves and I followed, frowning and confused.

"What's Sateekas doing here?" he demanded. "He was dead... we haven't even reported his death to the Core Systems yet."

"No, we haven't..." Galina said.

Drusus looked at her like she might bite. I could have told him from experience his instincts were right about that.

"He *knows*?" Drusus asked. "He knows what happened out there?"

"Not everything. I'm really not sure about the details."

Drusus was dumbfounded. "You would really go this far, Galina? You'd bring down the entire Earth to burn with you in Hell?"

"Such drama!" she responded. "Burning Earth isn't my intent, Praetor. I know you need a scapegoat to pin the Armor World failure on—but it's not going to be me. Sateekas has learned he died in this province after losing against the Skay in battle. Someone else told him about that a long time ago."

"It had to be Armel..." Drusus said. "Someone revived him somewhere, and he informed the Mogwa. Such a disaster."

"Don't panic," Galina told him. "All I did was inform him that the four of us were there when it happened."

"Why would you do such a thing?"

"It's a suicide pact," she said. "He will question us. If you agree to drop all charges against me, I'll go with whatever story you concoct for him. It's that simple."

Drusus looked desperate. He wasn't a good liar... that was putting it mildly. He was, in fact, a boy scout among officers.

But to placate the Mogwa he was going to have to lie fast and lie well. Frankly, I didn't know if he had it in him.

On the hologram, I saw Sateekas slap a cringing Nairb and badger him. Perhaps he was bitching about the lack of contact, and taking it out on his subordinates. I could hardly blame him for that. If the Nairbs worked for me, I'd probably kill one or two of them every day myself.

"Old Sateekas is young again," I said. "Really, I don't know why he's so sore about dying. It looks like an improvement to me."

Drusus didn't appear to hear me. He had wild eyes. He glanced around at all of us, eyes leaping from one face to the next.

"Tell me one thing," he said to Galina. "Did you, or did you not cooperate with that Skay invader?"

"I did *not*."

"What about Armel? He seemed to know what was going to happen."

Galina looked shy for a moment. I knew that was an act, but she did it so well it probably fooled most people.

"He was planning *something*," she admitted, "something with his squid officers. That's all I know."

"The sub-centurions?" Drusus asked in confusion.

She nodded.

"Wait a second!" I called out, interrupting. "I remember now! Old Sub-Centurion Bubbles was acting funny when I went up to Gold Deck that same day, before Armel pulled his trick. Bubbles pretended not to know me, and I clearly made him nervous."

"That's pretty thin, McGill," Graves said.

"It is," I admitted, "but you can beat it out of him. Don't go easy! Keep squeezing until there's ink all over the floor. It's the only way to handle one of these slimy squids."

Drusus turned back to the hologram. The Nairb we'd seen earlier appeared to be dead now. Sateekas was losing it.

"We can't delay any longer," Drusus said. "We have to begin the interview. McGill... try not to say anything that makes my hair turn white."

"It'll never happen, Praetor."

Sighing, he glanced at Galina. "If we get out of this alive, there will be an investigation here at Central—but it will fail to find anything. Do you understand?"

"Certainly. Now let's talk to the Mogwa before he nukes Central again."

Drusus activated the pick-up. We suddenly heard some clicking and barking sounds. The translators caught up a moment later and began interpreting the alien's speech.

"... you have earned this demise, creature! I will not be discomfited by a bureaucrat. All of you will live only as long as you are useful to me, contributing to the Glory of the Empire..."

Sateekas trailed off, having noticed that we were staring at him. Shuffling his limbs around, he eyed us in turn.

"This is the requested four?" he demanded.

"Yes, Governor," Drusus said.

I winced immediately. Sateekas considered the job of Governor to be a personal insult to his status. His prior office as an admiral was infinitely more prestigious, which was why I still used that title when I spoke to him. Drusus either didn't know that, or he'd forgotten. The long and the short of it was that Drusus had managed to insult the Mogwa with the first two words he spoke.

Sateekas shuffled his limbs in agitation. "It has come to my attention that I lived briefly onboard your pathetic ship, human. Is that true?"

"It's true, sir."

"And why was I not informed?"

"We've only just returned to Earth from 51 Pegasi. We don't have ships with the kind of speed your vessels from the Core possess."

So far, so good. *Go Drusus,* the words echoed in my head.

"Hmm... and your ship, *Legate,* lacks any kind of deep-link technology. And yet somehow, someone informed Mogwa Prime that I should be revived. How convenient..."

"It's all a matter of budget, sir," Drusus said. "We don't have that kind of communications tech on every ship. Possibly another ship came by and reported your death."

I cringed again. Drusus had stepped on another minor landmine. Sateekas hated anyone who whined about budgets.

"Every time I come out here to this beggar planet I'm assaulted by pleas for more funding. It's despicable."

Drusus blinked twice. "Oh... I'm sorry sir. I was only trying to explain the lack—"

"Please stop before you anger me further. I'm trying to be objective."

"Yes sir."

Sateekas turned away, looking off-screen. He demanded that a Nairb approach. Bravely, another of them did. The green, seal-shaped alien stood on top of the flappy corpse of his previous brother.

"If it pleases the court," the Nairb began, "this trial is now in session."

Graves, Turov and I exchanged worried glances. The Nairb's statement hadn't pleased any of us in the slightest.

White-faced, Drusus stared at the hologram.

"Who... who is on trial, sirs?" he asked.

"You are, human," the Nairb said. "All of you are... collectively."

"And what's the charge?"

"Treason. Assassination. War crimes and conspiracy to commit further war crimes. These are the major items, but the list is quite long and detailed. Do you wish to hear a full recitation?"

"No..." Drusus said, his voice small. "I'd rather not. What evidence do you have of these alleged crimes?"

"It has come to the attention of this tribunal that the species of primitives known as 'Humanity' did revive and assassinate the sitting governor of Province 921. Evidence of this was provided in visual form."

Immediately, a recording began to play. I recognized the scene immediately. It was of the Mogwa slaughter that had occurred aboard *Legate*. There was no sound, just action.

At first, I thought they'd somehow gotten a copy of my own body-cam recordings, as I'd been right there when it happened. But I soon realized the video was taken from the point of view of the killer.

"Armel was recording all that?" I asked aloud.

The others looked at me in shock, and I shut up in a hurry.

Even as I said this, however, my own face came onto the scene. I aimed a gun at Armel, talked to him for a few minutes, then shot him dead. The recording ended.

"The prosecution will now call its first witness," the Nairb said. "Centurion James McGill-creature. Are you present?"

"I am, sir," I said, stepping forward.

The other three humans in the room looked even sicker than they had before, if that could be imagined.

"McGill-creature," the Nairb said. "Was that you in the video?"

"Uh... yes sir. Sure looked like me."

"Did you shoot the assassin at the end?"

"Yes sir, I did. That was Tribune Armel, and I shot him dead. He has not been revived."

The Nairb seemed to take some notes. I felt a trickle of sweat under my arms. These bureaucrats were tricky. You had to handle them like live snakes.

"You spoke with the assassin," he said, "but we don't have the audio portion of this broadcast. What was said?"

"Uh... I don't rightly recall every word..."

"Wasn't it something like: 'that was a job well done, comrade, but now you must die.'?"

"What? No, no, no! I'm only a centurion. Armel was a tribune. I would have been executed for treason against humanity if I'd shot my superior officer without good cause."

349

The Nairb consulted with a few others who looked just like him. After a moment, he returned to face me. "Your point is accepted. Nevertheless, you didn't shoot him immediately. You spoke to him first."

"I had to find out why he was cracking the skulls of our beloved Mogwa officers. It seemed crazy to me. I had to know if there were any other assassins."

This statement perked up the Nairb. He'd been almost bored up until that moment.

"Indeed? And what was his response?"

"He said yes. He said he was in the employ of the greatest enemy we've ever seen out here on the frontier. He was an agent of another race of Galactics, in fact. They're the vilest of creatures, known to us as the Skay, and they're planning a vicious takeover of our Province even now."

At that, the whole bridge behind the Nairbs lit up with a wild wave of squawking. The Nairbs and the Mogwa were shouting at each other too fast for our translators to keep up.

-61-

After the Nairbs had settled down, Sateekas himself waddled forward to the camera pickup and spoke to us directly.

"Humans," he began, "there is something very odd about this province. My predecessor Xlur remarked upon this on several occasions, but I'd always assumed he was mad. Today, I'm not so sure. Today, I've witnessed my own butchery at the hands of your pathetic species."

He paused then, as if in thought. The Nairb prosecutor tried to wriggle past him, but he brushed the smaller creature away.

"Any sane Mogwa would destroy the lot of you just on suspicion. No more evidence of your foul natures would be needed beyond this visual recording. You're mad-dogs, and you should all be put down for the good of the galaxy... but still, I hesitate..."

The Nairb managed to slip past him and approach the camera pick up again. "If you would allow me, Governor. I have even more devastating charges to make."

Sateekas gave way somewhat. "How could such a thing be? What crime could be more heinous than the assassination of a sitting supremacy such as myself?"

Right then, I knew what was coming. It was crystal-clear in my mind.

My grandma always told anyone who cared to listen that I was a born genius when it came to mischief. I truly believe it was the ingenious part of my brain which sent a jolt of precognition through me at that moment.

There was only one move to make, and I made it without hesitation before the Nairb could say anything else.

"I know exactly what you're talking about, sirs," I said loudly.

Sateekas and the Nairb looked at me in surprise. Since I had their attention, I ran with it.

"McGill...?" Drusus said in a plaintive tone, but I didn't even look at him. I was in the zone, like when you've had your third or fourth beer at the pool hall and can't seem to miss a shot.

"The Skay have developed a poison," I boomed out. "They tried to give it to us, hell, they sprayed our ship *Legate* with it."

"A poison?" the Nairb said. "Are you confessing to my next charge before I can even state it? This is new territory for me as a prosecutor."

"No, you damned fool. The Skay came here to take over. You know that much, don't you?"

"That has been established, insolent human," the Nairb said primly.

"Right. They came out here, but they had more to the plan than just sending one ship at us. Do you think they'd dare to challenge the fleet strength of the Mogwa if they didn't have an ace up their sleeve?"

"Analyzing colloquialism... ah yes, a secret advantage. Are you stating you were aware that—?"

"The Skay are planning to do a lot more than just take over this backwater province. They plan to take you out, Sateekas— all of you. They've created a bio-terminator that kills only Mogwas."

"The existence of this biological agent is known to us, human," the Nairb said. "Your attempts to avoid responsibility for—"

A sweeping limb knocked the prosecutor from his perch. He flopped onto the deck, squirming weakly. It looked like he would live, but he was probably broken-up inside. His kind came from a low-gravity planet, after all.

Sateekas pressed forward, leering out of the hologram at us. "What proof do you have that this was a Skay plot?"

"It would have to be, sir," I said. "We don't have thousands of ships to fight our way to Mogwa Prime and dust your home world with the stuff. We don't even have the biochemical expertise to create it in the first place. No sir, this was the work of an evil mastermind above and completely beyond our lowly capacities."

Sateekas seemed to consider. At last, he made a definitive chopping motion with his foremost limbs.

"I believe the McGill. With my own orbs I watched you kill another human—your superior officer, no less—to avenge me. How could such a clear act of slave-love for one's rightful master escape the Nairbs? They never understand loyalty. Their mindset would blame firemen for starting every fire because they're always on hand when a building is blazing."

"That's exactly right, sir. They just don't get the warrior spirit."

"Just one more thing," Sateekas said. "We require that you furnish us with a sample of the bio-terminator that the Skay gave you so we can study it."

"Oh…" I said, turning slowly to look at Drusus.

He looked like he was going to puke, but he managed to nod in a stiff-necked fashion.

"We'll do it, Grand Admiral," I answered for him, since he seemed to be feeling poorly.

Hearing the title he liked much better than governor, Sateekas seemed to ride a little higher on his limbs when he next moved.

"This inquiry is at an end," he announced.

The channel closed, and I heard explosively loud exhalations all around me.

For my own part, I located Drusus' brandy cabinet and poured a round for everyone. They all drank a few, even Graves.

* * *

After the Mogwa ship left our skies, Galina was dragged through a series of investigations and trials, but she eventually was acquitted and returned to her rank and status. They just couldn't pin anything specific on her.

That didn't really surprise me. She hadn't seemed particularly guilty to me, but she had been involved in things like this in times past, which always brought her under suspicion when something new went wrong down at the capital. She had friends and enemies in high places, so in some ways she was like a ragdoll the politicians liked to fight over.

Even if she *had* been guilty, I figured there was a good chance she'd get away with it in the end. She hadn't gotten this far in life solely due to her looks.

She was not, however, promoted to imperator again. I knew that's what she'd really wanted, so after I checked in with Etta, who was happy with her new life at Central, I skipped town and went back home to Waycross. I figured Galina could cool off for a while on her own.

I lived without bloodshed after that for nearly a month. But one hazy night in late summer, I was sitting out on my creaking porch having a brew. The fireflies were winking, and the bugs out in the swamp were working it like a brass band, but I didn't mind. It was good to be home.

One set of fireflies, I noticed, were high, high up in a pine tree to the north. Twin glows, blinking, coming lower and lower, becoming bigger and bigger…

That was no firefly, I realized. It was an air car.

Now, for normal people, the arrival of an air car on their rural property was a cause for excitement. Maybe even for celebration. People around these parts simply didn't have that kind of money.

But I was a different sort. Often, when people came down to visit me, they did so with ill intent. Accordingly, I killed all my lights, got out my gun, and sat on my porch swing in the darkness.

The car landed out in the swamp. Not on the road, or in my parents driveway—it was in the bog itself.

Not moving, barely breathing, I watched the area to see what would come. In particular, I watched the foot-tall grasses that encircled my house. People often thought I was just too lazy to mow, and although that did factor in, there was more to it than that. The grass was a warning system for me in case someone came sniffing around my place in a stealth suit.

Don't laugh, it's happened before.

Waiting for maybe ten minutes, I was almost bored and annoyed enough to go out into the swamp to look for the driver—but then I heard something.

It was a curse. A female voice, releasing a series of very foul words. Thirty years back, that tirade would have turned my face red.

Finally, a splashing came up to the edge of the lawn, then walked onto dry land. She was young, small and wearing white pants.

I winced at that. Nobody down in Waycross was shit-off stupid enough to land in the swamp in white pants. It took a northerner to even think of it.

Straightening herself up as best she could, and still cursing now and then, Galina Turov made her way to my door.

I sat there still as a stone in the dark, like a gargoyle on a cathedral.

"You'd better be home, dammit McGill," she whispered to herself, and she knocked on my door.

"Boo!" I said.

She almost leapt off the porch, and I brayed with laughter.

Angry as can be, she stormed back off into the night. I went after her, caught her up in my big arms and swept her into the air.

After a few seconds of struggling, she let me carry her back to my place. We kissed, she slapped me once, and then we went inside.

It was a nice night for it, so we made love until the sun came up.

Books by B. V. Larson:

UNDYING MERCENARIES
Steel World
Dust World
Tech World
Machine World
Death World
Home World
Rogue World
Blood World
Dark World
Storm World
Armor World

REBEL FLEET SERIES
Rebel Fleet
Orion Fleet
Alpha Fleet
Earth Fleet

Visit BVLarson.com for more information.

22295816R00215

Printed in Great Britain
by Amazon